SOMETHING DARKER

A novel of the Inferi Dii

S.A. PRICE

This is a work of fiction. Names, characters, places, and incidents are products of the author's imagination or are used fictitiously and are not to be construed as real. Any resemblance to actual events, locales, organizations, or persons, living or dead, is entirely coincidental.

Something Darker
A Tease Publishing Print Edition

Copyright© 2012 Stella & Audra Price, S. A. Price
ISBN: 978-1-60767-200-5
Editor: Sascha Illyvich
Cover Artist: Stella Price
Interior text design: Stacee Sierra

Tease Publishing LLC.

*For You, Dear reader. Thank you for taking this
step into the darkness with us.
We hope you enjoy the boys as much as we do.*

Acknowledgements

Nothing in the writing world is done alone, not really. We are blessed to have a wonderful group of people that not only support us, but make this job worth having.

Thank you's go out to our editor, Sascha Illyvich, who rocks hardcore, our amazing street team lead by Damaris C from Good Choice Reading and the wicked staff from Authors After Dark for taking the reins, allowing Stella time to write.

Our friends Melissa Schroeder, Jennifer Armintrout ~the REAL one~, Jess Haines, The Amanda's and Tilly Greene: Thank you for your guidance, your patience and your support. Words cannot express how much we love you.

Last but not least, our partners in crime and conventioning: Lia Habel, A.L. Davroe, Leanna Renee Heiber and Jessica TTB. Thank you for keeping us sane, and the awesome car rides, brainstorming sessions, talks off the ledge and for just being the best girls we know.

Prologue

The Temple of Whispers
Sumerian desert

Twilight descended upon the temple. The fiery colors of the desert muted to dreamlike blues and lavenders as the last vestiges of sunlight touched the crystalline sands.

This was a place of worship, the in-between, and hidden in the deep desert on the mother continent. Time remained suspended here, hung in the embrace of the moon and the sun, caressed like a lover. Here it was always some semblance of fairy time, be it twilight or daybreak, for to exist in the in-between was to never be part of the extremes of night and day.

Five gods were before her, naked to the waist. She looked at her beloved Sumerian on his knees, the Etruscan as well, only with his arms affixed behind him. The Celt, arrogant but respectful, stood before her, his hand around a goblet of water. The Egyptian quiet and immobile in his place, proud and tall, resigned to his station, two of his priestesses at his back. Finally, the misfit, an elder god of darkness from the inner plateau's, whose powers didn't truly fit the decree, sat passively, chained at both the wrists and ankles. This was the best they could muster, and it would have to be enough.

Tiamat looked over at Orcus, the Roman god charged to be their leader, to guide them through the ages until such time as they were needed.

Orcus nodded to her and took her hand. After kissing her inner wrist, he released his grip and then turned to address the men before her.

"I thank you all for your sacrifice. Our lady goddess does as well."

She went to them one by one. Each spoke in low, respectful tones, before they bent their heads and kissed her wrist, pledging their allegiance to the cause, to her.

Here their training would commence. Here they would learn to use what was left of their bound powers, to fight for the world.

The banishment of the Velns was over but had left each pantheon weak, wounded. This action of giving up their dark gods, would wound each pantheon even more, was a necessary evil. Without this line of defense, the Velns would return and the world would be in chaos.

She walked back to her dais and addressed them all as Orcus took a spot in the line. "These items, in which your powers have been bound, will be hidden. Ask the fates that they never be found." She motioned to the six objects on the altar to the right of her.

"These objects shall now be known as Relics. To each relic a Keeper, the vessel of your powers for eternity. The first will appear when what is lost is found and the darkness draws near."

Her face was placid, devoid of emotion, all except the eyes. They swirled with the will of the cosmos, filled with the glow and power of prophecy.

"A Keeper to accept the face of darkness, one in chains, one found in lust, one found in compassion and one realized when that which has sunk to the depths is rediscovered."

The Goddess spoke, the words setting events into motion and the world shifted on its axis. She raised her arms to the sky above, the ceiling of the temple gone, the stars overhead twinkling with brilliance. "Those standing, kneel."

Magic filled the spaces between, and circled the gods before her, caressing their naked torsos and arms. When it dissipated, each was marked with symbols of power. "These shall be your reminders, to fight the darkness beyond."

Tiamat's powerful voice resounded through the temple once again, this time with a rich clarity that signaled the beginning of all that was possible. "Rise, my warriors, and begin life anew."

They stood, and she smiled. Those who were bound were release from the chains. The last defense against the darkness. The Inferi Dii.

Chapter One

Moonlight danced on the rooftops of the row houses, bathing everything it touched in an ethereal glow. Midnight in the city was rarely a quiet time, unless you lived in the few outlying neighborhoods that afforded themselves a measure of peace and calm from the non-stop action the city had to offer. Unfortunately, this wasn't one of those privileged neighborhoods, and that's why he was here. Something was not right.

Syrus leaned against the outer wall of the club, a hulking mass of a building that used to be a bank in its heyday, and lit a match. He set it to the end of his cigarette and drew off the other end. The tip glowed. The cherry flavored smoke filled his lungs as he inhaled and he smirked as he let the smoke out.

A woman walked by, giving him the once over and he inclined his head as she passed shaking her ass as she did.

Working girl? He shrugged. At any other time he would have followed her down the street, possibly into one of the seedy clubs and found out for sure if she was charging for that supple piece of ass.

He didn't need his mind reading powers to know what she wanted. Hell it was plain on her face, and in the way she dressed and moved. Women didn't wear skirts that showed off the bottom of their ass cheeks without expecting to get fucked, and hard.

But tonight he was the one working. Having drawn the short straw this evening, he was on call. While the rest of the Inferi Dii were patrolling the better parts of the city Syrus was stuck here, on this fucking back street in New York's Alphabet City, waiting for something to happen.

This was usually Arlo's gig, this part of town. Before they all suited up for the evening Bedit-Shari, or Sherry as she liked to be called, their soul Keeper, insisted that Syrus take the rather distasteable section of the city. As an oracle, and their indirect boss, her word was law.

Not that he didn't have other things to do. He knew his girls, the members of the sorority Psi Pi Chi, the front for his cult, were waiting for him at Minks. Psi Pi Chi was the closest cell of his cult to him, and he heartily indulged in its members. A group of willing females, all interested, none jealous, all fine with sharing. It was now as it was before, though through the ages the rules had changed. He no longer wanted just one. One wouldn't help keep back the loneliness.

He was starting the feel the weight of the years alone, and having one consort, one woman at a time was not the way to forget that he couldn't have the one woman he wanted, as the one thing that could make that happen for him was lost and gone.

He would rather be at the club, seeing the show, and hanging out with his priestesses. But no, the Soul Keeper's involvement with one of the other Inferi Dii had a tendency to fuck the other guys' plans when she was in a rut.

So Syrus and Arlo had switched it up, and only one of them was comfortable with their assignment. While Arlo was more at home in the seedy part of town, Syrus enjoyed the Village, which was only a few blocks over, but a world away in truth.

The quality of the people differed by blocks, like night and day, and Syrus wanted to be back with the emo kids, the indie kids and the audiophiles he preferred to hang around.

He spent a good amount of time at Webster Hall and The Bowery Ballroom.

Too bad both places were magnets for the unsavory Div demons that wreaked havoc about the city. It was just as well. Both had their silent protector, Syrus Alcot.

Syrus, who waited on a contact he had no clue about. Arlo's informant, a man who called himself Jingles, was supposed to meet him here at a quarter past ten. It was already ten thirty and the junkie was late, but then again what did he expect from a guy that called himself a verb.

Still if the man had info on the Div he wasn't going to knock it. The demons had been getting bolder of late. Div were the servants of the Velns, the elder gods who were once meant to rule this plane of existence. Since the old pantheons had bound them in a vapor dimension, and left the Inferi Dii to watch over the earth, the attacks had come in waves.

There were years and decades on end that they fought constantly, and years where the Velns lay quiet and left the realm alone. This decade though, they had gotten their balls up. Syrus had no idea why they were stepping it up now, and neither did the rest of the elite god force. So they had to rely on those who could find out for them, even if they sometimes were the world's undesirables.

Syrus let his mind wander back to earlier in the day when he had been happily abed with his high priestess and one of their new initiates. Simone, his most recent high priestess had been pouty at the fact that their relationship would soon be over. She was in love with him, though he could do nothing about it. Simone was hot, knew what he was and embraced it. And he felt absolutely nothing for her. She was the favorite to end up in his bed and his heart for all time, and he couldn't bring himself to care.

The Cult of Osiris was ages old, the memberships passed down from mother to daughter. They were all born with the knowledge needed to help their deity protect the world, by possibly being his Keeper, the woman that would hold and activate his relic, and take possession of his heart and soul. He thought it all piffle since his relic, a lapis Scarab, had been lost to them eons before.

For all he knew, Simone was his Keeper, but it didn't matter. Stolen out of his most secret and sacred temple, it always irked him that he might never find that special woman. Damn his priestesses for not hiding the relic better. No, in his heart he knew it wouldn't be Simone. His high priestess possessed so much he did prize in a woman, but she wasn't his Isis.

She wasn't too keen on training her replacement and in all honestly he didn't expect her to be. Their conversation could have gone better.

"You need someone experienced to take care of you."

He smiled. "True, but unless the Scarab surfaces, and accepts you, it won't be you Darlin'. So let's not worry about that okay. I have learned to live in the now, as you should. Have you picked your successor yet? Graduation isn't far off."

He couldn't keep them. They were all passing faces, women he would forget in the long run. Her mother had been a favorite, as was her family line. She was a goddamn legacy, and it didn't matter, The Scarab wasn't hers, and neither was he, so he accepted it, and looked towards his next best options.

"Of course," she sighed huffily. Changing her direction to sit away from him, She crossed her slender legs at the ankles. He could easily see the topic of her successor didn't sit well with her.

"I have one or two girls that I think worthy lined up for you to interview. Georgia isn't one of them." She nudged the girl with her foot.

"I should hope not." he sat back and grinned at her pouty attitude. "She's hardly ready for me full force. Don't be pissy with me Mone, you know the rules, as did your mother, and grandmother. And the others in your legacy. We had our fun, and will still until you get married to birth me the next generation. So who do you got lined up, and are you going to help me audition them?"

In the end she had been okay. He did need her, and he knew it, but not in the way she wanted. Simone wanted forever, and he couldn't give it to her even if he wanted to.

She had given him her top line up for which girls could replace her for his perusal, but really it didn't matter. He liked his girl's fine, and they were all just a means to an end, a passing fancy. Her choices were to be at his disposal soon, and he would help make the final choice on who would grace his bed most often once Simone was gone. So at least he had an illicit encounter to look forward to later on that week, something to keep his mind off his loneliness and burning need for his Keeper, his Isis.

It was then that Syrus caught sight of Jingles stumbling down the street; his eyes glazed and starry like his fix had been a good one. Syrus sneered. People who valued their lives so little that they would poison themselves so carelessly disgusted him. It was lucky he didn't deal with the waste of life on a normal basis. No, it was usually left up to Arlo and after tonight it would continue to be, he hoped.

Jingles stopped a few feet from him and leaned against the wall, and Syrus sighed and pushed off where he was standing, stubbed out his cigarette and went to him, eager to get this damn set up done.

"Where is Arlo?" the junkie slurred, his eyes bright, pupils huge as he stared at Syrus.

"Other commitments. What do you got for me?" Syrus inquired, leaning against the building. He stood far enough away to ensure intimacy of both words and touch was discouraged. The less he had to deal with this waste of life, the better. Perpetuating the myth of friendship between them wasn't the quickest way outta this situation.

Jingles frowned, and then smiled as recognition washed over his face. "Right." He dug in his pocket and pulled out a grubby piece of paper, gingerly handing it to Syrus.

Syrus looked at the paper, an address and set of numbers were on it and a name, Marrow Industries. He looked at the junkie and frowned. "What the hell is this shit?"

Jingles sighed and shrugged. "Arlo asked for the info. I told him Marrow was the central hub of the Div, he said give him proof."

Bombshell. While most humans didn't know anything about the silent war being raged throughout the world, or about the reasons why, few, like Jingles, did, and that knowledge was what drove them to alternate means of medications and of mental help. The majority of the humans that knew of the battles were committed to several maximum security institutions, screaming of humans who turned into fanged and winged demons who killed indiscriminately, spreading despair and hatred wherever they ended up.

While Jingles hadn't ended up housed for insanity, he was no better off.

Syrus looked at the sensitive, a man who drowned out his psychic abilities with the drugs he consumed, and felt sorry for him. If he had a stronger constitution he would have been a powerful ally, but as it was he was a mediocre informant, though if this tip panned out, Syrus would have enough respect for the man to consider him an ally even if it wasn't mutually advantageous.

Syrus nodded, frowned and slipped the paper into his back pocket.. There was a subtle change in the air, quiet, but that feeling of wrongness was growing.

Div. Shit, not now.

Jingles sensed it too and whimpered, shrinking into himself, trying to become one with the building. Odds were they were tailing the junkie because of the information he had, and Syrus, while he partially doubted the Intel, knew it must be close enough to the truth for them to be following him. He needed to get the guy out of there, and quickly.

"Jing, hide," he said quietly. "Get in the club, stay at the bar. I'll come and get you. Don't fucking leave."

The junkie understood and nodded, his face paler as he stumbled his way into the club, fresh cigarette smoke enveloping him. At this point, it was the safest place for him.

Syrus scanned the darkened street and caught it again. Malice. Someone else was the target; some unknown person was about to get a wakeup call into the world they didn't want to know.

He hoofed it toward the resonating sinister echo, hoping he wasn't too late, that whoever the target was, it was still innocent to their surroundings.

He found the scene minutes later, the dark parking lot before him held three cars, two women and three street punks.

He advanced, the energy coming off the punks wasn't human and his first assessment was correct. They were Div, and this meant trouble.

They were shadowing the two women, who seemed oblivious to the stalking. Talking and laughing as they walked toward the furthest car in the lot, the one on the right was purely human, while the one on the left's aura held a bit of the mystic. He wasn't sure if she was just sensitive like Jingles, but there was something about her... He was sure that was what was drawing the Div to her.

Syrus rolled his shoulders and palmed his weapons, his adrenaline peaking. When the leader of the Div took point and lunged, Syrus was off like a shot, his daggers in his hands.

The first two went down quickly as they didn't even hear him coming.

Acolytes. He slipped the blades of the daggers into the bodies of the newly turned Div, where the shoulders and neck met along the spine, and they clouded, fading into nothing.

He propelled himself upward, hearing the head Div speak to the girls, a gravelly and pain filled voice. Div in human form were constantly in need of blood and feelings of hopelessness, and when they didn't get enough, they went into withdrawals like an addict.

"Evening ladies. Think we can walk you home?"

The girls turned stiffly, realizing that they were in some deep shit.

Syrus landed silently in front of their car and walked out of the deeper shadows with his daggers hidden.

"Now friend, I think you might wanna leave the lovely ladies be and move along," he offered with undisguised menace to the Div leader.

The leader smirked, recognizing what Syrus was. "You're outnumbered Inferi."

Syrus shook his head and pulled out his dagger and spun it in his hand. "I think not. You're all alone."

Realization broke on the Div's face and then he snarled. Grabbing the girl closest to him, he pitched a switchblade, and held the point to her throat. "One fucking step and she dies."

Syrus scoffed and stood his ground; his feet place apart, the beginnings of a fighting stance. "The fuck do I care if you kill her? Honestly. Grabbed the wrong one there, Buddy." He smirked and looked at the other girl and threw the dagger. It imbedded itself in the Div's arm, and it the contact made the metal smoke.

The girl screamed, dropped and rolled and ran for the car, grabbing the sensitive as she did.

"Fuck Gwen let's go!" she screamed and didn't even bother to look back at the two men squaring off.

Alone, Syrus threw off all context of Good Samaritan, and let his powers writhe around him. True, they were bound, but he could still kick ass with what he had. "Now Div, where were we?"

The Div snarled and rushed.

Syrus coolly stepped aside and grabbed the flailing demon around the throat. "Do me a favor? Tell your boss to go fuck himself." He plunged the other dagger in between the Div's shoulder blades. It clouded as well, passing to vapor and then to nothingness. It was too easy. He and his team were fucking gods, and they were all wasted on what passed for Div these days.

He spun around, looking for and found the girls, terrified by the car furthest from him. The redhead kicked the vehicle, while the other, the sensitive, hugged herself.

"Son of a bitch what are we going to do now?" the redhead then looked up to see him walking towards them. She narrowed her eyes and stood protectively in front of the sensitive, Gwen.

She took a fighters stance, sizing him up. "All right asshole... I don't know what you think..."

Syrus stopped walking and held up his hands. "Please relax; I'm not going to hurt you. Christ I saved you from some rather unsavory asshats. Not a shot in hell I'm going to turn into a damn predator. Why the hell didn't you peel out already?"

The red head relaxed a bit, but kept her stance wary. "Car is toast. Flat tire and some motherfucker stole the damn stereo!" She kicked the door again and shook her head.

Syrus sighed. Leaving these two exposed on the street was not in the cards. The redhead was a fighter, the brunette; she looked like she was going to throw up. "Great. Look I can give you guys a lift if you want, my car is just out front, No tricks."

"Cause predators tend to be up front about their intentions." the brunette answered her voice clear despite her shaking. "What the fudge just happened?"

Syrus shrugged. "Junkies. I was meeting a friend of mine at Kanto and saw them outside. When you walked out they followed you. Probably that purse you're clutching in your hands there," he motioned to the redhead's wristlet. "Shitty area of town to be flaunting that."

She shook her head not buying his story. "I don't think so; I mean where did he go? I think we should call the cops." she told the last to the red head.

"Where did he go? He bolted; People do that when you pull a knife on them."

The redhead seemed to consider it.

"Yeah, fucker probably ran off. And calling the cops, shit Gwenny what the hell is that going to do? They going to take our statement? Tell us to get a tow?" she looked Syrus over and licked her lips. "And what kinda grateful would either of us be if we didn't thank this nice guy for helping us. Thank you Mr...."

"Syrus, just Syrus, and it was my pleasure, really. Those fuckers won't be bothering you again, that I promise you. So look, if I can't offer you a ride, lemme get you guys a cab. I don't think you could drive with a broken window."

The redhead gesticulated wildly. "Fuck the window, the back wheel looks like it's been chewed the fuck up."

He looked around the car to see the flat, and it looked like the wheel well had been bent, apparent sabotage. Odds are the Div didn't even know whom it was they were trapping, just laying the trap to catch some poor soul to devour. It looked like Gwen and her fiery friend were just victims of circumstance, though it was a bit of a coincidence the one called Gwen had that little bit of an auric twinkle.

He looked at her and their eyes met, and Syrus felt it. His soul woke, or what was left of it, blearily attentive to the dazzling aura before him. She was more than stunning; she was alive, vibrant, and extremely sexy. Her breath hitched, and he felt resonation, the space between them filling with almost imperceptible thickness... Gwen was a Keeper.

He smiled at her.

She took a deep breath quickly averting her eyes, she'd felt it too or at least she'd felt something. "I don't think it's such a good idea..." she looked at the redhead, her resolve seeming to fizzle. She turned back to Syrus and sighed. "Fine but promise me this, if you go all psycho killer please take her first."

Syrus laughed and shook his head. The redhead, for all her come hither and fuck me looks, was nowhere near what he was interested in. "Fair enough, though you really have nothing to worry about."

The redhead leaned into the car and grabbed a pair of sunglasses and CD, all that was left of the apparent theft and then came around, a sway in her hips. "I'm Ansley, and this is Gwen. It's very nice to meet you Syrus."

Syrus smiled. "Indeed Ansley, Gwen. Come on, the car is out front of the club." He pulled a cell out of his pocket. He clicked a button as he walked and then spoke quickly into the phone, giving Blaine instructions to get a tow for their car and a pick up for Jingles. Blaine wasn't too happy about the outcome, or Syrus playing the knight in shining armor, but he obliged, albeit grudgingly. Syrus hung up when they made it to the car, a midnight blue RSX that looked just off the lot.

"I'm surprised we got broken into with this sitting just along the street. And here you said Ansley's purse was asking to get stolen, no wonder you're carrying a knife." Gwen mused..

Syrus laughed. "Well I was standing by the car, they tend not to break in if the owner is close by I think. I always carry a knife when I visit Alphabet City. Speaking of which, you girls don't seem the type to be frequenting the clubs down here, like ever. Far too posh." He unlocked the car and motioned for them to get in. "And I meant you, not that rat hole you walked out of. So where am I dropping ya?"

Gwen gave him the address, slipping into the passenger seat after Ansley climbed into the back. "Wasn't my idea, I wanted to stay in. This night was fucking doomed from the start." her lip curled adorably over the expletive, it was obvious Gwen didn't swear often.

Syrus grinned at her. "Trust me if I didn't have to be here tonight myself I wouldn't have been, though lucky I was." He winked at her.

Ansley pouted. "Don't listen to her Syrus; she needed some time out and away... She would be a hermit if I let her."

Syrus laughed, "I doubt that." He pulled out of the spot and roared up avenue F towards Midtown.

They bickered a bit and Syrus watched them both, letting his powers seep out and get him the intel his eyes couldn't. Ansley's Aura was bright, flecked with gold and silver, ever moving and his powers couldn't get a read on it. Gwen was a shine in the darkness though. She was sensitive, something about her essence screamed to him. He felt it again, that pull at that hidden part of his essence, tugged as if to say 'look at me, pay attention to me'. How could he not?

She was sexy and sweet but sadness permeated her aura, sapping her will to live. He felt that pull again, this time to stop it. She had to be his Keeper; there was no other explanation. .

Knowing you had something you needed so close, yet so far away was the worst kind of torture. Without the Scarab, it didn't matter who she was, she couldn't help him, and he couldn't keep her.

"There's nothing wrong with being a hermit. I'm perfectly happy as a shut in. You're the one determined to thrust excitement upon me, and look at how well you've done." Gwen checked her watch. "And I'm later than I said I'd be..."

"Well we did have an ordeal." Ansley leaned forward onto Syrus' seat. She caught his eye for a second and licked her lips. Yes, the redhead was interested and he could care less. He looked sideways toward Gwen. Now that was an interesting female. He felt the tug again, slight, and saw her squirm in her seat.

"So what is it you do for a living Syrus? You look like you're in a band."

He looked back at Ansley. "I'm in security actually."

"Like money?" she leaned her head on the side of his seat, a clear invitation.

"Sometimes, I work for a security firm, in their IT department." He offered but made no move to lean closer to her.

"Really? I wouldn't have had you pegged as an IT guy, but then I guess you never really know a person just by looking." Gwen smiled at him, meeting his eyes again, the sparkle just peeking through the dark fringe of lashes.

Bingo. Girl was good at getting her flirt on. "Oh yeah? And what exactly did you think I did for a living. And you can't say band member, Ansley already guessed that one."

"Well let's see," her grin lit up her eyes. "Just enough stubble to be darkly sexy but not enough to look hairy. Expensive haircut and impeccable clothing, if a bit hipster. The knife's a worry though even without knowing you're carrying, you do scream dangerous. I'd go with mobster...although high-class escort was right up there. I'm sure Ansley would pay a lot to have your company for the night." She sat back in her seat crossing her arms. It seemed Gwen didn't like the thought of him spending quality time with her friend.

Syrus arched a brow. "Interesting. Though I have never heard mobster before. And I suppose I should probably shave." He turned his head as he took a turn onto Broadway. "And both of you don't seem the type to pay for it, which is good."

"Oh I pay in other ways, the true folly of a relationship I guess." She fidgeted in her seat, clearly uncomfortable with the admission.

She gave a little frown, as if she realized she divulged information best left unsaid and was upset with herself for doing so. Unable to sit still she wrung her hands momentarily, and then laid them in her lap, one hidden under the other.

Syrus frowned. He didn't like the sound of that or the idea of this woman in a relationship or so forlorn about the prospect. "Don't know what kinda relationship you got love, but I have never made a woman pay for anything, in any way." He shot her a kind smile, though the tone of his voice held an edge of clear malice to anyone that would do such a thing. For all his aloof behavior, he never treated his women, priestess or no, with anything but affection. He might not love them, but he liked women, and knew how to treat one. His Isis taught him as much. Women were to be worshipped, not held responsible for the world's ills or just a man's.

Ansley grinned. "Ooh one of the good ones...well see Gwen here..."

"Ugh, don't go off on Tom again Ans, you just never see his good side." Gwen cut her off sharply. This was obviously a conversation they'd had before. "You see Ansley and Tom don't get on, they've never gotten on. And he pays his way," she sounded defensive. "It was just a joke."

Syrus kept quiet and let it rest. She threw off such feelings of despair at the mention of this mysterious Tom; he couldn't bring himself to dig further.

"Tom is a complete piece of shit who wouldn't know a good woman if she was on fire in front of him. You think he would have dropped to save two total strangers? Fuck no. Tom is a waste of life, plain and simple."

After hearing the conversation so far, he had to agree. Syrus took a right and rolled onto the street they had given him the address too and stopped in front of a nice brownstone. He turned the car off and sighed. "Well ladies... home sweet home."

Without the car on, they heard a ruckus coming from the building, or more specifically, the second floor window that was open. Ansley cursed.

"And that would be the asshole in question."

"Might not be," Gwen said with no conviction. "Maybe someone's broken into my apartment...on poker night...while I've been out gallivanting." Her shoulders slumped dejectedly and she shook her head.

"Right that's about as likely as a well-hung hottie waiting for me in my bedroom." She smirked and turned to Syrus. "You wanna come up?"

Syrus smirked. Girl was persistent. "Tempting but no, I still have to meet up with my friend tonight, petal." *And you are just like every other girl in my acquaintance. No, I think easy isn't best.*

Ansley pouted but recovered quickly, then leaned in and kissed him on the cheek. "Thanks for the rescue hottie." She got out of the car, leaving Gwen to sit back down after letting Ansley past her.

"It's not often she gets turned down." her smile lightened her features but they were still shadowed by something. "Thank you for not turning into a psychotic killer that collects livers. Although it would have been a much more interesting end to the night than I'm going to have." Her lips curved in the beginnings of a wicked smile, the girl, for all her sadness had a black sense of humor.

He frowned. "Ansley, for all her bravado, is not my type. So, you going to be ok? I'm no expert but it doesn't sound like they are in a jovial mood in there."

The smile disappeared and she looked up to the window with a shrug. "I doubt you'd alleviate the situation. Thanks though. I'll be fine." she shook her head, clearly not believing her own statement. "I'll sneak into bed and they'll never know I'm back until I make breakfast for the terminally hung-over in the morning." she gave another shrug then leaned into him for a moment before pulling away and holding herself stiffly. "Well goodnight Mister Syrus, thank you again for the ride."

He smiled, took her hand and kissed it. "It was a pleasure Gwen, believe me." He let his lips linger, the feel of her on his skin sending little sparks he was sure she felt as well. Her breath hitched, and he let her hand go.

"Sleep well Gwen."

She climbed out of the car and waived back at him, a small smile gracing her lips.

He turned on the car, trying to ignore the niggling feeling that something was going to go down when he drove off down the street. He didn't make it two blocks before he turned left and made his way back to her street. Across the road from her brownstone, he turned off his car and tucked in, waiting to see that both girls would be ok.

***

"You nailed your set Raine." Simone grinned at her friend as she slid into the booth next to her. She slipped her hand onto her knee and gave it a squeeze. "And I got it all on film for him to watch at leisure. Not to mention now we have the camera think of its multipurpose uses. If he doesn't make it back by the time we go home we can make him a little movie to show him exactly what he missed." She lifted her martini glass.

Raine pouted. "Song was wasted though... Syrus was supposed to see it firsthand. Live, not on Memorex." she pouted.

"Oh honey I know." She gave a wan smile, brushing a stray hair from her face. "You can give him a live performance when he comes around later. But you know how he is, important things come up. He's our god; it's our duty to worship him not to expect things from him. I'm sure he tried."

She nodded and sighed. "Still it's not fair. You get so much time with him, I miss being around him."

"True but I'll be graduating in the summer and then I'll never really see him again. Hell after Tuesday I'll be training my replacement." She shook her head as the familiar pain cut its way through her. She didn't want things to end in the summer but she'd held onto him for as long as she could.

She was dragged out of her thoughts as Tony and another girl walked up to their table sitting a tray of drinks down as they took seats in their booth. "Look who I met." Tony laughed, tipsy. "This is... what's your name again?" She slurred her words and sat her empty drink on the table. Miraculously, it didn't tip, or slosh. Simone frowned at her, putting a check in the negative column mentally. Osiris didn't need a girl that drank too much; it was odd though, Simone hadn't ever noticed her getting drunk before.

"Carina." The girl smiled, tipping her own glass to her crimson lips.

She was dressed in slut chic, a red leather bustier and a short black skirt that flashed the red tops of black stockings. Her hair fell beyond her shoulders in dark silky waves. Hazel eyes were heavily lined, giving them a smoky, sexy appearance.

She wasn't exactly Simone's type but with a little work she could be beautiful. She found herself licking her lips. She reached for her glass then passed Raine one.

"My name's Carina." The girl said again with a wild smile at Raine. "I heard your set, your voice is amazing, so haunting."

Raine nodded, puffing up with pride. She was determined to touch the world with her voice. "Thanks. I love your skirt. Where the hell did you find it?"

"A friend of mine made it; she's real handy with a needle and thread." She sat closer to them, bumping Tony along in the seat. "You guys look pretty familiar though. Have I seen you around before?"

"Maybe." Simone smiled, taking a gulp of her martini. She sucked an olive into her mouth. "I work here so that could be it."

"Or maybe At Mercury Lounge? We hang out there a lot as well." Raine appeared to be sizing the girl up.

"No I don't think that's it...This is my first time here. What one's the Mercury lounge again?" She tipped her drink, sipping from it.

Raine took a sip of her drink and grinned. "That little hole in the wall on Houston? Bartender is from London? Perfect ass?"

Carina grinned, "Yeah that one, I'm pretty sure I've been there. At least an English bartender with a great ass sounds familiar."

Raine giggled again and leaned into Simone. "She's hot..." she placed her hand on Simone's thigh and slid it up.

She felt warm and fuzzy, her drinks hitting her quickly; two dirty martinis were definitely her limit. "She is." Simone finished her last gulp, dismissing the bitter taste.

"She's very hot. Slutty but we could work that." Raine leaned in and started kissing Simone's neck, her hand sliding up her inner thigh and under her skirt.

Tony watched and chuckled, then leaned into Carina.

"Hey girls, why don't we go somewhere more private?" Carina smiled, then wet her lips. She wrapped an arm around Tony. "My place is like five minute from here and I have a super hot roommate who'd love to meet you all."

Simone nodded, trying to think of why it'd be a bad idea but her brain came up short. It wasn't as if Osiris wouldn't meet up with them later and she always had the camera handy if anything very fun happened. "Sure, sounds fun, Raine? Tony?"

Tony grinned and turned to Carina, kissing her

Raine slipped her fingers into Simone's panties and moaned breathlessly. "Why not... Sounds like a good start to the night." she leaned in, "And you know he will love seeing this...more so then the set...Let's go play."

Carina smiled her agreement then kissed Tony forcefully. "Excellent. Bottom's up." She grinned, toasting her glass up to them before finishing it.

Raine pulled herself away, drank down the rest of her drink and giggled. "Wow, I never get this drunk this quickly. But it's a party." she turned back to Simone and smiled.

"A great party." Carina laughed, helping Tony out of her booth. "My car's just outside."

Simone nodded and kissed Raine as she pulled her up.

They all made their way to the door.

A black limo was waiting at the door.

Simone climbed in next to her, her arms and legs feeling weighted. Once Raine sat safely next to her, the door closed and the limo pulled away.

"Wow, what the hell did Tony drink?" Simone's voice sounded different when she pointed to her passed out friend next to Carina. Only minutes before she was alert, pawing at their new friend. Raine looked over with a puckered brow.. "Tony doesn't drink much. Yeah what did she drink?"

Carina smiled evilly at them both, tucking her legs primly under her, "About the same as you two, unfortunately she drank it faster so it's hit her quicker. Give it time; I'm sure you're already feeling the effects."

Simone tried to move but she couldn't, The effects of the alcohol dragged her body down. Then fear coursed through her.

Raine blinked and grimaced. "Mone? What's going on?" she whimpered and looked at Carina. "Why? What did you give us?"

She shook her head gleefully. "Just a little something from me to you, or from me to your master." She laughed coldly. "Enjoy the numbness girls, it's my gift to you, you'll be begging for it in a few hours."

Simone felt the blackness sweeping her under and she prayed for Osiris to save them. The last sound she heard was Carina's evil laughter.

***

Nathan Danvers smirked at the video screen showing the luscious sex kitten of a woman winking at him as she went through the door into his private sanctuary. Her being here meant only one thing, that she had succeeded, and the priestesses were in their custody.

It was a ballsy move, grabbing some of the Egyptian god's best and brightest, but he couldn't take credit for it, not really. He had planted the seeds in his little pet's mind, and she was the one that suggested the plan to both him and the head of his army, Caine.

Carina. She had been an asset to the organization ever since he found her brooding over the death of her family. She was a project almost fifteen years in the making, and she had come along nicely. Her rancor and ire were firmly placed against his enemies; she was a brutal ally to have on his side.

And she had helped to strike a serious blow against the damn Inferi Dii. It was going to be a multi-faceted plan he knew, but breaking the Egyptian was his first task. Caine hated him most of all, though why always eluded Nathan. Not that it mattered, Caine's issues only helped to serve the cause.

He turned and his door opened.

Carina stood in the doorway, picking at her nails.

"I trust everything is perfect?" his voice was smooth as silk as he strode across the room towards her.

His office was nothing short of industrial splendor. High concrete walls unpainted, severe, austere furniture in black, leather and chrome peppered the large space. Modern art sat on the long wall, between video monitors and a large flat screen television imbedded into the wall's face. The only proof of the room owner's personality was the overlarge wooden desk, stained a rich brownish red, the color of old blood. This room served to disorientate his business partners, being cold and sterile. The desk was meant to give a sliver of hope, something he rarely gave to the those he would conquer both on the battlefields of industry and destiny. As the head of a multimillion dollar corporation, and the high priest of the Veln's cult. The man was a force to be reckoned with.

"Everything's just peachy." she pouted briefly, "It was almost too easy. No challenge at all. I delivered them to Caine just like we talked about."

"What did you expect with a bunch of horny women? You're sex on legs pet." He took her face in his hands and kissed her hard. "And you did well. Not bad for your first op."

"Mmmmm not bad at all, but then did you expect any less?" She rose on her tiptoes kissing, him then nipping on his bottom lip. "So what now?"

Nathan smirked. Reaching down, he pinched her nipple through her shirt. The chit never wore a bra around him anymore. He had broken her of that soon after meeting her.

Finding those who were easily corrupted was a talent of his. It was the same with his lieutenants, and the other people that were pawns in his employ. Some were more useful than others in several different situations, like Carina. Not only was her hatred for the Inferi legendary, something he continued to cultivate, but the girl was a nympho, and kept his baser needs met as well. Well, her and few others he had for just that reason.

"Ahh... Oh that." she purred, leaning into him. Her eyes slid shut. "No baby," she opened her eyes and danced away from his touch. "I meant with those sluts. How else can we hurt the Inferi?"

She really did hate them, but her obsession wouldn't force his hand any faster. He was on a timeline damn it, and everything was calculated, precise enough for his chess-like strategy to work even with unforeseen circumstances. "All in good time my little tart. We can only destroy one life at a time; even with all my resources I don't like to be spread thin. This will play out nicely I think, Caine has his methods." He grinned evilly.

"So we're back to being patient?" she sneered. "Forgive me for not having too much faith in Caine's methods."

"Well then what do you suggest, pet? Calling too much attention to the company will negate all future planning." He frowned as the phone to his office rang. He moved away from her and went to his desk.

He hit the button the open line sending a crackle across the airwaves. "What it is?" he said in a clipped tone. He hated being interrupted.

Stark, one of his lieutenants sounded tinny coming through the speakerphone. "We have a problem."

Nathan sneered. "And just what would that be Stark? Another convert get smashed to ash?" Nathan had gifted Stark, Cain and Luther with the ability to create hosts for the Div demons out of the dregs of society and while Caine and Luther had completely embraced their powers without conscience, Stark was still riding the edge of humanity and mourned when one of his carefully selected Div were felled.

"No sir. We have had a breach of protocol. Someone leaked information."

Nathan balled his fists and gritted his teeth. This indeed was not good. "Leaked to who, Stark." His tone was even, measured. It wouldn't do to let on to the other man the level of his unhappiness, not yet.

He heard the other man swallow, a thick, meaty sound. "That junkie, Jingles. I don't think they realized it was him."

Nathan swore and threw his letter opener against the wall, where it embedded into the concrete wall close to Carina's head.

The girl looked at him with lust in her eyes and squirmed. Little slut liked it rough. "Indeed. Track him down, and have him exterminated, before he gets to the Inferi scum. I won't have our operation discovered."

"Yes sir. I'll have him tonight." Stark said with resignation.

"You better. And Stark?"

"Yes sir?" he swallowed audibly.

"Kill the asshole that leaked to the junkie. I want his traitorous tongue." He clicked off of the call before his henchman could comment and looked to the slut running her hands over her torso across the room. The violence had turned her on, he could smell it. Potent, dangerous, the woman held a magic of her own anyone that was acquainted with the gods would be able to detect. She was his, firmly ensconced on the side of the Velns.

And his regular bedmate.

"Come here. And crawl."

"Ummm yes sir," Her pink tongue flicked out, wetting her bottom lip as she slowly dropped to her knees and made her way towards him. Her hips swayed, full of sex, and her eyes never left his.

Nathan watched her with chained violence. He wanted to throttle someone, but would settle for a devious fuck where he could both get his rocks off and inflict pain.

She made it to him soon after she sat back on her heels and he scowled down at her. "Stand up." He hissed deeply.

A shiver ran through her as she did as she was told.

He grabbed her hair and pulled her to him, teasing her with a kiss that would never come. He turned her forcefully and bent her over his large mahogany desk, her ass high in the air. The desk was his one weakness in the room. He loved the history behind it, loved how it had belong to so many powerful men before him, men that had achieved their goals, and become titans in the world.

She moaned loudly, her hands taking the edge of the desk to brace herself. "Well someone sure is eager tonight." She pushed back against him, grinding her ass.

"Shut the fuck up whore." He held her in place by her hair, and opened his pants with his other hand. He was inside her seconds later hard and fast. He didn't give two shits if she was uncomfortable. Not that she was, her moans and gasps told a totally different story.

"Fuck!" she cried out, pushing back onto him.

He wasted no time using her for his own needs, working off the frustration and anger that lodged itself inside his stomach.

She took it all, begging for him to go harder.

He did, pulling her hair till she screamed and came hard under his ministrations.

He came then, deep in her, his magic canceling out any hopes of impregnating her. He could afford to be reckless. He was barren, his sacrifice to the Velns for the power he quietly wielded.

"Nathan!" she screamed, following him over the edge as he spilled into her sweaty, writhing body.

He pulled out soon after she stopped pulsing on him and let go of her hair. "Get cleaned up." He bit out as he righted his clothing.

"Well I'm hardly going to walk around with cum running down my thighs," she straightened. "Though it wouldn't be the first time."

"Which explains a lot. Go." He dismissed her disgustedly and walked over to the windows overlooking Manhattan.

He growled. Working off the aggression with the tart was good, but he was far from sated. No, this new development with the junkie wasn't good at all. It could ruin everything.

Chapter Two

The call from Nebacanezzar slammed into Nathan's psyche as it always did and he gritted his teeth through the pain of it. It was urgent, and it was loud. He sat up in his bed, thankfully alone in the darkness. Times like these were best dealt with alone, as to not to make known the extent of his powers. His followers knew he was in direct contact with the Velns, but they didn't know how.

He steeled himself for what was to come next. His essence would be ripped through the veils to a never-region, where they could converse in relative secrecy. It was because of this dimension that the Inferi Dii hadn't pinpointed him yet as their emissary on earth. He counted it lucky.

Nathan closed his eyes and took a deep breath careful not to scream when he was ripped from reality and into the never. His masters were not soft, and while they took his life seriously, needing him for their plans on earth, they weren't forgiving or gentle when they transferred him to their consciousness.

He traveled quickly, knowing his body was inert on the bed, almost in a deathlike trance. He gathered his psy-strength for when he stopped moving. He slammed into the nothing, which felt like a concrete floor rushing up to meet him at two hundred miles an hour, or would have had he not cushioned himself from the jarring pain with the power of his own mind The least amount of bruises on his physical body after an audience with his masters the better. He did need to keep up appearances of the steel handed asshole that ran Marrow Industries and a worldwide cult.

It was a bumpy ride, but his landing was as smooth as he could make it. He stilled his mind for the scant seconds it took for Nebacanezzar to materialize before him and boom his voice throughout the mists and space.

He waited, and watched. A figure came through the mist. He was lucky they did respect him enough to appear as humans, their real physical bodies a ruin of tentacles and sickly grey flesh and fangs, everything needed to rule over a world that was beneath them. They were the pantheon of nightmares, and despair, and because of the power they promised him, Nathan was a full convert to what they wanted.

He always found power alluring. And a little taste only made him greedy for it. It was only after he found the forgotten temple in the Sudan dedicated to the Veln's cult that he learned real power. Something had been calling him through his dreams, and led him to the long forgotten place among the sands.

As the leader of a prominent business of imports from the seas, he was able to handle the excavation and extraction of the antiquities held therein.

What he found was largely useless, except for the vase. It depicted monsters with tentacles floating in the air, of a world below in torment and decay, and while it scared him a little, the pottery radiated power. Seductive power called to him even more than the compulsion. When he had touched it, he had been given audience with their leader, the entity called Nebacanezzar..

He agreed to give his soul and life for the power they promised. Nathan had walked out of that tomb brimming with power, and a new purpose. That was back in ancient times. He was almost as old as the Gods he fought.

The Velns promised so much, and had delivered for every bit. He was now the head of a multimillion-dollar corporation, an international playboy and a bull on the corporate front. Women flocked to him, Men wanted to be him, and everyone wanted a piece of the Marrow Industries pie. Life was good, for as long as he had been alive, and it was all thanks to the Velns.

Seconds passed until Nebacanezzar fully materialized in front of him. Nathan went down on one knee, as he had done since their first meeting lifetimes ago, and waited for his lord to speak.

Nebacanezzar stood tall, wide like a linebacker, his skin golden like Nathan's, his hair straight and long, a black curtain behind his head. His eyes were a molten purple, with black slits for irises. He wore a pair of black linen pants and no shirt, the tattoo of what he really was wrapping his torso, two tentacles curling around his belly button.

Nathan bowed his head at the god before him, and then looked up at him once again.

Nebacanezzar took a head bowed too long as a sign of sniveling weakness in his minions and Nathan had been punished before for not heading the Gods wishes, and once was enough.

The God looked down to him with a sneer. "Rise. Meet me head on."

Nathan did as he was told, though meeting the entity head on was impossible as he was at least two feet taller than Nathan's bulky six foot four frame. "My Lord?"

"Your lieutenants are making a mess of the city, and in turn bringing much more attention to us. This is not acceptable. New York is the perfect place to hide, so much despair and pain here.

Your Div should be feeding, and your lieutenants should be building our earthbound army, not losing them to skirmishes with that infernal Inferi Dii!"

His voice boomed in the space between and Nathan did all he could not to wince. No weakness. None. He nodded. "The Inferi have become tenacious recently."

"Caine is your biggest issue with them, but we will deal with him at a later date. One of your fallen Div returned to us and had a message for you he couldn't bring you himself due to expiration of physical body."

This was interesting. "Yes?"

"They seem to have found one of the Relics of the underworld gods. I don't have to tell you how important this information is."

No, he didn't. Acquiring a relic was one step closer to bringing his masters back to earth. "So the Prophecy of that smug winged bitch is coming to pass then?"

Nebacanezzar nodded. "The time is at hand. Your lieutenants will be working overtime. We want more Div to receive us." "Yes lord. And the Relic?"

"A woman has it, or so we are told. The Div said the Inferi, the Egyptian from the feel of the dark energy still flowing from the final death of the Div, also sent you this gesture," he flipped Nathan off, "Or that could be for us, we are not sure what it means."

Nathan suppressed a smirk. He knew what it meant, but he would be damned if he was going to tell the God before him. No, he liked his spleen right where it was thank you very much. "Understood." He frowned. "Where should we start looking?"

The God closed his eyes and the spaces between shook with power. Nathan felt his body, so very far away, stop functioning, as the god used him as conduit. Had he not already been in a near death trance he would have choked and sputtered, but he was safe from the throws of asphyxiation on this plane.

The sensations only lasted seconds and Nebacanezzar came back to himself and opened his eyes, the purple a murky mass of expended energy. "Towards the middle of the city, a large tenement. Follow the path from the beginning of words, though it is not the slums." He sneered anew. "Send Caine; see if he can redeem himself in our eyes."

Nathan was sure that after this, Caine would be granted more power, as his brutality and evil had kept him alive through the ages. Nathan had found him in Turkey in the fifteenth century and had had him by his side, if just as a thug ever since. "Redeem?"

"He has been sloppy as of late. Do not allow him to kill any of those he has taken. It will bring too many complications for us."

Nathan wasn't sure how he was going to do this, but the gods had spoken. He nodded.

The God backed away, dematerializing into the mists and darkness surrounding Nathan.

He closed his eyes, readying his essence for the trip back through the void and took off as his masters let go of him. He snapped back like a rubber band, moving at extreme velocities, back to his physical body.

He woke with a gasp and cough, his muscles feeling achy and sore. It would pass with the rest of the night's sleep but before he could let the sweet oblivion of sleep claim him, he needed to carry out his master's orders.

He willed his cell phone from its perch on his dresser to his hand and flipped it open, hitting the speed dial for Caine. Using any kind of mind speak after an audience with the Velns was spotty at best, and he didn't want to project to the entire population of Div. Addressing the hive mind wasn't something he planned to do until needed, as it would take a lot out of him to touch so many souls, so he saved that for when it was needed, and that time hadn't come yet.

Caine picked up and he heard whimpering in the background. "I have had word from Nebacanezzar." "Nathan?" Caine's voice sounded strained.

"Who the fuck else would it be?" he growled into the phone. "What the fuck is your problem?"

"Just really getting into my job," he chuckled maliciously. "You sound like shit, if you don't mind me saying, lord."

"Comes with the territory. Like I said, I had word from Nebacanezzar. It seems a Relic has been located."

"A Relic?" he paused. "Where?"

"Midtown. Apparently that fuck Osiris sent one of our soldiers to their just rewards and he caught scent of the Relic. A woman has it."

"Osiris," he growled an oath down the phone. "I'll get it."

"Too true. Now, what exactly are you doing? I have been told to tell you not to touch any of those girls. Nebacanezzar orders."

"Ah... Well..." he could hear Caine frown. "They're as good as untouched. I'm sure you won't hear them complain."

Of course not. Gagged women rarely did much more then whimper and shed tears. "I mean it Caine. They were adamant. You're to start looking starting from the beginning of words, though I have no fucking clue what that means. Alphabet city most likely. Take a normal contingent, but don't draw attention. Get the relic, and the woman that has it. I wanna know how she got it. Clean, and by the fucking numbers Caine. No witnesses."

The man had been his associate and comrade for a long time, but Nathan never knew him to be much more than a psychotic lunatic.

He was a calculating son of a bitch some of the time, but his brutality was what had kept him a Div this long, and why he was a lieutenant. But if the Gods were not happy with his performance, or the way he was handling business, well...

He hated to think exactly what that meant. Whereas Stark was a bleeding heart still holding onto his humanity even after the last hundred years since he'd been turned, and Luther was the best showman they had, bringing in the largest volume of new recruits through the street missions, Caine was the one that was always with his hands in everything.

"Of course, I have just the Div for the job. I'll start right away."

"Indeed. And apparently, the Egyptian sent the Div with another message as well."

"A message?"

Nathan chuckled. "Yeah, he flipped the bird, though that could be aimed at them or me, either way I wasn't telling Nebacanezzar."

"No, I should think not."

"So the smarmy fuck is lurking about. Be on guard. And check in with Stark. Apparently while you were out we had a information breech."

Caine made a frustrated sound between a sigh and a growl. "One of his or one of mine? If it's his then it's his fault, I swear he coddles the little bastards."

"Didn't say. But I gave the order. The junkie is still at large. Put out the word."

"Maybe that's something you should put your pet whore onto."

"Possibly. She has to be good for something right?"

"If you say so."

Nathan snorted, "Says the man entertaining three priestesses."

"Entertaining myself with them all in the name of the cause. There no comparison to fucking with them like this and what you're doing giving the cunt free reign. She's got an attitude, prancing around like a fucking queen. You shared power with it and that's... Disconcerting."

"All in the name of the cause. She's an ally that they wouldn't see coming. You would do well to respect the fact that in brutality and effectiveness, the slut rivals you."

"Of course I trust you judgment. You've never steered us wrong so far... I'm just not too sure as to which part of your anatomy you're steering with."

"Does it really matter? Carina, Lorelei, and Eve... they are all the same, useful until proven otherwise. Carina though, she's something special. Not to me mind you, but they have told me she's important."

"That's a whole other matter then. Still you could work on that attitude of hers."

"Which is the least of my worries these days. Either way we need to be alert. That junkie, depending on what he found out, could make quite a mess for us. I have to assume that they know who is in charge here, but that doesn't mean we have to prove their suspicions. So like I said. No killing of the girls, keep a low profile. You have your orders."

"They're noted. I'll let you know when we have the relic and the woman."

"See that you do." They hung up and Nathan replaced his phone across the room with a though. He flopped back on his bed sighing. Fatigue was setting in, and quickly, and the only thing that would help the exhaustion was the sleep claiming him. He surrendered the tenuous hold he had on consciousness, and sunk down into blissful oblivion.

Chapter Three

"He give ya a goodnight kiss?" Ansley went up the steps to the door to the building. "Not a bad way to end the night if ya ask me, Guy was super hot."

"No, of course not." She didn't think Ansley had noticed her lean, she'd been so close, had wanted to so much. "I wouldn't do that to Tom." No matter if he'd done it to her, repeatedly. She didn't blame him though; she'd cheat on her too.

Syrus had been hot though, molten, and if it weren't for Tom he would definitely have tickled her fancy, maybe more than that. Sometimes Gwen didn't feel like the mousy Librarian she was, just sometimes though.

"Right." Ansley startled her from her thoughts of the sexy stranger's eyes. "I don't know why you are so loyal to that fucking leech. Look let's just forget about this ok? Superman can have our silent thanks, and if we ever see him again we can thank him properly. Several times." she smirked and licked her lips. "Guy was hot and moved like a wet dream."

"Hmmm." She'd had that wet dream before, the kind that you woke up from panting heavily and feeling completely satisfied, if not a little guilty for Tom's sake. Her dreams could touch her in ways Tom never could.

"And his eyes, not like anything I've ever seen before. A girl could never get tired of gazing into those."

Jealousy and defeat crept over her at once, of course he'd choose Ansley, men always did. Although maybe that was for the best.

Gwen knew full well that real relationships didn't consist of adoringly watching your partner's soulful eyes, losing yourself in them for hours.

The cold hard fact of relationships was that nobody was perfect. Relationships were all about compromising yourself. She'd just have to accept whoever was stupid enough to love her, and that man was Tom. Tom had his faults but she had her more than her fair share too and for all his faults, he truly loved her. "Anyway it's not Tom's fault you really never do see his good side."

"No one sees his good side, least of all you. And don't you dare tell me you stay with him because he's a fucking stallion in bed. No, that man's good side has got to be his ass as he's walking out of your life for good. You do know you're a goddamn doormat right?"

"God Ans, I don't need this from you right now." Not before she was about to walk into bedlam.

"Gwenny, I love you to death, and this man is toxic to you. You think Tom would have jumped to save us? Nope. He would have run his chicken ass away." Ansley crossed her arms over her chest.

"That's because Tom's not a heroic idiot." *With amazing eyes and a rock hard body. Not like Syrus.* "Tom's just a normal average guy. A Clark Kent to my Lois Lane. I'll never be you Ans; I'm not out looking for some god-like hero. I know my limitations and I've settled with the best I can do. It's realistic." The words tasted bitter in her mouth as some part of her, deep down, tried to rebel against them.

She turned and walked away, mostly needing to put distance between Ansley and herself, rather than and deep-seated need to get home quicker.

Ansley followed, blocking her. "Tom is not the best you can do. Tom isn't even the best a junked up prostitute could do. He's lower than the floaters in the toilet at a club! And you stay with him!

You don't ever have to be me Gwen, but you do have to have some goddamn self respect." She frowned down at Gwen. Ansley was statuesque while Gwen was just this side of five-five.

"Self respect?" she forced a laugh, stepping into her so she invaded her personal space. "I have plenty of respect for myself but I lose any I have for you every time you open your mouth against him. Nobody's perfect Ans you're just going to have to accept that, especially if you ever plan on meeting someone stable. No wonder supermen don't exist. Sometimes you have to compromise your dreams and goals to be happy. I hope I'm not there when that realization finally hits you because it's gonna hurt." She took that step back, her hands moving defensively to her hips.

"You deserve a man that doesn't cheat on you, or hit on your friends." she offered quietly as she looked up at the building they both lived in. A five-story brownstone sat in Chelsea, a stunning area of the city.. They were both lucky to have family that bought there when it was still up and coming. Ansley was on the fifth floor, while Gwen's apartment was on the second. Both girls had lived there since they were toddlers, and been friends since first grade.

At first, Ansley had lived with Gwen before her parents had decided to move to Boca, then moved upstairs to her own bachelorette pad that kept appreciating as the years went on. Both of the women had nest eggs worthy of American nobility should they ever decide to sell.

She threw her hands up into the air. "Whether I deserve him or not, I want Tom." she sighed, almost believing herself. "And he only hits on you because he knows you'll say no. It's like a joke." One it wasn't funny.

Gwen knew for a fact Tom would jump into bed with Ansley in a heartbeat. Most straight men would. Syrus had turned her down though, but then he was meeting friends. She didn't believe for a minute his statement about her not being his type though. She was every man's type. Her red headed best friend was gorgeous where as she struggled just to look pretty. "Anyway none of it matters much. We should get inside before anything else happens."

Ansley rolled her eyes. "You think inside is any better? Gwenny. If he's an asshole when we get there, you're staying with me tonight." They walked up the concrete steps and through the ornate double doors of the building. A few seconds in the elevator and they were standing in front of Gwen's door. The boisterous sounds of several inebriated men filtered under the door and Ansley frowned. "I'm not joking Gwenny." She shook her finger at the closed door.

"You don't have to walk me to my door, I'm a grown up." She glared at the door trying to hide a wince as something smashed. Dread filled her like molten lead; she'd half hoped they'd be finished by now.

Ansley scoffed and stood a little stiffer, ready to do battle. "Right. Like I'm going to leave you until I see the state your place is, and the state Tom is in." Something else crashed to the ground and she frowned. Her hands flexed into fists. It wouldn't be unheard of for Ansley to get physical where Tom was concerned; she had once hit him over the head with a watermelon at a block party when he said something rather unsavory.

"Yeah right so you've got more ammo for the next Tom bashing round that you have."

Gwen didn't want to open the door, she didn't want to see what mess her boyfriend and his friends had made in the house.

She didn't want to see if they'd brought any women or strippers in but she sure as hell didn't want to have to face whatever was behind the door with her best friend standing behind her judging her. "Just go. I don't want you here"

Ansley laughed, a bitter sound, tinged with sadness. "Not a fucking shot in hell. Imma take a peek, then I'm going to bounce." she took the key from Gwen and opened the door, pushing it open to bedlam.

Tom and two of his friends sat at the kitchen table playing poker. Gwen let out a sigh of relief that there were no women but it was short lived when she saw what had made the crash. Her grandmother's pot was in pieces, the yucca plant that it contained strewn all over the place, soil covering the cream carpet. It would take hours to clean and no amount of glue could fix the plant pot. Her grandmother had made it when she'd gone through a phase of working with clay. It was irreplaceable. Apart from that there wasn't much else wrong with the place, she noted with relief. The pot was her own fault; she shouldn't have kept the pot on the stand anyway. It was stupid of her to put something so valuable to her in such a position, Gwen told herself. It was easily knocked over. "So?" She turned to Ansley. "Satisfied?"

Ansley frowned and narrowed her eyes at the mess. "What shit is this? Honestly have the three of you no manners?!"

Tom glared up at her, causing Gwen to wince.

Ansley shouldn't have shouted at him when he was this drunk he always got volatile.

"Manners? Like I need you to come into *my* fucking house and lecture me on fucking manners. Mind your own fucking manners."

Ansley hit him on the shoulder, clearly unafraid of his malignant gaze or what it could mean. "Go to hell Tom. This isn't your house. You broke something and are too fucking lit to fix it or care. Fucking useless," she frowned with distaste.

Tom barred his teeth, then, when he saw Ansley wasn't in any way intimidated by his display, gave a chuckle to play it off to his friends. "Why should I care? It was an ugly pot and if she didn't want it knocked over the daft bitch should have put it somewhere where it wouldn't fall so easily."

Ansley wasted no time slapping him upside the head. "Watch it! You're not a fucking child; you should be able to move about an apartment without knocking shit over."

"Fuck Ansley!" he grinned, grabbing her hand and held it to his chest. "Baby you know how hot I get when you touch me. Gwen's frigid touch doesn't ever get me that hot."

Ansley rolled her eyes and scowled. "Take your hand back Tom unless you wanna lose it." "And if you feel like that about my best friend, then why the fuck are you here, you goddamn leech?"

"I stay for Gwen baby. How could she ever live without me?"

"Much better then she is now I can tell you that. Hands off, last warning." She positioned her hand for what Gwen knew would be a maddening assault on Tom's genitals.

He let her go and pushed her back. "Yeah, you would say that. I bet you've been telling her that all night just so you can get it back to things just being the two of you. You're so transparent you've always resented me. I just hate the way you manipulate her, it makes me so angry."

Ansley laughed and put her hand on her hip. "Yet I'm not the one that's sitting like a lump of shit in this apartment with two balding assholes who couldn't find the open end of a paper sack. Don't you guys have jobs?" she looked at Gwen. "Well?"

"I'm going to bed, Ans." She'd had enough of this. "Good night." She hugged her briefly.

Ansley smiled and nodded. "I will see you in the morning." she turned and frowned at the other men. "That's your cue to get the fuck out as well. Up!"

They grumbled and traded barbs with her as she herded them out of the house, slamming the door behind her. Gwen was alone with Tom then, and the silence was deafening for about five minutes, until Tom started the whirlwind once more.

"How the fuck can you let her talk to me like that Gwen? You know I love you right baby?" he stood up shakily and went to her, wrapping his arms around her, his lips sloppy on her shoulder.

"Of course I know that." She stood stiffly knowing better than to relax into him. "Ansley just does what she wants, I asked her not to come in." She hugged him back, trying but failing to feel safe in his arms. The acrid smell of alcohol wafted off of him. From experience she knew he wouldn't be done ranting.

"That's right baby. The bitch is just jealous of what we have." he rubbed against her, whisky dick rearing its ugly head yet again. "Now what were you talking about going to bed?"

"To sleep." She sighed and pulled away from him. "It's late and I'm due in at work in the morning. It's been a really bad night; we were attacked in a parking lot you know." Looking up at him she smiled knowing he'd be concerned for her.

He frowned and scoffed. "So what is it? Enjoyed yourself so much at the bar you can't come home and show me some attention? After all I fucking do for you?" he went over and kicked what was remaining of the pot and it shattered against the wall. "I have been hurting for you all night baby, and you're just going to do me like that?" he tried to look hurt, though the rage was bubbling up, mottling his skin.

Her eyes widened as she shook her head and dragged her eyes away from the remnants of clay. She hated when he got like this, if Ansley had kept her nose out of her business she could have snuck off to bed and he could have finished his poker game.

"No, it's not that." She lifted her hands to placate him. "You know I'd never do anything to hurt you Tommy. I just have to be up early and you're drunk. I don't want us to do anything that we'll regret in the morning. Please. Let's not fight. I don't want to fight." she pleaded with him to let it go. The last thing she wanted to do tonight was have sex. "I'm just not in the mood."

"Fucking never are!" He turned from her and grabbed his jacket.

Panic leapt in her chest, "I'm sorry!" The last thing she wanted was for him to spend the night someplace else. With someone else . She stepped towards him. .. "Look we can tomorrow. When I come home from work I'll cook a nice dinner or we can order in and have a bottle of wine, just the two of us. Something really special." Her heart pounded in her chest but she forced a smile at him. "Come to bed, we'll cuddle."

Tom turned to her and hatred filled his eyes. "No thanks Darlin. Nights still young think I'll go for a pint." he smirked cruelly. "See what I can see."

She shook her head, knowing exactly what that meant. He'd go out prowling find himself somebody else all because she'd been too lazy to give him what he needed. "No. Don't go out. Baby I'm sorry, come to bed with me. Please. We'll have sex."

Tom sneered. "Don't do me no favors Gwen. I don't need no frigid bitch tonight." he turned and went to the door. "You just have no fire, no matter how good I give it to you."

"Well maybe it's not me!   Because I don't feel any fire, no matter how "good" you give it to me." She made air quotes furiously.

"Cheeky bitch." The venom in his eyes instantly doused her anger. "Just proves you're frigid is all. You know what? Fuck this. I'm tired of the fucking charade. It's about time I move on to greener pastures. Hotter, younger, sexier pastures that enjoy a good fucking. Seriously you're frigid Gwen. Never gonna change that's for damn sure." He snorted with disgust then walked out the door, slamming it shut and rocking its hinges.

She winced at the sound; her fists clenched tightly her body ridged.

The dust filtered slowly down from the ceiling, drawing her eye. She stared numbly at it unable to move or feel. So this was it. He'd finally left her, hell; she'd practically driven him out. She knew in her heart of hearts that she'd be much better off.

No longer tearing herself apart trying to please him, cleaning up after him, justifying her actions to everyone, including herself. There was also another traitorous part that screamed she couldn't live by herself, couldn't be alone. It told her this was it; Tom was the only man who'd ever want to be with her. She was going to end up an old cat lady.

She'd be spending the rest of her life alone if she didn't run after him begging him to come back proving that she didn't have to be frigid. The first part of her stayed her feet. There was no going after him when he was like this. He'd go off and do what he wanted. No point in letting him hurt her any more.

Instead she closed her eyes letting the tears flow freely as she sunk to the ground sinking into the strewn soil and bits of terracotta.

Chapter Four

Syrus stood silent sentinel as the ruckus in Gwen's apartment went from extreme to non-existent. Seconds later, several men exited the building, though none of them held any energy signature that related to Gwen. *Ah Gwen*, he thought as he leaned casually against the RSX and watched the other men amble down the block. *Lovely Gwen.* The building across from him blazed with her essence. Bright purple, with swirls of magenta and silver, radiated from the second floor windows.

He frowned. She was distressed.

His powers were interested in what was happening across the street, something that had not happened in some time. Usually it was quiet, unmoving, unless he called on it for some issues with a battle or something similar. Rarely did it awaken of its own accord.

He crossed the darkened street and quietly scaled the fire escape, making it to the second floor to peer into the window.

The brunette that tugged at his heart and other things was there, seemingly engaged in an argument with a very inebriated man. He listened, his hands going to fists as he heard the asshole insult her, call her frigid. Her aura said differently, but what would a callous human know about a bright light such as her?

He watched her, the way her body moved and the defeat in her stance, and swore under his breath. There was only one reason for that, abuse. The woman was a shining light and the clod was intent on stamping her out with his behavior and infidelities. He didn't deserve a woman like this anywhere in his rotten life.

He watched as the fuck said his goodbyes and slammed the door. When she turned, he saw tears shining in her eyes. Syrus watched them fall, rage pouring through him. His heart pounded when he got a good look at her face.

She was so beautiful. Brown hair in shining waves, sad green eyes, that probably glittered when she smiled, really smiled. A perfect body any man would be privileged to hold close to him. Her lips were full, and he watched them as she cried silently, hugging herself. He couldn't comfort her, not and get away with it, but he could go and make that fucker pay. She walked into the bedroom.

He moved away from the window and the hairs on the back of his neck stood up. *Div. Shit. Here again? Don't these fuckers ever quit?*

It then dawned on him that the attack at the club and the contingent he felt close might be related. He sighed and cloaked his presence, intent keeping a covert eye out to see what the next move would be. He watched the doors to the building to see the drunk fucker leave, hoping that he wouldn't have to step in if he decided to come back for round two with the girl, Gwen. *Gwen...*

***

How dare that bitch talk to me like that! Tom sneered at the thought of her growing a backbone after all these years. She'd be nothing without him. She *was* nothing without him. Stupid bitch, he'd wasted enough of his life on her. He staggered along to the elevator, getting in and leaning against the wall.

"Oh well may as well see if the redhead wants to play." He pressed the button for the top floor.

He palmed himself roughly easing some of the ache in his cock. He'd take her so fucking hard. No way would she be fucking frigid like Gwen the fucking ice queen. The redhead had fire, something Gwen could never posses. He grinned and the elevator slowed to a halt letting him off.

"Hey bitch, come out here for a sec. Gwen needs you!" He slammed his fist on the door, standing close so she couldn't see out of the peep hole.

Ansley came to the door in her fluffy robe and bunny slippers wide eyed and pissed off. "What the fuck Tom? She throw you out? Go sleep it off you prick." she said frowned at him, her door open in total defiance of his seeming need for dominance.

"Stupid bitch, come here." He lunged at her, grabbing her arms. "I'm through with her. She's nothing but a frigid bitch."

"So what? You thought you would bring your sorry ass up here and get you a little some-some?" she scowled. "Hands off me Tom or you're going to be hurting..."

"Like a tiny bit of a girl like you could hurt me." He laughed in her face.

She brought her knee up and connected it with his groin and smirked. "Told you, you prick."

He doubled over, pain spreading through him. Falling to his knees he threw up on her floor.

Ansley scoffed. "Yeah that's sexy, you need to bounce Tom or I'm going to make you lick that shit up. Christ what the hell have you been eating?"

"Fuck you..." He rolled out of the way of the kick she sent at him and stood to his feet before hobbling in to the elevator. He punched the button for the ground level.

That was it, he was going out to Merry's and he was getting laid. She was one girl who appreciated him. *Fuck Gwen and fuck her fucking bitch friend.* The elevator stopped letting him off and he staggered back out stumbling hazily out the doors and down the stairs.

***

The Mortal's fate was sealed the second he stumbled into the alley between Gwen's building and the next. Not much bigger then a hallway, it looked well traveled by day, but looked even more abandoned at night then some of the crack houses in the Bronx.

Syrus stood against the brick of the building, still on the second floor fire escape, watching Tom get stalked. Son of a bitch didn't have one clue he was walking headlong into his death, and Syrus couldn't feel anything close to remorse.

He heard the guy grumbling to himself and then smirked as three Div blocked his path.

"What the fuck?" He looked them over. "Get outta my way stupid punks." He muttered with a slight slur.

The one on the right looked at the one in the center and smirked. "Your right, he's got the scent all over him. What do we do boss?"

Syrus went cold. Caine. The son of a bitch was still alive. He tampered down his rage and listened, intel was first and foremost. What did they want with the drunk?

The leader, Caine, stepped forward and Syrus got a good look at his face. Scarred, more than the last time they tangled, he was dressed much like his cohorts, dirty jeans, black boots, t-shirt and leather jacket, which was all standard issue for Div, much like the skinheads uniform of suspenders and Doc Martens, but his eyes were black, soulless.

Being a Div had agreed with him apparently, As he was still in complete control of himself, something the rest of these sad sacks wouldn't be in the next year if they lived that long.

Caine opened his mouth, his teeth brilliant white. "He also smells heavily of alcohol, I'm surprised you could sense anything on him at such a young age Brander. You show promise." he turned to Tom and smiled, a mouth full of needles. "Why do you smell like you have been in Egypt? I know you haven't left this city, so how is it you have come to smell of the dark sands of the deep desert?"

Tom blinked at them several times looking from one to the other ignoring the one who hadn't spoken. "What the fuck? What the fuck are you talking about?" He took a hesitant step backwards then another.

Syrus watched two more Div come up behind him, cutting off his escape. This was not going to be pretty.

Caine took a step forward and cocked his head. "Answer the question and maybe we will kill you before we dine on your flesh."

He frowned, "I don't know what the fuck you're talking about. I've never been to fucking Egypt, just came from my ex's apartment though, there's tons of old junk in there."

Caine smiled and relaxed. "Really? Anything from Egypt? Maybe a Scarab?"

"That's like a bug right?" the words slurred out of his maw.

Caine chuckled. "Yes, a beetle, a Lapis, or blue Scarab."

Syrus froze listening to the conversation. If what Caine was hedging at was true, then he was in the right place at the right time.

His Relic. His Keeper. He *was* reading it right. He nearly vibrated with hope. "Yeah she's got something like that. It's on a necklace, gold one too. I tried to get her to pawn it, bitch said no. Bet its worth something right?"

"Oh more then you know. Thank you." he smiled again, his eyes going blacker as his teeth got longer. Syrus shook his head. The guy was a whelp that wasn't getting out of this one. Served him right for selling Gwen out.

***

Gwen heard noise coming from outside. Tom. Smiling, she knew he'd come back and now was her time to kick him back out. If he was in a groveling mood there was no way in hell that she planned on missing it. She sat up, throwing on jeans over her sleep cami and boy shorts then went to the door.

He wasn't in the hall but she wouldn't put it past him to have changed his mind. Rolling her eyes, she grabbed a pair of sneakers and put them on making her way to the elevator. It was a mess, clearly someone had a tantrum and she wasn't taking any bets who it had been. Her neighbors were going to kill her, not to mention make her pay for the damages, all the more reason to make Tom suffer for his actions.

Maybe if she could just get him to admit that he was wrong and really mean it this time. She growled, shaking her head at her naivety. This false hope was getting ridiculous. She had to get stronger starting from now. She had to stop blaming herself for his mistakes. That was the old Gwen and starting from now she was the new Gwen, not a doormat or an enabler but a strong independent woman. New Gwen deserved better. Sure, and if she could just keep telling herself that she might believe it.

The cold air from the hall hit her and she hugged herself. She stepped out, going to the door and onto the street to see which way he had went. She could still smell the alcohol in the air so he couldn't have went very far. There was a scuffle from the alley way and she smiled, shaking her head. "Always was an alley type of guy." She decided to investigate.

The noises got louder as she walked towards the corner of the building. She couldn't quite place the sound of squelching and cracking. She blinked in confusion, it sounded like someone was enjoying a good meal. There was a deep slurp and an undeniably familiar moan. "Fucking hell." It was just like that bastard to go off and get himself a cheap whore to blow him.

Well that was the final straw. She couldn't live like this anymore, Ansley was right she deserved better. An amoeba deserved better than this. Gwen had officially grown a spine. She marched the rest of the way and, despite her new spine and the fury coursing through her; she gingerly looked around the corner. What lay there made her blood run cold and her stomach seize in terror.

Five figures knelt down over a sixth; they were covered in something that looked brown and sticky under the light. Her brain, horrified, refused to process the information giving to it, they were eating it... Tom. Oh God. They were eating Tom. She shook her head unable to get her body to work. They looked vaguely like the junkies from earlier. Though they had never been junkies. She'd known that from the start. Demons.

No Demons didn't exist, they just lived on TV and in books, this couldn't be happening. There had to be some rational explanation. Cannibals or kids out for Halloween. Only it wasn't anywhere near Halloween and Cannibals didn't have black eyes and shark-like teeth.

An arm wrapped around her waist and a hand covered her mouth as the body behind her hauled her back. "Shhhh... Gwen the last thing you wanna do is call attention to yourself." The man whispered in her ear as he pulled her into the shadows.

She swallowed her scream; her whole body tensing, fighting the masculine body behind her. She dug her nails into his hand trying to pull it away from her mouth in sheer panic. There was no way in hell she'd go without a fight. She kicked at him but still he persisted in dragging her down the street. Away from the mess in the alley, from the monsters eating Tom. Oh god poor Tom. He would have fought; Tom would have fought with his own shadow. For all the good that it did him. The defiance drained away from her and she let herself be led away.

Once back in front of her building, he let her go, cursing at the scratches on his hand. He turned her and smiled. "Calm down, ok? I need you thinking clearly, not freaking out. We need to get you outta here."

"You think?" She looked up at Syrus, and scowled at him. "I... you're not going to tell me that they're junkies, are you?" Her arms wrapped around herself hugging tightly.

"No, I'm not, just like I'm not going to insult your intelligence and tell you I was just happening by."

"Stalking then..." she shook her head. Now wasn't the time to stand around and chat. "We need to call the cops... or get a gun or a bible or something." Gwen could hear the shrill of panic in her voice but could do nothing to stop it, nor did she want to, she was panicking.

He smirked. "I'm going to go for door number 4. None of those things are going to help. We need to get you the fuck outta here."

Against her will her eyes dragged back to the corner her legs seizing and her stomach retching again. "I'm not sure I can... where?"

"Anywhere but here?" he guided her towards the door into the building. "Look we don't have much time here ok? Those fucks won't be occupied forever and I would much rather be well away from here when they pick up the scent."

"Scent?" Shaking, she let him guide her, his large hands burning through the thin fabric of her cami. Taking deep even breaths she forced herself to remain calm. Now was not the time for a mental breakdown.

He guided her to the stairs and hustled her up quickly. "Div can scent magic." He opened the door to her floor and looked around cautiously.

"How would you even know that, you're not like them are you?"

"Like them? Hell no, cannibalistic demon doesn't look good on me. Div are the dregs of the demonic underworld."

"Demons?" She shook her head grasping for rationality. "Sure and I bet you have a zombie butler... this isn't some kind of horror film, I'm not sure what that was out there but..."

"Look, Sweetheart," he calmly cut her off in mid rant; "I'll answer all questions soon, but right now we gotta get ya outta here." He smiled. "Get a bag packed, I'll be right back."

"No. No way are you going back out there." She gripped his shirt.

Syrus pulled her to him and lifted her chin up and smiled again. "Concern for me? Don't worry Gwen," he moved closer, his mouth inches from hers. "I'll be back.

Now get your fine ass in that apartment, pack up, no dawdling."

In a moment of madness or despair she reached up on her tiptoes, and pressed her lips gently to his for a second. If there was the possibility of never seeing him again, she didn't want to regret. "You better come back."

He groaned and kissed her harder, hauling her body to his. The kiss was pure intensity, but he pulled back too soon, and smirked. "For another one of those, I would crawl back from the afterlife."

Wow. This new Gwen was pretty ballsy. "Let's hope it doesn't come to that." she smiled timidly as her lips tingled from the kiss. "Just be careful."

"Always. Now go."

✳✳✳

Syrus watched her duck into her apartment and stole back down the stairs and around the corner to see if the Div were tipped off. Dear heaven that kiss. Perfection. She was ripe with magic, with the echo that strong, he did read it right, she was a Keeper, and if the scarab information was to be believed, his.

But that little truth would have to wait till the danger had passed. He cloaked himself in darkness once more and moved into the alley, drawn by the murmurs of the Div.

"Do you smell that?" the Div called Brander looked up and scented the air.

Caine looked up at him from the corpse, and then scented the air. "Indeed I do. Enlighten the others on what is it you scent." He smiled darkly at the boy baring his bloodstained teeth.

"The Relic... or a semblance of it... stronger. Like it is right here."

Caine hissed, his scarred face contorting. "Something like that. That boys, is the scent of one of the Inferi scum. The one with the closest ties to the Scarab."

Syrus backed up. He hadn't been made yet. Brander sniffed again. "But the relic... The scent, it is stronger... Like it was right here..." he lifted his head once again. "It's coming from the mouth of the alley.

Caine head jerked up towards him, meeting his eyes with his black soulless ones. "Indeed it is." he smiled at him as he stood from the corpse. "Well done Brander."

He nodded to him. "What is your will Lord Caine?" he stood and wiped his mouth.

"Kill the girl, get the relic." He smiled. "Watch out for the Inferi."

Brander nodded. "There's a back entrance, with your permission Lord Caine?"

Syrus tensed and backed up, not waiting to hear the rest of the conversation. He scaled the fire escape once more and stood at the window. He closed his eyes, willing himself into darkness. His god powers bloomed and he slipped into non-corporeal form, traveling through the open window, He materialized completely as Gwen walked out of her room. "Love, we need to get going. Now."

She started at seeing him in her apartment, and then shook it off, too amped to process it. "Go where? Aren't we safe here?" she a frantically stuffed some clothes into a bag. "And what about Tom?" Tears streaked down her lovely face.

Syrus shook his head. "I think that kiss rattled your brain, love, but it's something we are going to have to revisit at a later date. The fuckers are on their way up the stairs."

"There's nothing wrong with my brain except for the part where some type of... I don't know, zombies are eating my boyfriend and I kissed a complete stranger. But why would they come up here? Why won't they just walk on by once they've finished."

"Not zombies, demons. And your saintly fuck of an ex told them you have something they want before they tore into him. So let's go ok? I can't take all of them on now that they have fed. Think of the licker in Resident Evil." He went to the door and listened. "Chop -chop sexy, and bring that Scarab..."

"That game scares the hell outta me, why did I have to bring zombies into it..." she shook her head, "What scarab? Is it a pendant?" Without waiting for him to answer she hurriedly ran back to a drawer, taking a small box out and tucked it into her pocket. She ran to him, "Ok what now?"

He grinned. "Fire escape... and quick." he grabbed her bag opened the window, and pushed her through. "Slide down the ladder, my car is across the street. Get there and get in. I'll be right behind you."

"Slide down the ladder?" She said, her voice laced with doubt.. "You say that like it's an easy thing." Peering over the edge she grabbed the ladder in a death grip.

"We don't have time for me to give you the finer points of action star etiquette Gwen. Get your ass down that fire escape, and quick. We got about 2 minutes before they bust the fucking door down." He kept his tone neutral so he wouldn't scare her.

"Well if I'm going to go I guess a broken neck is quicker and possibly less painless." She took a deep breath then stepped off the ledge, dropping to the ground with a hiss of pain and a few choice words. She picked herself up and made her way swiftly to his car.

He smirked, his eyes momentarily trailing on her ass. He groaned. Woman was sexy as hell, and her heart shaped ass had his blood pumping loud in his ears. Sassy and sexy, gods had she been underutilized. Well no more.

He gripped the edge of the window, climbed out and turned back as the Div burst into the apartment. Syrus smirked and gave their leader the finger, then jumped down as he heard a roar from behind him. He laughed and hoofed it across the street and jumped into the open door. "Too late ya fucks!" he tore out of the parking spot, roaring down the street.

***

"Shit," Gwen swore at the pain in her arm while she sat in the speeding car. She'd caught her arm sliding down the ladder and blood now ran out of a large gash. Her jeans greedily soaked up the blood making a mess she absently noted as her head began to feel lighter. Apparently sliding down a ladder was easier said than done. Then again the man sitting next to her had managed just fine; he managed to do a lot of things just fine. She looked dubiously over at him, just who the hell was he? And why did he bring those things with him, the things that had killed Tom.

IT technician my ass.

She felt herself retch again, Gwen had thrown up as soon as Syrus had left her to go back and check on those creatures... her empty stomach threatened to find some long lost eaten piece of food at the thought of poor Tom.

He looked over to her with a concerned frown. "Shit your bleeding. We need to staunch that." he nodded towards the glove box. "There's one of my t-shirts in there, use that."

"Thank you," she lifted her uninjured hand towards the glove box, thinking better of it and reaching into her pack. "I have my own though." She rummaged until she found a T-shirt and took it out, gingerly wrapping it around her arm and holding it as tight as she could manage. At least she knew her t-shirt's were freshly washed, no telling what types of things she could pick up from a dirty cloth against a wound this deep. She could feel the two sides of skin rubbing together every time she moved the arm. "I'm going to need stitches."

He nodded. "You are going to need that looked at. Blaine will be more than happy to I'm sure. Can't say no to beautiful women." he looked at her sidelong and took another street, his eyes straying to the review mirror several times.

"Is this Blaine a doctor?" she quickly dismissed his beautiful comment. "The hospital might be a good stop, but if I could avoid a trip there..." she frowned at her arm. Hospitals always freaked her out; they kept you alive when all you wanted was to be at peace. Her Grandmother had suffered from dementia and had lain in bed on and off for years being cared for while her mind slowly degenerated. In the end, once she'd forgotten how to feed herself and who Gwen was, the machines were all that kept her alive; suffering, trapped and afraid in her own mind. The smell and claustrophobic atmosphere of a hospital always reminded her of how hopeless her Nan was. Of how every time her Nan became ill Gwen had prayed with all her heart for the woman she loved so much to die. She loathed hospitals. But there was no need for her to share any of that with him but the idea of meeting some back alley doctor didn't sit well with her.

She'd rather suffer a hospital than get some blood disease from unsterilized equipment. "Sorry about the mess," She motioned to the drops of blood which had fallen on the upholstery.

"Trust me, it will be fine, this isn't my only car. And as to Blaine, he's a doctor of sorts, a healer actually. Fix you up right, probably won't even be a scar." he smiled reassuringly at her.

"I'm not all that worried about a scar, more infection and being eaten alive." she smiled oddly reassured by him. "So you're not one of those things?" she looked him over her hand still pressed firmly to the bloody t-shirt.

He shook his head. "I told you before I wasn't. I would have offed myself ages ago if I was anywhere near that." he sneered. "Is it throbbing? Hold pressure on it."

"I can't get much more pressure on it." She spoke mostly to herself, looking at the whitened knuckles of her good hand. "Ok, so you're not planning to kill me?" she turned to face him. "So what are you planning to do? You were exactly where those things chose to show up... twice. Why?"

"That's a bit more complicated, and the last thing I wanna do is freak you out so you jump from the moving car. As cool as it would be to see you get all action star, it wouldn't be wise for the wound."

Anger flared at his response, "And that isn't supposed to freak me out? Work on your people skill buddy, because you just told me that I'd rather jump out of a moving car than sit here and listen to your explanation. Look, I don't know who you are or what kind of things you're into but maybe you should just drop me off at a hospital and we'll go separate ways. Thanks for the rescue, both of them, but I'm starting to wonder if I'd have needed them if you weren't around." The fear she felt etched into her words making them sound brittle and harsh.

"Well look at you, Miss Sassy shows her face. I knew she was in there somewhere. This is much better than the forlorn wallflower that I drove home earlier... and a hell of a lot sexier."

"Thanks for the critique I'll have to write that down in my diary," Her lips tipped in a smile her eyes narrowing, "I'm not trying for sexy, I'm trying for informed. Just how deep in shit am I?"

Syrus sighed. "You know, it's hard to broach the subject when the chances you will believe me are slim and none. I mean you completely threw the idea of what ate Tom out the window, what makes me think you're going to believe a word I say now?" He looked over at her. "And I wouldn't even consider dropping you at the hospital so forget about it. You would bleed out quicker than you would be admitted. I can't have that."

She shook her head; no she didn't want that either. His words confirmed, more or less, her thoughts on her arm. The blood had well and truly soaked through the t-shirt. "So I'm going to need more than stitches... just great." She said with as much enthusiasm as she felt, which was pretty much none. "Just so you know I'm not sliding down any more fire escapes."

She shifted tenderly rearranging her arm on her leg. "So what is it that I wouldn't believe? I mean I've been known to be pretty gullible in my time, I've pretty much already accepted the existence of," she paused, swallowing before saying the word. "Demons. And you got me into this car already, and you didn't even entice me with puppies, granted the aforementioned demons were about to... eat me... but still that smacks of gullibility."

Syrus gave her a sidelong glance. "No it doesn't. Actually it smacks of self-preservation, and something to be commended. You can take direction when it will save your life. It's a damn good thing. But your right, demons are real, just like I said. I guess the easiest way to answer you is to say that me, along with my friends are the ones that hunt the Demons."

"Ok," she relaxed a little bit. "That makes sense, I guess. At least it explains how you were around for them attacking." He was just trying to help, this was his job. She smiled settling further into the seat closing her eyes for a few heartbeats. It still didn't explain how he knew about the Scarab pendant but it explained enough for her to give in a little to her exhaustion. "But just so you know, I know how to protect myself and I have pepper spray." She wondered if she'd actually thrown the canister in her pack or not. Probably not but he didn't have to know that.

"That's a damn good thing. When I give you some pointers later you won't be completely clueless." he grinned. "Though the pepper spray is a bit of a futile attempt. Now a tazer, that's a good idea."

She stared at him not sure if he was completely insane or just pulling her leg. "I'll be sure to keep that in mind."

"See that you do." He took another street at breakneck speeds and shook his head. "So you got more questions?"

Of course she had questions, but what was the point in asking them. She shrugged holding back a sigh. "Will they be answered?"

He nodded. "To the best of my ability sweetness."

"To the best of your ability," she repeated the words that didn't exactly fill her with confidence. "Fair enough, so where exactly is it that you're taking me?"

"Simple enough question. I'm taking you to headquarters, the secret Inferi Dii honey comb hideout." he turned to her and grinned. "We are a few blocks away, and before you ask, no it's not in some sewer. I'm not a Ninja Turtle."

His manner made her smile for a second or two before she remembered she really shouldn't be smiling, not after what had happened to Tom. She had no reason to be enjoying herself while he lay half eaten in some alleyway. "I'm glad I don't have to add visited sewer to tonight's lists of firsts." She hugged herself as best she could while keeping pressure to her stinging arm.

He shifted once again and tore down the street. "I'll try to spare you any more unpleasantness. I don't have anything to hide from you Gwen. You're more a part of my world now than I would be happy to admit, and I don't think having you go in blind is a good idea. Best to err on the side of caution and have the knowledge you need when you need it."

"Oh ok..." She felt herself frowning as she tried to sort through his words and their meaning. He'd spoken about his world as if it was a separate thing, granted demons weren't exactly an everyday occurrence for her in the normal world. Then there was the Scarab, "How did you know about my pendant?"

He turned his head, giving her a genuinely happy smile. "The Scarab is tied to me in a number of ways, and when in close proximity with me, it's like a homing beacon. I can feel it now, and see it, like an aura, in places it's been."

"Tied to you? But how is that possible I've had it all my life?" she felt a little twinge of disappointment that her knight in shining armor was in reality, just that, and not her personal hero. She hadn't really expected him to be but hearing him say it smarted. He obviously saved women from demons and kissed them all the time it was, after all, what he did. Why should she expect to be any different? Why should she deserve him all to herself? It was always the way, Tom was the only person she'd really let in and look how that turned out, and he'd been a decent guy when they'd met.

He gave her a sexy grin. "I'm a lot older then I look. And that brings me to my big question, how the hell did you come by it? Found it in an antique shop or something bizarre out of *Needful Things*?"

"No it's nothing like that. It's been in my family forever. It doesn't matter how young you look there's no way you could have seen it. It's the only real heirloom we have, passed down from mother to daughter for..." she shook her head and smiled. "Well, ever. It's lucky, at least my Nan used to say it was. She wore it as a necklace; it still smells of her sometimes." She looked to the pack longing to touch the warm Lapis; one of her earliest memories was of sitting on her Nan's lap playing with the Scarab. Before she'd become ill, her Nan had told the most amazing stories of her adventures, she was so vibrant and alive. Gwen had sat for hours cuddling into her and playing with the pendant, watching the way the light played with the gold flecks. The scarab was attached to one of her best memories, the way the hospitals were linked to her worst.

"I can feel your need. Grab it if it makes you feel better." he turned and flew up First Avenue. "And trust me, I'm a *lot* older then you think. I did see it, because I was there when it was turned into my relic. Its older then you think even, a real antique, just like me." he winked. "Ever date a really old guy Gwen?"

Her body reacted to his simple question as if he'd asked something far more inappropriate. "I... I guess not." She stammered, feeling her cheeks heat up. "I've really only dated Tom." She reached into her pocket and pulled out the Scarab's case while being careful not to knock her bleeding arm. The blood on the t-shirt had dried but she could still feel blood seeping out of it. She opened the case and took out the long gold chain with the Scarab pendant attached. It fit solidly into her palm its gold shining up at her in a familiar comforting way.

"Want to?" he grinned at her and nodded to the Scarab. "It looks perfect on you, very at home. So what If I told you it's over fifteen thousand years old?" he said quietly, his voice still that dirty caress that made her think of things done in the dark.

"Fifteen thousand?" she stared down at the Scarab in disbelief. "Wow that is old... I sort of wish I'd taken better care of it now. It should be in a museum or... Wait did you really just ask me out? I find that a little inappropriate, Tom's barely cold or... digested..." she barked out a bubbling hysterical laugh which was, in her opinion, long overdue. "Oh God that really happened." Her vision clouded over, soon followed by the sensation of hot tears running down her cheeks. "This is crazy," she told herself, her hand tightening around the Lapis, even its comforting warmth couldn't do much to make her feel better.

The air in the car fizzled with errant static electricity. "Don't you dare shed a tear for that piece of shit! I hope he gives the Div indigestion. He got off light by them eating him. Fuck like that didn't deserve a woman like you." he shook his head and made a right onto 70th, the static abating as his tirade did. "And yes, I did ask you out. You telling me you would rather mourn that preferred abortion then hangout with me?"

She shot him a glare but couldn't put much feeling into it. "That's what happens when someone you love dies, you mourn... Things weren't perfect with Tom, not even close," she wiped the tears. In truth she felt a little relieved Tom was gone, relief mixed with a whole lot of guilt. "But we had some good times, I'm almost positive we did. He didn't deserve that, no matter what you think." The Lapis burned in her hand or perhaps it was her imagination. She had to stop thinking about Tom and how awful his final moments must have been. "How could you have been around fifteen thousand years ago?" she forced her mind away from Tom.

"I'm a god." he said matter-of-factly. "And before you say the requisite 'yes you are, hottie' lemme clarify, I'm a dark god of the Egyptian pantheon."

"Uh huh..." she smiled at him, "Well that explains everything. A fifteen thousand year old god running around fighting demons with my grandmother's pendant..."

"And by the way, you didn't love that piece of shit, you were comfortable with the situation, not that I have any idea why. A woman like you is bound for so much more."

She pinched the bridge of her nose tightly and chose to ignore his statement. It was something she would have to revisit at another time. "Well you did say I wouldn't believe you. So let's go the other direction and say I do believe you," she shook her head, "What's the significance of the pendant? You said it was your relic? What does that mean?"

Syrus spoke slowly. "A relic is an object of power used to store power and the essence of a god in order to keep the balance of the universe."

Ok this was tipping the scales into crazy town. "Your essence?" The Scarab seemed to pulse in her hand. "But why?"

He looked over at her once more, his eyes taking her in, softening when he met hers. "So it's time for a bedtime story? Once upon a time when the world was young, different pantheons were set to rule the world. Think like the president here, every few hundred to thousand years; another pantheon would become the ruling power on earth. Following so far?"

"I think so," she smiled, listening to him tell stories was far better than when Ansley started one. His voice was practically hypnotic, very soothing or that could have been the blood loss.

"Well while we all had our turns, there was one pantheon set to rule called the Velns. They were a nasty piece of work. Didn't wanna be worshipped, no their smarmy asses wanted to enslave humanity. So all the other pantheons got together and decided something had to be done about it. Their idea was to banish the Velns, which would cost them a great amount of power, and then leave immortal caretakers to ensure that they would never take their place among the humans we all loved so much. There are six of us, and we all gave up our lives for the good of you all." He spoke with what sounded like thinly disguised regret.

His expression had become sour half way through his story leaving Gwen feeling cold. "That's very... noble of you all. It couldn't have been easy."

He nodded. "Believe me it wasn't. But we knew what was at stake, regardless of what we left behind, and who faded from us." he turned down another street, close to the garment district and eased up on the gas.

"So why are you telling me all this? I'm guessing you don't explain all this to every woman you save from being eaten... If you want the pendant back, it's yours... I guess. It'll be sad to see it go, but it's only right." She held on tightly to it, not willing to give it up just yet.

He chuckled. "Ah see it isn't that easy. The pendant is yours, and as that goes, you and it are a package deal." he grinned. "And I don't explain this to anyone, but the right woman can get anything out of a man." He gave another of those heart-stopping smirks.

She returned his smile , "I doubt I'm very talented in that area, but you seem to not do so bad. You're a very smooth man, god... person."

"Man works, person works, and I'm a god in every sense of the word." He laughed at her incredulous look. "Sorry."

It was refreshing, his pseudo ego and arrogance. She could tell it was just this side of an act, but the man beside her knew his worth. She couldn't say the same for herself. "Don't be," she laughed, "It's just living proof that men are all the same, no matter their linage." She shook her head. "Ansley is all about the ancient cultures and archaeology. She would have loved to hear that bedtime story."

"I'm a god almost as old as the world, of course I'm cocky, and not all men treat women like that fuck Tom did. Fucker wasn't worth the spit to put him out if he was on fire. And as hot as Ansley is, and she is, don't get me wrong, she doesn't interest me, though I'm sure the guys would be." He looked her over and licked his lips.

"Ah so you're gay then..." she winked at him. "You'd have to be not to be interested in her and here I thought that was just the Romans?"

He stopped at a red light and leaned into her, capturing her lips quickly before she knew what he was doing. "You know I have been called a lot of things over the years, but gay isn't one of them. I know a beauty when I see one." He nipped her bottom lip. "And I'm looking at the definition of it right now." He frowned and then his eyes lit up with recognition, and then shook his head as if to clear it. "I'm sorry, I shouldn't have done that, I didn't have the right."

"No," she gasped, as he moved away not wanting him to stop. Her tongue ran along her bottom lip, savoring his taste. Deep, with a hint of cherry. She blinked and swallowed clearing her head of the dozen or so inappropriate thoughts that poured into her mind the second his lips had touched hers for the second time. "It's ok, it was ok... better than," she stammered her face flushing once again. "You shouldn't have, but I shouldn't have teased, I asked for it really..." Right now she was totally thinking about asking for it again, though maybe harder and without the having to drive the car.

Wow she thought with a pause that was the first time she'd ever rationalized that she'd deserved something good. She hadn't asked for it at all, but she'd wanted it. She'd never wanted any of the things she'd told herself she deserved with Tom. But for some reason she wanted Syrus and, whether any of the things he was telling her was true or not, she intended to have him. Whether or not she deserved him was something to come back to later. She didn't have any of the old doubts when it was just the two of them. It was as if they had possibly died with Tom.

"Did you now? That's the first time my advances were turned around on me. I believe I shall enjoy seducing the Keeper of my relic, especially when she's so responsive." He winked at her.

Fear leapt in her throat as his tongue rolled off the word seducing. He was so sexy, so in control and so experienced. She was none of those things. It was one thing deciding to have him but getting him was a whole 'nother ball game. She could barely keep Tom satisfied and all that took was a bottle of scotch and a hooker or two. Ansley threw herself at men but they were all happy for her affections, Gwen wasn't like that. She'd most likely embarrass herself if she tried anything remotely seductive with Syrus.

"Keeper?" she moved away from him physically putting as much distance between then as she could. "I think I've missed something there, but I doubt seducing me would be worth your time." It was never worth Tom's. His taunts of her frigidness still rang in her ears. Sex was never like it was in dreams; in real life it had mostly been awkward and frustrating. She didn't need to add a disappointing fumble with Syrus to her crushed ego; although he talked such a good game maybe there would be nothing disappointing about it. If she wanted to change she'd have to put herself out there, risk total humiliation. She shook her head, being new Gwen was tough.

He laughed. "Somehow I disagree. Gwen, I don't know what kinda shit people have been shoveling at you, but trust me, seducing you will be a worthy pastime."

"If you say so, but don't say I didn't warn you." she sighed dejectedly then looked out of the window.

He pulled around the corner, down the ramp to an underground parking lot and stopped the car close to a pair of elevator doors. She was stiff next to him and he took off his seatbelt and turned completely to her. "Whatever that fuck did to you and for how long, you need to know something. You were meant for so much more Gwen." he reached out and turned her face to him. "You think what you want darling, but I don't often compliment women on anything. You're a very bright light in the darkness." he ran his thumb over her bottom lip and smiled.

"And you are my Keeper. You just stepped into a war here Gwen, and whether you believe it or not, you're now part of it all. As Keeper of the Lapis Scarab you're linked to it, and through it, me. It is mine, but your family, and apparently you have been holding vigil over it these many years. So it's only right that you continue to do so. Just gives me a damn good reason to hang around you. As if I needed one." He sighed contentedly, as if he had found home.

She smiled gently. "You really are a smooth talker Syrus. I'm your Keeper and a bright light? Let's just hope I'm not a train." She wanted to be worth more, she needed to be but at the same time she didn't want to be hurt. Syrus seemed to be nothing like Tom. She couldn't go through that again.

"Too late." he grinned and winked. "Let's get you patched up ok? Then I can get on with the seduction. If you faint on me I wanna know it's from what I did, not from blood loss."

"I'm likely to faint?" She laughed shaking her head, "Exactly what kind of seduction are you planning?"

He leaned in; mischief danced in his eyes. "The kinda seduction that makes you pass out from pure and raw pleasure." he wagged his eyebrows. "I am a fabulous lover you know." he blinked. "I'm going to call in right now, make sure I can get you inside the compound, so just stay quiet."

***

Syrus got out of the car, pulled out his phone and hit a button. Blaine picked up on the first ring. "B, yeah, we got a major situation."

"You're telling me? Shit man you said you'd be in ages ago. Even by Dezi's standards you're late, and he's been here for an hour already. The guys have been hanging around waiting, and you got to know that never goes well. I've been getting my ass whipped at pool." He laughed. "Your just lucky Kaid ignored the call in or you have him after your hide. So what happened? And Jingles is fine by the way, freaked out to hell and back, babbling about Div, but he's sleeping it off."

Blaine sounded exasperated, but dealing with Jingles for any amount of time would do that to anyone. Syrus likened the junkie to a needy five year old, one that ran you ragged with its nervous energy.

"He's coming down off something, leave him where he is, we can question him once he's sober. Glad I sent you in to get him, he missed all the fireworks, thank Tiamat. If he saw it he would have bolted."

"Fireworks?" The noise of pool balls cracking off each other as someone took a shot sounded in the background. "Anything noteworthy?"

"I'd say." he laughed. "It's been an interesting evening to say the least. Kaid still not call in? He's going to wanna be there for this."

"Nah he's out doing his own thing, as always, I can call him again though if you like."

"Yeah call Kaid, Div are out in force and are hunting, I would hate to have him caught with his pants down so to speak," he sighed.

Blaine laughed. "What's your ETA?"

Oh yeah. This was going to be fun. "I'm here, parked."

"Well what the fuck are you waiting for?"

Syrus ignored Blaine's hostile tone and kept talking. "I'm on my way in, but make sure all the wards are down, I'm bringing in a Relic."

"Fuck!" Blaine whistled and Syrus could hear him moving around. "I'll sort it out. So who is the first to get a chance at heaven?"

Syrus turned and walked a bit away from the car and then looked inside to Gwen who was watching him with confusion. "Me."

"Shit it's yours?" He gave a low whistle. "Well that is good news, and calls for a celebration. Just try not to do a Kaid on the way in here and pitch it down a well, ok?"

"Not a hope in hell. I have been searching this for the last seven thousand years; Kaid always knew where his was. There's more though. A girl."

"You bringing in more strays?"

78

He ignored the comment. "No, she's not a junkie, and she's going to need some medical attention."

"Oh *is* she?" Syrus didn't need to see him to know he was grinning. "Is she hot?"

"Extremely. Hands off, spread the word." he closed his cell and turned back to the car, opened the door and got back in. "Sorry. Had to make sure the wards were down. Shall we?" he got out of the car and grabbed her bag for her then came around and opened her door with lightning speed, offering his hand. "Come on, the guys are waiting."

She looked at his hand; well it was now or never. Never maybe being a little more permanent due to the wound on her arm. Gwen accepted it letting him pull her up out of the car.

Chapter Six

Gwen was amazed at how quickly her arm had healed. There was still a mark and a bruise but that was fading fast. Once they'd left the car Syrus showed her to a guest room. He'd managed to flirt constantly and Gwen, for once in her life, flirted back. It came easily around him, a little too easily. Maybe because he'd already declared his intentions and those intentions she really wouldn't mind sharing. He made her feel, really feel, for the first time in years.

Around him she had the confidence to flirt back. Dare she believe that she was even starting to feel a little sexy around him, blood stained clothes and gaping arm wound not withstanding? To have a man like Syrus showing extreme interest was a confidence boost they should sell in bottles. He'd told her she was meant for more, agreeing with that part of her that screamed that affirmation every day. Gwen had to give it to him, if it was a line; it was the best one she'd ever heard. She wanted everything, everything his body and words promised and more.

When she was around him all she wanted to do was let herself go and wrap around him. She'd just been telling Ansley that she wasn't looking for superman and here one showed up right on her doorstep. Not only that but he was attracted to her. He actually wanted *her*. Somebody like her should have to beg somebody like him to notice her, or pay him. Not that she'd ever consider paying for sex.

She couldn't have him though no matter how much she wanted to. He was very complicated;. She'd seen demons eating Tom.

Every time she closed her eyes she could see it, still hear the noises that they made. It still made her stomach retch up its thankfully empty contents and her want to hide somewhere dark and safe. That was why she'd followed Syrus, had let him take her here. Despite how complex he made things, he was safe.

She couldn't believe the way she felt just hours after Tom's death. Again shame flooded through her. Syrus was right, Tom wasn't the best boyfriend around, hell, he was pretty much one of the worst. She could admit that, if only to herself. But none of that meant that she'd wanted him dead, let alone eaten alive. A fate which was mostly her fault, if it hadn't been for her and the Scarab, Tom would most likely still be alive. It was her fault he'd died so horribly and yet here she was flirting was a self confessed Egyptian god and feeling great about it.

Without Tom she was alone. He might have been an asshole but at least he'd been there for her when she'd needed him... to an extent. She'd never been truly alone. She was terrified of it. Frightened of it even more now that she knew there was demons and god-knows-what out there just waiting to eat you up, quite literally. She couldn't just go latching onto the first available male that passed her way. She refused to let herself be so clingy. Gwen was many things but she didn't want to be the type of women that was clingy. Especially with Tom gone, it was just too fast to jump head first into something she knew next to nothing about.

Syrus had led her to the so-called guest room but it was far from hotel quality. It had everything in it that it needed to be called a room: a bed, an empty wardrobe and a bathroom, but everything was sterile and unused.

White walls, white sheets, white tiles the whole place felt cold. It lacked personality and life like a prison cell or a dreaded hospital room.

A blank canvas so they could ship in and out as many customers as they could. Her lips curled in distaste, nobody lived here and nobody ever would, the place had no soul.

Looking around she instantly missed her home and all her things. She's always loved colors and clutter, that's why her apartment was decorated with things from her Nan's travels and Ansley's expeditions. Anything she could put a memory or a happy event to she'd kept surrounding herself with a comforting visual story. Before Tom she'd imagined sitting with her daughter or son on her lap telling them adventures or reading them tales from her favorite books. It was Tom who' decided they weren't going to have children and at the time it had crushed Gwen but now it was probably the most intelligent decision he'd ever made. No baby deserved Tom as a father even Gwen could see that. So why had she been so adamant that she deserved him?

Blaine had come in behind them. Gwen had liked him instantly with his sandy blond hair and infectious easy smile.   He reminded her of sunshine on the happiest brightest day of her life. His presence was an instant mood lifter if they could bottle Syrus's sexy ego boost then they should certainly bottle some of Blaine too. That Syrus was a dark god was believable but there was nothing dark about Blaine. She'd bet he could make spiders seem cuddly.

She'd sat on the bed, trying not to get any blood on the blankets. She'd seen enough blood tonight to last her a lifetime. The thought of having to sleep in sheets covered with her own didn't sit well at all. She had always been fastidious; this mess really grated on her. The thought of sleeping here at all didn't appeal to her. She wanted her own bed, not because it held so many memories but she needed something familiar. Something that didn't feel so clinical and hard.

Syrus and Blaine had spoken to each other in a language that she hadn't understood for several minutes before apparently coming to a decision. Smiling, Blaine had knelt in front of her asking to see her wounds. The shirt that she'd wrapped around the deep wound was thick with crusted, fresh blood and had been hard to take off, not to mention painful. Finally, after soaking it in the sink, they managed to remove the shirt and reveal the deep cuts.

With his head bent over, he inspected the arm then the other one gently probing them with his oddly warm fingers. Then he'd closed his eyes. The heat from his hands spread over her wounded arms and through her body. It felt amazing, drawing a moan from her throat as she sank back letting the heat work through her. It subsided quickly leaving her feeling rejuvenated and fresh like she'd just woken up from the best night's sleep she'd ever had.

"Almost good as new." He sat back with a smile guaranteed to make any woman melt, and gave her a glass of spicy orange liquid to drink. Once he was sure she'd drank it, he left her alone taking Syrus and his smoldering look with him. The things that look promised left her panting in anticipation. All thoughts of not getting entangled went totally out the window that was if there was a window, which there wasn't. The only thing she wanted to get entangled in was Syrus. Yes she was going to enjoy him and everything he had to offer fully without getting clingy and attached, a one, maybe two night thing at the most. Ansley would be so proud.

She inspected the fading bruises in the shower, amazed. Syrus had said he was a healer but that anyone could do this was truly amazing. It had to have been magic, maybe god magic?

That's if there was such a thing. Syrus had said his powers were bound to the Scarab. Maybe Blaine still had his powers.

The water ran cold fairly quickly, signaling to her that she should end the shower. She stepped out, grabbing a white towel as she did. She wrapped it around herself and wrapped a second around her hair. Her bag was next to the bed where Syrus had left it so she picked it up, rooting through it anxious to see what she'd grabbed in a hurry.

Underwear. Apparently her panicked addled brain packed enough panties and bras to last her the better part of a month. *Why the hell did I have to start in my underwear drawer?* Cursing the fact that she didn't think to bring any pants because her jeans would do, she settled on a grey knitwear dress that she must have grabbed by accident. But hey, at least she had underwear. Tom had hated the dress so it wasn't something she'd worn often or at all since Ansley had talked her into buying it.

With a cowl neck that scooped low enough to flash a little cleavage, it was a little shorter than she liked but it would have to doLifting her blood soaked jeans, she sat them in the bathtub taking the black velvet box from the pocket.

"I can't believe Tom nearly had me sell you." She opened the box. The Scarab inside was a deep blue lapis flecked with gold. It had always radiated warmth but tonight it burned with the same heat that she'd felt from Syrus. She slipped its long gold chain around her neck and under her dress out of sight. She'd never even considered selling it. Tom had been furious with her. It was one of the only things she'd ever denied him and it was because the pendant just meant so much to her. And now it seems it might mean even more.

She searched her bag for something to tie her hair back with, coming up with a clip which she used to pin half of her hair up. She left the bulk of it loose curling around her shoulders. She smiled weakly at her reflection and couldn't help but notice that she looked different. Tired and worn but that wasn't it. The dress gave her a shape, not a stunning shape like Ansley's, but a shape none the less, and her hair looked good in loose curls. It had been so long she had all but forgotten that fact.

"This is it Gwenny." She told herself. "Just you and this mess you've found for yourself."

Here she was alone.. When her parents had died there was her grandmother and when she fell ill Ansley had moved in with her, helping her with the care arrangements, the payments and eventually the funeral arrangement. Once Ansley moved out she'd met up with Tom and he'd made all the decisions from there. He'd taken control deciding what to eat, when to go out. Hell he'd even helped her choose her job.

Being a librarian had hardly been a calling. She loved books but surrounding herself with them? She didn't exactly jump at the chance but Tom had decided and she found out that she enjoyed it. She loved setting up the rooms for visiting groups of children and now she was learning to care for the oldest of books the library owned. Restoring long lost words to page and bringing something previously lost back to life had became a passion and she couldn't help but get a thrill every time she discovered something new.

Sometimes Tom got things right. But Tom was gone now and she had no idea what to do. She wasn't strong enough to make life-changing decisions. She wanted to be but she just didn't think she could run her own life.

Deciding she couldn't sit in the cold room facing her reflection any longer, she opened the door, stepping out into the darkened corridor that was the "compound." Syrus had taken her in from the parking lot, to the left. She went right, following the sound of men's laughter her stomach in nervous knots. Hopefully it would take her to Syrus, if not she'd be in trouble.

She padded barefoot along the corridor, turning one corner and then another. As the voices and laughing got louder, the Scarab began warming between her breasts. Silently, she peaked her head around the corner to see five of the sexiest men she'd ever laid eyes on playing pool.

Blaine she recognized, who sat reclined in a computer chair of some sort, his feet resting on a table strewn with papers and drawings. He was dressed as she'd seen him last but he was cradling a bottle of beer between cupped hands on his lap.

Next to him on the table sat a darkly sexy man in jeans and a black shirt unbuttoned and hastily pulled on. He had tattoos all over his tanned chest and shoulders and was barefoot. He looked like he'd just been dragged from bed. Gwen accepted her first assessment as he stretched out, showing bright red nail marks scoring over his abs following the dark trail of hair under his belly button. He'd been in bed all right. And yes, he'd been dragged, and by the looks of those livid marks, he had been enjoying himself.

Playing pool was a tall wiry guy with short straight black hair in a choppy cut. Green eyes shone under the lights as he bent to take a shot. He had his bottom lip pierced in the center and honest to god black leather pants with a black wife beater. Dark scrawling tattoos curled up his arms. Beside him was another tall man, solidly built with nice abs.

She could tell this because he was completely shirtless with low rider jeans hanging on his hips flashing two tattoos of birds. Gwen could feel the intensity of those dark grey eyes from across the room and thanked God that they were focused on the pool balls.

Man these guys were showing entirely too much flesh. Syrus had his back to her but she knew it was him. He'd changed since they'd last met, opting for faded dirty washed jeans and a tight, black T-shirt of a band she had heard of once or twice, The Faint. The t-shirt rode up as he bent to take a shot showing a small tattoo of a black and purple flame on the small of his back. She smirked remembering Ansley calling a tattoo there a tramp stamp, she didn't really thing it applied to him though, or she hoped.

She took full advantage of the really good view of his ass. Nice and tight. She had to wonder just how it would feel under her hands. She felt herself flush thinking very impure thoughts. Forcing her eyes away, she met the grey eyes of Mr. shirtless and fought a whimper. She'd just been caught gawking by a stranger she'd been gawking at a few seconds ago. Her cheeks burned red as she fought to look away, fidgeting.

Out of all of these men, all perfect specimens of male virility, Syrus was the one that called to her most. It was more than the air of danger about him, more than the peak of ink and flesh and a nicely taught backside. Syrus was her physical ideal. Hair cut short and choppy, longer in the front with blonde chunks, his skin that perfect light olive that tanned to golden in the sunshine. His physique screamed that he had strength enough to kick some major ass, but didn't need to advertise. It was something she always liked in a man.

It was the green eyed Adonis that broke the silence. "Holy shit. Sy, man, since when the hell do you bring presents home?"

Syrus chuckled. "Our stunning houseguest is no one's present. Well maybe mine." he turned to her and gifted her with a heart stopping grin. Dear god, his eyes were a grey green that was so startling, she hadn't noticed it in the darkness, but now she knew she would never again make that mistake. He looked at her with a hunger though, one that had her blushing harder. "I take it she got enough of an eye full as we have." He turned and leaned against the pool table, crossing his ankles. "Speechless?" he quirked an eyebrow at her.

She shook her head swallowing hard. "No." She flushed, brighter embarrassment and arousal coursing through her, one feeding the other.

"Well fuck me," Mister just outta bed grinned brightly his dark blue eyes searching her. "An honest to god blush. I haven't seen one of them in..." he mentally counted off something using his fingers he gave up at seven. "Years. You know Sy, presents should really be shared. I bet that goes all the way down her chest, from what I can see already it does." His tongue ran along his bottom lip and Gwen fought the urge to adjust the cowl of her top.

Syrus barely glanced at him. "Stow it Dezi. Gwen? Shall I introduce you to the boys?"

Boys? Unless they had Peter Pan syndrome she was pretty sure none of these males could be mistaken for boys. She took a deep breath her body calming down. "I guess, yeah. Though the muscle show in here is pretty alarming." She smiled, stepping close to him and tugging his t-shirt down so it covered his studded belt.

He grinned and took her hand and then turned back to the room. "Dezi," he pointed to the guy at the table. "Half naked guy over there is Castor," he pointed to the green-eyed hottie, "Arlo. You know Blaine, and the last of us, Kaid, decided to be a slippery shit and not show tonight. May I introduce the Inferi Dii?"

Arlo smirked. "Old dragon boy missed a damn fine surprise that's for sure. Welcome to headquarters Darlin." he winked.

Dezi tipped an imaginary hat to her sitting back up on top of the papers. "It's a pleasure, love," he said silkily.

Blaine nodded and gave her a wink. Gwen smiled at them all. "Thank you." she took a deep breath her mouth dry as she asked a question that'd been preying on her mind for some time. "Syrus do you think the people in my apartment building were safe? Those things were only after me, right?"

"I would think so. And they aren't people, Div haven't been people like you know since their conversion. They really are just demons walking around in human husks, think *Invasion of the Body Snatchers*, though no aliens."

"Conversion?" She shook her head, "Ansley lives on the top floor, are you sure they're safe? I don't want her to get," She swallowed dryly not wanting to start retching again. "Dead. Even the old lady next floor up is annoying but she doesn't deserve to... you know."

Blaine broke in. "Div are single minded creatures, they don't actually have much by way of proactive behavior. Once they ransack your place they will try to pursue the car and the Scarab's relic signature.

Once that fails they will go to ground. Plus, it's close to morning, and Div don't like daylight much, shows the fact that they really aren't the humans they are masquerading around as.

We can send someone to clear people out if you want." he offered and cocked his head.

"The old bat'll be fine, it's more Ansley. She's my best friend, has been for as long as I can remember. I don't know what I'd do if something happened to her, especially if it was because of me."

"Is she fuckable?" Dezi asked from his perch showing interest.

"Very." She nodded.

"Dibs!" Arlo said as he broke another shot.

"No way can you call dibs." Dezi growled. "It's not in the rules. Besides you already got some earlier, I was rudely interrupted."

"So interrupted that you were what? An hour and a half late? No dibs, from either of you guys, she's a civilian. She doesn't need to know about us." Blaine sat up, grabbing his phone. "Are we bringing her in?" He looked at Castor. "I can call Kaid; chances are he might answer this time."

Castor nodded. "Might as well. Can't have our darling guest here all in a tizzy over her friend, and it might be smart to do it anyway, in case the Div are getting creative." he looked at Gwen. "Do you need anything else from your apartment? Provided they can find anything?"

It touched her that the big old shirtless badass would even ask her. "Clothes would be nice. Ans knows her way around my place I can call her and tell her what to grab."

"Kaid?!" Dezi pushed off the table, "Seriously Kaid? Come on, really? Sy you trust him to bring her in in one piece? He's not exactly subtle."

"And he's not going to try to seduce her into staying and letting him show her a good time either." Castor said and looked at Syrus for conformation, who nodded.

"Fuck me, he hardly has a way with women either. Shit the last time he had a real conversation with one he fucking sacrificed..."

"Jesus Dezi!" Blaine slapped the back of his head as he hung up the phone. "Enough! Keep on going down that route and I swear to fuck when Kaid gores you, you can heal on your own! I'm sick and fed up of you two. And you're outta luck because the fuck actually answered this time. He'll pick her up on his way in."

Dezi glared at him for a heartbeat then broke out into a grin. "Shit, B, I'm only kidding. Get Kaid to bring in the girl, see if I care." He laughed. "Seriously though, Jesus?"

Blaine shook his head smiling, "Shut you up didn't it?"

Syrus watched them with dry amusement and then to her. "Cool?"

"Yeah I guess." She nodded.

Syrus moved closer to her, wrapping his arm around her waist in a loose way, though the visual was lost on nobody in the room. She was his. "You look a lot better, Feel better?" he walked her over to an overlarge stuff chair in cerulean blue suede. "Drink?"

"So Kaid?" she frowned yet nodded to Syrus' question. This was the man they were sending for Ansley?

"Broody motherfucker of the highest order." Dezi rolled his eyes. "Deserves a good bitch slap if you ask me. Which nobody did." He grinned, ducking Blaine's half assed swipe.

Blaine snorted shaking his head and taking another sip of his beer. "I bet you a grand you wouldn't say that to his face."

"Ansley's more than capable of dealing out a bitch slap." Many of her encounters with Tom proved so. She turned to Blaine, "Is she safe with him?"

"Kaid's a mean bastard but he wouldn't hurt her. Just stay out of his way and don't worry about it, you're friend will be fine. If you say something that pisses him off he might take it out of Sy's hide but he doesn't hurt women... without good reason." Blaine added the last bit quickly. "He knows how to behave himself. he just doesn't do it all too often but he's fully capable of it."

Syrus frowned. "Ok gents this isn't scare the hell outta the lady time. If Sherri heard you guys being so fucking shady she would have all your asses."

Dezi smirked, "She'd have Arlo's ass regardless."

Arlo smirked. "Jealous?"

"Of you? Never... Now of Sy... it's possible." He grinned.

"Better not let Sherri hear that." Syrus winked at Gwen. "Don't let them get to you, it's not often we have women here at all, aside from the Soul Keeper, and none have been as attractive as you."

She smiled getting another much needed ego boost. "No, I don't mind. I like watching the interaction. It's cute. So what is it you all do? When you're not pursuing women and or demons in human husks?"

Castor answered her in his gruff but honeyed voice. "Ever hear of Briathos Securities?" he took a sip of the beer he just opened.

"Nope." Something twitched in her memory. "Wait, they do all the university and public building security right? I'm sure I've seen their box on the building I work at."

Castor blinked, and smirked with an incline of this head. "She's perceptive. Yes. Well that is us. Blaine here is the public face of the company, and the rest of us run different departments."

"So Syrus wasn't lying when he said he was an IT tech. So you guys are linked to pretty much most of the city? That must come in handy." It was pretty damn clever when she thought about it.

"Anywhere that has antiquities, yes. We also do virtual securities for several of the major auction houses as well as their physical offices. Any place where a Relic might show up, we have our hands in the pies."

"And you all have a Relic?"

Castor nodded. "Yep."

"How many of you have found yours?"

"They all aren't lost, Gwen. Some are in the permanent collections of several museums. As of now all but Arlo's and Kaid's have been found. But that's his own fault."

The more she found out about Kaid the more worried she was about sending him after Ansley. Still though, Syrus didn't seem to be too concerned which was reassuring. "What did he do, Kaid I mean?"

"He threw it down a well or blow hole or cave or entombed it. He claims not to remember or care, for that matter." Blaine answered. "Either way protecting it wasn't high up on his list of priorities. There's issues there that he hasn't entirely dealt with."

Syrus nodded, took up his stick again, and lined his shot up, then turned his head and winked at her. He shot, sinking the nine ball. He moved around to the other side of the table and set another shot up.

Arlo leaned on his stick and looked her over again. "So you are the Keeper of the Lapis Scarab? Funny, you don't look like a Scarab priestess."

"No?" Gwen smiled, trying her hardest not to be distracted by Syrus's bending. "And what exactly does a Scarab priestess look like?"

Arlo grinned. "Well for starters you're not a mummy, and you're not holed up in some musty forgotten tomb buried from the world. That's a good thing. You would be wasted as a mummy."

"I guess most people would be." She laughed finding herself liking Arlo.

"Gold." Dezi grinned. "There was a lot of gold involved, I remember, and a little heavy on the eyeliner. Not necessarily a good look though. I'd always thought that they'd be rocking the panda look in the morning."

Castor smirked. "Bitches never woke up. Egyptians had a way of keeping their big secrets secret, eh Sy? So how did you end up with the Scarab?"

She frowned. They didn't exactly speak highly of the Egyptians. She wondered just who was from what pantheon. "I don't know, it's been in my family for generations. There's no real story behind it." She scrunched up her face, not really knowing how to feel about the whole priestess thing. The Egyptians had some brutal customs but then most of them did. Ansley could ramble on for hours about the correct brain extraction for mummification and sacrificial plate placement of the Incas.

The idea of women totally devoted to Syrus really didn't sit well with her. Gwen had never thought of herself as the jealous type before but now with the evidence in front of her she couldn't really deny it. That and there was her ego and battered self esteem.

He was thousands of years old and it was likely that he'd had three times as many women. How could she ever add up to that? When he'd had a legion of women who literally lived to serve him, that would do things for him that she just wouldn't. It kind of killed any type of a relationship off before anything had started.

Which was why there wasn't going to be any relationship, no clingy over thinking. She was just going to enjoy herself and that was that.

Syrus grinned at her, breaking her thoughts, and took another shot. He didn't seem too broken up about the conversation, or the way his friends regarded his priestesses. In the course of their conversation he was running the table, an action that caused Arlo to frown.

"Leave her be guys. She has it. Doesn't matter to me how she got it, or why. It's been missing for so long I never expected to see it again. It's a bonus its Keeper is Gwen."

"Yeah, I'm a bonus." she beamed at him glad he'd stuck up for her, the guys; Castor, Dezi and Arlo were intimidating and pretty intense. They were nothing compared to Tom in a drunken rage, but they were still intimidating. She supposed it came with their sheer size. She'd seen heavily muscled men before, but whereas they looked gross, or sick in some way, each of them wore their weight and size better than anyone she had ever seen. They were all images of male perfection, each a little different, each the ideal of a certain style of woman. Syrus, for his wiry muscles and strength, and sarcastic candor, was hers.

As for the mention of priestesses she hadn't really given them much thought but she supposed all gods had had them and worshipers at one point. What their roles had been she could only guess at though. She wanted to ask but she'd wait until she had Syrus to herself before she did. Her heartbeat quickened at the thought of having him to herself. "So is this what you guys do around here for fun? Play pool?"

Castor smirked. "That's the PG-13 version."

"I can imagine. Well actually I can't but I don't need any help on the matter. I'm sure you're all very virile."

Blaine choked on the beer he'd been in the process of swallowing.

Syrus grinned. "She got you Cas."

Castor smirked, seeming to relax a bit. Apparently being razzed by her agreed with his sensibilities. "Yeah. You'll fit in well here; just don't let her mouth off like that to Kaid. You know he might eat her. And not in the good dirty way either."

"Noted." Syrus took another shot.

Arlo grinned at her. "So what do you do?"

"I work in the New York Public Library." she shrugged. "Cataloging, restoring old books and setting up groups. That sort of thing, it's not really fascinating."

"Actually that's pretty cool, and explains a lot." Arlo took his shot, cursing when he missed.

"It does?"

Syrus looked at her. "Arlo has this theory he's been trying to perfect for the past two hundred or so years. You know that saying 'it's always the quiet ones'? Well Arlo here thinks it's true, and more so in women librarians."

Arlo wiggled his eyebrows. "Care to help me test the theory?"

Syrus moved lightning fast and had the thin end of the pool stick at Arlo's throat. Apparently there was only so much flirting he would let his teammates do with her and Gwen liked that. "Do yourself a favor Februus, stick with the Soul Keeper okay?"

Arlo laughed. "Shit Sy, you need to remember the rules brother. Ladies choice."

Syrus sighed and they both turned toward Gwen waiting for her verdict.

She looked blankly at them both still trying to take in the scene. Syrus had moved so fast. She looked to the others. Castor was watching her expectantly a slight frown on his face whereas Dezi just looked smug that he wasn't involved.

Blaine chuckled and motioned to them."They want you to choose between them. We don't have many girls back here, let alone a relic Keeper, so we don't often get into situations where girls can cause any arguments. Chances are if you don't choose they'll rip each other apart at some point... and most likely Dezi will throw himself in there too." he gave her a long suffering sigh.

"It'll just get messy." Dezi grinned.

Syrus, always Syrus. She thought to herself."Ok... Well as flattered as I am Arlo, I kind of know Syrus a little better. So I choose him... on one condition." She looked to Syrus.

Syrus raised an eyebrow in question.

"That we could get something to eat? Sorry, but I kind of threw up everything that I think I've ever eaten."

"Shit, you want a date outta it?" Castor smirked. "Not a bad condition when you're talking about forever..."

"A date?" she frowned at him, shaking her head, plainly ignoring the way her heart skipped at the mention of forever. She felt her face go red again; damn it and she'd been doing so well too. "No, a piece of toast or some chips would do."

Syrus grinned, clearly happy he was the victor. "I think we got just the thing in the kitchen.Come on, you can grill me for information while I make you something to eat." He dropped the pool stick and went to her, helping her up by her hand and lead her down another hallway to the music of cat calls coming from the room behind them.

"Sorry." she told him once they were in the kitchen. His hand was warm against hers and she held onto it.

He walked to the fridge and looked at her quizzically. "For what?"

"I don't know... for whatever was my fault." she shrugged, her stomach rumbling. "I'm not even that hungry, I'll probably just throw it back up anyway."

"Nothing is your fault Darlin, trust me. Throw five underworld gods who all were considered their pantheon's Don Juan and you're going to get some posturing when it comes to the fairer sex. Now how about a sandwich? We got some roast beef, Turkey, chicken and some salami, though shit knows that's going to repeat in the end. Something lighter maybe?"

"Some chicken would be good." She took a seat. "I should have stayed in that room."

"Why? You didn't like meeting the guys?" he set to making her a sandwich, grabbing the bread and working on layering the meat. He put cheese on and then looked up. "Really they aren't so bad. Each one of us has a relic, and well, a Keeper too, though the Keeper isn't bound to us like the relic is. Arlo was putting his order in so to speak, just in case we don't work out."

That was interesting. "Order? Desperation must make a guy do strange things."

Syrus shrugged. "I wouldn't call it desperation. He is a collector of beautiful things. You happen to fit into that category." He\ offered her the mayonnaise and mustard.

She nodded, though far from accepting of what he'd just said. Sometimes in life it was better just to agree with people. "Lip piercings just don't do it for me."

"Just lip piercings?" he smirked and put the top on the sandwich, on top of the tomato and lettuce.

She thought back to what she saw of him already. "I'm ok with tattoos. I just wanna feel lips when I'm kissing...depending on what I'm kissing." She grinned.

He raised an eyebrow. "And other piercings?"

"Piercings?" She frowned wondering what in hell he was getting at. "What other piercings could you have? Your ear? Belly..." She trailed off swallowing hard her body tightening as she thought about it. "You're kidding. Wouldn't that hurt?"

He winked. "Nope."

"But why?" Her curiosity got to her. Why would any man do that to himself? Unconsciously her gaze moved to his groin and she licked her lips.

"I could show you why." Mirth shone brightly in his eyes just before they set to smoldering, his gaze penetrating, setting things low in her body to flutter.

Oh she bet he sure could, would, will. She swallowed hard again, lord he made her react like an oversexed teen. "Ummm..." she worried her bottom lip between her teeth, laying both her hands flat on the table. "Maybe that wouldn't be such a good idea."

Syrus gave her a knowing look. "I think it would be a fine idea, but that's just me. And despite what your voice is saying, your body is saying something much different. It seems to agree with me on this. But you're probably right, though," he sighed and gave her an easy smile. "You're so accepting of this." "Of what?"

"The fact that you just pretty gave me free reign to show you a very good time by choosing me."

"There wasn't a choice, I know you better than any of the guys in there. Which doesn't say a lot, for how well I know you. Although I did just find out something I'm not sure I wanted to know about you."

She smiled taking a bite of the sandwich. "I don't think you really want me, but that's neither here nor there. I guess we could put it down to shock; it's been a pretty rough day. You called Arlo Februus. Was that his name?"

Syrus nodded. "Arlo is the Etruscan god Februus. Each of us are considered underworld gods, hence the name Inferi Dii."

There was just so much information to take in but still she needed to know more. "What is an underworld god? And how did you guys end up this way? It seems a bit harsh. What happened to the rest of your pantheons? Are they still around?"

"And now you're just full of questions." he laughed. "We are all the dark gods. Darker powers, over death, the elements. Most that you would know would be Hades, or the Devil. And yes, they are still around, and real, they just don't deal with humanity anymore, not really. They left that to us. As to how we got this way, well that's far from a bedtime story."

"And it's way past my bed time." She finished her sandwich and drank some water. "Thank you."

"Anytime pet. I think I should walk you to your room then, yeah?"

"It's hardly my room, it's hardly anyone's." She shivered as she stood. "It's cold."

Syrus nodded as if he knew exactly what she was talking about. "You're welcome to use mine, I think it might be safer in the long run." he grinned. "It's far from cold there."

"Really?" She brightened. "Where would you sleep? I couldn't take your bed from you."

He considered it. "The bed is big enough that we could share, though failing that, there's a couch in the room as well."

"No, thanks." She shook her head, not wanting to steal his bed from him or sleep with someone she hadn't met before today. "I think I'll be fine where I was, it is tempting though. Where is yours?"

He shrugged. "Shame then. You really won't be putting me out. And my room is one door down from the guest room we put you in. Sure I can't tempt you? The room is really nice."

She shook her head and laughed. "You already know from experience that you can tempt me, but no. I need to at least try and spend the night myself. I'll need a phone though so I can tell Ansley to expect..." she trailed off, "What will I tell her?"

"You wanna call her now?" he pulled a cell phone from his pocket.

"Yeah it's best I do it. Give her time to pack, for some reason it's impossible to pack in a hurry. You should see the stuff I threw into my bag." She took the phone. "So what will I tell her?"

"Anything you want. The truth, that after Tom walked out you were propositioned by a sexy guy whom you couldn't say no to, and he's got friends?" he grinned and winked. I'm hitting the bathroom... I'll be back."

She sighed and shook her head. No way would Ansley believe that. No way would anyone who knew her believe that. Plus most likely she's already seen the mess of her apartment. Dialing Ansley's number, she waited for her to answer.

"Who the hell is calling me at three am? This better be an insanely sexy man offering favors for no reason."

She laughed. Ansley's voice relaxed her. "Sorry no one insanely sexy here. But I could offer you a favor if you want.... but only if you'll do me one?"

"Well shit. You ok? I heard a tussle downstairs after I sent Tom packing. You know that piece of shit came upstairs and tried to proposition me. Please tell me you didn't take him back and have gross drunk sex with him. I will hang up on you."

"No nothing like that," She took a deep breath a steeled herself for the lie she was about to tell. "Tom smashed the place up. I tried to fight him off but..." She sighed. "You remember the guy from earlier?"

"Girl I have been dreaming about Syrus."

She didn't like the sound of that. Ansley could have anyone she wanted; her taking an interest in Syrus was very bad. Syrus was hers. The guys might not be able to call dibs on girls but if it came down to it she was well and truly calling dibs on Sy. Ansley couldn't have him and there was no way in hell she was Jolie'ning her man away from her. Even after she'd had her fun.

"Yeah tell me about it. Well I dropped my purse in the car. He was returning it when Tom got aggressive. He sent Tom packing but we had to leave in case Tom came back; you know how he and his friends can be. I doubt even Syrus could fight them off." She rolled her eyes; Sy could take those wimps on blindfolded. "So anyway I'm at his place and I'm not sure if Tom and his friends will pay you a visit once they figure I'm not in. You know how I worry, it'll be better if your here with me... besides he has some very sexy friends. Plus I need clothes." she smiled, surprised at how easily she could lie to her friend.

"No shit? Superman he is that's for damn sure. Saving damsels in distress. Ok. So you want me to go to your place? Pick some clothes up? Hell I'd need a change of panties every hour or so. I'm in, so what's the deal?"

"I need clothes that I can wear, maybe a few pairs of Pj's and some jeans. Please don't pick out lots of frilly things that you think I should wear, I'm trusting you. He's sending somebody to get you, he's... well I haven't met him but he seems like a loose cannon. Just be on your best behavior. Ok?"

"Can do. A gentleman of danger? I'm in. He got a name?"

"It's Kaid, and I mean be nice."

"Gwenny I'm always nice. Very nice in fact. I'll be there soon Okay?"

"Ok see you when you get here." Hanging up, she squashed the guilt she felt at lying. Ansley was safer this way.

Syrus leaned against the wall watching her. "I'm a big fat liar."

"Big fat? Don't think so. And you're not a liar, you did what you had to do, and I didn't even have to threaten you about keeping our secret safe. Neither did the rest of the guys. You didn't hesitate, didn't even think to spill did ya? Proves you're supposed to be here. With me."

"Well as long as I have this." She pulled out the Scarab and held it on its chain. "So what does it do anyway?"

He groaned when he watched her slip her hand out of her dress. "It actually does nothing. But the right invocation can unlock my god powers, and another can break the seal on it my pantheon used to help bind the Velns. Otherwise, it's worthless, to anyone but you, and me."

"Ok," she nodded and slipped it back inside her dress. "So what now? Ansley will be here in a few, maybe I should get that sleep?" She felt exhausted, physically and emotionally drained. "Is that offer on your bed still available?"

He nodded. "With or without me in attendance."

She shook her head with wry a smile. "I really should get some sleep; I'm guessing if you join me there wouldn't be much sleeping involved."

He chuckled; a very manly chuckle. "You guessed right. Come on I'll show you to the room."

"Lead the way." she followed after him, staying close enough to feel the heat that radiated off his body.

Chapter Seven

Ansley frowned as she got up out of bed and went to the bathroom, grabbing her toiletries and toothbrush. She looked at herself in the mirror. She frowned again and sighed.

"I look like ass." She turned the faucet on, grabbing some of her face cleanser before doing a quick clean up. Minutes later she patted her skin dry and was pulling the shock of red hair back into a twist with a barrette.

She opened her medicine cabinet and considered the condoms she had living there, trying to figure out which ones would work best. The Magnums? *Right I should be so lucky.* She threw them in anyway. Gwen had said Syrus' friends were good-looking guys, so she might have a chance to try them out after all. Who knew?

There was a time where she bought them and was searching for a guy to use them on, but everyone she thought a likely candidate had either been a complete disappointment or a pleasant interlude. Not one of them rocked her. Ansley wanted to get rocked.

And that Syrus fellow. Lord he looked like he could rock a girl. She smirked, remembering how his package looked as he stood there threatening the street punks. She sighed. "A superhero. Sexy, witty and kicks ass." Shame he didn't look at her twice though. No he had only had eyes for Gwen and that suited Ansley just fine. The girl needed a quality guy that could take her to heaven and back. And if his friends looked anything like him, and were as heroic... well she could deal with that.

She smiled and then used her mouthwash, gathering everything she figured she would need and then left the bathroom and went back to her bedroom and grabbed her large overnight bag.

Not knowing what to expect, she packed some jeans, slacks, shirts, blouses, a couple pairs of shoes, and then grabbed several pairs of underwear.

As she zipped up her jeans, a pair of low riding huggers, she heard a knock at her door. She slipped her feet into suede flats and pulled a black fitted tank top over her naked breasts before going to answer the door. She was greeted by a tall surly looking man that radiated sex on multiple levels.

Her breath caught. *Jesus Christ.*

"Please tell me you're Kaid." *And you're single.*

"I guess." he mumbled, stepping past her into her apartment and looking around her place.

"You guess? Well you are or you aren't."

He paused in his search, looking her over focusing his dark eyes on her for the first time since entering. "I am Kaid. You're very short." He dismissed her, going through her apartment again pausing at her bookcase.

"Hey I'm five-five. You on the other hand could be a goddamn Viking!" a sexy as sin Viking. Hell if all Syrus's friends were like this it was going to be a good time away that was for damn sure. "And what are you doing, casing the joint?!"

"I'm not a Viking." He smiled at her the simple gesture lighting his face. "I'm satisfying curiosity. What exactly is it that you do?" He fingered one of her texts out thumbing through it lightly.

"Like for a job?"

"Maybe, what is it that you do that you need all of these?" He moved to throw the book at her feet then seemed to think better of it. "Never mind, it's not my place to ask, or know, or even care. I'm just picking you up." He tucked the text into his jacket and looked around again. "Do you have a car?"

"And you're stealing one of my reference texts? What the hell?" she walked into her room and came back with a jacket and her overnight bag. "I hope you're not driving a bike, we have bags to carry with us. And to answer your question I'm a research assistant at the natural history museum while I'm getting my doctorate in anthropology."

"I'm not driving a bike, do you have a car? Mine had a little... accident." He smiled brightly, taking the bags off her. "You don't need the book; it's pretty much full of shit anyway. Theories some professor or another had fifty or so years ago."

"Regardless it is my book. And what the hell do you know about Sumerian mythology? You look like you don't know much about anything except breaking and entering, or maybe how to be an exotic dancer."

"Exotic dancer?" he laughed, "Looks like you found me out. I'm really a stripper, although if I looked like you and was dressed the way you are I wouldn't exactly play the stripper card." He casually leaned against her high backed couch.

Her? A stripper? She wasn't sure if that was a backhanded comment or a compliment. "Hey buddy I just was woken out of a deep sleep to hear that you were picking me up to spirit me away from here for safety's sake. I didn't dress to impress. Hell you're lucky I did my hair. So shall we? You still going to nick my book?"

He gave her a wolfish grin. "Let's say I'm going to borrow it for a little while." Something crashed outside and he swore. "Fuck, did you hear that?" He frowned and moved quickly to the window. "Fuck! What did you need from downstairs?" he barked the question at her.

Wow did he have a potty mouth. "Clothes? A toothbrush, some shoes..." She ticked off the rest of what she figured Gwen would need.

"And you couldn't have lifted that already?" He sighed, clearly trying to hide his agitation. "Fine come on."

She smirked and walked out, grabbing her keys and locked up as he darted down the stairs. Man has quite an ass on him. "What's your damage? It's probably some dogs or some drunk." she hoofed it after him to the mess that was Gwen's apartment and frowned. "Fucking Tom did a number down here."

"Hungry dogs." he moved to the window watching outside. "And I have lots of damage thanks for asking. Hurry it up will you? I wouldn't mind getting to bed before dawn."

Neither would she. She looked him over as he moved about the apartment seemingly checking for threats. Whoever he was he was probably nuts. Gwen did say he was a bit unhinged. She waded through the war zone that used to be Gwen's apartment and grabbed a few sweaters, jeans, shoes and sneakers, t-shirts and her hairbrush, along with her poor excuse for a make-up bag and her iPod, knowing she couldn't live long without the music. She came out and Kaid was looking down into the alley with a frown. She stuffed the remnants of what she gathered into a large carpet bag Gwen had in the hallway and then zipped it, picking up Gwen's phone that she saw lying on the floor of the kitchen. "Ok then that's it. See? I was quick."

"Well done." He straightened up and moved to her. "Is your car out front?"

"No. It got chewed the fuck up earlier this evening." she walked out and shut Gwen's door behind her.

"Great, just fucking great. We're not going out the front, where's the back way out of here? We're gonna have to take a walk, if you don't mind?"

"As long as you are carrying the bags."

"All the way." he grinned, "Now where's the back exit?"

"One more floor, make a left. What the hell is going on? We could take the fire escape otherwise."

He turned to her and gave her a sidelong glance. "I owe some guys money; they've been tailing my car. I really didn't think that they'd catch up to me this quickly." he put his hand on her waist, hurrying her along. "I really don't wanna chance getting caught, especially not with a little sweet thing like you. They aren't you average bad guys."

"Uh huh." she held back a shiver at the heat that washed through her from his touch. Lord she did have a thing for bad boys. "Look whatever. We can always hail a cab. It's not like we are in the Bowery here, we get cabs all night."

"Let's walk a few blocks first," He pulled her a little closer. "You're not in any desperate hurry to leave me are you?" He chuckled into her ear, his fingers flexing on her hipbone. "We could talk about Sumerian mythology if you'd like?"

"Again, what exactly do you know about it?"

"A few things, try me."

"Well I don't know. I'm working on my doctorate thesis."

"Oh on what?" He directed her around a corner his body tense and alert.

"The goddess Eskirgal."

He let out a hiss of surprise and his fingers tensed, digging sharply into her side. He stood frozen to the spot with her bags hanging loosely forgotten in his hand.

The touch was explosive and set her off, her body waking up from its usual bored slumber and took notice of the man next to her. "Whoa... Ease up sexy... please?"

"Shit, sorry." He snapped out of it. "I just thought I heard something." He let her go.

"No harm no foul. Everything ok?"

"Yeah it's ok. Must have been a cat or something. Come on." He led her faster down the street.

As she walked she moved closer to him, partial to the tingles he gave her when his skin was close to her. "So what do you do Kaid? We have established that you're not a stripper."

"No I'm not. I'm in security."

"Figures, like Syrus. What kind?"

"Ever heard of Briathos security?"

She smiled. "Yes, they handle all the security for the New York Museum where I work. All the cases and such."

"Well I work for them, in a roundabout sort of way. I set up the cameras and boxes from a strategically sound point of view. I don't do the computer shit but I do work with the layouts and plans, fitting alarms and so on."

"Ah so you have probably been to the museum then." *And it's a damn shame I haven't met you before.*

"Yeah I have."

"Well that's good to know." she looked at him sideways. "So where are we going now? Can we get that cab, I don't know about you but its freezing out here and I'm not wearing a bra."

He stopped pulling her to a halt next to him. "Shit why didn't you say so?" Setting the bags down, he shrugged off his leather jacket handing it to her. "Put this on." His grey wife beater was stark aganst the darkness surrounding them. His hevily muscled arms flex as he moved, making his vaguely familiar tattoos dance in the struggling light.

She let a smirk tug at her mouth. "A gentleman all the way." she shrugged into the leather and inhaled the scent of him. Her head swam with dark and naughty thoughts. If it was possible, her nipples went from hard to achingly hard all with the scent of him. "You sure you won't be cold?" She gave him the once over and grinned.

"I'll live. I'm a big strong man." They crossed a road, hurrying down an alleyway. "So about your thesis?"

"What about it?" she rushed alongside him, noticing that he was far more alert than most men were to a football game, and there wasn't a patch of anything to worry about.

"How far into it are you?"

"About twenty pages. I'm thinking it will be around 80. Once I get more information I have been looking for that is. I have been working on this since undergrad, Sumerian mythology is my passion."

"Passion?" He grinned at her. "You don't look the type."

"Meaning?"

"You just don't, you're petite and beautiful. People who are interested in long dead cultures and mythology are old and fussy. Mostly male in their sixties." he flashed a smile. "You should be doing some pop culture thing on the rise and fall of Britney."

Right. Cuz that's exactly what she needed. It was bad enough that her attractiveness had gotten her in trouble on several occasions; she didn't need anyone to think she was a vapid twit that got her degree by fucking the grades outta some must old fuck professor.

"Just because I'm hot means I can't have real interests? Please this world isn't real; the worship of stupid pop tarts with less talent then my right ass cheek isn't real.

History, if we don't study the past, we are doomed to repeat it. I study what calls to me. Sumerian culture always has."

"I'm sure both of your sweet ass cheeks have a lot of talent. You're hot and that means you don't *have* to have any interests." He grinned wolfishly. "I just doubt that studying the fall of Sumerian pantheon would give us any insight into our current culture."

He was flirting, and doing a damn fine job of it. It wasn't often that she met someone that had any sort of brain that looked like him, so she supposed stereotypes went both ways. "On the contrary, but that's not my thesis."

"So tell me about your thesis. Tell me about," He paused swallowing, "Eskirgal." The way he said her name was a reverent whisper, sexy and pained.

She shivered and a jolt ran through her. "She is my favorite of all the goddesses throughout the world. Strong, powerful, graceful and adored. Her sacrifice for her people was epic, and her life is a legend few know. So my thesis is the correlation between her sexual allure and powerful will against women of power now. She wasn't afraid to be beautiful, sexy and wield her body like the temple it was. Women today that use sex to get what they want are scorned for it, while she was revered and emulated by countless millions." She sighed and blushed, as she always did when she talked about the goddess. "She was the ultimate powerful sex kitten. I admire that."

He was silent beside her as they hurried onwards though the dark streets. "What did she sacrifice?" "Her life... and the love of her consort, Nergal." she sighed. "You should know this if you know Sumerian myths. Their love affair was better than Paris and Helen, better then Zeus and Hera, better then Shiva and Vishnu. They are timeless."

"And they are dead." He sighed bitterly his mood souring. "As are their people and everyone else you mentioned. If there's anything to be taken from history it's that life fucks you over at every given turn. Eskirgal was naive and ignorant of life's ways and she died painfully for nothing but a dying pantheon to save face. No one should dare try to emulate her. She's closer to Britney than any powerful female leader of today."

Well that struck a chord with her companion. "See I disagree, but that's beauty of thesis, you don't have to agree, only agree that the argument I pose is a viable one. And you speak as if you knew firsthand of the sorrow. You couldn't be more then what, thirty?"

His mouth audibly snapped shut and he glared across the street into the darkness. "Yeah I'm thirty two but I watch a lot of history channel."

She smirked. "You look damn good for thirty two. So? We going to zigzag across the city eluding an enemy that's not there for the entire night? Cuz I gotta tell you, I'm seriously tired. Bed is calling me."

"We're almost there."

She nodded. "And Kaid,"

"Uh huh?" They walked across another street, stopping in front a large brownstone.

"Don't bullshit me. The history channel hasn't done anything in depth on Sumerian culture. You're hiding something but it's ok. I'll just take it as a student of the world kinda thing." she looked up and smiled. "Where the hell are we?"

"My place." He typed a code into a keypad and put his face up to a lens. "Retina scan," he explained. "It's a little James Bond but fuck it why the hell not. It would be bad for business if I got broken into."

"You think?" she grinned. "Why the hell did you bring me here? I'm supposed to be meeting up with Gwen. There was nothing in the brochure that said I would be locked down alone with a guy I hardly know." Not that it really bothered her.

"Well that was before we were being followed. Look suit yourself, you can stay here and get some sleep maybe have a snoop around my history texts and in the morning, when its daylight, we can head over to meet Gwen. Or you can wait in the hallway until I source a car. If you feel threatened you could always shoot me."

Kaid was a weird guy, weirder still with the offer of plugging him one should she desire it. She frowned. "Far be it from me to turn down an invitation to spend the night with a hot guy." Ansley might be *Perfect 10* model material, but she hadn't had a real date in ages, and hadn't gotten laid in more than ages. "And the possibility of snooping through your own texts intrigues me. So color me staying.".

"Excellent choice." he opened the door and stepped aside to let her into the house. "I'll call Syrus and let him know that we're going to be late." he took his phone out, and flipped it open. "The library's down the hall to the left. Snoop away."

Chapter Eight

Syrus slammed the eight ball into the right corner pocket and threw his stick on the table. "That's game Arlo."

Arlo took a swig of his domestic longneck and then grimaced. "Slippery shit. How is this fair? You win the game and get the girl?"

"If I'm not mistaken, He hasn't gotten anything yet." Castor offered. "Unless you count getting transplanted from his room for the evening with nary an invitation."

Syrus rolled his eyes. "Will you both just can it? Did anyone get any information out of Jingles or is the fuck still passed out sleeping off his fix?" he sounded disgusted.

Arlo shrugged. "Well aside from the paper you gave us, which Blaine is already running an online data mine on, no. He's still seventy underground, and I don't plan on seeing him about and useful till tomorrow sometime."

"So who is taking babysitting duty then?" Syrus blinked.

Arlo shrugged. "Blaine can, he's stuck here anyway. Castor has an appointment with Sotheby's and Kaid is on the docks for the new exhibit coming to the New York Museum's Paleontology department. Why we are on that detail I'll never know but I doubt they are going to find any relic's in a dig in an old tar pit."

Syrus nodded. "And Dez?"

"The usual."

Syrus frowned. The usual meant he was seducing someone or another, by way usually of lunch and an early round at the plaza. And he didn't mean drinks. Dezi had gotten a lot of their clients that way, women just loved to trust him, and he loved to give it to them.

"And you?" Syrus said to Arlo.

"I'm over at Whickham and Trust to assess that goddamn cache of Etruscan pottery. Why they keep digging the shit up is anyone's clue. The Torpus Mirror isn't anywhere near the old homestead." He frowned. "Though where it is, is anyone's guess. So why not start looking there eh?"

Arlo was very bitter over losing his own relic, or rather allowing the Etruscan priests to hide it from him. Whereas Syrus had known where his was, but it was taken, and the rest of the guys had been kept appraised of the location, should they need it, Arlo's pantheon hadn't thought it prudent to let him in on the particulars. They had sacrificed him to this life and this calling, but they didn't trust him for shit. Now cut off from his own Pantheon, the location has been lost completely to antiquity, which meant the possibility of finding his keeper and getting back to his powers was slim and none. Still, stranger things had happened.

Syrus and Gwen were living proof of that.

"Ok so it's Blaine and myself then. I'll deal with the girls; Blaine can sober the junkie up."

"Hey," Arlo looked up. "Jingles is a pretty decent person when he's not medicated. Give him a break."

Syrus shrugged. "So back to the task at hand then, what do we know about Marrow right now?"

Blaine walked in. "Aside from the name of the CEO, nothing much. Their public face is cleaner than a preacher's sheets. Nathan Danvers has the company involved in a lot from mergers right down to street missions and soup kitchens. They are a fortune 500 company, same as us."

"So that means that like the almighty transformers..." Syrus smirked.

"There's more than meets the eye, yes."

"Great. Well this doesn't help does it?"

"Actually," Arlo grinned. "It does."

"How?"

"With the info and the data mine we should be able to directly link the Div activity with some of the company's smaller divisions and charities. Maybe help us put a lock on them. Figure out where the Div are coming from. I mean they aren't upper crust coeds or trust fund babies from the fucking Hampton's. Every single one I have sent to his hellish reward has looked like a runaway, young, emaciated and full of anger. If you think about it, it makes hella sense. Take from the forgotten ones, the ones that aren't going to be missed. In this throwaway culture, it's the perfect cover. And they were using urchins and street kids back east when they emerged remember?"

Syrus grinned. Arlo was a devious son of a bitch and it helped to have a hoodlum on the team who thought like that. It had saved their lives many times in the past, and now his darker, sinister side opened possibilities Syrus would have overlooked. It wasn't his fault that he looked on the brighter side of things; he just had more to keep his spirits higher for longer.

Castor nodded to Syrus. "Now, why the fuck are you here with us? That woman is a stunning specimen of what heaven is supposed to be. Strength she doesn't know she has. Sherri is going to love her."

Arlo looked up, and wicked glint in his eye that Syrus quickly squelched. "Don't even think about it A, I don't think Sher or Gwen are the type of girls to get off on that little fantasy."

"What?" he asked innocently. "Honestly I wasn't thinking anything."

"The hell you weren't," he grumbled. Not that the idea didn't cross Syrus' mind, it just wasn't with Sherri.

Dezi snorted, "I know I was. Seriously though, if you don't I will... you know, just check up on her. Give her a good tucking down; it's all part of the service." He laid his hands wide with a shit eating grin.

Dezi, for all his big talk, wouldn't front on Gwen now, not when Syrus was her clear choice, whatever the reason. Syrus grinned at him. "You really only have one thing on your mind don't you?"

"Not much else to bother about these days. I love being worshiped and I'm not above putting the effort in to getting it either. I work fucking hard at it."

Dezi's god powers were a direct result of his followers, and being the supreme god of darkness in the Welsh pantheon; he was also their god of lust. And he enjoyed the full scope of his secondary powers on a daily basis. Women never said no. The man didn't know the meaning of the word rejection, except when it came to his fellow gods. Still, Syrus felt the need to reinforce his claim. "Indeed you do. Just don't work on Gwen, Cool. I would hate to tear your heart out. Sure it won't kill you but it will hurt like a son of a bitch."

"Eh I've had worse for less," he grinned, "By the looks of her it'd be worth it. I know that type, wildcat. Arlo isn't too far off with his "quiet ones" theory and a fucking librarian? Fuck, I don't know a man out there who hasn't had one of those fantasies at least once.

All prim and proper with a tight bun and wire rimmed glasses. Not to mention those pencil skirts. Mmmmm..." He grinned, losing himself in his daydream.

"Does she look like she wears buns, glasses and pencil skirts? That woman is at home in Jeans and t-shirts. She's way outta your league. Mine too." Syrus offered.

"Well at least I'd be trying. Besides she's one of those low self-confidence girls, she'd let anything fuck her after a few sweet words. She doesn't know how hot she is." He groaned, "Man that's just so rare, I bet you any money that my Keeper's some sort of whore... it's no less that I deserve but still. A nice girl should be cherished." he laughed, finishing his beer.

And that was the crux of it. The women that would be each of their Keepers would hold a bond with them; could be the woman that held their lives and hearts for all time. There was no doubt Gwen was his Keeper, and there was even less doubt that he was overly attracted to her.

But she was delicate. Fuckers like Tom had really whittled her away. Dezi was right, a few kind words and he would be buried between her thighs making her scream for him. But he didn't want that. He wanted her to want him on a level playing field. That was going to be tough to accomplish, and he knew that.

"And she's *my* Keeper. I can't help that I was the first to find mine. She's a challenge alright but she will be cherished."

"Then you should cherish her." Dezi grinned picking up the pool cue. "Come on Arlo it's my turn to beat you."

"C note says I whomp your ass big time lust bringer."

Syrus laughed and then frowned as the cell in his pocket began to vibrate. He fished it out, not liking the feeling it it produced. He opened it. "Yeah?"

"It's Kaid."

He sat back and grabbed a cigarette out of the pack on the side table. "Yeah? And where the fuck are you? You better not have her tied to a bed frame." Though it would be a new one if the Sumerian admitted doing that. As far as they knew, Kaid was celibate. Ansley however could tempt the most pious priest to sin.

Kaid gave a disgusted sigh. "Not my style Egyptian. We ran into a little problem of the Div kind. They followed us from the apartment. We're holed up at my place but they followed us here. My place is pretty much fucking compromised. We'll head over at sunrise."

"Shit. Cas did mention that they might get a brain between them. This is not good. You guys going to be ok? I mean she doesn't know what's up does she? Castor was clear; she gets the cover story, that's it."

"Not yet, she's not an idiot though, I'm not sure what she believes but for now she's content with my story. She's in my library rummaging through texts and whatever else is thrown in there. You ever ask your girlfriend exactly what it is that Ansley does?"

That was interesting. Kaid called Gwen his girlfriend and used her friends name, not 'the girl' or 'the bitch'. "Um, it never came up while we were running back here, nor when the guys were hitting on her hardcore. What the fuck does it matter?"

"Ask her sometime, you might find it amusing, I sure as hell don't." The line went dead.

He frowned, set the phone down and lit his cigarette. "So apparently Kaid is not going to make it in tonight."

Dezi missed the shot and swore. "I fucking told you he shouldn't have brought her in."

"Apparently Cas was right. Fuckers were waiting and followed them."

"Are they ok?" Blaine looked up from his laptop.

"Well they're at Kaid's brownstone, so you decide. He said they will be in in the morning."

Blaine nodded then flashed him a grin. "Maybe you should let Gwen know." The hint wasn't wasted on him.

He smirked as four sets of eyes laughed at him. "Yeah I guess you're right." he stubbed out the cigarette, the cherry scented smoke enveloping him as he got up and walked toward the hallway that would take him down to where she was sleeping.

Gwen. Jesus he wasn't sure how the hell he got a woman like that. She was stunning, sexy, especially because she didn't know it, and sassy. It had taken everything he had to spend time with the guys in the pool room, acting normal. Truth was he was jonesing for her again, her smile, her scent, the shine of her hair. This was not a new feeling, but it wasn't something he had felt in longer than an age. The only woman that had ever illicit such a response from him was his late wife and lover, Isis, almost to a T. That it was exactly the same shored up his courage.

But she was delicate. Life had been hard emotionally, and with the recent unpleasantness, he would have to treat her with kid gloves. She calmed him, stoked his inner fire and roused his powers. He only hoped he could do the same for her. Truth was that for all his arrogance, he knew there was the slight chance that she wasn't into him, and that this could end up being a tender friendship. Sure she responded to his kiss earlier, but that could have been anything from the adrenaline to the fathoms of blood loss. He had to know, her being so near and out of reach was torture.

Not remembering his trek, he stood in front of the door and listened. Not a sound came from behind the door, and he was sure she was in fact sleeping. In his bed, on his sheets, snuggled on his pillows. The thought made him heady. He tried the handle, found it unlocked and grinned. Even if it was unconscious, Gwen was still giving him an invitation. He entered silently and walked into the bedroom to a sight that made his knees weak.

Syrus' mouth went dry as he watched Gwen writhe in her sleep. The dress she had on earlier was wrinkled, and her bra was lying on the overstuffed chair next to the bed. The dress had ridden up to just under her breasts, and her silver thong was peeking out from under the sheet that barely covered her perfect thighs.

The cowl of the dress was sitting to the side flashing the top half of her nipple to him, a rosy offering against the grey of the dress and creamy sweetness of her skin. Her hair was a cloud around her and her arms were thrown over her head as she whimpered. He groaned and reached down, adjusting himself in the confines of his jeans. Sweet Tiamat she was a sight. A Sexy, unadulterated wet dream waiting in his bed.

There wasn't a shot in hell he could not respond to the sight of her undone like that. Her sleep self showed him the passionate woman she hid behind in her waking life. He approached the bed and crawled up as her thrashing got worse. He leaned in, placing his lips on hers as she moaned and gasped for air. It wasn't voluntary; his essence was driving him, pushing him towards the woman that kept his powers close to her heart.

She stilled under his lips leaning into him, her moans turning gentle.

His hands went up to hers and he settled down, his hips between her splayed thighs, holding her down. He kissed her deeper, lost in the sensation of her satin lips on his, of her sweet breath on his face. In her dreams she was accepting him, but when she woke, well that was completely different.

Her moans grew more urgent as her legs wrapped around his waist as she ground herself into him through his jeans. Her hands slipped down her body, cupping her breasts, rubbing them through the knitted material.

Dear goddess, she had some powerful thighs.

This was torture. Her legs were a vice around his waist, and he groaned anew, his hands now on her waist as he kissed her. She was so responsive, she moved just like he thought she would. He slipped his hands up to where hers were and broke the kiss, licking a wet line down her neck, over her collarbone, before dipping into the area of her dress. Her nipple was exposed now, and he attacked it with his mouth and tongue. His hand kneaded the globe of her breast while the other slid down her body and lifted her hip so he pressed more fully into her searing heat.

She cried out softly, exhaling in pleasure a peaceful smile gracing her. "Mmmmm Syrus." She sighed in tones only a woman could make. "Please..." She ground into him her hips circling as her thighs held him tightly.

The girl was saying all the things he wanted to hear. Too bad he had morals, and wouldn't fuck an unconscious woman no matter how much her dream self begged. He tore his mouth away from her pebbled nipple. He kissed her again, sweeping his tongue into her mouth and rolled his hips into her once last time. He might have morals, but he was still a man. She was too tempting for words. "Gwen... baby I won't do this with you sleeping... it's not a dream... wake up..." *and please say yes.*

She woke with a start, her body tensing as her eyes darted open. Fear washed over her as she realized her position moving to fix her dress trying to cover herself.

He rolled off her and blushed, sheepishly, swearing under his breath. "Shit... I'm sorry. I... Shit." he stammered. What was it about this woman that could make him feel so damn awkward?

She sat up and immediately tucked her legs under herself, pulling her dress over her ankles covering every piece of flesh. "I..." She flushed, breathing heavily. "It's ok."

He smiled and cocked his head. "You're an amazing kisser." he winked.

He saw her throat move when she swallowed. "You're pretty amazing yourself... kisser that is. Amazing kisser. Though you probably know that already. How long was I asleep?"

"I don't know, I came in to talk to you, and you were lying here like an offering. I couldn't help myself. I'm sorry. Then when you moaned my name... were you dreaming about me?"

"I..." She shook her head "Not at first."

"What where you dreaming at first?" he scooted closer to her.

"Demons," she told him in a quiet voice, shaking her head. Her eyes glazed over, "Tom was one of them and he..." her voice cracked. "I don't want to think about it."

"So when did it turn to me?" he grinned.

"I don't know, but I'm glad it did." She leaned into him, looking to him for comfort.

So was he. If he could spare her any unpleasantness he would. He captured her lips in his and kissed her once again, setting his hand on her hip. "Do you have any idea how hot you are?" he murmured and then smirked. He wanted more, but after that little show, he would do well to wait for her to come to him.

She was willing, but the question was how far to go. She was the only one who could answer that, and he would let her come to it on her own time. "I feel hot when you touch me." She breathed against him.

He groaned. Oh this wasn't going to be easy. "And do you like it?"

"When you touch me? I do." She rested her head against him.

He pulled her closer to him and settled down, stroking her side and smiled. This felt right. "Then I'll be sure to touch you a lot then."

"Mmmmm," she moaned softly "If you want. Please."

He grinned. *Bingo. Permission granted.*

"Did Ansley get here? Was that what you wanted to talk to me about? Is she ok?"

"She's fine. Kaid called in. Div were following them. Kaid took her to his place and they are hold up till morning."

"Will she be ok?" she lifted her head from his shoulder.

He nodded. "Kaid's place is Fort Knox. She's safer there then anywhere in the world. Which is really fucking odd to say in general. Gwen, what does Ansley do for a living?"

She screwed up her face. "She works at the museum, at the moment she's getting her doctorate in anthropology. She's got a real hard on for Sumerian culture, she's working her thesis on some Eskirgal goddess.

Getting her to shut up about its pretty hard." she frowned up at him, "Why?"

Syrus almost choked. "Shit. You're kidding." he sat up. Kaid was stuck with a woman who was researching, in essence, his life and had a passion for it. He was fucked.

"No... Why?" She shot him a look, "Is she ok?"

"Oh she's fine... but... well Kaid is Sumerian."

"Oh... well she's gonna love that. Like I said, she has a real hard on for it."

"Yeah well... She can't know so... it's moot."

"I guess..." she pushed him onto his back, curling up next to him. "So tell me about you."

"About me? What's there to know? I'm the Egyptian god of death and the afterlife. I was sacrificed for the good of the world, left alone till now. See? Not much there to tell." he said quietly. There was more, but it was not a story he enjoyed reliving. He might have been the lone god to volunteer, aside from Castor, but that didn't mean that he had enjoyed his life till now. Gwen could change it all, and she was well on her way to proving that.

"I know there's more to you than that." she smiled. "I know you like to play pool... or at least you're good at it. I tried once and I was useless at it."

He grinned. "Ummm well we will be here today, If you wanna learn, I could teach you. Let's see. I do like pool; I also like porno, hard cider and cherry flavored cigarettes. As for my less lascivious pursuits, I enjoy sushi, Central park when it snows and a good concert in the village."

"We'll see? That's something now isn't it?" She smiled. "So you had priestesses huh?"

This was going to get tricky. "A long, long time ago, I had a temple dedicated to me."

"Just the one?"

"Yes, most dark deities don't have much more than one cult."

"Ah..." she tucked herself under his arm. "So what was it like?"

"What exactly are you asking about?" Amusement filled his voice. He leaned forward, grabbed the blanket and pulled it up around then.

She shrugged and shook her head. "I don't know really, what was it like back then? Being worshiped? Being a god? You don't have to answer if you don't want to."

Lying there with her, he realized he couldn't deny her something so easy. Not that it wasn't going to be awkward. "It was different. I am still you know, there are Osiris cults all over the world, even here in New York, small but they are always women."

"Why?"

"Apparently I was known as quite a lothario back in my day. My priestesses kept me safe when I had my godhead, and when I was inducted into the Inferi Dii I was weak. They took care of me, said they always would. Back then, each year I would choose one of them as a lover, and there was never any issues or anything. I was married, to Isis. She didn't mind sharing, come to think of it, neither did I. It was nice. I was given some of the most beautiful women as my priestesses. When the Scarab was created, twenty two of my most loyal priestesses gave their lives to keep it safe for me." he sighed. "When it went missing, and I heard about it and went looking." he paused. "Looks like my new priestesses kept it safe for me."

"Not that safe I was close to ebaying it a few times." The look in her eyes told him otherwise.

"But you didn't. And if you could have, then you would have. You kept it because you were meant to be my Keeper."

"Maybe." She sighed. Running her hand over his belly frowning a little as she moved her hand over the stud that lay there. "So what did you do? The death and afterlife leaves a lot to the imagination."

"The usual. When I was working, the dead were my responsibility. Some would go to the afterlife, some would be reincarnated. Some souls went to Dis. others stayed in the realm I lived in, and lived out their afterlife. When priests would curse people, I was the one there to oversee it. When death prophecies were written, I was the one that put the stamp of approval on them. And when I wasn't working..."

"Priestess orgies?"

He laughed. "No. I never had more than one of them at a time." *Not like now.* "But they were my constant companions. I *took* them to orgies and other sort of debaucheries. It worked out well. Isis was there when they weren't."

"Ah so you're off time was filled with beautiful women throwing themselves at you. Nice, I'm sure, if you like that sort of thing."

"I did for a long time. It's my nature. There's a fine line between sex and death."

"Really?" Her eyes glinted with sarcasm. "And I'm sure that's a line you use a lot."

"No line, apparently. The French call orgasms *Le Petite Morte*, the little death. Your heart stops for half a second when you come. Did you know that?"

"Half a second?" she sounded impressed. "That must just be the really good ones."

He smirked. "Oh the really good ones are epic... Those half second ones, Child's play."

"Oh I bet." She laughed, her body tensing next to his.

He grinned and kissed her sweetly, shifting slightly. She was under him again seconds later, and he resumed the position he was in before she woke up, only this time she was aware, and she was not telling him no. The kiss grew in intensity, and he slipped his hand to her hip.

She gasped, his tongue gaining entrance to her mouth eating up her moans. Her hands slid down to his waist, holding him firmly as she lifted her hips up to meet his.

"You sure about this Gwen? " he asked against her ear.

"I don't know..." She shook her head and pulled back just a touch. "I don't know what I want anymore. Everything terrifies me, I've so many doubts."

Syrus looked down into her eyes; the bright beauty of them tightened his chest. He wouldn't sit there and say meaningless words, wouldn't give into the pillow talk. Instead he licked his lips. "Gwen, you never have to be scared with me. If anything, I have to be scared of you."

She shook her head, "I don't want to disappoint you. sure you like me now but that could change..."

"I don't see how. Not after that stunning preview you gave me before."

"I was sleeping."

"You're using that as an excuse?" he grinned. "All that proved to me is your passion is so amazing you have had to hide it from everyone... saving it for me." *Like Isis.* Syrus kissed her and nibbled her bottom lip. "Your body wants me, I can smell it." He whispered in her ear. "It's soaking through my jeans. You are the best kinda tease Gwen." He licked the lobe of her ear, catching her little stud earring and tugged playfully. "Be my Keeper Gwen... please."

No he was not above begging with this woman, not when she was turning out to be everything he wanted in a partner. Her passion bubbled just under the surface and he knew the walls hiding it in from the world were cracking.

She moved against him, rolled her hips into his and he almost lost it.

Syrus reared back and pulled his t-shirt over his head. "Gwen, tell me, those silk and lace panties I spied before, how do they feel all wet and rubbing against your clit?" He nipped her bottom lip again slid his hand down her hip and over her thigh between the two of them and pressed his fingers against her, the heel of his hand firmly on her tight bud.

"Good," she gasped rubbing herself against him. "Very good. But it might feel better without them." Her hands moved up over his chest, delicately exploring, her soft touch driving him crazy. "Yes, I think we need to take them off." she told him coming to a decision. "And these." she tugged at his jeans and met his gaze. "These need to go as well."

He grinned and hooked two fingers under the wet flimsy fabric and pulled, a thick tearing sound filling the space between their labored breaths. Hepulled them up and swung them around his finger. "I'll buy you another pair." he murmured and then hissed as he replaced his hand feeling her heat double. He swore and kissed her as she worked at his belt and zipper. It was when both her legs reared up and her heels gripped his hips and pushed the jeans down his narrow hips that he lost it. "Bad girl..."

She gasped as she realized that he wasn't wearing underwear under the denim. "We need to get this dress off you.

As naughty as it is to see you undone and wanton with this cowl exposing your breasts, I want the full scope of you... I need to feel and lick each part of your skin."

Taking her hem of her dress in hand she slowly slid it up her body, wiggling herself closer to him with each deliberate movement. Her gaze locked on his cock, never leaving as she pulled the dress over her head and throwing it to the floor. With both hands free she reached down.

"Wow." She reverently thumbed over his piercing, her tongue running over her lips. "I'm not sure if he'll fit." Her hands never left him, her soft touch feather light. He groaned.Syrus looked down then up at her and chuckled. "Oh I disagree." he hissed and closed his eyes as she stroked him. In seconds, she turned from nervous wallflower, a front she wore like armor, to the smoldering temptress that she was in her sleep, the real Gwen. "If you're worrying about the piercing..." he trailed off and looked sheepishly at her.

"I'm not... well a little bit..." Again she rolled the piercing curiously with her thumb. "But I trust you not to hurt me."

He grinned. She trusted him. It was the first step he knew and he couldn't disappoint her. "It won't hurt, promise. You'll like it a lot."

"If what I've seen already is any indicator then you're right, I will."

He kissed her hard, rolling them so he was on his back. "Well then we should get started shall we?" he gripped her hips and pulled her to straddle him; his cock nestled between her thighs. He groaned. Syrus reached up and palmed her breasts, his thumbs working over her nipples with deft purpose.

"Here?" She looked down at him uncertainty clear in her eyes. "No. I can't be on top." She shook her head, her body going stiff even as she leaned into his palms.

He smirked. "No? I beg to differ. But that's hardly the point." he slipped his hands down her soft skin and growled grasping her hips and pulled her forward, so her sweetness was parallel to his mouth.

Her hands went to the wall steadying herself. He felt the slight tremors moving though her, something that had nothing to do with nervousness. "What now?".

Syrus didn't answer; just kept her eyes locked on hers as her hooked his arms around her thighs and pulled her down to his mouth, his tongue darting out to lick her already slick and throbbing flesh.

"Fuck Syrus!" She swore as her body buckled above him.

He chuckled and worked her taught flesh.

She writhed above him.

His tongue searched her flesh, his lips sucking at all the right places, especially that little bundle of nerves begging him for attention. He couldn't get enough of her scent, of her taste. The woman above him was a goddess, truly worthy of a god as her lover, more so because she had denied her true self so long. And here she was, giving it over to him. Luck had nothing to do with it, and he silently thanked the goddess whom he served under, for sending this woman to him. Being inside her was going to be epic, earth shattering... and if she agreed to be his Keeper...

But that would come later, and now all he wanted was to make her boneless, exhausted with satisfaction. With the way she was moving, she was well on her way.

She tore her hands away from the wall, running them through his hair as she rode his mouth wanton with need.

"Please!"

She moved faster, harder. Reaching her peak, she cried out his name as she came, grinding herself down into him.

Syrus moaned into her as he tasted her, really tasted her for the first time. She was intoxicating, and he was greedy with it. It was only after her tremors subsided that he pulled away from her and slid her down his body with one hand, and pulled her down to kiss him with the other. A quick flick of his hips and he was inside her seated to the hilt, his mouth absorbing her scream. She was tight, but the snugness was quite welcome. He groaned into her mouth and broke the kiss, Panting. "See?"

"Yes," She moaned breathlessly kissing him again. "Snug." She sat up on him her fingers moving experimentally over his body as she began to move, accepting him fully into her.

***

Syrus was in heaven. Pure heaven. This woman was beyond measure the best choice for him. He watched as the Scarab lolled between her breasts as she rode him, cradled between, close to her heart. He swore and licked his lips. "Your perfect Gwen... you like that... like how that feels?" he bucked up into her feeling his frenum piercing slide against her inner walls and he bit his bottom lip. The sensation was maddening.

"Mmmmm I do... feels so good." She rode him harder her eyes closed as her hips rolled in a controlled rhythm.

Stunning... just stunning.

He growled and bucked up again, then gripped her hips and rolled them, so he was on his knees and she was on her back, He pulled her further onto his cock and then leaned down and kissed her hard, his lips blazing a trail down her chest and latched onto her right nipple.

She cried out, her body arching up to him. Never missing a beat, her legs came around his waist, her thighs latching onto him as she met him.

"Perfect," he moaned. "You're fucking perfect."

"Mmmmm less talking more kissing." She murmured with a smile pulling him into a searing kiss, her arms snaking down his back cupping his ass.

He hissed, gave a very creative curse and kissed her, his tongue mimicking what his cock was doing elsewhere on her body. This was the real Gwen, a woman he planned to keep around. Need built in him. The need to mark her with his symbol, to make her his Keeper in every sense of the word. He held back, his willpower stronger then the cosmic pull. She would have to choose, though it wouldn't be this first time.

He could feel her getting closer; already his instinct about her body was being honed to a razors edge. He changed tactics, swiveling his hips for a deeper angle, knowing that he would bring her closer, his piercing scraping against that magic, sensitive flesh that would make her explode in sensation.

"God yes Syrus!" she hissed, coming hard around him her body clamping vice-like down on him. She scored her nails down his back in passion as her orgasm took her wave after wave.

Syrus rode the sensations and groaned letting himself go. He followed her over the edge, his seed pumping deep into her and panted her name, licking the sweat off her shoulder.

The need to mark her as his Keeper subsided with his orgasm, but he knew it was just a temporary reprieve. The need would grow stronger each time they made love, and soon, he wouldn't be able to do a damn thing about it, whether she wanted it or not.

He panted anew. "I didn't know making love to you was going to be an earth shattering event, though I had my suspicions."

"Mmmmm..." She agreed breathlessly. "My heart definitely stopped for more than half a second." She flashed him a satisfied smile.

Syrus chuckled and kissed her, slipping out of her body. "Told you." grinned and then looked at her. "No more hiding Gwen."

Shaking her head she sighed. "I don't hide, not intentionally."

"No, but you use it as a shield from the world. You're stronger than that."

"Maybe," she answered doubtfully.

"You are. You couldn't have the relic if you weren't."

She smiled pulling him into a kiss. "Your relic."

He grinned. "Mine."

"And mine seeing as how I have to keep it for you."

He nodded. "It's not that simple, but yes."

"Not that simple how? Isn't that what a Keeper does?"

"Part of it. A real Keeper not only holds dominion over an Inferi's relic, but his powers, soul and his life. She... She becomes a part of us, our other half, or so says the doctrine. A Keeper allows us access to our full powers, and shares our godhead, ensuring that the Inferi is happy, cared for and loved." he sighed. "The six of us have spent countless lifetimes alone, with the hope of finding our Keepers."

"Oh..." She frowned unhappily looking away. "I can see why you would be searching for her then."

"Not her, you. Regardless if you choose to become my real Keeper, you hold my relic; it chose you, your family. The rest is up to you." he turned her head and kissed her on the lips. "I found what I have been looking for, but I won't make the choice for you, ever. This is your life Gwen, and you have to make a conscious decision to either be with me, or hold my relic in name only."

She nodded silently. "I don't think I could share god powers that I barely understand." She sighed. "I want to be with you though, this was fantastic."

He chuckled. "I said godhead. Meaning my immortality. But that's neither here nor there at this point. You don't have to decide now. What matters right now, is keeping you and Ansley safe from the Div and the Velns. You are a target now, your life signature."

"Because of you?"

"No, because they detected the relic." he sighed and pulled her to him.

"Why is this one so important? There's five others, three in museums and places. So why focus on ours?"

"Because the others they aren't sure of. We have gone through a lot to hide the reality of these relics. Over the years the names have been changed to protect the innocent, so to speak, like ours, though mine and Dezi are the only ones that stayed close to our real names. Yours is accessible, because you are a civilian, and the relic hasn't been kept under armed guard or enchantments. Its raw energy, radiating the power of a very potent binding spell.

"The rest have been cloaked, well except for Kaid's, and Arlo's, but Arlo's... that's another story. All I'm saying is that if you chose to be my Keeper, my lover and the woman that holds my heart, or if you don't, things won't ever be simple for you again.

Not until we possess all the relics." And the women that would activate them, but he couldn't bring himself to tell her.

"Things weren't exactly simple before. So then what happens? What happens when you have all the relics? I mean you have what now? Five? Four?"

"One. You. A relic isn't activated until it comes into contact with its Keeper. Which is why for the longest time they were protected and coveted by our Priestesses, priests and oracles... In the hopes that one of them would be the Keeper, or bring the Keeper to the relic, and the best match for each of us. I will be honest, when the Scarab went missing; I lost all hope of finding you. And yet here you are and I'm the first. Odd how things end up. We had thought Castor would be the first, he is our leader, but it seems the goddess had other plans."

"Granted, but what happens when you have all the relics," she repeated slowly adding, "And their Keepers?"

"Your guess is as good as mine. I just work here. The one to ask about that would be Sherri. She's our go between."

"Between what?"

"Us, the lowly foot soldiers, and the supreme dark goddess, Tiamat." he said as he turned and opened the bedside drawer and grabbed a pack of cigarettes. He took one out and lit put exhaling the smoke in rings.

"Gods with a goddess. That's a little unusual is it not?"

"Not really. This venture was set up between the goddess and the Roman pantheon. It wasn't till about one hundred or so years later that they realized Orcus, Castor, couldn't do it all on his own.

"They enlisted the other pantheon's that helped imprison the Velns to sacrifice one of their own to watch the spaces between the worlds, and hold back the darkness. What better than their own dark gods? We understand the darkness, and that makes us the best defense. Sherri is a Soul Keeper. She holds a piece of each of us, until our Keeper makes the choice."

"The word sacrificed doesn't sound so good." She said quietly cuddling down into him.

"Believe me it wasn't. None of us had a say in it. Except Castor and myself."

"It must have been hard." her fingers worked comfortingly over the flesh on his arm.

"It was." he said in a clipped and quiet tone. Reliving that hell wasn't something he wanted to do ever again. Not for Gwen, not for anything. He stroked her side as he took another drag of his cigarette and exhaled slowly.

"So do you have a place like Kaid does? Or do you live here?"

"I have my own place. We all do, except Blaine. He stays here most of the time. Fucker rarely sleeps, though we all have a room here just in case, like tonight. My place is downtown, on St. Marks."

"What's it like?"

He grinned, loving how she changed the subject; she could probably detect his unease. "I own one of the brownstones, right next to the building that used to be the Continental club. Place is closed now though. I liked being close to the music. It's got a stunning roof garden; I had it decorated, though I'm never there. Every time Castor comes by he tells me I gotta stop living in dorm room squalor, though compared to his uptown penthouse in Trump Towers I guess I do." he chuckled. "As if I have ever been to college."

"I'm sure you could teach the lecturers a thing or two." She laughed, "Do you have plants in your garden or is it all tiled. I've always wanted a garden. I've never understood how people could call a place devoid of plants a garden. I'm pretty good with plants or at least I tend not to kill them."

"It's an enclosed greenhouse with a small koi pond." he grinned. "I'll have to take you and show you."

"One day when demons aren't trying to kill me..." she paused thoughtfully drawing lazy circles on his arm. "Will demons ever not be trying to kill me?"

"Yes." he grinned. "But that's a choice you'll have to make. Life with an Inferi isn't always safe, but it is interesting. "

"I'm starting to see that."

"But safeguards go into play as well. I can't get into it cuz I honestly don't know." he smiled. "I wish I had all the answers for you. And I'm glad you're looking at this from a level place as well."

"True but that could have just been the unbelievable out of this world sex."

He grinned and pulled her into a kiss. "I don't doubt it, but this can all be dealt with. In a few hours Kaid will bring Ansley in, and then we will have to deal with that. First and foremost though, your safety is paramount. I think we both need some sleep." he turned and stubbed his cigarette out and went to get out of bed.

"Are you leaving? And here was me thinking that I was just a little more than an easy fuck. A little wham bang thank you man..." She smiled jokingly at him but there was a tension in her voice that he couldn't miss.

"Far be it from me to presume that, but no, I was going to lock the door. Now that my brain isn't as lust addled I realize that I didn't lock it when I came in." a smirk tugged at his mouth.

"So you just presumed that you could stay?" she grinned at him scooting over in the bed to give him more room. "Well good, I hate sleeping alone."

"No, I anticipate the need for some really great morning sex." he winked and locked the door then walked back to the bed and slipped in, and pulled her naked body against him. "Goddess your perfect love."

"I love it when you say stuff like that." She smiled back at him snuggling deeper into his arms.

"I only speak the truth pet." he nuzzled her throat. "Sleep, nothing can harm you, not with me here."

Chapter Nine

He was there, standing across the way, his chest bare, a loving look in his eyes as he moved closer and levered a large goblet to his lips. He drank deeply of the liquid therein, and then lowered the cup as he stopped and sat on the large pillow on the floor, parallel to her gaze.

"Isis, can't we enjoy the time we have?" he said and offered the glass to her.

"I am allowed to be melancholy, Osiris, I'm losing the love of my life."

He sighed and got to his knees and pulled her into his arms, nuzzling her throat and placed his lips on the nape of her neck. "Not losing, never losing Isis. You are my love, losing you is to lose a piece of myself."

"That's just it though, your powers will be bound my love, your link to everything you love severed. How will you manage being away from Abydos? Away from my love and adoration?"

"I will muster through. The Velns cannot be allowed to rule. We already lost much in the banishment; to lose the world we love would not be wise."

"And us? Do you not care that I will fade?" her shoulders slumped in his grasp.

"Of course I care Isis; life without you will be a pale shadow of what it is now. This has to be done. And steps have been taken, right? Your priests have bound a piece of you into the Scarab right? We will see each other again. Love like ours is eternal."

"And what will you do without me?"

He frowned and shook his head. "I suspect I shall live, and do my duty, and pine for you."

"And the priestesses? Promise me none shall capture your heart my love... that belongs to me."

"None could. They are loyal, and useful, but only you will ever make my heart beat."

He pulled away a little and grabbed a curved shallow bowl and brought it closer, taking a small comb out of the basin and held the shiny inside of the pottery up to her and proceeded to use his other hand to comb through her hair.

She blinked and gasped, looked to him quickly and he smiled at her.

"So beautiful, my Isis... never anyone before you my love." He moved in, his lips pressing to hers firmly as his hands dropped his props and went to her waist and pushed her backwards as she arched up to his.

Gwen woke up with a start, her heart hammering in her chest. The woman in the crude mirror was she, or a semblance of her, one made up in the old Egyptian style, her hair cut bluntly and her eyes dark with kohl. She could still feel his lips, his body bringing hers to life. *Where the hell did the dream come from? Isis? Seriously?* She wondered and turned over, slipping back into sleep nestled into Syrus's chest.

The ringing of a phone brought Gwen out of her peaceful slumber. Syrus's arms were still cradling her; he was so warm and right. It was better than waking with Tom ever was. She lifted her head up searching for the location on the noise.

The bottom of the bed. Ducking under his solid arm she scooted down to the covers and found his jeans. She slid the phone out of his pocket and rejected the call. Whoever it was that wanted her god's attention would have to wait. He was hers for the morning, possibly forever and, freaky dreams aside, she was planning on waking him up properly.

Thorough morning sex was firmly in her mind after all he had promised. They'd went over a lot of things last night, some that still made her blush, but she'd decided that she wanted to change so old Gwen was officially no more. He could help her with that she was sure of it. He already had in a way. She felt so much better today.

Last night's incident with Tom was now feeling like a nightmare, as was the past few years. Maybe life with someone like Syrus wouldn't mean she'd have to compromise herself for their happiness. She could stay with a man like Syrus; someone who was Tom's polar opposite.

She pulled back the covers admiring his sleeping form as the phone started blaring once again. Growling grumpily she checked caller id, an unknown number. It could very easily be Ansley.

"This better be good." She growled down the line.

"Mistress Sherri? I need to speak with Lord Osiris!" the hysterical voice on the other end said.

"Lord Osiris?" she repeated slowly letting the words sink in. "Why?" She glared though the girl couldn't see her so she turned the glare on Syrus, sorry, Lord Osiris.

"They are gone! They didn't come home! They don't stay out! Not Simone and Tony. Please Mistress Sherri I need to talk to My Lord!"

She frowned confused the girl was obviously in some distress something that Gwen was starting to feel herself though she had no doubt it was for different reasons. "You're kidding right? This is a joke?" *Please be a joke, please.*

"No mistress Sherri, Our high priestess and two of our adepts are gone. Please, please let me talk to him. This is his phone right?"

"Oh god," She swallowed bile as it hit her. "You guys are priestesses, right? That's ok," she forced herself to calm she didn't want to just to the wrong conclusions. It couldn't possibly be a sex thing. "Sure that's ok, it's not like he has a captive harem of women." She said casually her eyes narrowing for the girl's response.

There was a confused pause at the other end of the line which did nothing to ease Gwen's state of mind. She began to tap her fingers impatiently. No way could it be a sex thing, he'd said himself that he'd only chose one a year so if that was the case it wouldn't be so bad.

Maybe he just kept then like a band of taggers on. *Yeah Gwenny, sure*, she thought to herself bitterly. *What would any male do with at least four girls worshiping him? Yeah he wouldn't take advantage of that at all.* She reached her conclusion as the girls' silence stretched on.

"You're with him? Aren't you?" she replied at the girl's silence. "Sexually." she added because the girl didn't sound too bright or maybe she was just being bitchy. She had every right to be bitchy by the sounds of things. Syrus had his own harem, his own stock of fuck bunnies. Why hadn't she seen this coming? She tasted bile again. "How many of you are there?"

The girl hesitated. "This isn't Mistress Sherri is it?"

"Answer the fucking question." She snapped angrily causing Syrus to stir.

The girl on the other end panted. "Apologies. My name is Georgia Comstock. I'm part of the New York cell of the Dark moon society. Osiris is my Lord, I live to serve him. Please, please, whoever you are he needs to know!"

"That doesn't answer any of my questions." she sighed, "Well maybe one. That's all I need." she considered hanging up, smashing the phone but instead she got up wrapping the sheet around herself and lifted her dress. She needed a shower, she felt dirty.

"Here, you can have him back." She kicked him sharply, harder than she'd meant to and threw the phone on his chest. "One of your whore's is on the phone."

The word coming from her mouth shocked her. Sure she felt used and cheated but it was no reason to take it out on that poor girl who was probably in the same boat she was or worse because her friends were missing. A small evil part in her soul rejoiced that fact but it was quickly squashed down under worry for them. Syrus wasn't some Jerry Springer prize for her to fight over. He might have been a catch but she was better than that, now anyway. It was funny how you could get so attached to an idea so quickly.

Syrus woke up blearily and frowned. "Huh? Gwen? What the hell is going on?" he looked down at the phone and picked it up. "Gwen where are you going?" he put the phone to his ear. "Hold on." He looked at Gwen. "I don't know what's going on, thanks for the kick in the ass, Just wait ok? Logical explanation ahead." He watched her glare at him but stay where she was. "Who is this?" he asked as he hit speaker phone.

"It's Georgia, my lord. My apologies for interrupting you but Simone, Tony and Raine didn't come home last night. They're not here... they're not anywhere."

He sat up quickly and frowned. "That's not like them. Raine isn't at Jared's Place? Call him, she usually crashes there after a show, Simone might be with her, you know how involved they are. Shit. Make a few calls.

"In Simone's office is a list of places and the parent's numbers. Call me back when you have done that. Georgie, I'm counting on you, find our girls."

"They're aren't at Jared's, I've called all the numbers I could think on but I'll go and check the list, My Lord. I'll do my best."

"I know you will Georgie. You have my love." he hung up and looked at Gwen. "Now what the hell is wrong?"

She shook her head her hands going to her hips, "How many is there? Obviously it's a pretty big list. One that you've just added my name to. Where do I come?" She asked shaking her head again her anger flared inside her a living thing threatening to consume them both. "Dead last? Middle of the range? How could I have been so stupid? I'm practically the whore nevermind that poor little girl, what is she twelve? Just old enough for you to take advantage? To swoop in and be all I'm mister big god with an even bigger dick, come worship at my feet?" She threw her hand in the air. "What a fucking line, seriously."

"Gwen honey I think you got this wrong..." he sat up and grabbed a cigarette. "Sit love. We need to talk. Tell me what you're thinking?"

"Don't you dare," She couldn't stop shaking her head, her whole body moving with her. "Don't you dare pretend that this is normal! Sit there and tell me nothings amiss, well something is fucking amiss! I believed you," she told him, "Oh gods help me I fucking did! You told me I was special and I just opened my fucking legs. I'm such a stupid easy bitch... I liked you." She stomped her foot. "Damnit I really did! Here I was ten minutes ago thinking about..." She growled stomping again then spun away from him.

She stepped away tripping on the sheet and landing on the floor. "At least Tom was only fucking the occasional whore and here you are, you have a whole society of them. Dedicated to your..." She shook her head again pulling her dress over her head.

"Hold it!" he stood up and went to her, getting to his knees to be level with her. "First, you are special ok? I feel you here." he pressed his hand to his chest. "Second, I never once hid from you that I have a cult. They are my responsibility, the world throughout, but not like you think. Yes, the cell here has acted like my harem for a long, long time. It's how they thought me to find my Keeper.

I did, and it's not them, it's you. They are still my responsibility, even more now that my high priestess and two others are fucking missing, and with the Div activity in the past 24 hours surrounding you..." he sighed. "Shit. I haven't been so secretive with them because I knew they weren't going to be my Keepers. That kept them safe in my eyes. Now they are missing. You think that's a coincidence?"

"I can't bring myself to care." She said wincing at how cold it sounded. "No that's not me. I care that the women have disappeared. I really don't want anything bad to happen to anyone. I also care that they've been used by you, you're just fucking around until you found one that fit." She took the pendant off with shaking hands throwing it at him. "Well you can just keep looking, no matter where you feel me. I've been used and I don't care to repeat the process. I'm not that person anymore."

He frowned. "No, you haven't, and neither have they. They go into this life knowing full well what it entails, and what happens. What you don't realize is I care about each of them, but they aren't mine, and no matter how much I like them as people.

"You are mine; you are the one I have been waiting over ten thousand years for. My society is much, much more than a harem, as you put it."

"Oh no? So you're not fucking them?"

"The New York cell, honestly yes, I *was*. Emphasis on was."

"Then how is that not a harem? A group of girls that you fuck on regular basis? How many is there? How often do you visit? Monthly? Weekly? Daily? Fuck... did you even shower before we were..." she swallowed hard gasping for air.

Her chest felt as if it were caving in from lack of something, oxygen maybe. Suddenly the room felt too small for the both of them. He was far too close to her radiating that heat that she felt so much comfort with.

"Calm down. You know I'm a god not a saint. I have a very high sex drive, very high. Without a Keeper I, like the rest of the guys, have nothing to regulate it. We all have our ways for it. But you know what; I'm not going to give you excuses. I did what I did before you, and yes, I was with them a lot, no one of them could handle me, not like you can, my Keeper. And yes, I did shower." He shook his head.

"I can't apologize for something I did before I met you Gwen, I can tell you that my relationship with them in that capacity is over. I found what I was looking for in you. But they are still my responsibility. Especially now."

"You stopped seeing them as of when? Yesterday?" she shook her head. "That doesn't exactly cut it. When would you have told me about them? Today? Tomorrow? Next week? Would you have bothered? Don't answer that, it's not important." She shook her head feeling very far away. "In the interest of full disclosure. I've only ever had one boyfriend and you let him get eaten alive."

He sighed. "I did tell you about them, and I planned to take you to the society house and introduce you, as the society has been looking for you as long as I have. And that piece of shit wasn't fit to lick the dirt off your high heels let alone be called something as amazing as *your* boyfriend. Gwen I don't know what I can do or say to prove to you that you're not some girl to me. You are *the* girl, the one."

"I don't want to talk to you right now. I can see that I might over reacting," she told his as calmly as she could manage with her body still shaking. "I'm just disappointed. It's my own fault, you were too perfect. Of course you'd have a whole society of girls dedicating themselves to you. Why wouldn't you?" She tasted bile again. "I need to shower." She told him evenly.

He nodded. "Fair enough. Look use the bathroom, though the door there, I'll have Sherri bring your stuff in, If that's cool." he sighed. "Look for what its worth I'm sorry we had this as our first morning together. I feel like an asshole. I'm sorry."

"Yeah it's kind of typical of men, always letting you down; don't beat yourself up over it." She told him walking into the bathroom and shutting the door.

Chapter Ten

Things were not proceeding according to plan.

Nathan looked out of his office windows in the bright sunshine, disgusted with the night's disappointments. The Inferi had beat them to the girl, and the relic, all because his minions felt the need to eat a human. Caine was truly fucking up, and this was not what he needed right now. Not when the prophecy had been set into motion. If they could acquire the relics, all of them, then no matter what, the Velns would be denied their birthright no longer. They would rule, as they were promised. The girl could be the Relic's Keeper though and if that was true, then they were in a whole shit load of trouble.

Caine had found out from the human before they ate him that it was the Lapis Scarab, and now both the Scarab and the girl were in the hands of the Inferi, in the clutches of the damn Egyptian. If she was his Keeper, and there was a very good possibility of that, getting her away from them before or after the Inferi consummated their relationship was not going to be easy. It was lucky for them they had a bargaining chip. Three actually.

Still, Caine had lost the girl, gotten flipped off, which Nathan was seeing as a recurring theme with Osiris, and none of it was encouraging. The Inferi was getting bolder than usual, and it only served to remind him that while he felt he was the real power in this city, he did have rivals.

Desperate times called for desperate measures. If things kept going on this line of fate, where the Inferi would win this relic, he was going to have to rethink his strategy and use a bit more of the powers he had been keeping covetously cloistered from his associates for the better part of his lifetime. No, they couldn't be allowed to succeed, not when he had so many advantages at his disposal. Even if he had to deal with Div that had become loose cannons.

Caine, while proving incompetent of late, was still needed, and his task now was indeed simple. It just depended on whether or not his lieutenant was going to see it as he saw it.

Nathan turned from his spot at the window and sat in the large black chair behind his desk and hit a button on his office phone and it dialed into Caine, who picked up with a grunt on the second ring.

"Caine. I think we need to step this up a notch. We need to provoke the Inferi, and I believe sacrifices will have to be made. Open your link with your Div. Let them know what's going on by way of the females your entertaining. I have a feeling we are going to be hunted this coming evening, and I want the Egyptian on edge, making mistakes."

"What do you suggest?"

He leaned back, setting his feet on the cherry desk; the shiny leather of his Kenneth Cole's winking in the soft light of his desk lamp. "Taunt him; tell him what you are planning to do, bluff if you have to."

He could hear Caine's agitation a mile away. "Why should we bluff? We have three girls to bargain with. He'll be more desperate to save two if we kill one with gusto. Let's send the Inferi a message... Then offer a swap for the two left over."

Nathan rolled his eyes. *Asshole.* "Remember, you can't kill anyone, Caine. I don't want a fuck up because of your bloodlust. But the more the Inferi thinks his precious priestesses are in grave peril the more unhinged he will be.

If we are lucky he and the girl aren't destined, though I think our luck ran out the second you ate that dipshit." He growled and shook his head to the empty room.

"Did you have to eat him before you acquired the relic? Honestly?" Nathan sighed. Caine's insanity and recklessness would compromise this operation, he knew it. "Look bluff the fuck outta him, I don't care if they are a little worse for wear, but don't fucking kill anyone. Do whatever is necessary to get the fuck to agree to a trade, but don't *kill* anyone, get me?"

"The boys were hungry, Nathan, I could hardly deny them. The drunk was abusive though in hindsight he'd have made an interesting convert. Osiris will agree to a trade I guaranteed it."

Nathan was starting to get that little headache between his eyes, the exact same one he always got when he spoke to him at length. "Then do what you have to Caine, but don't fuck up, less I send you to see Nebacanezzar himself."

He felt Caine shudder, "That won't be necessary."

"Let's hope not." He looked over to see the intercom button blinking on his desk. "Get it done Caine."

Nathan growled as canceled the call only to have his secretary, Faith, call into him. "Mr. Danvers, your eleven o'clock is here."

Nathan smirked. He enjoyed how his secretary made it sound like another business meeting. Come to think of it, it was very much like a business meeting when he stopped to mull it about his brain. "Of course, send her in." He clicked his phone again and swiveled his chair towards the double doors that lead to his inner sanctum.

Carina walked in wearing a long black trench coat. The only thing visible was her fishnet covered hands and the black stilettos with the ribbons wrapping around her slender ankle. He knew she was all but naked under the coat, as she always was for their morning fuck sessions.

Normally he was amused and interested in what she had in store for him, she was nothing if not creative, but today, the worries of the day pressed heavily on his mind. He didn't need to have another audience with his masters because of Caine's issues, and he had this distinct feeling that was exactly what was going to happen if the Div didn't calm the fuck down.

He pushed the unpleasant thoughts of Caine from the forefront of his mind and focused on the girl that was standing in front of him, feet apart, coat open, held shut by her gloved hands.

"Show me." He said and motioned to the jacket.

"My aren't we impatient? But then when are you not?" she slipped the coat over her shoulder letting it slide low exposing the tops of her fleshy breasts. "Though I'm not sure I should be so quick to obey. Last time you didn't exactly pay me the attention that I deserved." she pouted.

Nathan frowned. Oh she got the attention she deserved all right. "Then why are you here?" he asked and smirked. "Oh I know why you are. Little slut needs the cock doesn't she? Can't go a full twelve hours without it. That's okay, come here... and take that fucking jacket off."

"Uh huh, damn right I need your cock." She let the jacket drop to the floor moving lithely over to him.

Nathan watched her with interest, feeling smug down to his black soul.

The woman was such an easy mark. She might feint anger or sadness but really she was just a cock slut always looking for a good dicking. As long as she remained useful, in and out of the bedroom, then he would keep her around.

One thing was for sure, Caine might disapprove, but the woman before him had never let him down, not like the Div had. No, he wasn't going to change her, not when she was more useful exactly the way she was. She might be a radical variable, but she always sided with him, so long as he kept giving her what she wanted. Her Nymphomania was off the charts, but so was her need for revenge, and to get both, she would do anything he said.

She was dressed, or rather, undressed, to perfection. Clothed in nothing more than a silk tie he knew was from his closet, and the fishnet gloves, she was a perfect midmorning distraction. "Stunning as usual pet. Now, hop up on the desk."

"Mmmmm," she smiled happily in anticipation as she rolled fluidly onto the desk. "So, how should we start?"

Nathan smirked and settled between her thighs and looked the length of her body. She was a beautiful creature. If things had been different... he shook off the woulda, coulda, shoulda lamentations and licked his lips. "That depends on how wet you are."

"Well I could tell you." returning his smirk she drew her gloved fingers up the inside of her thighs slowly parting them. "Or you could come and find out."

He grinned and his eyes followed her opening thighs. Yeah, she was ready for him. He moved in, laying a kiss on the skin of her inner knee and he felt her shudder.

He had bound her to him, partially, as a present when he met her. She would feel his emotions. His anger, his pity when it chose to surface, but mostly his arousal. It was a perfect set up. He got horny, and so did she, and she showed up and took care of it. No muss, no fuss.

He trailed his lips in hot scorching kisses up her inner thigh, hearing her whimper. He stopped just short of her pussy and looked up.

She glared breathlessly down at him quirking an eyebrow. "Such a tease..."

His eyes never wavered. "Tell me what I wanna hear."

"I thought I already had. I need you Nathan; I need your cock... What only you can give me," she whispered shivering. "I'm yours, body and soul."

Yes she was. He smirked. "Good girl." Nathan moved the scant inches and tasted her, his hands going to her waist. She moved a tiny stilettoed foot to the arm of his chair, and the other hung limp from where she was sitting, allowing her to open her legs wider.

Gasping she arched her back running her fingers through his hair. "Sweet gods Nathan." she cried out.

No, there was nothing sweet about their gods, but he got her sentiment. He nibbled and sucked and licked, feeling her quiver minutes later and pulled away before she could teeter over the edge. He stood and released himself from his pants, and gripped her hips and entered her swiftly.

She cried out welcoming him into her body her hands going around to his back clawing him deeper.

Such a dirty slut he thought to himself as she wrapped her leg around him and dug her heels into his side. It was fast, and he was unforgiving in the using of her luscious body. He came hard, not waiting for her and panted, then kissed her.

She cried out into his mouth as she found her own release, she really got off on being used. He didn't care either way. He pulled away and cleaned up, tucking himself back in his slacks and smiled. "What's on your plate for the rest of the day?"

"Not much," she smiled primly leaning back on the desk and crossing her legs. "You got something to keep me busy?"

"Perhaps. I'm sure you heard they located a Relic?"

"I might have heard something about that." she answered vaguely picking at black painted nails through the fishnet. "The Egyptian's?"

Nathan turned from her and rolled his shoulders. "Indeed. Or so we think. Caine was too late to acquire it. So I believe both the Relic and the Inferi's Keeper are safely ensconced with them. But it made me think that the rumors we have been hearing about relics might not be rumors at all. With the prophecy coming to pass, I believe we might be able to get a leg up."

"How so?" she asked looking up at him. He now had her full attention.

He turned back to her with a smile. "I need some more intel, by any means necessary, but If we can find any of them, even one before they Inferi do... well then..." he smiled. "You think you can handle this?"

"I think I can manage that. What do we know about the relics and the women? Of course I'll have to be careful; fuckers will be looking for me now." She grinned gleefully.

Nathan sat back down in his normally easy way, watching her sit there, still naked and picking at her nails. "Indeed. But we've got some info on the Torpus Mirror and the Chalice of Vapor; I would start looking for those."

She nodded and uncrossed her legs. "I'll keep an eye out and I'll make a note of the women the Inferi visit. It might be an idea to get proactive in taking them out. Make the bastards fear getting close to others."

This was the third reason he kept her about. The woman was always thinking, figuring ways to hurt his enemies. "Always thinking. I'll leave that in your capable hands."

"I try. What do you want me to do if I find any of these women? Bring them in? Or dispose quickly of them? Personally I'm a fan of killing them on sight. Less chance for escape if they're dead."

He considered it. "Just recon so far. If we do find any, we will deal with it on a case-by-case basis. I will confer with the Gods and let you know."

"Of course Nathan." she smiled. "But if I get the chance to make any of them suffer I will strike. It's what the murdering bastards deserve."

Nathan nodded. "No killing though. We need an activated Relic for things to work in our favor love." He smiled and looked down at the intercom button, which was once again blinking.

"Yes?"

"Royston Fletcher from Arrowmark is on line two."

He looked at Carina and feinted regret. "I have to take this."

"Sure thing." she hopped off the desk dipping to pick her coat up. "I'll get busy with the recon boss. Call me if you need anything else." she slipped the coat on.

He nodded. "Expect a call."

He watched her get the coat closed around her still sex blushed body and walk out without another word. Yes, Carina would excel at the task he had given her, and it was only a matter of time.

Chapter Eleven

Syrus was not enjoying today in any way. Gwen was mad at him, for being something he had always been, for doing something with someone before he met her, and three of his priestesses were missing. This was not the way to start off their relationship.

He had grabbed a pair of sleep pants from the dresser and slipped them on, hearing the shower in the other room start. Seven shower heads at once. His cock got hard as he yearned to be in there with her. In his mind's eye he watched her step into the stone enclosure of the shower, heard her sigh as the water hit her and felt her unease and sadness that was all about him. Yes, he fucked up, but he didn't know how to fix it. She was his Keeper, in truth, he felt it deep inside him, and if he lost her, after looking for so long...

He adjusted himself and miserably willed his hard on away, then padded out the door to her room and was back minutes later with her bag, and put them on the side chair so she would see them when she came out.

His task done, Syrus walked into the common area of the underground complex. Dezi was passed out cold on the pool table, drooling and ruining the felt, and Blaine had the back end of a pool cue wedged under Dezi's side to pry him off the table. It wouldn't do for Gwen, Ansley or Jingles even to see the Welsh Inferi succumb to whatever issues he had drowned his sorrows in, and Castor, if he saw it, would be furious.

He walked up and frowned. He knew why Blaine was approaching his task this way. Dezi had a tendency to get all horny when woken up by human or semi human hands.

And that was never a good thing. There had been several times that they had tried to wake his ass up only to have him change into his altered form, the large black horns and tail not encouraging. Then there was the last time Sherri shook him awake and Dezi had grabbed her. The girl was all for it, but Arlo saw red and the sparks started to fly. Arlo and Sherri had an open relationship, but he didn't tolerate any of the other Inferi Dii touching the Soul Keeper.

Syrus leaned against the door jam and smirked. "What was it this time? He was fine when I went to check on Gwen."

"Yeah well..." Blaine shrugged giving up with a sigh. "We all have our cracks. Dez's coping technique just doesn't do it for him any longer. I might not agree with Arlo's but at least it keeps him in check, and Kaid, by not coping, does rather well. Dezi's just stuck in a rut and he's starting to destroy himself. He heard you and Gwen, we all did, it was quite a show. Though not as explosive as this morning's..."

Syrus sighed. "Tell me about it. Georgia called and fucked my world up. In numerous ways. Simone, Raine and Tony didn't come home last night. I was supposed to meet them at the bar for Raine's set and never made it, and now I feel goddamn responsible."

Blaine frowned, "Really? I take it that's not like them, could they be playing you for not meeting them?"

Syrus shook his head, quite sure. "No. The girls know the deal. Hell they all have been trained in basic combat and Simone has taken out a Div on several occasions. No. This doesn't ring of pouty women trying to punish men. Georgia wouldn't be in on it, she's too new."

"Could they know about Gwen? Stands to reason that that could tip them over the edge. Women are unpredictable. I'm only saying to be absolutely sure, because if it's not then the shits hit the fan."

Syrus grabbed a cigarette and lit it, inhaling the sweet cherry smoke. "Not a chance, and If they did they would be fine with it. My girls aren't jealous catty bitches. They know they are part of something bigger, like their mothers before them. I was taking Gwen to see them tomorrow, to meet them, you know, once I explained everything." he sighed. "Shit, I think, has hit the fan cuz I haven't gotten another call from Georgia. Throw in the fact that Gwen thinks I'm a man whore, and today seriously sucks."

"And it's barely past dawn." He prodded Dezi with the cue drawing a grunt. "We need to tell Cas. The Div have slowly been organizing for years but this, this takes brains and a lot of control. Once Kaid comes in I can send Arlo to the bar where the girls were last and seen what he can sniff up. If dragon breath here's woken up by then, then he can go along too."

Dezi snarled rolling onto his side presenting them with his back. "Not a dragon." he growled in tones no human throat could manage. "That's Kaid, send him to fuck."

Blaine shook his head speaking to Dezi's in ancient Gallic then shook his head. "Well your day could be worse; you could be starting his hangover, which," he said to Dezi, "I'm. Not. Healing." He punctuated his word prodding him with the cue.

Syrus grinned. "Serves him right. He knows not to get this fucked up. And Cas is going to stroke about the table felt. That shit is expensive to replace."

"Not to mention he binged in Cas's private collection." Blaine smiled at the fact.

Syrus swore and shook his head. Castor had a thing for collecting rare vintages, and most were stored here at headquarters, and only opened on special occasions. "Well you screwed the pooch there Dez." he looked at Blaine. "So what do I do now about Gwen?"

Blaine prodded Dezi again. "She'll calm down, eventually. She's new to a lot of things and you're just going to have to let her adjust. Once she sees that you're all about her then she'll understand that the girls aren't just about sex. You can't force that decision on her though; it has to come from her. Concentrate on the things that you can do and focus your attention on finding the missing girls."

Syrus scoffed. "Yeah cuz that's not going to set my Keeper off or anything." he grumbled. "Why was it that I found mine first? I mean did I have to be the guinea pig? Castor is the leader..." he whined but it was half hearted. He knew he was lucky to have found Gwen, regardless of the issues surrounding them. Nothing worth anything was ever easy, and this was just a situation proving that. He had to win her over, his future depended on it.

Castor walked in dressed in a slick black Armani suit with a briefcase. He looked at Dezi and frowned, then turned. "You're paying for that Devil man..." he said as he walked out the side door, only to be replaced by Kaid and Ansley. Syrus smiled and nodded, and then took a gander at Kaid's mildly amused face. If he didn't know better he would have sworn the Dragon god liked the redhead's company. "Kaid? Ansley, you look rested love. Gwen is in my bedroom showering."

She smiled and nodded. "I figured. I'll just bring her this." she turned to Kaid and smiled. "Thanks for everything Kaid," she went up on tiptoe and kissed his cheek. She then looked at Syrus, who motioned down the corridor. "Third door on the left."

Syrus watched her go and then turned to Kaid. "Spill."

His eyes narrowed dangerously as his usual scowl settled onto his face. "Spill what?"

Syrus grinned. "Gwen told me about Ansley's thesis. You ok? You look stung the fuck up."

Kaid gave him a dismissive wave. "I've been through worse. Although I'm pretty sure she's robbed me blind of several irreplaceable writings and artifacts. Don't worry I'll send you the bill." he sneered looking over Dezi and then Syrus. "I see you two didn't fare much better."

Syrus had to admit Kaid got that right. "No, my evening was bittersweet. My Keeper is a bit pissed at me." he sighed. "And apparently three of the sorority girls have gone missing, my high priestess one of them."

"Missing? If the Div got a hold of them you better hope they're dead already."

"Thanks for not sugar coating it ya dick." he pinched the skin between his eyes, feeling the headache that always came on when he talked to Kaid start to fester behind his eyes.

"You want sugar coating talk to the healer, don't bitch to me about your fucking girl problems, I ain't your mother."

Syrus took another drag and then stubbed the cigarette out. "Thank the goddess... Look I know you're on the docks today, but lend me a hand with the girls will ya? I gotta figure something out and keep my Keeper from completely rejecting me. And it seems you had a pretty decent time with Ansley, I mean, if that kiss was any indication."

Kaid walked past him and turned his head to give him a long-suffering look. "You really don't want me to baby sit with you Syrus."

True, but nothing about the situation was hardly ideal. Kaid was the kinda guy that spending time with him made you wanna visit the dentist and have a long slow root canal. "I don't wanna sit here alone with them either. Especially when I should be finding the girls." he sighed.

"They're your problem... Get the ladies man there to sit with them."

Syrus smirked. "Dezi? You sober enough to show Ansley a good time?"

Dezi smiled rolling onto his back his eyes still shut, "Not sober but I don't have to be to show a women a good time, just get her to hop on..." he patted his hips then lifted his hands up into the air pretending to hold a woman waist as he began rhythmically pumping up into thin air. "I'm replacing the felt in this thing anyway may as well fuck it up good."

Syrus laughed. "Well I don't give two shits; just leave Gwen out of it."

"There's room for her too." He squinted his blood red eyes open against the dim light before squeezing them shut his hands going to cradle his head. "Might have to turn a light or two off though. Fuck that's bright."

"Got a little bit of your other self leaking through there Dez." Kaid smirked. "Ladies are gonna love that."

Syrus shook his head. "Yeah Dezi I think you need a shower, and maybe a cool down... less your horns and tail come for a visit. And quit thinking about Gwen like that. She's my goddamn Keeper."

"Don't smell your mark on her, but I do smell the frustration on you." he started to chuckle but stopped wincing in pain. "Fuck. Blaine, gonna do something about this?" He slowly rolled off the table.

Blaine moved off past them, to his desk with a smirk on his face. "Not a damn thing."

Syrus shook his head. "And it serves you right. Regardless Dezi, you touch her and I'll cut your fucking eyes out."

"You know that'd be a mercy at the moment Sy." Dezi grinned. "Anyway I can't help you. Cas will have my nuts if I don't make this deal today and I ain't gonna make that the way I am. I need my beauty sleep before I go out schmoozing the clients."

Syrus swore and shook his head. He was going to have to go at this alone, and that meant bringing Gwen with him. "Fine, Kaid, since she thinks you're just the gentleman, take her to lunch or something ok? Or see her to work... I don't know."

"I'll take the redhead to work and watch over her, but I ain't taking her out to eat and you're on your own with yours." The Sumerian growled.

"Fair enough." he sighed. "I need to get in the shower, in the goddamn guest room." he grumbled and shook his head.

"A shower sounds fucking good." Dezi mumbled as he rolled off the pool table and staggered off.

"Stay outta my room ya fuck." Syrus called after him. He turned to look at Kaid. "Just make sure neither of them leave." He looked at Blaine. "We got something around here for breakfast for them? Shit, or Coffee?"

"I'll manage to sort something out for them. You want me to talk with Gwen?" Blaine asked softly. The Healer hated dissention, and keeping everything status quo was his normal M.O.

"I don't know... maybe... if I'm not out by the time she is..." he trailed off and shrugged.

Blaine nodded as Kaid laughed, "I'll talk to her if she comes out. Maybe having her friend here will ease her view on things."

"We can only hope." he sighed again and turned towards the hallway and the blessed massage of a hot shower.

***

Gwen let the showerheads wash away her tension as she massaged shampoo into her scalp. Syrus had been right; he didn't have to apologies or make excuses for how he'd been before he met her. She wasn't a prude in any matter but the thought of him with so many other girls made her see red.

It wasn't a good way to start a relationship, any type of relationship. It wasn't even logical. She'd never been jealous of Tom before, not even when she'd known he was out with other girls. But Syrus she'd hardly knew and she didn't want to share him with anyone. That could never happen though; she couldn't demand that he cut all of his priestesses off despite her feelings on the women.

Sure she'd known that he was bound to have had other lovers, but a whole society of them? Of living fresh girls, fresher than her no doubt, and they would all be just waiting for him. Waiting for her to slip up. There was nothing to stop him from leaving her for them. The first real argument that they had or the first time she didn't feel like sex he'd be off. Running to them. Not that she could ever see herself not wanting him. Even now she wanted him; she'd never gotten that great morning sex he'd promised.

Her body sang for him, begging to be touched. Last night had awoken something that she hadn't know was there. Something Tom had never dreamed of. It was something that wanted Syrus and only Syrus.

But she couldn't let herself commit to something based on great sex. Especially not when it had the potential to end to horrifically. She just wasn't ready to commit to anything right now especially Syrus an all his baggage.

Still he needed her. They all did if she was to be believed and she did believe him. A story like his was crackpot insane, way too insane to be made up. So what was she supposed to do? Well that was the million-dollar question. What was the old cliché, stuck between a rock and a hard body? She sighed rinsing her hair before the shampoo ran into her eyes. If she left she'd most likely cause the enslavement of humanity and end of the world, but if she stayed? Well if she stayed he'd only break her heart. Trusting any man with that right now was just not wise. He had offered her friendship, she could work with that. Sure it wouldn't be as satisfying as hot god sex nightly but she'd be safe. Her heart would be safe.

So it was decided, she'd be his Keeper in name only, for the time being. She'd need to ask him for the Scarab back, she still couldn't believe that she'd thrown it at him. With her luck it'd been chipped or broken. She missed its familiar weight almost as much as she missed Syrus's touch. They had to slow things down, take it slowly. She needed to trust him. She slapped on some conditioner lathering it gently through her hair. No wonder Syrus's hair was so soft he had like a grand's worth of products in here and it smelled like him too. Spicy and warm with just a hint of cherry.

Deep in contemplation she barely blinked as Ansley opened the shower door. "Holy shit, Could they all be hotter?"

"Hotter?" She asked still lost in her thoughts.

"Syrus and Kaid and good lord the guy sleeping on the pool table... and the other two... Hell one of them was walking out as we were walking in; he was dressed in a four thousand dollar suit... I almost came looking at him!"

"Oh the guys," she grinned, "Yeah, I thought you'd like them. I take it you had a good night?" she stepped under the water rinsing her hair.

"It was... interesting." she grinned. "I could ask you the same thing."

"My night was amazing," she smiled back. "My mornings been a little bumpy though. So what did you do? Was Kaid ok with you? He sounds a little rough."

She giggled. "Rough? Hottie was a complete gentleman, even gave me his bed to sleep in."

"I bet. The question is if he slept in it with you?"

"Nope, he took the couch." she grinned. "Total gentleman. Bed was huge though, He could have slept there and I wouldn't have known it though." she blushed. "Which is probably why I had the damn dreams."

"Damn dreams?" She asked picking up on Ansley's tone change. "Flying heffalump dreams or sexy dreams?"

"Full blown kinky sex dreams about my smoking hot gracious host. Good lord I don't know where it came from but..." she whistled.

"And you didn't act on them?" she asked amazed Ansley hadn't tried anything; she was normally so loose when it came to sex and that was putting it politely.

"I don't know... I don't think he's interested in me. Dream Kaid was a fucking sex monster but real Kaid..." she shrugged. "And the dream kept me through the night. It was full on vivid too..." she shivered and grabbed a large towel for Gwen.

"Like?" She grinned getting out of the shower and wrapping the towel around her. "As in details, I need the cheering up." She felt so much more at ease now that Ansley was here.

Ansley grinned and sat on the large counter and swung her feet. "Well it was weird; it was like I was in some large stone keep. There were large fire sconces; the stone near it was blackened like that's where the light came from. And Kaid was there, half naked his pants weren't hiding anything though, they were like painted on. He was standing against the wall and turned his head to look at me, and gave me this sexy ass look. Next thing I knew it was me against the wall and he was licking down my chest."

"Nice." She grinned moving out to grab clothes. The Scarab was laying next to her tooth brush; she lifted it slipping it over her neck to rest back between her breasts. "What next?"

"I don't know he spoke to me in some language, Which I could swear was Sumerian, and I understood him, and I let him take my dress off, I mean I was wearing this sheer white and blue frock with a heavy gold belt. He ripped the gauzy material off my body, which was so fucking hot, and left the belt on. It was so erotic, so heavy on my hips." she shivered and Gwen watched as color came to her face. "He took me right there, told me in Sumerian he would always need me... always want me... It was so hot. I woke up totally in need. Still am."

Gwen grinned, that certainly was hot and the Sumerian twist was closer to Kaid's real nature that it was scary. "And you didn't just jump on him? That's so unlike you... maybe we've switched personalities." Now there was a scary thought.

"Meaning?" Ansley grinned. "Ooh you got you a little some-some?"

"Uh huh..." her insides threatened to melt at the memory. "I got a lot of it. More than enough." She shrugged mentally distancing herself from everything, "Not surprising seeing as how he's just a big old man whore." She sighed bitterly.

"What the hell does that mean?" she asked and checked her teeth in the mirror.

"Nothing." She lifted her toothbrush and started to brush her teeth.

"Ah-ah. Spill, I did... come on Gwenny."

She spat out in the sink rinsing her mouth out. "He just... I don't know we had a fight. Or I had a fight. He has women... lots of them."

"What guy doesn't?" Ansley asked and then sighed. "Gwen, no guy that looks like that is a virgin, and seriously, Lemme ask you... did he spend the night with you? Was he apologetic about things this morning? Cuz I got to tell you, he looked miserable when I saw him a few minutes ago. Hot, and half naked, good lord he's got the body of a god, but miserable none the less."

Body of a god was right. "He was really miserable?" She smiled feeling a little better despite her better nature. If the thought of losing her made him miserable then there might be hope yet, maybe for more than a friendship. "I don't know but things have been going a too fast. I just don't want to jump strait into anything. I like so think I've learned a lesson and things are just a little too raw. Anyway shouldn't you be all worried for me? And interrogating him and shit?"

Ansley shrugged and hopped up on the counter. "Nope. I think he's a good soul. He didn't look twice at me when I walked in, the other guys; even the guy partially passed out on the table cracked an eye when I walked in. Syrus wasn't interested, at all."

She already knew that, but hearing Ansley say it reinforced it. "Yeah well you have to take my side regardless, you're my friend." She grinned going through the bag Ansley had brought. "So what did you bring me?"

"All your favorites, Jeans, that big fluffy sweater you adore, shoes, some sexy t-shirts, ooh and nail polish, I noticed last night you needed a new coat."

"Thanks." She smiled going through it wishing she'd asked for something a little sexier. Looking her best can go a long way to boost a girl's confidence, true it's not the stuff Syrus could bottle but it helped to look presentable.

Ansley grinned. "And just incase..." she pointed to the inside pocket. "Some play clothes." she winked. "Regardless of what you said, I couldn't have you near that fetching man without some come hither clothes."

"You're the best; you know you dress me better than I do. What should I wear?"

Ansley laughed and grabbed a pair of vintage washed hip huggers and held them up. "They show off your ass perfectly. And that sexy shirt... Where is it?" she rummaged through the bag until she came up with a boat neck black shirt with a wide band at the bottom. On her it reached her belly button and the outfit would show off the smallest enticing band of skin. "No bra. Your tits are too perfect." she winked and handed over the shirt.

She took the shirt slipping it on. "So you saw all the guys then. Who was on the table?" she slipped on her jeans leaving her hair loose.

"Not sure. Black hair, half opened shirt, Looked like her was made to fuck?"

"Dezi, I'm guessing. He is hot, but then they all are."

"You said a mouthful there," she giggled. "So what are the chances I end up with one of them tonight?"

"Good... very good." She grinned. "Have you eaten yet?"

"Nope. Kaid let me use his shower, which is almost as divine as this one, and then I got dressed and we came over here. Did you know we are in a midtown office building? I don't think Barathos' clients know there's a bachelor fuck pad under the offices. You think they got coffee around this place?"

"With a little luck. Come on." She took her hand and they left moving through the halls.

Ansley and Gwen held hands as they entered the common room. She squeezed her hand as they found the area void of life. Ansley walked around checking stuff out. "No coffee here, though there's enough cigarettes and beer bottles it could be mistaken for a frat house."

"You're not the first person to make that assessment." Blaine said from a doorway. "The kitchens through here."

Ansley looked at Gwen and her eyes went wide. "And the first hottie of the day." she walked through the doors, Gwen following close behind her. Ansley went to the island seat in the large kitchen that Gwen had had a sandwich in with Syrus the night before. She grinned at Blaine and cocked her head. "So I didn't catch your name before." Ansley said and licked her bottom lip while checking Blaine out.

"This is Blaine." Gwen introduced smelling fresh coffee. Any thought of protecting poor Blaine from Ansley left her mind in favor of pouring a fresh caffeine laden cup of heaven.

"Nice to meet you Ansley, I hear you robbed Kaid blind of artifacts last night. I hope you got into his good stuff in the vault?"

Blaine flashed her a smile guaranteed to melt any woman. "Coffees in the pot." He told Gwen nodding to the brewing coffee.

"The vault?" she frowned. "He neglected to mention one. Where is he?"

"No clue, I couldn't keep tabs on him if I tried." He gave a teasing smile.

She frowned. "Well poo. That's not fun. So what's the deal are we stuck here? Don't get me wrong I'm not mad about it, six stunning specimen of the male species all to ourselves does have its appeal, but I do have to be at work by noon."

"Kaid's going to take you; he even said something about lunch." He grinned, "So what do you guys eat?"

Ansley beamed. "Ummm so I *can* hit him up for his vault." she a dreamy and satisfied look and grabbed the coffee Gwen offered to her. "I don't eat in the morning, but coffee is life." she took a sip and grinned at Gwen. "Gwenny? So if I'm going to work are you?"

"I don't think so, I haven't taken a vacation in years and I think now is as good a time as ever." She shook her head. "I'll have whatever you're making... Unless it's leftover pizza."

"I wouldn't deprive Dezi of his staple diet." Blaine said his head in the fridge. "Looks like its bacon."

"That'd be great." Gwen sighed looking around. She missed Syrus.

"He'll be out soon, he's having a shower." He told her noticing her change in mood.

"She that obvious eh?" Ansley grinned. "Our Gwenny here is a bit forlorn Blaine. Maybe you could shed some light for us?"

"Light?" He asked with a quizzical look.

"On Syrus. Gwenny has some issues with his extracurricular activities."

"Of course, may I have a few moments alone with her? I'm sure you'll find Kaid in the gym working out. If he's not in the common room it's the only other place he could be. It's through that door and down the hall."

She grinned. "Naughty Blaine, you said you didn't know where he was..." she downed her coffee and shook her head. "Maybe I should pick up a camera. Find me when you're done okay?" She winked at Blaine and walked out of the kitchen and towards the hall.

He waited until she had left before talking as he put the bacon on to cook. "I'm sorry Gwen. I'm sorry you had to find out the way you did. What he did was necessary to keep him sane. It's gotten really lonely for us." He turned to her taking a seat. "An eternity with nobody to share it with eats at you. It seeps into us and there's not really anything we can do... we weren't created like this. Gods by their very nature need others. Even the dark ones were social. We loved, even married. This is something that's been forced onto us. It's not natural for us to be so cut off from everything. Worse even for those of us like Kaid and Sy that lost their wives.

"We may never have our powers returned to us; even now after so many years I reach for mine daily only to find that they're gone. Our people and our ways are long dead." He sat back with a forlorn sigh.

"Syrus was lucky in that the Egyptians put measures in place for him, mostly because he was so devoted to Isis. The priestesses were entrusted with his sanity, as charged by his wife. We weren't all so lucky. We all have different ways of dealing with it, Dezi fucks and when that doesn't work he drinks. Kaid's an oddity. Arlo likes to escape from it all through medicating himself. I don't want to know what Cass does but it probably isn't pretty and he was different."

"He had a choice?" she said remembering what Syrus had told her the night before.

"Yes, although I've never been clear on how that took place. The Roman always was Tiamat's little favorite. Syrus did too, though for the longest time he regretted it. Losing your wife does that."

It was a lot of information to take in but she did. So Kaid was married as well and Cass was Roman. Blaine didn't seem to like him as much as the others for some reason. Syrus had said that he was they're leader of sorts so maybe that had to do with it.

"So what do you do?" She questioned curiously, she might as well get as much information as she could Syrus wasn't the most forthcoming of people. "You're not like the others. I can't imagine you being a dark god."

He shrugged noncommittally. "Darkness has nothing to do with evil just from where your powers originate."

"How do you do it? Do you have your own special clan of women?" She wanted to know.

Blaine shook his head, his stance getting a bit stiffer, as if he didn't like where the line of questioning was going. "No, but I wish that I did. What I do is far worse than that. Far, far worse. It's something that, if the others found out..." he trailed off shaking his head. "It only hurts me, don't worry about it."

"Should I be worried about you?" she asked him.

"No." he said in a clipped tone. "Worry about Syrus, like it or not there are women out there who pledged to give their lives for him and if the Div have gotten a hold of them that's probably going to be the case. I'm not sure he could take the guilt."

***

Syrus stopped short of the kitchen doorway and listened to Blaine explain things to his Keeper and sighed. She didn't answer, and he had a feeling she wouldn't, not and give the game away so to speak.

He steeled himself and walked in and stopped dead, floored by what he saw. She was stunning, the sexy little outfit, naked feet with perfect silver nail polish on her dainty toes, her silky hair shining around her. She caught him staring, and he smiled then leaned against the door jam.

"Hey." He said and looked down. "You look amazing."

She smiled at him. "And you look like crap."

"Comes with the territory. Blaine? Can we have a few minutes?"

"Sure, knock yourselves out. You might want to turn the bacon though." He sent Gwen a reassuring smile before walking out.

"I'm going to leave that to you. Me and bacon, don't hangout." he winked and pushed off the wall, shaking his head. "You still cross with me?"

"I don't think so." She took a fork turning the bacon.

"Don't think so?" he asked and arched a brow. "What does that mean exactly?"

"It means not entirely no." She leaned against the counter crossing her arms.

"Well that's completely confusing. Look, Gwen, I was thinking..."

"Me too."

He smiled. "What were you thinking?"

"I don't want my actions to enslave the world." She smiled back at him. "That and I really like you. You?"

"At the risk of sounding like a big old puss, I do too." a smile graced his lips, "A lot. And I'm sorry about this morning, seriously sorry."

"You do sound like a puss." She grinned at him moving next to him. "So we should take things a little slower, I think. Friendship first." She ran a finger down his chest. "For as long as we both can bare it."

He grinned. "The ultimate test of wills." he pulled her to him and kissed her greedily, his hands roving her back before settling just above her rump. Gods it felt good to have her back in his arms, her scent filling his being with longing. "So?"

"Mmmmm. Good friend," she cuddled into him. "So? Busy day?"

He sighed. "Unfortunately. I have to find out about the girls, I was hoping you would come with me, meet them, see that they aren't just..." Syrus looked down at the floor, something close to guilt heating his skin, "my harem."

"Ok." She smiled up at him. "I'll come with you. I'd like to do that."

A weight partially lifted off his heart. The woman in his arms was amazing; willing to do what was needed regardless of her feelings, for the good of the all. She was a Keeper, his Keeper, and a woman strong and able to be part of their world.

He kissed her sweetly, and pulled her closer to him, her heat radiating through his body, reinforcing that feeling of home. "I was serious before when I said you looked amazing. Those jeans on you should be illegal." He palmed her ass in the tight denim and grinned. "I think we need to finish that bacon." He went to the fridge and pulled out eggs and cheese and some chopped vegetables. "You like omelets?"

"Sounds good." She gave him a strange smile.

He cocked his head. "What's that look about?"

"Nothing, I just like that you're cooking. It looks good on you."

"Well you're going to keep working on the hog there, I don't know how to cook what I don't eat." he winked.

"You don't eat meat?" She smiled turning it again.

"Oh I do, I just don't eat pork. Never have. They used to sacrifice animals to us... you know, to curry favor? It was widely known that I didn't dig the swine... so" he grinned.

"That's weird. Very weird."

He popped a piece of cheese in his mouth. "Why?"

"It just is... You don't like it at all?"

Syrus shook his head. "Never have. Big fan of beef though." he grinned.

They cooked side by side, Syrus taking over the stove, and Gwen grating the cheese. It was domestic, something he had wanted for a long, long time. You couldn't get domestic with twenty girls in a sorority house, not when they lived on coffee and takeout. He watched her as she grabbed some of the cheese and popped it into her mouth, the same with the diced tomatoes and mushrooms. Her smile, so carefree, was infectious. He grinned along with her, flipping her omelet, and adding the cheese and vegetables, folding it and then let the cheese melt as she watched.

He made his quickly after, opting just for cheese and tomatoes, and they sat at the breakfast bar to eat. Every little way she moved, he watched and took stock of. She was graceful, sexy and completely oblivious to it. Exactly the kind of woman he always wanted, she emulated Isis so much. She was proving every second why she was perfect for him, and he was powerless to resist the siren's call screaming to his soul. She was his, and he would have her.

They ate in silence for a while the tranquility broken by a high tinkling laugh as Ansley and a very sweaty and seemingly distressed Kaid followed her in.

Syrus cocked his head in interest and noticed the flushed color in Ansley's face. They had either been sparing, or kissing. Syrus was leaning toward the former, but with Kaid you never knew.

"So she forgiven you for your whores yet?" Kaid smirked going to the fridge.

Syrus looked at Gwen then at Kaid. "I dare you to call any of Psi Pi Chi whores to their faces." he kicked Kaid in the shin and spoke to him with his mind. *Careful Nergal, unless you want me to tell Ansley why you're so interested in Sumerian history.*

You could, he frowned eyeing him up, *but then you'd have to face Cas and tell him why you let her in on our little secret. I believe your leader has decreed that she was to be kept out of the loop. Kick me again and I'll rip out your spine in front of your pretty little Keeper and make her and her friend watch while you re-grow a new one. I have no such qualms about keeping secrecy.* A loud he said. "They're not my type, I'd have to be drugged and or knocked unconscious before you'd even get me in the same building as them."

Ansley frowned. "Hold on, you're talking about the super exclusive sorority at NYU aren't you? Shit, Makes sense." she grinned and then turned to Kaid. "So what's this about lunch Kaid?"

Syrus chuckled in his head. *Now don't get pissy dragon... she's hot, sexy and it looks like you rev her engine. Do yourself a favor and tap that ass before Dezi does ok? You seriously need your pipes cleaned.*

Don't concern yourself with my pipes. She's too clever to let Dezi touch her and no I'm not indulging. I have no interest in her, other than to keep her safe. Which I've already said that I will.

Gwen frowned up from her omelet. "Sorority?"

Syrus looked at her and gave her a small smile. "My ex's belong to Psi Pi Chi."

"Oh... of course." She stabbed at her plate. "Why not. So Ans, you and Kaid are going to lunch?"

Ansley grinned. "Blaine said so, though when I found Mr. Muscles here in the gym all hot and sweaty, and I do mean hot, I mentioned it and he just sneered at me, as if it's a hardship to take me out to lunch and ensure my safety?"

Kaid laughed baring his teeth in an almost smile, "That wasn't the intention of the look. I'd be honored to take you to lunch anywhere you'd like. I was merely deciding which of Blaine's kidneys I would cut from his body first."

"Why? You into that back alley organ harvesting?" her eyes shone with mischief.

"Depends on where you want to go for lunch, it might get expensive." His smile turned genuine as he poured himself a coffee, he liked bantering with Ansley.

She shrugged and Syrus noticed Kaid studying the motion with interest. "Someplace close to the museum. Hell I wouldn't be adverse to Gray's Papaya for some hotdogs. I'm a cheap and easy date."

"Well then it's a good thing I'm expensive and hard to please. I've seen sewer rats that look more appetizing than hot dogs. Choose something else."

She laughed. "Hmmm... Then I'm going to say Runa that Japanese place? Appeal to your expensive side."

"Better, much better."

She smirked. "Don't forget to make the reservation." she winked.

Syrus finished his omelet and looked at Gwen. "Are you finished?" he smiled. "You have a bit of cheese on your face pet..." he leaned in and kissed the corner of her mouth, sucking the cheese off.

Gwen leaned into him her eyes closed, "Ummm yeah I'm done." she grinned kissing him back.

"Any more of that and I won't feel like eating." Kaid rolled his eyes standing. "I gotta pick up some stuff; we've got a stop to do before the museum."

Ansley grinned. "Kidney stealing instruments?" She asked and Syrus laughed.

"No papers for work. I was due to do some today but I should be ok just handing in some plans and blueprints."

"Well don't let me stop you. You do what you gotta do Kaid and we can have a rain check on the lunch too." she said with a hint of disappointment in her voice. Syrus grinned and grabbed the plates cleaning up and slid them into the dishwasher.

"Why would I do that?" Kaid frowned. "The papers are in my room here and the sites not that much of a detour out of our way."

"Ooh so I get to see your room here as well?" she bumped her hip into his. "And what's this about a vault I keep hearing?"

"Vault?" He asked looking panicky at Syrus for help.

"Umm hm. Blaine said you had a vault full of goodies at your place. Said I should take a gander." she grinned. "Why didn't you tell me, or were you saving it to make sure we had a second date?" she winked.

Syrus chuckled and went to Gwen. "Go get ready to bounce." he said softly, "And I will explain about the sorority, and why it is what it is." he winked and kissed her again. "And if you're a good girl we can come back here for lunch."

"What I don't get taken out for lunch?"

Syrus grinned. "We could, though dessert would be another matter." his eyes glowed with sexy promise, and he leaned in to whisper to her. "We do have unfinished business you know."

"And what might that be?" She tugged playfully at her hair.

Syrus pulled her flush with his body, his erection pressed deliciously against her.

She let out a gasp, "Mmmmm so much for taking things slowly."

"I told you it would be a test of wills love." They both looked over as Kaid cleared his throat. "What?"

"Don't you both have somewhere to be? Some purpose other than making me want to vomit every meal I've ever eaten?"

Ansley whacked him. "Jerk. Gwenny? I will see you tonight right?"

"Sure will. Barring disasters."

"Which are a dime a dozen." Syrus grinned at Ansley then gripped Gwen's ass. "Go get ready love... "

"I can do that," she said brightly rising up on her tiptoes to kissed his cheek.

He turned his head and captured her lips. Ansley laughed. "Ok you two."

Syrus turned with her and looked at the clock on the wall. "Shit. We better motor if we don't wanna be late, and you gotta call into work still."

"Yeah I guess, though that's not really a conversation I'm looking forward to. Can I borrow your phone again? And I need to put some make up on. No way in hell am I going to walk about like a frump."

Syrus gave her an amused look. "You could never be a frump love. And yes, you just gotta fish it outta my pants. My phone I mean."

***

Gwen smiled over at Syrus sitting in the driver seat of a blue Volkswagen R32. It was one of many cars that'd been in the garage though she was sure that they hadn't all been his. She didn't think she could do this, but she was willing to try. Knowing the girls were out there was one thing but meeting them was another matter all together. She couldn't help but think that Blaine was right. Syrus made her feel amazing and had been wonderful and patient with her at every turn. And if being with the girls had helped him stay the amazingly sexy great man that he was then she at least owed them to try to get along. With a bit of luck it would end up to be nothing like the creepy scene that she had in her head.

"So a sorority?" She asked watching him shift gear. "They always had that cultish vibe." She teased trying to lighten the mood.

"A cover. Nothing more. Easy way to keep the society close to me and not with me. The idea was instituted in the early twenties, been a good way to hide them, and still be able to have access to them. Apparently secret societies outside of college campuses are frowned upon these days. Unless its television."

"Ah and you're the only one with one? Blaine said so, more or less. So what's their other purpose?"

"My followers were good to me and me to them. The society started the sorority as a way to keep the girls close to me, but not all go there. As I know it, descendents from the original twenty two, albeit removed, attend college and are inducted to Psi Pi Chi. Apparently they are the best my society has to offer, the best bets for finding my Keeper.

Thought they were pretty off the mark. Anyway, Not only is the sorority the closest to me, but they are also my personal guard, or so it says. Not that I need them. They are all versed in combat, and some have even hunted with me. They also become the ones that run the society businesses.

"It's all very regimented. My most recent high priestess, Simone, one of the missing, is graduating this coming May and will be taking over one of the textiles businesses the society runs." he gave a small smile as if remembering the predicament they were in. "Depending on where the Inferi moves to, the sorority opens a chapter. It's the easiest way to bring them with me. Not that I need them anymore, well not for the reason I did."

"You better not, or I'll get Kaid to help me geld you." she smiled not knowing where that thought had come from but it sounded pretty accurate to her.

It was getting harder and harder for her to stick to her decision of friendship. It shouldn't matter to her that he had other girls waiting for him and he shouldn't be giving them up for her. But it did and he was. She knew deep in her heart she there was no chance she could stick around while he porked the others. But was what she was asking of him fair? To give up what he had for some friends with benefits scheme? And there would be benefits. It was taking all of her will to fight her attraction to him and keep her hands off him now.

It was pointless to deny the attraction that they both felt and so if she followed that logical conclusion they were going to end up in more of a relationship than her and Tom had ever had. But with even more of a chance of getting her heart ripped out and, in some cases, actually eaten. *Ugh.* She wrung her hands. This was getting very complicated.

He looked at her and grinned sexily. "Gwen, if you think you're walking into a vipers nest it's not so. My girls aren't like that. And I found what I was looking for. They were fun, and I will have fond memories, but they aren't and could never be you."

"I know that." At least rationally she did. She turned to look out of the window her mind full of things she shouldn't have to worry about. "I just don't know what to expect... plus losing your balls is a good threat to have on the table. Just in case you're tempted."

"Not a chance." he winked and sped down the street to the large house that the Psi Pi Chi sorority called home.

"You never know. Nice place." The building was more than impressive. A large brick faced brownstone with a dark wrought iron fence that protected it from the sidewalk, the front stoop was lined with begonias, hosta and potted ferns on both sides, making a lush entrance to the building beyond. It looked like every other place on the block, except for the Greek letters that adorned the keystone above the door. No one would ever know anything more than a sorority lived there.

"Yeah I think so. And before you ask twenty girls live here."

"Wow that's a number and a half. So what do we do? Go in and have tea? Pimms on the lawn?" she swallows hard nerves creeping up on her.

He laughed. "No, though I believe that wouldn't work as there's really no lawn. We need to see what Georgia knows and who else. And you can see the girls aren't a threat."

She thought about denying it and telling him that she didn't feel threatened by them but it would have been a pointless lie. All throughout her life girls like the Psi Pi Chi had looked down on her. She knew the type, perfect hair and nails with bodies finely toned in the gym.

Ok granted she could also be describing her best friend but that Ansley was her friend was a fluke.

These girls had perfect lives and every opportunity thrown at them, they would take one look at her and instantly know that she never went to the gym and her pedicure was six months overdue. They'd know that she wasn't worth this, not worth Syrus. She took a steadying breath then another trying to ease the dread. Chances were there that they'd all be lovely, sure they were slim but they were there.

"Do you think we'll find out anything useful?" She asked keeping to the serious stuff, she could deal with the serious stuff.

"I hope so." he opened the door and got out of the car putting his sunglasses on. His hair flopped straight over one eye and he looked over the house with a frown. "I'm sensing agitation inside. Come on, this can't be good."

And clearly missing the agitation right here, she thought wryly, *or ignoring.* "Well if some of them are missing I'm sure there would be agitation." She smiled what she hoped was a reassuring smile as she stood beside him.

Taking her hand in his he walked up the small walkway and went to the keypad and punched in several numbers. The pad beeped and then went green, and the door opened. "Come on," he said and entered the house closing the door behind him. "Georgie? Merla? Lydia? Anyone?"

"My Lord!" A blond squealed, running through into the room. "Bless us, you are here." She said making it sound like a swear. "We can't find the girls anywhere and I mean anywhere! They're just gone. Disappeared since Raine's set."

Syrus caught her and hugged her close. "It's okay Lyds... Calm down. We will find them. Now where is Georgie? I need a status report."

Two women, presumably Georgia and Merla, came down the stairs and launched themselves into his arms and he held them. It just had to be a blonde that threw herself at him first. There were two blondes to be exact and a brunette and while there was hugging there was no sign that it was anything else going on. It was just a hug. No groping or pelvic grinding. She'd been here a few minutes and nobody had ripped off any clothing, in fact, and this was the best news she's day all day, the girls weren't devastatingly beautiful. They were pretty but in an average sort of way, maybe about a 6 in the guy-scoring card. Georgia even had the soft belly folds normal people got and the beginnings of a double chin. They were normal average girls. She felt the tension within her ease as she watched them and then it came crashing back as she remembered the reason she was here. Their friends were missing.

"Georgie? Honey don't cry. We need a clear head about this. I need to know what you guys have found out. First though... I have a surprise."

Georgia and Merla looked over to where Gwen was standing, just off to the side of Syrus and cocked their heads. "Um, my lord? Who is this?" Merla asked and frowned at her.

Georgia detangled from Syrus and stood watching. Syrus looked at Lydia. "Well your perceptive Lyds, who do you think this is?"

"A present?" Lydia smiled wiping her tears with the heel of her palm as she assessed Gwen the way a shark would its prey. "She's pretty hot."

Gwen ignored her struggling not to squirm under the intense assessment from the gathering girls.

Syrus laughed and shook his head. "She is indeed." He looked at her with a smoldering gaze that weakened her knees. "And as for present, kinda, but not for you guys. For me. Ladies may you be the first to be introduced to my Keeper, Gwen Stapleton."

"Wow... really?" Lydia looked Gwen over assessing her even more intently. "Are you sure?"

Syrus grinned and nodded. "Show them the Scarab."

Gwen reached behind her neck taking the chain and pulling it over her head. She didn't blame the girls for wanting proof, they were just looking out for Syrus, something, she reckoned, that they always did. She took the Scarab out showing it to the girls.

Merla and Georgia grinned and Merla palmed the relic and closed her eyes. She gasped and then looked at Syrus. "It's real. My lord bless it its real!" she dropped the relic from her hand and launched herself at Gwen and hugged her close. "Welcome sister." she whispered to her and kissed her square on the lips. Georgia looked at Syrus and then Gwen with joyful tears in her eyes.

"Uh... thanks." Gwen smiled awkwardly at the girl wrapped ferociously around her. It felt weird to be this close to a stranger. The only person whoever really hugged her was Ansley and it had never been this tight before. She patted the girl's back.

"Fuck sake Merla, let the woman breath, wouldn't do if you went a suffocated her. I'm sure our world is hard enough for her to take in at the moment without that to add to it." Lydia joked pulling her away then grinned. "It's nice to finally meet you, you've been long awaited you know."

Georgia smiled and went to Gwen and grabbed her hand. "I'm honored dear sister." and then she went to Syrus and hugged him. "Things are going to be better now right? She will help?"

He held her close to him and rubbed her back. "Of course Georgie." He looked at Gwen and smiled his eyes awash with undisguised emotion. Love, happiness, sadness, anger and regret. They were all there.

Gwen couldn't help but agree. As much as she tried to find fault with the situation, she couldn't, the girls were genuine and she found herself liking them. "I'll do what I can." She promised. "But I'm afraid that I won't be much good. I'm not a fighter."

"The Keeper doesn't need to be a fighter, just strong enough to love her god, like Great Mother Isis before her. But you know, I could teach you some moves, you are our sister after all." Lydia gave her a hopeful look.

Gwen grinned back at her. "That might come in handy, thanks." Plus it would give her more time to get to know the girls. The mention of Isis tweaked her memory bringing back thoughts of the dream she'd dismissed earlier in the morning.

"Anytime you wish, My Omah." she bowed and so did Merla and Georgia.

"Maybe once we have the other girls back safe." she smiled sadly for the first time truly feeling their pain. And she'd acted like such a bitch to Georgia and Syrus.

Syrus let go of Georgia and went towards Lydia. "Indeed. Lydia? Petal, will you take me to Simone's study, I would like an update. Merla, Georgia, I trust you can keep Gwen company? Show her around? Maybe some tea?"

"We have fresh coffee too." Lydia said as she started walking. "The study's just up here but there's not much in there, I even picked the safe lock and still nothing."

Syrus chuckled and kissed Gwen. "I knew there was a reason why the girls kept you around Lyds..." he winked and walked after Lydia and was gone seconds later, and Merla cocked her head at Gwen.

"So? Shall we retire to the kitchen? Lorraine is making soup, big old vat of it, we could eat while we talk? No doubt you have questions."

"Just a few, I'm sure you have some yourself." She shrugged. "Though I think I may owe Georgia an apology for this morning."

Georgia shook her head. "No apologies Omah, I was wrong to assume you were Sherri, though I don't think she has ever answered Sy's phone. I was frazzled. I'm sorry if I was short with you, or hysterical. Osiris deserves better in his priestesses."

"Well he sure didn't deserve the way I talked to him this morning. What's with calling me Omah?"

Merla turned to walk towards the kitchen and they followed. "Because that's what you are. Our supreme priestess, our goddess Isis is called Omah. She is the one that our beloved lord is coupled with, the one that holds his life and love. You're very special to us, and to him."

"So he keeps telling me. It's good for the ego but I'm not really sure how that equates into real life."

"It's true. Syrus has been looking for you for a very long time. I suspected when I was a freshman here that he wouldn't find you among us, and I was right. You're the missing legacy Omah, You're family."

"I doubt very much that my family are descended from priestesses. We're more likely grave robbers or some sort."

"That doesn't matter. The Scarab chose you, chose to stay with your family till you acquired it."

"I guess it did. But you can call me Gwen if you like, there's a better chance on me answering to it."

Merla laughed. "Very well, Gwen then. You can call me Merl, and Georgia here we call Georgie."

Georgia smiled genuinely.

"I feel very lucky to be here, I mean in the Sorority. I don't know if you know, but I was the last to be inducted, and it looks like I will be the last." she giggled. "My sisters are going to be pissed."

"So you were inducted?"

Georgia nodded. "I was. By Syrus and our high priestess, Simone." she sighed and closed her eyes. "Dear Isis, I hope she's still ok."

"I'm sure she will be," Gwen said reassuringly despite her reservations. "Syrus told me that she was an expert fighter, he says all his girls are. He's really proud of you all." She squeezed her hand wanting her to feel better.

Georgia smiled through unshed tears. "Thank you Gwen. We all love him, and to hear that he's proud of us..." She looked toward Merla and the other girl picked up the thought.

"It just means so much to us. He's never been cruel, never harsh to us. But we knew he didn't love us, not in that way anyway. He loves you though; I can see it in him." She gave her a genuine smirk. "So you probably wanna know why twenty women in this day and age would be ok with sharing one man for so long right?"

"Well it had crossed my mind, though I understand why you could share that man. He's mine though, just to be clear. I've just came from a really dark path and I can't go that way again." She told them. "I hope he likes me, as for love... it's a little too early for that. I'll settle for like at the moment."

Merla laughed. "You're exactly the right kind of woman for him. And we all knew, when he found his Keeper, we would bow out of sharing his bed, his Keeper, his newfound Isis, you, would be more than enough to satisfy his appetites and urges. And he has many." she winked. "Kinky thing."

"I'm not sure we've gotten to those yet but I can only do my best." Gwen blushed not really wanting to hear more but at the same time she did. She wanted to know everything about his ways and his desires; couldn't wait to find out. But she'd do it the old fashioned and exciting way by being with him.

"Need any tips let me know." she smiled good-naturedly at her. "So? What else?"

"Well what else do you guys do?"

Merla shrugged and put the kettle on. "Tea?" she asked and continued. "We all go to school here, major in programs that will allow us to take over our families companies."

"Companies?"

Georgia nodded. "We all come from families that own companies, where Osiris is a silent partner. It keeps him living in the luxury he's accustomed to."

"Luxury?" She asked with a frown, she didn't see him as the type to go off on cruises and on holidays, she said as much to the girls. Aside from the mysterious brownstone downtown, and his apparent love of fast cars and cherry flavored cigarettes, nothing she saw from him screamed of luxury.

Merla nodded. "He likes his toys, cars, electronics, clothes," she shrugged. "Apparently his brownstone is pretty impressive."

"I think he said there was a roof garden which is impressive all on its own here."

Georgia shrugged and grabbed a few mugs and a canister of tea. "None of us have ever been there."

"Wow... well if I get there I'll take pictures for you all to have a snoop."

Merla laughed. "Oh you'll get there. It is your little love nest. You're going to be the envy of all the girls." she noted and pulled the screaming kettle off the range.

"I guess I will be." She gave a small smile. "Are there other sororities around the world?"

"Just one. Depending on where our god moves depends on where the chapter moves to. We have been in twelve U.S. cities since the twenties."

She nodded taking everything in. "So what is it that your family does?"

Merla shrugged. "My family owns a textiles mill. So after we go through school, and our serving under Osiris, we are sent back to our families, and find a man to marry us. Or that's how it did work. Now, we will still be his sect, and his personal guard, but we won't be his bedmates. That's all yours sister."

"So now you're free to find a man to marry? So what happens when you do? Do you tell him about this? Like your father, does he know?"

Georgia picked up the conversation. "No, daddy knows mom belongs to a alternative religion. We marry in the tradition of the man, so not to arouse suspicion. But Osiris comes and blesses the union. It's all quite informal." she grinned. "And every first born from a priestess and her husband is a female, as better to serve Osiris."

"And he doesn't even suspect a little?"

"Daddy? No. He has never even seen our Lord. He's a bit involved in his own life. We prefer it, or did, Now, things will have to change, but I think for the better." she smiled a small smile.

"I hope so; I mean shaking things up a little can't hurt too much."

"Well we haven't ever had a reason to, not when he was actively looking for you. Now that you have been found, you will lead us, and you will be the love of his life. It's all very romantic." Georgia said and sighed her eyes going glassy. Clearly she liked the idea of a happily ever after.

"Well not too romantic, my last boyfriend got eaten alive and those things..." she looked away remembering the girls that were missing. "Well maybe it's a little romantic."

Merla made a disgusted sound. "Div are the fucking dregs of the demon world. I don't think Div took the girls, they aren't stupid, not those three. But something did. I feel it." Merla said and shook her head. "I just hope they are ok. If they were taken for any reason we would hear, I know it."

"Well you'd think that we'd hear something. I'm not an expert but I watch enough TV to know that kidnappers normally contact you. Would it really be kidnapping if they're adults?" Gwen asked more to herself with a frown. "Abductors. Abductors normally contact you with a ransom."

"Yes, that's true but it hasn't been more than six hours since they are overdue, and that means we have time to wait." Syrus said from the open door. Lydia had her arm around his waist and smiled. "Coffee still there?" She asked and walked to the pot and grabbed a cup.

Syrus grinned at her. "Nice chat?" he asked and walked over to where they were sitting at the kitchen island, and accepted the cup of coffee Lydia gave him.

"Uh huh." She nodded grinning teasingly. "We were talking all about you."

"Naturally. I am their favorite topic... You too." he took a sip of the coffee with mischief dancing in his eyes. "And what did you find out?"

"Ooh you've got such a big head." She laughed poking him in the chest.

He opened his mouth as if to say something, and Merla threw a dishtowel at him. "Sy! Don't even!"

Gwen giggled shaking her head, "Men are all the same." She winked at him, "Well almost the same."

"Not all of them are gods." he wrapped his arms around her waist and nuzzled her neck and Georgia cooed happily, "Isn't that amazing?"

Merla nodded. "It is good to see you truly happy my lord."

Syrus kissed the nape of Gwen's neck and looked to the girls. "I am. You know you're all dear to me..."

Merla nodded. "You don't have to say it Sy, we know. And we embrace her as a sister."

"I like you guys too," Gwen told them. "I really didn't know what to expect, but I like you guys. We're going get along just fine."

Merla smirked. "You freaked when you found out he had a harem didn't you?"

"Just a little." She blushed and ducked her head, settling back into his safe warmth.

"Think of it this way, all we did was keep him in practice for you." Offered Lydia.

"And you did a pretty good job of that, thank you." She stroked his hand thoughtfully. "I was freaked out at first but I get it now."

Merla went to them then, as did Georgia and Lydia and they embraced them fully holding their god and their leader. "We will always love and serve you both," Merla whispered. "And the sect will be so happy to know you have been found Gwen."

There was no malice, no jealously, no hatred. These women were genuinely happy she was by Syrus' side, embracing a relationship and a woman that just came into their lives as if she was always there.

"Thanks for making me feel welcome." She hugged them back. They had made her feel like family, she was so happy that they weren't a nest of vipers as Syrus had so delicately put it. She leaned her head against him feeling totally relaxed.

"You always will be, here and every holding we have. But that's for happier times. Syrus what are we to do?" Merla asked and rubbed her cheek on his shoulder. It wasn't sexual, more of a comfort move.

Syrus kissed the top of her head. "We wait. I'm going to take Gwen back to HQ. If you get a call either way lemme know... Once we know what happened and what they want, if anything, and then I can take action. Don't worry loves, we will find them."

Gwen nodded silently letting them discuss things. This was her place but she had nothing further to add. Once they knew more than they could deal with it together but until then she'd be there for them. "I'll give you guys my cell number, just in case you wanted to chat." She said jotting down the number of the cell that Ansley had so wonderfully remembered to pick up for her.

Georgia grinned. "Once this is all over, you will have to come over for girl's night." she said hopefully. "We drink margaritas and do each other's nails and watch 80's flicks."

Gwen was touched they were already making plans to be with her. "That sounds great; I'm a sucker for a cheesy movies and margaritas."

Syrus shook his head. "At least I know you'll be well taken care of." he said dryly. "We should go. Merla, make sure to add Gwen's phone number to the doors code, just in case." He winked.

Merla nodded and then hugged him and kissed him on the lips, then Gwen. They each in turn did so, and Syrus smirked.

"You guys sure like to kiss a lot." Gwen laughed taking Syrus's hand.

Syrus nodded. "It's a sign of respect in our culture. That and I think they are sweet on you." he winked. "Now that would be hot."

"Oh no you don't." She whacked his arm laughing. "Don't even get that into your head."
"Too late."

Chapter Twelve

Syrus and Gwen made it back to headquarters before six, mentally exhausted and physically keyed up. Seeing his Keeper interact with his society, the women that kept him sane and normal for her was heady. She was good with them, gracious and seemed to truly care about their distress over losing three of their own. She was one of them, he surmised, but elevated and they all embraced her like a long lost sister, which in fact she was.

She didn't miss a beat once with anything they threw at her, or tested her with, and fell into a commanding roll with the girls that Simone would not be happy with once she got back. If she got back. He waved the fatalistic thoughts away, trying to focus on the fact that all three of the missing were seasoned fighters, hunters and brutal as sin when it came their lives and his. He had to believe that wherever they were, if they were in trouble they were actively trying to make it back to him and the sorority house. Losing them, even one, wasn't an option.

Headquarters was quiet, aside from the soft music filtering back from the recesses of the underground complex. It had to be Sherri, cuz none of the guys listened to that top forty bullshit.

Knowing she would wander out and meet up with them in her own due time, Syrus pulled Gwen to him and kissed her. "You were amazing today, took to the girls so well, they consider you their leader now, you know that right? I mean they not only serve me, but you now as well." He grinned. "And Merla offered to teach you some hand to hand combat."

"Which I fully intend to take her up in, along with the margarita night." She ran her hand down his chest breathing him in.

"I'm proud of you, you know, All the touching and such, you didn't bat an eye." he kissed her.

"Ummm well I didn't want to disappoint you by freaking out, you have enough on your plate." she nuzzled his cheek. "Besides they were perfectly normal, not mindless drones of any kind."

"They are. Though it is my fault they are oversexed."

"I'm sure it is." she told him wryly.

"I think they will be able to handle it in the long run. Whomever they marry will thank me, silently of course." he kissed her and picked her up, moving them both to the couch.

"Of course because they don't get to meet you... though I'm sure you're always there in the background lurking around."

"Something like that love." he grinned. "So," he settled her on his lap and wrapped his arms around her waist.

"So..." She sighed laying her head on his chest. "I take it you didn't find anything out?"

"Sadly, no. Everything is in order. Nothing taken, no extra appointments, no surprises written down in Simone's ledger... I'm baffled."

"Georgia said that the Div are too stupid to have taken them. Does that mean it was someone else, or are the Div working with humans? Do they do that?"

"Honestly? With the Intel we got last night, it's damn possible. Though the Div wouldn't take them. They would have brutalized them and left them to be found by us. as a message."

"So who else?"

"I don't know. Intel says that the Div are run by Marrow International. A corporation, but I don't see them attacking women at a club. I hope Arlo had some luck locating them." he turned his head as he heard the music cut out. He grinned at Gwen. "I think you're about the meet the Soul Keeper."

"Oh?" Gwen tensed under his arms.

He laughed. "Easy love Sherri is harmless."

"I'm sure she is, so she's like your boss right?"

"Kinda, she's like the bosses assistant."

"But that still ranks me above him." Sherri smiled from the doorway. "So yes, I'm like his boss. When he decides to listen to me."

Syrus smirked. "Well I'm glad I listened to you last night that's for damn sure. Sherri, meet my Keeper, Gwen."

"It's wonderful to meet you." Sherri grinned moving over to them and cupped Gwen's face. "You bring so much hope with you. And yes, he didn't want to replace Arlo's run the other night."

"Well I'm glad he did, things wouldn't have went so well for me if he hadn't. My friend and I were attacked. If he hadn't been there then..."

"Arlo wouldn't have stopped to save you that's for sure. He and his informant would have ran off somewhere."

Syrus looked at Sherri. "And you don't seem too upset about that."

"About what?" She asked simply.

"That your little fuck buddy wouldn't have done his job and kicked some Div ass."

"He'd have done his job, which was to get the information. Taking time out for a few Div isn't primary concern; he doesn't have to do it. And even if it was what would you like me to do? Leash him? Send him to the Goddess?"

"You would with the rest of us."

"You in a heartbeat. Blaine probably if he ever left the compound. Castor wouldn't shirk his responsibility. There would be no point to sending Kaid, he's been to see the goddess almost as often as I have. Personally I think he enjoys it and he put her in the foulest of moods. But no good would come from sending Arlo or Dez; they'd just retreat further into themselves than they already are."

"So I'm the whipping boy." he sighed. "Which is fine, I got you babe..." he kissed Gwen unashamed that the Soul Keeper was watching them with interest. "So I was supposed to find Gwen is that what you're telling me Bedit-Shari?"

"That would certainly be telling Osiris." she winked at him. "Let's just say that you should listen to me from now on eh?"

"You're going to milk this for all its worth aren't you?" he sighed. "Now where is your lover? He was supposed to check on shit for me."

"He's not back yet," she smiled sadly, "Maybe he found someone who caught his eye."

Syrus looked down. Sherri was head over heels for the Etruscan god, and Arlo, while he enjoyed fucking her, wasn't for the Soul Keeper. She wasn't part of the prophecy, and it irked her. She knew she would have to let him go, and now that Gwen had been found it was only a matter of time before she would have to give him up. It was a sad state of affairs. "I doubt it highly. Maybe some substance or another, but surely not another woman."

"Well you never know. It's going to happen one day and soon by the looks of things. You're the first and the others will follow after that. Congratulations."

"You will too Sher."

"Maybe." She smiled again, this time it managed to look hopeful. "I'll leave you two alone now. It was very nice to meet you Gwen; we'll have a longer talk tomorrow."

Gwen nodded. "Thanks, it's been nice meeting you too."

Sherri gave her a secret smile and then made to walk out the door before pausing. "If Arlo comes in let him know I'm home." she told him then walked back out of the door she came from.

Syrus sighed and looked at Gwen. "See? Totally painless."

"She was nice."

"That's one way to put it. But if she hadn't sent me out, then I wouldn't be here with you right now."

"Exactly. I like her." She grinned up at him.

He pulled her close to him and kissed her soundly, running his hands down her back.

A small gasp escaped her as she leaned into him. "Mmmmm that feels good." She purred, "You feel good."

"Of course I do pet, I'm meant to touch and please you."

"Here? On the couch?"

He wagged his eyebrows at her. "No better place... why, you afraid we will get caught?"

She nodded, "A little bit..."

"And you're not a little bit turned on from that fear?" his voice muffled by his kissing her neck.

He felt her body tremor and he knew she was. "That's beside the point."

Syrus grinned. "That actually is the point lover... You know I don't care if they walk in, actually it would be pretty amusing to see them all pissed off. But that's for later I think. "He kissed her again and pulled her closer.

"Ah..." She returned his kiss, her hand moving down to cup him through his jeans. "Mmmmm... The thought isn't bothering you at all." She grinned wickedly at him. "You know you owe me great morning sex."

"I do, though it is evening. Great morning sex will have to wait till morning, though perhaps I can interest you in some hot early evening sex?"

"Oh I'd be very interested." She swung her leg around him straddling him as she popped the buttons of his jeans and slipped her hand inside.

Syrus groaned and bucked into her hand, kissing her deeply.

She gasped biting his bottom lip and grinned at him as her hand fisted around him.

"Now Gwen... you keep doing that and you'll be naked and screaming my name right here..."

"Oh," she gasped, "I know."

"And you don't care if Castor and Blaine and Dez see you all strung up in your passion... those perfect nipples hardened to tight little peaks, your body begging for me?"

"Ummm not at this very moment I don't, especially not when you put it like that." She purred into his neck. "Mmmmm you're right I should, I did a few seconds ago... you're a very bad influence on me."

He smirked. "Obviously. But your body is just making up for lost time. It's begging for a good fucking... And as much as I would love to do it here, you're not ready for your public debut." he winked and shifted in her hand. "So? Our room?"

"Our room." She agreed.

"Then zip me up will you? I don't think I could carry you there with my pants around my thighs." he sucked on her bottom lip.

She moaned into her mouth as she zipped him back up fixing his button. "All better."

"Says you. I gotta walk with this hard on." he stood and carried her with him, and started walking towards the hallway and oblivion.

***

A while later He was woken up by a knock at the door. "Sy? Let's go." Castor's gruff voice sounded through the door.

Syrus sighed. "Duty calls. I will be back soon love." He slipped out of bed and she frowned.

"Where are you going?" she asked and rolled over.

"No doubt patrolling for some Div, which is smart, and I'm seriously surprised I didn't think of it."

She smiled. "Be careful?"

"Damn right, I have you to come home to." He winked and got dressed quickly, slipping into his leather pants and boots, both the color of oxblood, and his black fitted t-shirt and black jacket. "Back before you know it Petal. Go back to sleep, and you will see me soon.

***

Gwen turned over in bed for what felt like the millionth time. Sleep eluded her no matter what position she lay on in the bed. Somewhere out there Sy was out chasing Div looking for the girls. All of the guys were, except Blaine who was locked up in his computer fortress. She hoped they would find the girls, or some mention of them their disappearance had hit Syrus hard and after spending some of the day with the others she could see why.

Still though there were parts of her that weren't exactly thrilled at the idea of their existence. She just wanted him all to herself. That wasn't exactly a crime but with Syrus there was this whole other part to him. He was this amazing guy on one hand but with the other he was an ages old god. A god that she knew close to zero about. Damn her for not listening to Ansley when she got her scholar freak on.

But there was nothing to stop her from quizzing the woman now. She sat up almost slapping herself on the head. Of course it was so simple; Ansley could tell her pretty much anything she wanted to know about Syrus's other life. The problem would be shutting her up once she got started. She swung herself out of bed and grabbed one of Syrus's shirts to pull over her pajamas. Once she was protected from the chill and wrapped nicely in Syrus-smelling clothes she went in search of Ansley.

Ansley was in the common room, sitting in the lounge surrounded by texts and papers. "Jeeze Ans don't you ever give up on that? You brain's gonna leak out of your ear someday with all the thinking you make it do."

Ansley looked up and smiled, taking her glasses off and rolled her shoulders. "You know how I am when I get that wild hair up my ass, and these texts, I swear I don't know where Kaid got them from, but they are citable, and they are going to revolutionize my dissertation. So many questions that I never thought would be answered..."

"Yeah?" she asked genuinely interested. Her friend had put a lot of work into her dissertation and it was good that she was getting what she needed.

"Yes, So many new facts have come to light, I swear if he would let me I would kiss Kaid." she smiled wistfully. "Holes I have been very concerned about regarding the life and death of the woman that was Eskirgal, and her legacy, the Orb, I think I might know where it might be."

"Wow," she smiled nodding not understanding anything that Ansley was talking about. "That's great... what orb?"

Ansley sighed and pinched the bridge of her nose. "Never mind sweets. What's up? Can't sleep? And where the hell did they all go?"

"Nope, you know how I am about sleeping alone. Syrus told me they had a breach in some of the security at one of the businesses they monitor," she sighed, hating to lie to Ansley. "I kinda thought to come out for some warm milk or something stronger."

"I don't know about milk, but the liquor cabinet is stocked to hell and back." she smirked. "And it's not locked. Kaid took care to mention that when they all went out. What kinda breach of security needs four men strapped up like they are going to war in leather and blades?" She shook her head

What indeed...Gwen decided to change the subject, she couldn't explain even if she wanted to. That Ansley was even buying the cover story told her that her friend was even more engrossed in her work than ever. "We should take advantage of that for sure... that is if it doesn't ruin your concentration. As for the breach, they take their clients seriously, or so Syrus told me. There's a reason why they get all the big clients."

"Don't get me wrong, I think it's hot, and probably over the top but showing that kinda strength has to discourage those assholes looking to fuck shit up.

As to the alcohol, you know me; I can down a bottle of Johnny Walker black label and still rock a full day teaching the kiddies. "

That made her laugh, "And I'm sure their parents are fine with that." One look in the cupboard was enough to see that Ansley was telling the truth. "Wow, I don't think I've seen so many bottles outside of a bar. What'll you have?"

"Anything caramel in color. You know I like my drinks like I like my men, Strong, and they burn me up when they go down." she wiggled her eyebrows at Gwen and placed her pencil in her mouth.

"That's disgusting, seriously far too graphic. And wrong." she laughed pouring out two scotch's. Normally she'd mix hers with sprite but the boys obviously didn't go for mixers. "Remind me why were friends again?" She teased giving her the drink then sitting back on the sofa next to her.

"Because without me, you wouldn't be exposed to the finer things in life." she took a sip and then raised her glass to Gwen. "Oh and we wear the same size and I dress better then you."

"All very good points," she conceded raising her glass in a toast then sipping it slowly. "So tell me about Kaid. You really haven't kissed him? That's practically unheard of for you."

Ansley shrugged and relaxed back into her seat. "Tell me about it. The man is scrumptious, sex on legs, all danger and pent up aggression that I would love to help him with, but he's a boy scout as well. Hasn't done much more then touch my cheek. It's kinda creepy though. And Arlo was talking to me, and so was Dezi, and well, he growled when they did. Guy doesn't want me, but doesn't want his buddies to have me either. How the fuck is that fair?"

"Maybe he's just looking out for you, Dezi seems to be a bit of a womanizer and I'm not so sure they get on too well. As for Arlo well," she shrugged not able to sum him up to easily.

"Like I care. I'm not looking for Mr. Right; I'm looking for Mr. Right now. Even if Kaid is my vision of physical perfection and is as interested in the old world as I am. He doesn't have the right."

"Maybe he called dibs?" she grinned knowing how much Ansley would hate that idea.

She frowned. "What right does he have to do that." she groaned and shook her head. "Doesn't matter. So what about you?"

"Yeah things are good." she smiled.

"Yeah he seems enamored Hun. Way to go."

"He's great, really great."

"So what's the problem then? And before you say nothing Gwenny, I know you."

"I'm not sure," she frowned deeply into her glass as if it held all the answers. "It's all a little fast I think."

"Who says anything has to take time. Love is chemistry, something you never had with Tom."

As usual, Ansley had a point. "And here I thought you majored in history." she grinned looking at her glass once again then back up to Ansley. She really had no idea how to start this conversation without arousing her suspicions, which, knowing Ansley would already be on red alert. "Don't you ever study anything other than this?" she lifted a parchment scribed in what she assumed was Sumerian of some sort or the other.

Ansley shrugged. "By choice? No. But I do when I'm at work, and in school I had to deal with all the cultures anthropology has. I touched on them all. Some were more interesting than others.

Like the Babylonians, and the Mesopotamians and I know they are so cliché, but both the Egyptians and the Gallic pantheons were fascinating."

"Oh so cliché," Gwen agreed sarcastically rolling her eyes. But they were getting somewhere now, "Egyptians? They couldn't be that fascinating, I used to click them on the discovery channel every time I wanted something to help me sleep. Worked really well too."

Ansley took a healthy sip of her scotch. "Well yeah, the shit they put out there for public consumption is boring as fuck. I mean most people don't know what a bizarre society they were. Curses, hell some of the best curses came outta Egypt. Ooh and their relationships were the best kinda soap operas. They were weird. Children ruling millions, brothers and sisters having children to keep the royal lines pure... wild shit."

"Brothers and sisters?" she felt herself frown.

"Yeah, but most societies and pantheon's were like that. The Greeks were notorious for it."

"Yeah them's were the times I guess. So curses and soap operas?"

Ansley laughed and sat back, licking her lips. "Yep. They had some of the best curses. Now people think the gypsy culture, or the voodoo or Middle American religions have them. Nope, the Egyptians kick all their asses. And their gods were messed up. I mean dog heads, owl heads... come on now."

"That is certainly true, there was a dog headed one," she suppressed a smile thanking the knowledge given to her on documentaries. "What was he the god of again, the afterlife... underworld or something?" she shrugged.

"Anubis? Yes he was the god of the underworld, the ancient deity that oversaw death and the underworld. Later it was taken over by Osiris, who ruled both the night and the land of the dead.

It was later said that Anubis foresaw the mid-grade of the underworld, or their hell."

"Osiris? Why does he sound familiar?" she asked beginning to get the feel for being sneaky as she topped up Ansley's now empty glass.

"Search me; He's the more known god of the dead. I'm sure you saw on TV things about him, and his wife Isis."

"Wife?" she asked too sharply her hand sloshing the scotch, this was what she was looking for. This was what she needed to know. "I don't think the show mentioned a wife."

She nodded. "Isis. Some texts say she was also his sister, but I don't take that literally, I mean I'm a firm believer that the family trees were there to explain to the lower peoples so it made sense."

"Hmm," she nodded. "But back then there were marriages all the time, it didn't mean anything special right?"

"By all accounts they were devoted to each other, and were the only gods of their time to stay together for sheer adoration."

"Great," she downed the glass grimacing as the fiery liquid burned through her. Being sneaky didn't suit her at all; this had been a mistake, pure and simple. She'd known he'd been married and it was good to hear he could commit to someone but that someone wasn't her. "And kids? Because there's gotta be kids right?" New found Isis, that's what the girls had called her. Great, just great, she didn't want to be his replacement wife.

"Word was they had a child, Horus, the one with the bird head. Though I don't know if that's true. There's a few odd writings though, ones that have been all but dismissed by the academic community as being hoaxes. They were the most interesting, and telling if you want my opinion."

She really didn't, but still this was why she'd started up the conversation. "Odd how?" she asked pleased that her voice sounded interested and calm, maybe it was the scotch. Certainly none of this mattered, if she couldn't be upset about his priestesses then having a long gone wife shouldn't even blip on her radar. Widowers remarry all the time and Syrus had never given her the impression that he wanted anyone other than her.

"Well they were from a cult that most historians swear never existed; the cult of Osiris apparently had an offshoot, which loosely translated to the Dark moon society in modern times. Apparently they were written by members of said sect, and one supposedly was written by Isis herself, though there's no proof that a physical being that was considered Isis ever existed."

She frowned her tired brain trying to sort through Ansley's words before giving up; sometimes she had trouble dumbing down her words. "Meaning?"

"Well it's not really anything big, but what they say is important."

"Which is?" she glared trying hard not to snap. It was like getting blood from a stone, normally Ansley was so forthcoming with the old world stuff. Murphy's law for this to be the one time she held back the suspense was just about killing her. "What do they say?"

"They spoke about a dark time, when their beloved Osiris lost his Isis, and the rest of his pantheon due to some cataclysmic event."

"Cataclysmic?" Like how his powers were bound from him into a Scarab. At least that explained a lot, no doubt the cult of Osiris was made up of his priestesses and she'd met with several of them earlier. "And so Isis allegedly wrote one of these thingies?"

Ansley closed her eyes and took another sip.

"Scripts. Yes, a firsthand account apparently, something about how she was leaving this plane, and the love she adored or something, and how she would be born again to him when he needed her most. It was all very romantic, but that's why they dismissed it. Apparently the sky goddess wasn't known for her warmth."

"But she loved her husband." How could she not? He was wonderful but he wanted her, no matter his long gone wife. Gwen knew this in her heart despite any worries or doubts her life experiences may have led her too. Her mind swam back, blearily; to the dream she had had earlier. Ansley's word rang true, and she felt it in her soul.

"She did, she apparently gave him up for the good of the world."

"Lucky us." *And lucky me.* She smiled blandly lifting back up the parchment she'd lifted earlier. It was time for a subject change, "Can you actually read this stuff?"

Ansley nodded. "Yes. I can read several forms of cuneiform. Useless in the real world but it was worth it I think. It's not something I brag about though. Few people know it's a dead language."

"And I guess Kaid can too," she grinned sipping from her glass. "You guys could talk to each other in it... that is if you could figure out how to pronounce the squiggles."

Ansley grinned. "Well it's hardly useful as dirty talk, and I tell you that's the only kinda talking I wanna do with that man."

"I just can't believe you haven't already," she sank back on the sofa leaning against her friend, relaxed.

"He's resistant, well sometimes. It's like he wants to, let's some things slip like he's a monstrous flirt.

Other times he starts to be, then it's like he remembers he has to be a miserable son of a bitch and stops. That one blows hot and cold."

"If anyone can break him its you." she said through a yawn, the exhaustion of the day flooding through her. Carefully she sat her glass down tucking her legs under her and resting her head on the back of the sofa.

"Right. Well I don't think he really wants be a project that's for damn sure. But his library, man alive, I swear I need a week in there. Longer really but I will settle for a week."

"Extensive is it?" she heard herself ask as her eyes slid shut.

"Indeed. Almost as extensive as the library at Princeton. Gwen honey, you're drooping on me. Take your punk ass to bed will you?"

"Mmmmm I'm fine just keep talking, your having that discovery channel effect." she grinned slyly keeping her eyes shut. "You could make a fortune doing documentaries. Wear a tight top and bounce around a lot and you'll bring in a whole new kind of viewer."

"I'm going to pretend you didn't say that you tarty bitch." she laughed and downed the rest of her drink. "Go to bed I have another hour or so of research before I sneak into Kaid's room and pray he doesn't freak out when he gets back."

That made her laugh, "That's almost worth staying up for." Reluctantly she opened her eyes and sat up. "Fine I'll go and leave you to your musty pages, it's a wonder you don't smell like that." she stood stretching.

"I take steps," she said and pulled a body spray out of her bag along with some hand sanitizer. "See? All you need to not smell like the past."

"Ah I bow to your greater knowledge." she grinned taking a mock bow before yawning again. "Ugh ok, I'm going to get sleep. Try not to frighten Kaid too much and you might wanna keep an eye out for booby traps." She felt like a zombie, thankfully she didn't have too far to walk.

"Booby traps?" she asked in horror. "Well after seeing his house all locked up like fort Knox I don't doubt it. There weren't any earlier when I dumped my stuff in his room so maybe I got the green light."

"I'm sure you did." she rubbed at her tired eyes and started out the door. "Night Ans," she called back as she made her way back to bed satisfied with her new knowledge.

Chapter Thirteen

Syrus was torn. Torn between his duty to his priestesses and the need to be with Gwen. It was completely insane, how attached he was to her already, how utterly smitten he was that she was fast becoming all that mattered.

But she was safe now, holed up at headquarters with Blaine and Ansley, while he and the rest of the Inferi Dii were out looking for Div to capture and interrogate. If successful, they would accomplish two things. One, that they would be able get the assholes to spill where his priestesses were, and two, they would be able to work off a little bit of the violence that had been brewing since he got the call that morning.

Castor and Kaid were taking midtown, while Arlo took Alphabet City, his usual haunt. That left Syrus with Dezi staking out the east village, or more importantly, Webster Hall and then Houston. As Div were creatures of habit, they tended to structure their hunting without realizing it. Blaine had been working on a triangulation for some time, and thankfully his researching had paid off. They didn't have to blindly patrol sectors anymore and Syrus was praising the goddess for it more than ever now, because it wasn't proactive to be chasing their tails running about the city looking in places they rarely went.

They walked up to Webster Hall, Syrus tipping his head to the bouncer who nodded and let them both in. Syrus was more than a regular at Webster, he had saved one of the bartenders one night from being a late night snack for a group of fledgling Div a few years back, and they had never forgotten, especially when that bartender ended up being the music manager for the club this year.

Syrus and the guys drank for free there, as did the girls in Psi Pi Chi, and in return, Syrus kept the club pretty free of the vermin that called themselves Div.

Tonight though, they walked in and did a quick pass, running downstairs, then back up and to the second floor, each grabbing a beer and planting themselves close to the right side balcony door, just in case something happened and they needed to traverse the quickly filling club with ease.

The bands slated for the evening weren't a favorite of Syrus' or the Div for that matter. The Demons gravitated to the more aggressive music, the heavy hard core and metal that was getting more and more popular. Syrus's personal choice didn't run towards the metal side of it, but he knew they did like it so it was necessity. Anything that promoted violence, they wanted to be a part of it.

Even though the evening's entertainment was more towards the emo side of the spectrum, Blaine's research said that Thursday's Div activity was most likely to be at Webster or the general vicinity.

Syrus turned to Dezi who was taking a long drink of his beer. "Houston was a bust eh? I figured they wouldn't be there, but it was worth it to try. Not one sense of resonance. You think they are staying off the streets because of their little power play?"

"Fuck if I know, but we are getting nowhere fast." Dezi spoke scanning the crowd, "To think we're actually wishing Div on these folks."

"I'm not wishing shit on them, but Blaine has never been wrong. The sooner we find these fucks, the better."

"Yeah well Blaine's not infallible especially these days. How did things go today with Gwen?" He tipped his beer again. "Just for the record, there's nothing worse for a hangover than angry woman screams."

"Sorry about that. She wasn't too happy about the girls."

"Yeah no shit. Can't blame her though, I guess, things all cool now then?"

Syrus shrugged. "One can only hope." he took a swig of his beer. "So who do you have to thank for those scratch marks we all got an eyeful of last night?"

"Stripper." he grinned at him. "Well, part time stripper. Jenny's a whole load of fun; man was I pissed when I had to leave last night. Popped by earlier on though, finished what I started before heading off to work."

"Figured as much. I'm surprised you didn't try to get on Ansley. She seems your type."

"What with Kaid growling at me every time I looked sideways at her. No way man. That fucking no good shit guards like a pit bull with an electrode up its ass. Besides Jen knows how to look after my hangovers."

Syrus smirked and shook his head. "You seriously think Kaid is going to lift his imposed celibacy?"

"For her? Doubtful... Feel sorry as hell for her if he does. He must have a deadly case of blue balls... that or he spanks it more than a monkey."

Syrus grimaced. "Graphic. That was not a picture I needed..." he stopped talking and turned back toward the crowd and concentrated. Dezi followed suit. "Where?"

"Not sure." Dezi looked over the heads until he stopped pointing to the back exit door. "There. Prick with the leather on chatting up the busty blonde. Natural Double D's I'd wager, perky too."

"Sensible, considering those fucks don't dig the silicone implants. Keep it in your pants will you, at least till we save her ass from becoming lunch."

"Not a fate any natural woman should suffer, or the touched up ones."

"Agreed. Shall we?" he asked as he slipped a throwing knife out of his pocket.

"After you bud, I'm guessing you have some issues to work off."

Syrus grinned savagely and took the side stairs, the ones that would take them close to the Div and his possible victim. They made it down the stairs and hit the bottom floor just as the Div caught their proximity. He smirked at the girl and they walked out the doors, and both Syrus and Dezi followed on their heels. The Div was quickly leading the woman into a side ally just off Tenth street when they caught up with him. Syrus Looked at Dezi. "Get the girl to safety, then come back and help me."

"Can do... she'll be as safe as I can make her. Try to keep the fuck alive for me eh?"

"Oh I plan on it..." They entered the mouth of the alley and the Div had the girl against the wall, lifting her up. Syrus pulled another knife from his pocket and stood in the small light that came from the neon past the mouth of the alley. He cleared his throat and grinned. "Now I know I'm interrupting here... but you and me need to have a little talk Div."

Dezi moved away from him, his eyes locking onto the frightened girl with a gentle smile. "Don't worry about a thing Kitten," he told her smoothly ignoring the Div's presence taking a step closer to them. "Everything's just gonna be fine."

Syrus flashed his knife and kept his eyes on the Div. "Kitten, go with Dezi will ya? He's much more attractive then this punk, and a sight cleaner I do suspect."

"Sy I never knew you'd noticed my obvious attractiveness, I'm flattered, but you know I don't swing that way." He moved forward careful not to startle the Div who was clearly staying still trying to decide whether to lunge or run.

He held a hand out to the girl, "Come on over here, pet, Sy has to ask the bad Div some questions." he cooed lightly in a tone one normally reserved for frightened children and animals.

The girl looked him over and smirked. "Umm much more sexy..." she murmured, clearly drunk, and went to Dezi, wrapping herself around him. Syrus shook his head. Dezi had that effect on women, and used it to his advantage more often than not. Tonight though, it was saving this poor girls life, and he hoped it wouldn't be the only life saved tonight.

"Nothing but truth there." Dezi grinned into her ear holding her tightly to him. "Let's get you somewhere safe." he suggested his hand slipping down her back cupping her ass and giving a squeeze.

She giggled and went with him, nuzzling his throat and whispering to him. Syrus was soon left alone with the Div, and all the good humor that was in him quickly bled out. "Shall we have a chat?"

The Div hissed at him baring his teeth. He was young, freshly turned, and not too bright which was saying something for a Div.

"Look buddy I can make this quick and painless for you. Truth is you're not going to leave this alley. Tell me what I wanna know."

"Fuck you, ass wipe." He growled gutterly and launched himself at him.

Syrus shook his head and grabbed the Div by his collar and held him at arm's length. "See now you're going to make this difficult, and it's not going to end well for you. I was willing to be nice about this but you just had to be an idiot didn't you?" he sighed. "Tell me what I want to know Div...Now."

The Div turned his jaws snapping inches from Syrus's arms his hands snatching at him.

"Oh come on now... I'm a God older then time and you are what, a Div of a month? Maybe? No contest." he turned and slammed the punk against the wall. "Last chance to tell me before I start cutting body parts off." He brandished another knife at him to prove his point.

"Go to hell." the Div cried defiantly grinning. "Can't do any worse than what's happening to your women. Hurt me and they'll feel it tenfold."

The smarmy attitude never sat well with Syrus, though his patience this night was running thin for obvious reasons. "Uh huh. And is that why you're out all by yourself? No I think they just left the sheep out, not as bait but as pawns. If you matter one iota you wouldn't be running the streets alone tonight fucko. But we are getting somewhere. So you do know what I wanna know. So spill. Or this wonderful blade is going to be embedded into you in an unnatural angle."

"No way," he shook his head blood pouring out of his nose. "You won't risk it... your an older than time god, you're smart enough to know what they could be going through. Besides what make you think that a pawn-sheep like me is gonna be updated in all the masters workings?"

"Because I know something that you don't. Div have a hive brain... All you have to do is access the information... Like you did when you just dropped that little tidbit. Why do you think you were sent out as cannon fodder? Now tell me..." he stabbed the Div in the leg, rage coursing thought his being at what the Div was hinting at. Now that the Div had confirmed that they took them, it was more important than ever to get them back, intact, tonight.

"Fuck!" he cried out thrashing, "I don't know anything."

"The hell you don't... You're Div, you know."

He cried out as Syrus twisted the knife. "I swear it I don't..."

"See you think I'm an idiot. I have killed so many of you I know I'm right. So? Spill or the next one is going 5 inches to the left. Your balls won't appreciate it."

"They'll kill me worse than that." he hissed again showing his fangs, his rancid breath misting over Syrus. "What do you want?"

"Three things. Why did they take my girls, where did they take my girls and what do they want?"

He gasped and Syrus could feel the air pricking up as the hive mind clicked in, making his voice go flat, but raspy, with thick tones. "We took the girls because we were looking for your Keeper."

"Yeah, well none of them are her. I don't have a goddamn relic... so why look for mine." he bluffed, he knew, but hopefully the Div didn't.

"Prophecy," he shook his head. "You're the first. Caine scented your relic..." He breathed fearfully.

Fuck... which was why the Div had attacked Gwen. "Well he missed didn't he? My priestesses are my fuck toys, and I want them returned to me, tonight."

He bit back a laugh. "No, their Caine's fuck toys now. He's with them now... I can feel it." he whispered the last shaking.

And that bond went both ways, Syrus knew. Rage bubbled and boiled inside him. "Yeah? Well listen up Caine, return the girls to me, Now." his eyes burned with dark fury, fury he saw staring back at him through the irises of the Div's unfocused eyes.

The Div's expression changed smiling ghoulishly and its voice changed again to one Syrus knew. "You know, I don't think I will. I'm enjoying them far too much... they are alive for now. But kill my minion and you'll be killing one of yours."

Syrus knew Caine was fucking with him. "Last chance Caine. Harm one hair on any of their heads and you won't live long enough to enjoy the misery."

Caine's voice laughed through the other Div; "I think we're past harming hair on their heads." the Div shrugged. "How's the luscious Gwen? Does she taste as good as she smells?"

Syrus rolled his eyes. Seriously? This asshole was going to play that card? "Why would I tease you like that, honestly? Last chance Caine. Return my priestesses. They are innocents."

"Mmmmm not from where I'm standing. Do you have any idea how easy they were to get? Childs play, honestly. Which one do you want me to kill? In retaliation of course, you kill mine, I kill one of yours... do you have a preferred method? I suppose you'll want her organs intact for burial." He sighed. "Pity they hold so much power after joining with their god. Their blood too. It's quite a treat."

Syrus smirked. If he wanted to play that game..."Oh your minion will be alive and well when I done with him... but your hours are numbered Caine. Cut to the chase. Where are you so I can come kill you?"

"You couldn't take me alone Inferi, fortunately for you that's not how you play. No I'm not ready to have you storm my castle just yet... I'll be in touch. Just know that I'm enjoying your women." The connection cut off leaving the Div reeling.

Syrus swore as he dropped the Div foot soldier to the ground and sneered at him. "Your master bought you your life. Bring him a message for me will ya?" he punched him in the face hard, feeling his jaw crack as he did. It was a two-fold wound.

One the Div couldn't use his mouth to suck the girl's energy, and two, the blatant violence, even though he let the guy live would speak volumes.

True, it might make Caine retaliate, but the girls could take getting knocked about a bit, they were his lovers and bodyguards after all, and while they were not mutually exclusive, they could survive a lot.

The div shook his head screaming. "No" he lisped though the speech must have been agony. "No you have to kill me... I've failed him." he wailed begging him.

"I kill you, he kills one of them. No, no I think while humane, I'm going to bargain on them."

He panicked crying out, "Bastard!" The demon growled pulling the knife out of his leg and embedding it deep in his throat blood spraying from the artery.

"See that won't kill you puppy, just make you one hell of a mess..." he grabbed the knife and cleaned it off. "Have a good night there pal." he strolled off and found Dezi at the mouth of the alley, grinning like a cat that got the cream.

"Wow." Dezi grinned at him looking back at the Div. "You know they're supposed to try and stick us with the knives. Man, Div are stupid."

"Eh. Caine and I had a chat. I let the fuck live and he don't kill my girls. Not that I trust him completely but... He cut all contact, something about not wanting to share his sandcastle. Fuck is stupid."

"Sure is if he's living in a sandcastle... probably thinks it sounds clever."

Syrus shook his head. He wasn't happy in the least, but there wasn't much he could do. As some crazy cartoon once said, now was the time for negotiations, not violence. Violence comes later. "And the girl?"

Dezi shrugged. "She's fine, a little disappointed that she got cut loose but it's better than being Div food."

"Surprised you didn't send her on her way with a smile on her face and a number in her pocket... or wherever you can slip a piece of paper with that get up she was wearing."

He laughed. "Just how low do you think my standards are? Any girl wasted enough to go out back with a Div got to be minutes away from puking on my shoes. I don't wear vomit well."

That did get a laugh out of Syrus. "Yeah, something tells me that." his phone rang and he answered it all at once. "Yeah?"

Arlo drawled into the other end. "Any luck? It's quiet as fuck out here."

"Yeah, I got some info, and Dezi almost got puked on."

"Beauty. Cas called we need to meet back at HQ."

"Yeah. See you in twenty."

He hung his phone up and looked at Dezi. "Boss wants us back."

***

Caine cut off his conversation with the Egyptian with a snarl. That was one more useless Div he'd have to take care of at a later date. Sheep weak enough to get spotted deserved to get picked off. It only bothered him that it was one of his recruits. He expected more from his chosen. Osiris would be doing him a favor by taking him out. A pitiful whimper echoed in the small room and he had to smile, looks like his guests were waking up.

"About time too." He smiled to himself pulling a long blade from its sheath at his side and slowly making his way to them.

He scraped the blade off the metal wall the noise deafening in their confined space. If they hadn't already been awake he was certain they were now.

He could smell their fear; taste their essence filling up hazing over him. It wouldn't do to lose control though, Nathan would have his balls on a stick if he killed any of them, but it didn't mean he couldn't have his fun with them. It was good for his morale, his and his Div's. His latest recruits had to learn that there was punishment for the weak and the strong were rewarded.

"Awake at last I see." He beamed brightly in what he hoped was a false reassuring smile. Truth was he didn't do much reassuring so he wouldn't recognize it.

The three girls swung in front of him their feet maybe a foot or so off the ground. Strung up with a particularly harsh rope securing their wrists as an anchor point above their head. It was a particular barbaric way of stringing someone up, putting all of their weight on their fragile human shoulder blades.

The more they struggled the more likely they were the dislocate something. He'd had them like that since Nathan's pet whore had dropped them off. Of course they were let down occasionally but Caine truly doubted whether they enjoyed that time any more that their hanging state.

He watched their naked and bruised gagged forms dispassionately their wild eyes darting from place to place. Truth of the matter was that he'd grown bored of them. By now the women he took to bed were usually dead or lucky enough to have escaped. He'd done everything that he could have thought to do to a woman at least twice and hated to repeat himself.

The one thing that he longed to do, opening them up, was blocked to him so he was stuck fucking about till Nathan decided what he wanted to do with the whores. He could only take so much of their whimpers and sobs.

Thankfully they'd given up on pleas within their first hours. This warred with his every instinct. His inner demon was screaming at him to go for the meat, to open a vein and to hell with the consequences.

He caught himself taking a step forward before pausing and calling to the Div outside. Four of them piled in eyeing the girls Caine could feel their need almost as he felt his own. He calmed them down, doing so with his own demon. In many respects they were one entity, controlling one was controlling the other. He'd inducted these Div and so his bond was stronger at least for the first few years of their change, they were easily controlled. They calmed visibly all but the one at the front; Brander had managed to calm himself of his own accord. The young one was showing much promise and that would be rewarded, for now.

He turned his back to the girls feeling their anxious eyes on him. "By now I'm sure you can feel my disappointment. One of your brothers was weak enough to be caught by the Inferi." The stared back dully their glazed eyes accepting. "The fools let him go, I cannot accept such weakness from one of mine... Stark's fools I expect it, but not from one or ours."

"I shall hunt him down for you, boss." Brander declared stepping forward. "You shall have this weaklings head."

"No," Caine raised a hand tapping Branders shoulder. "Nothing so dramatic, he'll die when we're good and ready for him. I expect nothing but the best..." he told his men. "But I give as good as I get in rewards. Brander, you've been invaluable these past few days and for your reward..." he stepped away motioning to the girls. "Choose one and do anything you like with her."

Wide eyed, the Div stepped forward, "My lord... many thanks."

He moved towards the closest producing a knife to cut the naked girl down with.

"Just," Caine stopped him tapping his shoulder. "Don't kill her, or open her up... a taste wouldn't hurt but nothing damaging. Share her if you like but the rules apply. Do not kill her," her repeated to the nodding Brander. If anyone were going to open the bitch up it would be him.

The girl, Tony he believed, tried to scream as she was cut down, her ball gag turning the scream to noise. The pain in her shoulders of all things must have been excruciating. "Ah the price for cavorting with higher beings... humans never will learn." He smiled at the two left swinging as their friend was dragged off and soon put to good use.

He stood next to the smaller one, Rain or Raid, something like that. He pushed her making her cry out as her body started a swing her aching shoulders couldn't take. "Must hurt." He noted pushing her harder again.

The other girl made a noise and kicked out with her left foot, catching him on the shin lightly. It must have hurt, but that one, his high priestess, held promise. She glared at him, her eyes over the edge past defiant.

He met the girl's eyes smirking as he pushed Raid viciously. The girl screamed through the gag slumping down possibly unconscious. She was of no consequence to him, broken meat. What Osiris saw in her he didn't know. The high priestess though, she wasn't broken, not by a long shot and that got him excited if not a little hard.

"Nice to see your joining my party." he stepped up to her weaving his hands through her hair to hold her head still while undoing her gag with his other hand and ripping it from her mouth.

She flexed her jaw and her eyes shot daggers at him. "Fucking bully, what the hell is your fucking problem? You know, I get it that you got a hard on for pissing of Sy, but you do realize that him and the Inferi are going to kill you, and this will be all for naught. Where did they take Tony?"

"Out for some fresh air." he flashed a smile full of sharp teeth. "You could always join her if you like, I'm sure my boys would appreciate it." he smacked her face lightly. "And you're little gods aren't going to find me, not unless I want to be found."

She scoffed, or tried to, her throat raw and scratchy from lack of water. "Right, and the queen's wig isn't white. You do know that you're just a glorified babysitter right? I was awake when you spoke to Sy, you letting your little frat boys run a train on Tony is not holding up your end of the bargain. When he finds us, he's going to make you suffer and nothing those Velns fucks could do would ease your agony."

"I'm not worried about your little master, whore," he snarled anger flashing through him hot and thick. Once again his demon raged up against him battling to get free to tear at the worthless bitch and feast on her. He tamed it hard, not wanting the boys to go over that precarious edge. "I didn't bargain with him, killing that worthless pig shit would have done me a favor. I never promised not to hurt any of you."

"You are a coward. Harming innocent women. Could you be any more pathetic?

He laughed at her scornfully, "Yet here I am, with the power and there you are," he pushed her, "All strung up and in pain. If you could have, what's that term?"

he asked searching for the phrase he wanted, "Kept it in your pants you wouldn't be in this mess and neither would your delicious little friends. This is as much your fault as mine; you walked them into my grasp..."

She looked down at his pants and then back to his eyes. "And you should be careful to keep it in your pants, friend, seeing as you're so ready to go there. Ever hear of that book The Weasel Bride? Getting your cock bit off by a pair of vaginal teeth isn't the way to go. And you can hem and haw all you want you pig, all that pomp and swagger does nothing. Torture us, bleed us, you still can't kill us without bringing down the vengeance that is the Inferi Dii." She seethed. "You won't be able to hide, you or your fucking handler." she looked at his incredulous look. "Surprised? Like your pea brain could have come up with something so fucking dastardly."

Caine felt himself go cold, like somebody flipped a switch on his rage changing it to something darker. The bitch had a mouth on her, one that he'd soon break with the utmost of glee. "Kill you?" he asked his eyes bleeding black. "What an excellent idea." He mentally called Brander to stop what he was doing and bring the girl back in. "Such faith in her master's protection." He chuckled as the girl was dragged in by the hair she was covered in bite marks. "Let's see how confident you are after you watch your friend die. Your suggestion of course, I'm sure your master will be glad to know he's a whore less because his so-called high priestess couldn't keep her mouth shut." He happily stuffed the gag into her mouth using more force than necessary. "Now where did I put that video camera?"

Chapter Fourteen

It was morning when Arlo burst through the outer door, and into the common room with a wild look in his eye. He was covered in blood, and carrying two disks. "Sy, shit man. I have been trying to get a hold of you for hours."

"Yeah, phone died last night. Where the fuck were you? Last I heard you were on your way in, then nothing." he said as he went over some papers on the coffee table. When he didn't hear Arlo answer him he turned and looked him up and down and frowned. "What the fuck happened to you?" Realization hit him as he took in the entire scene before him. "Which one?" he asked his throat getting tight with anger, his voice even, measured, but dead.

Arlo took a deep breath and grimaced as he walked forward. His clothes were a mess of drying blood. "I was on my way in, but then Sherri called me. Told me there was a disturbance, to do another sweep. I did, nothing big, even went into Webster. Absolutely nothing. I walked around the club after..." he swallowed. "And I swear to you Syrus there was nothing I could do. Tony was lying on the floor of the alley like a broken doll, duct tape over her mouth and a disk tapped to her chest."

"Where is she?" Syrus asked quietly, his powers starting to thrum around him. Still bound, everything he had access to was raging.

"Uh-uh man. No you do not need to see that." Arlo shook he head, his eyes clouded with remorse and pain.

"Arlo I'm not going to ask again, where is she?" he bit out through clenched teeth.

The Etruscan god before him sighed and sagged, defeat clear in his stance. "In the operating theater, I couldn't leave her man. She..."

"I'm sure you did your best." Gwen spoke softly saying exactly what Arlo needed her to say. What Syrus could not at that moment. She touched his hand, "Syrus..."

He tore off down the hallways, Gwen calling to him and trailing behind. He broke through the doors of the room to see Castor suiting up in medical gear.

Castor, the big bastard he was, stopped Syrus with not so much as a glare. "Syrus, Oh no, not a shot in the ten hells buddy. You don't need to be here."

Syrus saw red, but stopped moving forward when Gwen reached him and held him from behind. He closed his eyes and steadied his breathing, then looked at Castor.

Gwen hugged him tightly, a slight tremor moving through her.

"No autopsy. You know that." Syrus said with finality.

Castor nodded. "I know, but I need to assess her wounds, and see if there's any clue, so we can save Simone and Raine."

Syrus nodded. "She has to be interred at the crypt."

Arlo stood behind them and sighed. "I already called Daphne; she's on her way to pick her up with two more elders of your sect. She will be well cared for."

Yes, her mother would be able to take care of it. Syrus squeezed his eyes shut, the rage turning to pain. He shook, knowing this was his entire fault. Had he just been a bit more responsible with them all, Tony would be alive and looking towards her next year of college.

It wasn't fair, but he knew he couldn't dwell on it. She was gone; he couldn't even feel her anymore. Her soul was gone, to points unknown. The fuckers were going to pay. "Where's the goddamn disk?"

"Blaine is running it through the analyzer. He's waiting on you." Arlo offered as he leaned against the doorframe.

Syrus turned into his Keeper's embrace and sighed. "I don't think you should see this Gwen. Fuck I don't wanna see this."

She shook her head. "No I want to stay with you."

He looked down into her eyes, shining with unshed tears for a woman she never met. Goddess, he loved her. Everything else aside, she was there for him, joined him in the pain of the moment, took the burden on herself as well, to lighten his load. All with a look.

"I'm really sorry." One of the tears spilled over down her face. "Come on," she pushed at him directing him away from the theater, "We'll go and see Blaine."

Syrus didn't know what was worse, seeing her body or seeing what was done to her. Either way he couldn't allow Gwen to see this, to watch him fall apart, not now, not when he had two other girls to find and help. He held her and nodded and Castor frowned. "Dezi is with Blaine right now, suiting up. You know we won't let you deal with this alone Sy. They were important to us too. "

Syrus nodded and shook off the numbness that was creeping up his limbs. There would be a time to mourn her, but right now he had to know the fate of Raine and of Simone. He sent a silent prayer to Tiamat that he and the guys would be able to save them. "Thank you Cas." he let Gwen lead him back down the hall and motioned her to Blaine's command center.

She entered before him keeping herself touching him. Blaine sat at his computer desk his face grim as he worked furiously.

Dezi stood behind him slipping knives into his rig. "Man I'm really sorry." He said angrily, the death of women always hit him hard. "We're gonna get whoever the fuck did this."

"Damn right." he said, his voice seething with menace. It was better to be angry, to let his powers rule him, let the darkness of his origins fill him, then puss out. He would be no use to anyone that way.

He looked at Gwen and his heart ached. She was going to see a very hidden part of him, something that only his fellow Inferi Dii had only seen a handful of times. They weren't bound yet, and she might not understand, but at this point it was all he could do to not break down.

He looked at Blaine, his eyes and tone cold. "What do you got for me?"

His eyes sidled over to Gwen then back, "You sure?"

His face softened and looked down at Gwen. "This is a partnership, Gwen. You sure?"

She swallowed hard then nodded threading her fingers in between his tightly. "I am." Her soft voice was thinly laced with steel as she made her decision.

Syrus looked over at Blaine, the hard lines back. "You heard the lady."

"Fair enough." He smiled grimly respect showing in his eyes as he turned back to the screen pressing a few buttons on his keyboard.

The tape switched onto the club stage. The lights were switched low making the picture quality grainy, the crowd hushed, everything focused on the stage. Rain walked on stage and began to sing, the band behind her all but disappeared her voice was clear and beautiful. Gwen shivered beside him rubbing her arms as everyone in the room and the club put their full attention onto Rain.

Quiet laughter bubbled from behind the camera as the song died to a close. "Ummm see what you're missing sire?" Simone's voice teased happily. "You'd rather be out fighting the good fight instead of here with us. She's amazing though isn't she? Maybe, if you're good, later on she can give you a private performance. If you'd like. Hopefully you'll get here soon though so she won't have to." The camera panned down showing a watch. "She was miserable when she found out you wouldn't be here. Never mind though, I'm sure you'll make it up to her, you always do and I've got it all here on tape." Simone sighed as Raine started to sing again.

The camera cut out flicking to another scene. The lights were harsh and bright a total contrast to the club, it was a small empty room the walls hung with sheet to disguise the location. Tony was naked tied to a chair bruises and bloody bite marks marred her pale skin. She had a ball gag in her mouth, which muffled her screams. In the background Simone and Raine hung naked and gagged from a pipe. Their wrists had cuts from struggling against their bonds otherwise they were relatively unmarked.

Gwen hissed from beside him turning from the scene and burying her face in his shirt. Blaine swore pushing his computer chair away from the desk; for once his feet were on the floor.

Syrus clenched his jaw tightly and held Gwen. "Fuck." he swore and growled, watching the tape unfold. He didn't want to, but he needed to, needed to see everything, needed to know just how one of his own gave her life... In old days he would have been fine with this, but women of this age were much softer and less the warrior, regardless of what they did to become them.

A vicious laugh echoed through the room and Tony flinched her eyes darting up to behind the camera. "That's it girl, smile, you're on camera. Wave to your master." the man laughed again, "Or at least shake your head from side to side."

Caine stepped into full view completely naked and hard. Healed scars marred over his body. "Now what should we do? Hmm?" He asked her running his bloodstained hands through her hair. "What should we show your master that we've learned?" he batted his cock suggestively off her arm the slap almost as loud as her whimper.

"You've been a good little whore for me haven't you? Enjoyed yourself." She tried to pull away as he slapped her again. Her thighs were covered in bruises and dried blood all consistent with rape, brutal rape. Dark black finger shaped bruises showed on her hips and waist. "That's right, you should tell him that you're mine now... You. Are. Mine." He emphasized each point with a slap of his hard on. "You know that don't you?" she shook her head and he slapped her hard with his hand the impact almost knocking the chair over. "You are mine! You and your little friends are mine. A gift. There's nothing your god can do about it," he looked up into the camera moving behind her. "Nothing but watch Osiris."

Tears streamed down her face. "So tell me peaches. Whom do you belong to?" he asked removing the ball gag simultaneously snapping her wrist from her bands. She screamed her voice hoarse and filled with agony. "Tell me." He commanded twisting her hand around.

She screamed again her hand threatening to rip off. "You!" she screamed, "Please god you!" she howled, "Stop please... please god," she sobbed her eyes looking directly into the camera. Directly at Syrus.

He let her arm go looking back into the camera. "See how willingly they renounce you?" He asked stepping away from Tony over to Simone. "I wonder how long it will take this one?" He stroked his hand up her thigh digging his fingers into her flesh causing her to cry out. "Maybe once she finds out that you have your woman and it's not her?" Simone gasped and he chuckled. "Oh this one is going to be a lot of fun. But you see, Osiris, old buddy, old pal, I don't want this one..." he slapped her ass, "or this one," He pushed Raine making her yell out as one of her shoulders dislocated under the weight. "Or that one." He motioned to Tony as he walked off screen coming back with a bag. "I want the one that you have."

He knelt down behind Tony who was begging incoherently. Pulling her head to the side he grinned showing his teeth before taking a bite out of her. Caine moaned chewing in her flesh savoring it as she cried out. "Delicious." His pink tongue flashed out lapping the blood from his lips then licking around the bite. "That blood is quite potent." He replaced her gag then took something out of the bag and attached it to her arm.

A blood bag started to fill with her blood as Tony looked on in horror. "I'm toying with taking her organs as well they'll make good rewards for my people and it'll be hard to give an incomplete body the burial she deserves. I'm giving you this one back but the next I think I'll keep for myself and who do you think that should be? I'll let them decide I think." He switched off the bags whenever they got full letting her heart pump out her blood for him as he neatly stored the packs away.

They sat in silence watching Tony's final horrific moments.

Just as her eyes were about to flicker shut Caine cut her bonds free and pushed her to the floor to die.

"Now let's be adults about this. I have something you want and you have something I want. Give me the Scarab and the woman and I'll give you your priestesses back and don't be ignorant enough to believe that these are the only girls that I have access to. I'll tell you what, since you woman put me in such a good mood I'll let you give me one, the bitch or the Scarab and I'll give you one of yours. Between me and you I doubt I could keep myself from killing another one of them anyway. I'll be in touch." He winked licking his lips as the camera cut off.

Syrus stood with his fists balled at his sides. He had since stopped holding Gwen and stepped back from her, His powers rising off him in waves, well what stunted powers he did possess. He looked at Blaine and pulled himself together; calming his inner chi "I want analysis. Sound, location, the fucking stone on the floor. Find Raine and Simone Blaine."

"I'm already on it." Blaine nodded, "It's an unusually small space but I don't think it's an apartment or a warehouse. The sheets are deceiving but I'll crack it. There's an echo I'm not sure about but I'll run it through and see if I can get any background noise. We'll get the fucker."

"So he wants Gwen or the Scarab?" he sighed and looked at Castor, who had walked in and leaned against the far wall. "Syrus, we can't abide either."

"You think I'm giving my Keeper or my godhead over to that fuck? He is out of his fucking mind. I can't sacrifice the girls though. Not after that." he sighed. "How long do you think we have till he wants the trade? And can we do a bait and switch?"

Castor frowned. "I don't know what the fuck to do brother. Dezi?"

"I don't know, they'll smell the real thing." He frowned in thought, "That place looks real familiar, sounds it too, I'm sure I've been somewhere like it. I'm drawing a blank though, sorry, I've been in a lot of places in my life."

"Keep thinking." Blaine told him. "Arlo did you find out how they were taken? What did Hannibal say?"

"Limo... with a tarted up chick. Said it was the usual for them, bunch of girls all over each other, He didn't think it was weird." Arlo sighed. "As to your bait and switch idea, they will know, Fuck your godhead radiates from between Gwen's breasts, and I know that it's the Scarab, no offense Gwen. We need to figure something out. When does the fuck want the exchange? I think I missed that on the goddamn message with his insane ramblings. I don't think being a Div is agreeing with him much."

"Being Div doesn't agree with anyone and he didn't say." Dezi growled. "Wants to be in control and have us tearing ourselves apart."

"But we won't," Blaine interjected. "We're just going to have to work with what we have. Can you get the security tapes from the club? See what we can find out about the tart and the limo. Take things from that angle."

Arlo threw the other disk at Blaine. "All here, Hannibal was very forthcoming once I told them the girls went missing. He knows Simone doesn't fuck about."

"Great." he flicked through them lifting the one from the door and putting it on. "Now to speed it up." he forwarded it till the girls poured out of the club.

The four of them staggered Tony half supported by a girl he didn't recognize with long dark curls and a short black skirt and a blood red corset top. Blaine paused it as she helped Tony into the limo, "Look like that's our girl. I can't see the driver though."

Dezi whistled, "Why do all the evil ones look that hot? Then again guess the girls wouldn't have went for it if she'd fallen out of the ugly tree... Shit looking at the four of them I'd have been tempted. They don't look in full control of their faculties though, especially Tony. She probably slipped them something."

Arlo growled. "You just said a mouthful. Woman has an ass ripe for a guys hands. Holy shit. Why *are* the hot ones super evil? But your right, it has to be drugs; the girls aren't the shy retiring types to go on pure physical coercion... And they aren't the kind to play outside of their own pond either."

"And to get in a limo with a stranger, no matter how hot she is, and go fuck knows where is just plain stupid. Unless you're me. Those girls aren't stupid." Dezi frowned

"Like I said, Sy's girls don't play outside their own pond." Arlo interjected.

Syrus nodded. "Why do you think there's twenty of them?"

"Plates are fake." Blaine swore throwing himself back from the computer in his chair and running his hands through his hair, "So all we have is the girl. I'll get the make and model of the car and see how many are in the city but that could be a few. I'll scan all the cameras we have for the limo last night but that's gonna take a while."

Castor nodded and folded his arms across his massive chest. "Get on it. Blaine this is all on you. Dezi, Arlo, I want you both to go back to the bar and check out the places we know Caine has been known to frequent... Clues here guys." he looked at Blaine. "When Kaid calls in, keep him appraised but have him keep Ansley out with him. Dinner, a movie, something. And then make sure they spend the night here. No slip ups."

"Kaid doesn't slip up, but I'll let him know. If that girl got half a brain she should be out of town by now. I'll check the passport records at the nearest airports. I can also run a check of Marrow industry employees, see if any of them will fit her description and photo. I can hack into some db's and check photo recognition but that'll take time and only come up good if she's got a record. I'll do it on the slow burner." He wheeled over to another computer and started typing furiously holding his pen between his lips.

"Good thinking. Now where the hell is Sherri?"

"I was looking over the body." Sherri called from the other room as she made her way to the doorway.

"And?" Castor said and looked at Syrus.

"She's incomplete, very little blood." She sighed giving Syrus a sorrowful glance. "She has organs missing. I doubt Caine is orchestrating this."

"He did call them gifts." Gwen spoke up her voice a little shaky. "Somebody gave them to him."

Sherri nodded, "We need to find out what happened to them after they got into that Limo. Caine isn't the type to associate himself with human women. Somebody has to be though, somebody's calling the shots." She sighed, "First things first though, Tony should be wrapped before her mother picks her up."

Castor nodded. "If you'll help me with that, though Syrus you need to lead the prayer, but you know that."

Syrus gave a grim, lackluster nod. "She needs anointing as well, Sherri? I will need her canobic jars as well. She will be given a royal funeral." he looked at Gwen. "Now what about us?"

Castor sighed. "After your duties are finished I suggest you both go and relax. I don't need you charging in half-cocked and with less than zero of your powers. You need to mourn and this might be the only time to do so." he looked at the other guys who all nodded. "We won't let you down, you know that."

Syrus nodded. "Directions from the goddess?" he asked Sherri.

"To do exactly as Cass asked." She spoke softly. "I'll contact her this evening to see if she can direct us further in this."

Syrus nodded and looked at Gwen. He took her hand and led her out of the room and into the hallway. Seeing where she stood in all this, and if she was ok. "Gwen..." he started and gave her a forlorn look.

She nodded. "Its ok." she threw herself into his arms hugging him tightly.

He held her, took the comfort that she offered and returned what he could. "I need to do this. Tony deserves to be honored." he said quietly.

"I know, I'm so sorry for her... for you. What will you do?"

"It's a ceremony, and an anointing. Castor and Sherri will wrap her in muslin soaked in rosewater, and she will be anointed with the interment oils."

She nodded, "Do you want me there? I can wait here if you wish; I don't want to get in the way."

He looked at her and smiled a very small smile. "You are my Keeper, and I would love the support of you there. But I understand that you might need the space, especially with all this death."

She shook her head, "No I don't want to be alone. I need you. Especially with all this death."

He bent his head and kissed her fiercely pouring all the affection he felt for her into the kiss. "You won't be alone Gwen. Thank you."

"Neither will you."

Syrus sighed and nodded and held her tighter. Strong, perfect, he could feel Isis radiating from her. It was a comfort he needed. "Come on."

Chapter Fifteen

Nathan was entertaining when Caine walked in with his perpetual scowl of a mean ass son of a bitch replace by the bright sunny disposition of a man who was content. Nathan was not happy with this development.

"And what small child did you run over on your way here?" he asked in an amused voice. Hopefully last night had gone well, and the Inferi were waiting for their call, and they would be in possession of the relic forthwith.

He looked down at the woman with her face in his lap and smirked, fisting his hand in her hair. With Carina on assignment, he had brought back an old standby, Lorelei, and she was proving to him why he needed to keep her around more often. Woman sucked cock like a fucking vacuum. The girl moaned and dug her nails into his thighs, and he hissed, enjoying the little bit of pain with his mounting pleasure.

Caine watched the woman in his bosses lap with interest, almost mesmerized. Nathan petted her head and looked down, then up at Caine. "I realize it's interesting to see a woman sucking cock, but there's more pressing matters at hand. How did last night go?"

"It went very well," he grinned happily. "The one we lost was of no consequence. Weak sheep."

"I suppose we have Stark to thank for those blunders then. They will have to be replaced. And how are our three... guests fairing?"

"Ah," he frowned. "Well we had something of an accident."

Nathan frowned and cocked his head. "Accident?" he asked in a slight hiss.

"A little one." Nathan stepped away from him moving towards the window looking out. "One of the girls sort of died. The Inferi got the message though, loud and clear."

Nathan grabbed the girl by her head and wrenched her off his throbbing erection and snarled. "What!? What the fuck did I tell you Caine!" he pushed the girl away and she sobbed gathering her clothes and scooting to the side. Nathan stood and righted himself, then strode the three steps to where Caine was standing and grabbed him by his throat. He slammed him up against the wall of glass that was his windows. "What happened, and don't fucking lie to Caine or so help me, you will pay for their life with your own."

Caine glared down at him chocking, his body rigid. "I lost my temper." he relaxed forcibly. "The Egyptian's little whore deserved it. The other two are still breathing and the Inferi got the message with her body."

Nathan saw red. "Excuse me? Caine what have you done?"

"They shot a film for him the night they were taken..." he choked out. "I added to it... Documenting her death... It was the unimportant one."

Nathan squeezed harder then let the Div fall to the ground and kicked him. "You son of a bitch! What did I fucking tell you! They are all important! You have just fucked us into a position they didn't want us in you fucking lunatic!" it was rare that Nathan lost his temper to this degree, normally settling for taking his anger out on a willing woman. But Caine had crossed a line that the Velns were adamant about. Killing the female was going to be a deal breaker, one that Nathan was not taking the heat for. If someone had to answer to Nebacanezzar it would be Caine.

"What position?" Caine spluttered not moving to defend himself. "If anything it's stronger... You wanted the Egyptian distracted and not thinking of the Keeper."

Nathan growled. "Caine, you have the fucking memory of a goldfish! Nebacanezzar said not to kill any of them. Your God, our boss, said not to, and you went and fucking did it!"

"I..." he growled his black eyes seething. "I lost my fucking temper... Now lay off me." he growled rolling away and getting to his feet. "I want the Egyptian in pain. He's in it. Fuck our boss Nathan... What does he know about here? I sent the message... They got it."

"I'll relay your felicitations to him next time I'm ripped through the fucking veils to deal with your incompetence. I don't know what this is going to drive the Inferi to do, but if we were specifically told not to do something, and then it happens, then it stands to reason that the outcome won't work in our favor. Did that go through your head? They are omniscient you know."

He snorted. "They're gods. Not infallible. This will work..."

The man's stupidity knew no bounds. Nathan looked over at Lorelei and went to her offering his hand. She took it and he lead her over to the couch where he sat down and brought her with him. She didn't even have to be told what he wanted. She perched on his thigh and set to work nibbling on his neck while her hand massaged him through his pants. She whimpered when his hand came up to toy with her newly erect nipple. She worked his pants open and then smirked at him waiting for direction.

Nathan patted the leather peaking out between his legs and she moved to the space he wanted her at. He palmed her breasts and rolled her nipples as he put his attention back on Caine who was frowning severely.

"Well I'll leave you two alone and get back to my, very much alive, charges."

"We aren't finished here Caine. What did you send him exactly?" Lorelei moaned and reached back to touch him and he stopped touching her.

"Like I said, a video." he took a disk front his pocket. "She was still alive when I started. I spoke to him then drained her blood. Its potent stuff... I have some for you. I took her organs too. They're full of power and it means he can't bury her properly."

Nathan frowned. "Bring the organs and the blood to Luther." He watched Caine start to protest and raised his hand to silence him. "This isn't negotiable. They will be used for important magic, and perhaps this sacrifice on your part will keep the Velns from skinning you alive."

Caine wince clearly deciding that he didn't want to be at the mercy of the Velns. "As you wish my lord. I'll send it immediately."

"Yes. Now, have you found the goddamn junkie yet?"

"Not yet, Stark said he'd look into it as it was his problem. I believe the Inferi have him though... The one they call Arlo tends toward the junkie side."

"Right." Lorelei gasped as he pinched her nipples hard. "Now Caine, do not touch the other two priestesses. I want information, but there's other ways to get it. Get the info from them."

"What do you want to know?"

"Anything you can get out of them about the Egyptian, the Inferi, anything. The smallest comment is often the most interesting. I would taunt them with a Keeper... get them thinking he won't come for them because he's found his Keeper and you'll see the songbirds sing."

"I'll get everything I can. I'll record it all too... Then you can pick up on anything I can't."

Nathan nodded. "Then get to it. Once they find that message Caine, our time table is cut in half."

Caine nodded. "I'll get to it then." he started to the door.

Nathan watched him leave and didn't say a word as the door closed and then pulled Lorelei back into his embrace. "Now, where were we?"

Chapter Sixteen

Syrus parked the R32 in front of his brownstone and shut the engine off, then turned to Gwen who sat smiling at him. His heart ached as he looked at her, feeling guilty about the issues at hand. One of his priestesses was dead, and while he appreciated her, he didn't feel one tenth of what he did for Gwen. He was upset about losing Tony, but he also knew that in this war, there were casualties, and his camp had long been without. Not saying that he was cosmically due, but he had the most to lose.

The Egyptians had made provisions for him, to keep him safe, sane and worshipped, but they didn't have the foresight that evil would evolve and not strike in a physical sense. Yes, the Egyptians were the most schooled in poisons but when it came to psychotropic drugs, they were at a loss. None of their training could help them when they were tied up and tortured like Tony was. He sent a silent prayer to his mother, Nut, and to Horus, that one of his most loyal would be taken care of on the other side.

Gwen was amazing through the ceremony, even helping with the wrapping and with the anointing, as Isis did for their fallen favorites in times past. It was as if she was working from memory. He didn't have to tell her anything, she just knew.

Both Castor and Sherri were pleased that she took such an active role, but none were more pleased then Syrus. She proved to him yet again that she was ready to be his; ready to live in the world she had been thrust into.

For that alone, she deserved to see the brownstone, but Syrus knew that even if she hadn't helped him physically, and just was his spiritual support, they would be standing in front of the building he had longed to truly call home.

He got out of the car and walked silently around to Gwen's door and opened it, helping her out onto the sidewalk. He turned as he closed the door and wrapped his arm around her waist. They looked up to the building that he had called his private sanctuary for the past seventy-five years. This was the first woman he had ever brought back with him, the only woman that should ever set foot in his private residence. It would be hers as well, if they bonded, and she agreed to be his Keeper in full. He knew this, and even though he had had little hope of ever finding her once his relic went missing, he still decorated his place in the way he hoped his Keeper would enjoy.

He kissed her sweetly on the cheek. "I can't wait to show you." He murmured and then guided her up the steps to the front doors. Minutes later he opened them after using the keypad thumbprint scan and whisked her inside. The foyer of the brownstone was tile, as it was for most of the city, done in blues, and greens. The tile went half way up the wall, while the rest of the wall was done in black, to really accentuate the iridescence of the tiles. He smiled and took off his sneakers and helped her out of hers when she gave him an incredulous look.

"Trust me; carpet is so thick you would be amiss to not feel it for what it is." He winked and they walked into an anteroom, complete with a round settee and the stairs that went to the upper floors. The wood was dark, cherry and walnut, and the settee was rich suede in oxblood. The floor was a dark stone, almost slate.

The door beyond opened into a brighter room, with windows along the far wall, covered in sheer silver and black curtains.

Two overstuffed couches in dove gray suede, in front of a large fireplace, dominated the room. A fifty-two inch plasma hung above it and the walls were done in charcoal and a cerulean blue.

He smirked and leaned against the back of one of the couches and looked down. "See? Carpet is totally lush. Something like five inches deep, and the color is wine, I think. Sherri helped me pick the color out. Said it was beyond decadent."

"It really is," She smiled wriggling her toes in the fibers, "Wow. I didn't think carpet this deep existed. It's amazing."

"So you approve?" he asked worried about how she was going to like the place.

"I do, it's wonderful."

He nodded. "Fireplace works too."

"It does?" she shook her hear looking around. "I can't believe you live here. It's like something you see on TV speaking of which, I've never seen a TV that size before. Not in a house."

He looked over his shoulder and chuckled. "Dezi says the only thing a TV that big is good for is pseudo-live porno."

"And I'm sure he'd know." She laughed.

"True. Though I'll be honest I haven't even turned it on." he shrugged. "Come on, lots more to see." They went back through the anteroom and he motioned to another door close to the stairs. "Kitchen is through there, along with the small breakfast nook. Kitchen is big though, and you can get to it though the living room too, though I had the door disguised as a wall panel." He grinned. "I'll show you upstairs."

"Secret wall panels," She smiled, "This is exciting."

He laughed and they scaled the carpet-covered stairs. Upstairs, Gwen was presented with three doors. Syrus grinned and shook his head.

"Now before you get all 'I'll take door number two Alex' on me, lemme tell you. To your right is my office, the center a closet and to the left is the bedroom."

"So door number two would be out, though I do have to snoop there eventually... what's in your office?"

"The usual. Surveillance equipment, a command consol for the security system, my computer, porn free of course, and a TV."

She laughed, "Oh the usual. Snap. That's exactly what's in my office as well. So the closet?"

"You can snoop in the closet all you want." He walked over to the closet and opened the door. "See? Jackets." he winked.

"Ah but what kind of jackets?"

He closed the door and went to her kissing her sweetly. "The kind that I can hide a lot of weapons in."

"Mmmmm." she smiled at him. "So I guess that just leaves the bedroom?"

He winked and walked her to the double doors that locked the bedroom suite away from the world and opened them, exposing the room no one except him and his decorator has ever seen.

Done in rich browns and tans, it resembled his bedroom in Abydos, his earthbound and ethereal palace. The walls were muted mustard; the overlarge bed in browns gold and bronze. The bedclothes were sumptuous silks and Egyptian cotton, with tons of throw pillows and a carved headboard. The wall behind the bed had what looked like a fresco of the Nile, and the wall in front of it a large sand stone fireplace.

There were overlarge pillows and beanbags strewn about, over thick throw rugs, and the floor was laid sandstone to match the fireplace. He walked in with her by his side and grinned. "The stone has heaters under it, so it's never cold."

"Wow..." she looked around in awe. "Just wow... I've never seen anything like this before."

"I should hope not." he grinned and wrapped himself around her from behind. "Otherwise my idea of a one of a kind Egyptian bedroom would have gone to waste."

"Well it certainly hasn't." she moved to her knees running her hands over the stone. "I love it. It seems, familiar somehow. Homey for all its grandeur."

Pride swelled in his chest and he grinned. "Really? Well go on, explore..." he winked and leaned against the wall.

She did, moving through the room feeling all the different textures.

She looked stunning among the finery, and his brain was flashing images of her naked on the bed, calling to him, of her lying back on the large Love Sack beanbag, sweating and moaning for him, of her on the chaise in the corner on her knees as he took her. He watched her with interest and reached down and adjusted himself, enjoying the ideas but enjoying seeing how she reacted to this haven he created for her more.

She ended up sitting on the bed amongst the silks and cotton. "How often do you stay here?" She asked him petting the pillows.

"Never. I mean I haven't ever slept here."

"Why not?" She looked puzzled getting off of the bed.

He pushed off from the wall and walked toward her. "Because I didn't have you."

"Ah... well that makes a whole lot of sense."

"You like it though?" he asked and wrapped his arms around her.

"Of course I do." She cuddled into him. "So you plan on spending the night here tonight?"

"I hope *we* were planning on spending the night here. Together."

"Oh we are... I was just checking. I'm still holding my IOU for great morning sex."

He smirked. He was too. Her body was a temptation he wouldn't have to hold back from... a temptation that he could heartily indulge in. "You wanna see the bathroom?"

She nodded grinning. "Uh huh."

He led her into the bathroom, through a dimly lit doorway, and smiled at her response. The Jacuzzi tub was large enough for two, and everything in the bathroom was the same sandstone as in the bedroom. Large potted ferns sat in all the corners, and there were many, the room an odd shape, almost a hexagon, but with a small hallway. Gwen walked around looking at everything, her face awash with the soft light of the room, coming from the recessed lamps. He had five foot pillar candles in green, peach and cranberry, and smaller pillars as well on the steps that lead up to the tub and strewn about the room. It was opulence in its purest form.

"My god..." She shook her head looking around. "Its amazing." she swallowed hard.

He let out a breath he didn't realize he was holding and smiled, the grin reaching his eyed. "Really?"

"How could it not be?"

"Well it's yours."

"Mine?" She frowned shaking her head. "No it's yours..."

He went to her. "No, it's yours, This house is a present to my Keeper, a place for us to be together, a safe haven, decadent, wonderful...You're my Keeper, the woman that holds my relic, and my soul. And my heart. Everything is yours, well except for the lucky charms in the pantry. The cereal is mine." he winked.

She blinked at him shaking her head. "You're insane."

"Yeah age does that to a guy." he kissed her. "Why do you think I'm crazy?"

"You can't just give me a house... I don't want the place, I want you." She kissed him back wrapping her arms around him. "And if you're in the house at the time then that would be great too."

"How about you getting both?" he grinned and kissed her again.

"Damn your lips should be illegal. I'll only stay here if you do."

"I sure as shit ain't going anywhere, not when I have you here with me." he lifted her up and wrapped her legs around his waist. "I need you Gwen."

"Let's go to that giant bed of ours." She grinned taking his face him her hands kissing him.

A finer idea he had never heard. He turned and left the bathroom carefully traversing the minefield of pillows and bean bags and made it to the bed with nary a stumble. A smirk tugged at him. "You know I had some ideas when I bought those things. I didn't expect them to impede my walking."

"Ideas?" She asked wrapping her arms around him and nibbling on his neck.

He grinned. "Lewd and illicit ones involving lots of naughty sexual positions."

"Tell me." she gasped as he let her down onto the bed.

He stood to his full height and pulled his hooded sweatshirt off, then his t-shirt. He stood there half naked, and unbuttoned the top button of his hip hugger 501's and watched her eyes traverse his chest, linger on the piercing in his bellybutton and then lower to the Black flame tattoo.

"Tell you what? How I want you naked lying on that large bean bag chair, your thighs apart, with my face between them? Or maybe with you on your knees, pillows under you as I sink into your soft body..."

"Mmmmm yes." She licked her lips pulling her top off and throwing it to the floor. "All of that... I want all of that."

He smirked and looked her over. "No more bras, I insist..."

"Not even sexy ones?" She asked taking hers off and throwing it after her top. Her jeans slipped down her hips to her feet and she nimbly stepped out of them. Left in just her silk panties she got to her knees before him boldly taking the edge of his jeans and pulling him to her. "Tell me about this." She traced over his tattoo with her tongue.

He shivered, the touch setting his body temperature to skyrocket. "It's a symbol of my power. Dark fire is my main power, something I haven't had access to since my godhead was bound to the relic."

"What exactly are your powers now?"

"Same as the rest of the guys. Read minds, rapid healing, heightened abilities like running, jumping..."

Her eyes rolled up to look at him, "Can you read my mind?"

"No, though I would love to... With the girls I could when I concentrated, but I never needed to. I usually just use it to talk to the other guys. With you, a real partnership means that both are independent of the other. If I could read it, it wouldn't be fair. So why did you blush? And why are those pants still on?"

"Because I'm taking my time, that's why." She pulled him to her, her tongue once again flickering over him.

"You're stunning sitting there you know that?"

She grinned wickedly, her fingers playing with the top button. "That's the desired effect."

He shivered and growled. "Naughty Keeper..." he said with a gasp. "Get me out of these so I can show you what I have been dying to do to you all day."

"Mmmmm with pleasure." She undid his jeans slipping then down his narrow hips.

He was naked in a matter of seconds and grinned. "Now, about that scrap of silk..." he motioned to the underwear.

"I think you should take care of that." She lay back on the bed offering it up to him.

Syrus loved how sexy she was, how unashamed. Such a change in her in two days, though it suited her. This was real; this was the woman she was meant to be. He leaned in and nibbled a line down her stomach and grabbed the silk with his teeth and yanked, ripping them off.

"Damn that was sexy." She purred cupping her breasts and teasing her nipples.

"I don't think you should wear panties either. Unless you don't mind them getting ripped off."

"I don't mind at all... not if you always do it with your teeth." She pulled him up into a kiss her legs wrapping around him.

The woman was a tiger. "You know I quite like the real you... that timid wallflower thing you had going on didn't suit you love."

"I've been through a lot since then. This is the new Gwen... I guess the real one, whatever that means."

"I would say so... and you're going to go through a lot more... but that's for later. Tonight, I need to feel you, I need to bond with you Gwen." He kissed her shoulder and started nibbling at her collarbone.

"Hell yeah we're going to bond..." she moaned and pushed against him. "Wait you don't mean that in a sex way do you?"

"Be my Keeper fully. Share my life with me; unlock my godhead, and my powers."

"And just how do we do that?" She asked running her hands down his back.

He nibbled down her body and looked up, his tongue finding her nipple and laved it, then sucked hard on it, his hands on her hips.

"Mmmmm very nice," she arched into him. "But I take it there's more to it than that?"

Syrus chuckled. "Oh that has nothing to do with it... I just couldn't resist."

"Oh... so how do we do it then? How do you make me your Keeper?"

He grinned. "You already are my Keeper. You accepted the relic, and it resonates my life force and yours. But to bond... It's instinct..."

"That's not an answer... You don't know do you?" She pulled back to look at him. "I mean it's not like you've done it before."

"I have no fucking clue. So I'm going to go with the instinct answer. God you smell so good..." he nuzzled the swell of her breast.

"You do too." she scratched lightly down his back. "So instinct? That sounds easy enough."

"Let's hope so." he murmured and nibbled down her torso, letting his tongue play lightly on her hipbone and then the soft dip of her abdomen. His hands went to her thighs and he parted them, settling between them as his mouth dipped lower. He tasted her.

Her body arched under him.

He made quick work of bringing her to the edge and reared up pulling her hips flush with his own as he sank back on his knees. Her thighs hugged him, cradled his cock as he watched her fully.

"Ummm that's very sneaky." She panted hard, bucking her hips up to him looking for some friction. "Very good and very sneaky..." She sat up, gliding against him her arms wrapping around his neck.

"Yeah it's about to get better." he shifted them both, sinking her down on him with a satisfied groan. Nothing felt better than this... nothing felt more right.

"That's it," she moaned riding him hard. "Mmmmm so much better."

Syrus kissed her letting her take the lead and find her pleasure. She rode him harder and his hands on the small of her back, keeping her close to him, ensuring as much sensation as they can both muster.

Her cries became louder as she neared the edge. "Harder... Please!" She dug her fingers into his shoulders.

Syrus growled and gasped. "Baby your driving this car... Take what you need, give yourself over to me." he growled and bucked hard into her. He reached between then and worked her with his thumb, while his other hand still held her at the small of her back. Words flowed from him, words he didn't ever remember using, but knew within the depths of his soul. "Tell me you want this; open your soul to me."

"It's yours, completely..." she cried out, taking his face in her hands kissing him deeply. Her tongue worked into his mouth joining with his as he filled her.

Syrus was close to losing it, but he wasn't going to shame himself and her in the process. He kissed her hard, moaned into her mouth and then he felt it.

A hard tingle invaded his body in one instant and they both exploded, shattering into the haze of the room. His powers rushed back, burned his skin and soul, with her essence and his. They were one, a mix of emotion. He felt her there, in his mind, in his body. His body got the old familiar feeling of warmth, dark warmth and his eyes opened, and he panted. "Holy shit."

"You can say that again..." she laughed breathlessly.

He kissed her hard. "Fucking epic."

"How do you feel?" she gasped, astonishment clear on her face, "I know how you feel, I can feel you... you feel amazing."

He grinned. "Yeah so do you. And check this out..." he closed his eyes and willed his full powers to his call. His hand conjured a dark opaque flame, with a small ball of what looked like electricity in the center. "I'm back."

She gasped, "Dark fire? Is it hot?" She lifted her hand to it without touching it.

"I don't know... but you can touch it... it's part of you too now..." he pointed to the tattoo that mirrored his under her bellybutton. She was Isis now, his equal, his wife. She just had to access that part of herself.

"I didn't sign up to get inked." She looked down at it in surprise then looked over her shoulder to see if there was one on the small of her back.

"There is." He paused, " I think it's how we are linked. Fucking sweet hell it's sexy..."

"Hmm well it is on you. So what does it do? The fire?"

"On me it's functional. On you it's fucking sexy. The fire is multifunctional... I mostly have used it for fighting. But... there's something I have always wanted to do... and I can now I think."

"Can what?" she cocked her head curiously.

He smirked. "Lie back."

"Ummm ok." She gave him a dubious look while lying back.

He leaned over her and licked a line up her torso, starting at the tip of her little tattoo. He then placed his fingers on her stomach and willed his fire on to her skin. The little flames licked over her skin and he moved back and watched them as they danced.

She gasped, writhing on the bed. "God that feels so good..." She linked to his mind letting him feel a ghost's version of the flames licking over him.

He grinned and moved his fingers, sending the flames up her body and concentrated them on her nipples. They licked at them, twirled and pranced on her skin. "And that? You like that?"

She cried out fisting the bed sheets sweat beading on her skin. "Yes damn..."

He watched her body respond, and sent a few of the flames lower, back past the little tattoo, to play on the sensitive flesh between her thighs. "Goddess this is erotic."

She thrashed around on the sheets as the flames licked over her, building with intensity. Her breathing peaked as she fast approached her climax.

Syrus groaned. "Oh that's it... Sweet hell Gwen that's hot..."

"Syrus!".

He grinned and watcher her tremors fade. The look of satisfaction on her face, the rise and fall of her chest as she panted... He leaned in and kissed her, pulling the fire back into himself,. It felt as if it was happy to be of use again, even if it was a new use.

"And it has other uses you say?"

"Yeah... Mostly to burn and kill people, though I'm really liking this new one." He kissed her again.

"So, my lovely Keeper, was it everything you hoped it would be?"

"Mmmmm and much more." She reached up to kiss him. "And you?"

"I have my godhead, my woman to share it with, and a Keeper who understands me. I couldn't be more happy."

"Perfect." She yawned stretching out. "And tomorrow is another day."

"And tomorrow, and tomorrow and tomorrow..." he pulled her to him, lying down on the bed.

She curled up against him and rested her head on his chest. "And after that too. You think Ansley got on ok with Kaid today?"

"I think so. I mean neither of us got a phone call that someone was killed..." He held her closer and sighed. "Is it bad that I'm so damn tired from making love to you that I can't even move to get us under the covers?"

"Ummm nope." She kissed his neck, nuzzling him. "It's very good." She sat up pulling the covers over them both.

Syrus nestled her into the crook of his arm, spooning her. "I'm going to need my sleep, I did promise you some fantastic morning sex." he murmured. "You sure you like the place?"

She laughed, "I do. It's like one of those places you dream about staying in but never quite make it to. So familiar, I can't shake the feeling like I have been here before. I love it... Ansley's gonna be so jealous."

Syrus choose to let her feelings go. She would figure it out on her own. Now his godhead was unlocked, and Isis was out of the bag, she would figure it out soon enough.

He felt Isis, felt the little piece of her lock into place in Gwen, the missing piece of her soul, the one that she needed. It wouldn't be long now. "I don't doubt that. And what are you going to tell her about us? This is much quicker then whirlwind romance..."

"Eh she'll get it. All she cares about is that you're not Tom and that you treat me the way I deserve. And that you're super hot with hot friends helps her decision along nicely. Ansley's pretty shallow when it comes to the details. As long as I'm happy she won't dig too much into things. With any luck she'll spend most of her time chasing after Kaid or one of the others. Maybe Blaine, I like him."

"Blaine has some serious issues, but yeah, she would be a good distraction for any of them. Well maybe not Castor. Son of a bitch is so starchy that he farts flat handkerchiefs. Though I doubt she will get very far with Kaid. He doesn't indulge." He sighed. "I know this is real, but Ansley isn't stupid. She is going to question it someday, especially with you moving in here."

"Then I'll tell her that I don't feel safe at my house anymore. I wouldn't be lying to her, I really don't and it's with good cause. She'll accept my choices. It's not like I'm quitting my job either. I'm still going to do all the things I used to. I'll just be happier when I do it. I'm still keeping all my goals I might even go back to school."

"You should. Anything you wanna do I will support it."

"Can you..." She frowned when a thought occurring to her. "Well, can we have children? Is it possible? Should we be using protection?"

"Already talking kids and I haven't even proposed yet..." he kissed her shoulder.

"I think the answer to that is yes, we can but we don't have to worry about that until your immortality is cemented. We can't procreate unless you can support an immortal child. The Romans and Greeks had different rules with their pantheons, but ours is adamant. No young unless both parents are immortal. A human couldn't support the child, Hell we have people with dog heads and shit. Not exactly easy to pass lemme tell you. And when we do have to worry, it's only at certain times. Tiamat has her own rules as well."

"Ah ok... just checking." she nodded, "I don't want kids just now but eventfully I'd like to."

"And you shall have all you desire love." "Then it's a very good thing I'm not demanding."

"Even if you were it wouldn't matter to me. I now have two reasons to be on this earth. Keep the Velns from coming forth, and spoiling my Keeper."

"Hmmm you better watch or I'll get to like being spoiled, come to expect it."

"That's the plan pet. See? You're already hip to my game."

She laughed. "You plan to make me demanding and bratty?"

"No I plan to keep you happy and content."

"Ah there's a big difference." She kissed the tip of him nose. "Well right now I need sleep." She yawned. "Someone wore me out but I'm very happy and extremely content."

"Sleep." he nuzzled her, and settled in, content himself with how the night worked out. He had his Keeper, his powers and the woman that was quickly becoming the love of his life. Tomorrow they would come back to earth, and deal with the issues at hand, but tonight, he could look towards the future without any issues, even if it was just a lie.

Chapter Seventeen

Gwen watched him sleep peacefully with a small smile curving his lips. She'd been awake for some time now propped up on her elbow. Syrus looked so innocent while he slept, a total contrast to his awake self. The sheets pooled around them both covering very little and, even though his bottom half was partially covered, the teases of his flesh were just too much for her to bear. She could feel him in her head now. Not in a scary big brothers watching you kind of way, but in a comforting warmth sort of way. They'd never be alone again. His powers were restored to him making him whole again. Her heart had just about broken when she'd seen the look in his face as he'd called his fire.

They'd both slept in his giant bed after making love. The room around her a lush paradise beyond anything she'd ever dreamed of. That he'd never spent the night there made their time shared even more special. He'd taken her in and showed her around; even let her snoop in his closet, though she'd made a note to go back in for a proper snooping.

Indulging herself, she ran her fingertip down his chest to see if he stirred. He didn't. Grinning wickedly to herself, she sucked her finger into her mouth then repeated the process, leaving a wet trail down his chest, circling around his belly button and lower.

He groaned softly under his breath but otherwise didn't wake up any. Now was the time for her to play with her thought from the other morning. She pulled the sheet away from him revealing him in all his glory.

It didn't take her long to lie between his legs and lookup the length of his body.

Still no movement.

She nuzzled him, taking his cock into her hands massaging gently as it grew in size, hardening before her. She'd always hated doing this with Tom but Syrus was different. She breathed in his sweet masculine scent before gently sucking the tip on him into her mouth.

His hips arched and he growled, his hand went to her hair and caressed her. "Fucking sweet hell Gwen..." he licked his lips.

She loved that he knew her enough after so little time to only mention her name, not the several others that had shared his body over the years. Not his wife's, but hers. He wanted her. She purred a smile up at him, sending vibrations through his shaft as she took more of him into her mouth. With her hands, she kneaded the soft flesh of his thighs.

His eyes opened and looked down at her with a sleepy grin gracing his lips. "Now that is the best sight to see in the morning love. Goddess your talented." he arched again and hissed.

He felt like wet silk under her tongue, so smooth and hot. She rolled her eyed up to him. *I wanted to do this the other morning.* She sent the thought to him wondering if he'd pick up on it.

And I wanted you too... He sent back and moaned. *Sweet darkness you're amazing.*

So high on the praises. I guess I better earn them then. She bobbed her head up and down sucking his harder applying more pressure to him. The feel of him passing though her lips drew another moan from her throat. She was already soaking wet and on the edge. Her body thrummed as she moved faster, one hand palming his balls, massaging them gently.

Syrus swore and shuddered. "Baby as much as this feels amazing... I think you need some attention too..." he grinned. "Swing around..."

Kinky. She chuckled into his head. She moved around so she lay on top of him, never once breaking her contact with him.

Syrus groaned and pulled her down to his face, her thighs close around his head. His tongue found her quickly, sucking her sweetness into his mouth with a relieved moan. He worked her tirelessly, lovingly.

She cried out around him, redoubling her efforts as she felt the tension mount in her own body.

Come with me... he called to her in his mind, his voice a sensual caress.

His silken voice brought her over, sending her orgasm crashing into her as she sucked desperately on him.

Syrus moaned and bucked up into her, his body following hers over. He held her close, kept working her slick flesh as she shuddered over him.

She moaned around him, swallowing everything he had to offer her. "Mmmmm..." She pulled off him once he was finished. "And a very good morning to you." she rolled slowly off him, feeling spent and boneless..

Syrus chuckled. "Very good indeed. Ummm." he stretched. "Come here."

She crawled up into his arms cuddling him. "We should do this most mornings."

"Every morning." he pulled her up and kissed her. "You are quite addictive love."

"Speak for yourself god-boy" She kissed him back.

Syrus laughed and then sighed. "Ummm I don't remember the last time I have slept so good... or was woken up so perfectly."

"It's quite a bed, I'm glad as hell you haven't used it with anyone but me."

"Me too. I'm glad I waited till I found you. Though truth be told, this room has gone through several incarnations."

"Oh yeah? No black pvc I hope."

He laughed. "No, that's Dezi's fetish. I was never happy with it. But when I got it to a replica of my old quarters in my palace Abydos long ago, it stuck."

"It's beautiful." She stretched her arms over her head. "I've never been to Egypt but this is what I would expect."

Yes you have... but you will figure that out soon enough. "Back when I was a ruling god, it was, well minus the giant bean bags." he winked.

She nodded, looking around with even more appreciation. "I don't suppose they had those back then."

"No, though I will say that the sheets have gotten much better. Four hundred thread count Egyptian cotton was never even heard of then. It's a luxury I believe we both like?" he kissed her again, toying with her nipple.

"Mmmmm..." she moaned her agreement, arching into him.

Syrus leaned into her again, his mind telling her he intended on round two when his phone rang. "Shit." he grinned. The song, Black Sabbaths *Iron Man* blared into their quiet room. "It's Arlo, Answer it will you baby?"

"Why me?" She asked grabbing the phone and answering it. "Hello?"

"Now that is a voice to hear first thing in the morning. Sure I can't entice you to the dark side? I do have cookies... and edible underwear."

She laughed, "Like the sound of cookies but edible underwear squicks me out. You'd do better enticing women to the dark side with puppies and muffins."

"Puppies and muffins... got it... though the muffin part might not go so well seeing the connotations to a woman's... You know what? Never mind it is a bit early and I haven't been to sleep yet."

"Did you find anything?"

"A little. Tell your lover that Dezi is on his way over, and he's expecting either breakfast or a threesome. I will let you decide which, though if you pick the latter, I'm going to be jealous."

"Oh I don't think a threesomes on the cards," She looked to Sy, "But I'm pretty sure breakfast is."

"Whatever. Just tell him to lower the goddamn static shield ok? And I'll see you later sex pot." he hung up.

Syrus gave her an amused look. "So what did the Etruscan have to say? I think I just caught the word threesome in there. I hope you said no."

"I did. Dezi's coming over and he wants breakfast and I agree with him. What's a static shield?"

"Arlo's attempt at being funny. He swears both Kaid and I have far too much security at our places, but where either of ours haven't been broken into, his has. Ass. So breakfast? How does pancakes sound?"

"Pancakes work." She swung her legs over the bed and sat up. "Don't suppose there's a robe lying around anywhere?"

"Bathroom, down the little hall, there's a closet, robes, sleep pants and tank tops." he winked and shook his head, his sleep tousled hair falling about his face. "Grab me the black ones too if you can, I don't need Dezi freaking out from seeing my ass again. Last time was total drama."

"I can't imagine it'd bother anyone, I love your naked ass." She laughed moving down the hall to the closet and picking out a few things.

"Besides Dezi strikes me as someone comfortable with nudity." She threw him the pants while pulling on a smaller pair and a cami.

A scoff came from the bedroom. "Yes, his own, or scores of women. I remember when he walked in on me dressing a while ago, flipped out. Shouldn't have walked in if he didn't wanna see cock." he winked and went to the door.

"Is that a rule you have? Along with the no dibs one." She followed him out. "You know you're still going to show me the garden, maybe after breakfast."

"True, the stairs are in the office if you feel so inclined... Pop up, I'll get breakfast started."

"Oh no, I'll save that for later. I want to watch you work, all half naked and sexy like."

"Can't fault you there. Come on."

They walked down the stairs, the anteroom bright from the partially hidden skylight. Syrus looked up and grinned. "That skylight is actually the Lucite pond upstairs, so every once in a while the sunlight will flicker with the water when it moves. Its tranquil." He made it down the stairs and walked into the kitchen with her hot on his heels. "And I know your checking out my ass love." "What else am I supposed to do?" She gave his ass a little pat and a squeeze. "Plus it's so firm and ripe. So pancakes?"

"Buttermilk, from scratch. Nothing but the best for my Keeper...And Dezi." He snorted.

She giggled. "And Dezi... can he get in?"

"He has the codes, so yes. Why? You afraid he's going to walk in on something indecent?" He wiggled his eyebrows and set to work on the batter, pouring the flour and egg and buttermilk and used an overlarge spoon to stir it.

"No I just don't want to answer the door wearing this."

"Why not, you're stunning, love."

"Maybe to you, but I'm a mess. Plus answering the door would spoil my view of you."

"He can get in himself. And trust me, he won't think anything past the fact that you have the perkiest tits in creation, and he's jealous as fuck." He bent down, grabbing the butter spray and then set the griddle on the range on and sprayed it. "Now you want sausage, bacon? And no they aren't pork."

"Oh no?" She hopped onto a stool. "What are they?"

"Turkey." he smiled. "I meant it when I said I don't dine on swine."

"Don't even try arguing the point with him." Dezi grinned from the doorway, his eyes worked over her. "He's got a sickness in him. How anyone who hasn't had pork for... how many thousands of years has it been?" he asked then shook his head. "Not important, it's been a few, but how he can still be adamant after all these years that he dislikes it is beyond me. Food preparation has changed greatly over the years."

"I see your chipper as ever this morning Dez. So? What's the verdict? Meat or no?"

"Meat, and plenty of it, I haven't eaten all night." He rooted around in the fridge. "Any beer?"

"Dude you are not sullying my homemade pancakes with that swill. Now what happened last night?"

"Well there's good news and bad news." He grinned sitting up next to Gwen.

Syrus poured some batter on the griddle. "Well, start with the bad."

"No sign of the girl, she's a fucking ghost. Me and Arlo can find just about anyone especially if she's female but this girl... We tried all night, not one deviation but," he shook his head. "She has to be long gone by now."

"We can worry about taking this out of her ass later; I'm not so much worried about her than Caine and the girls in his tender care."

"Well that's the good news, I remembered that room. Or one like it."

"Yeah? Been there?" He flipped the pancakes and the turkey bacon.

"Yeah a couple of times, but you don't wanna hear about the crazy sex parties we had in the eighties. Most recently it was with Kaid, and no not a sex party with the fucker. It's a container, like the ones they have at the docks. When that shipment from Nepal came in for the museum, it came in a steel container. Blaine checked the surveillance that we have down there and spied the limo that we've been looking for. We've found them...we'll not exactly. But we know their general location. We'll need you to show us exactly where."

Syrus frowned. "You think I can do that?"

"Well sure, you're all powered up now aren't you?".

Syrus piled the pancakes on a plate and walked over to them. He wrapped his arm around Gwen and kissed her shoulder. "Jealous?"

"Extremely." Something dark flickered behind his eyes for a second, then he grinned brightly. "But then who wouldn't be." he grabbed a stack of pancakes, putting them on his plate. "But I promise not to fall out with ya if you keep feeding me." He lunged into the plate eating ferociously. "Congrats by the way. And good luck Gwenny, you'll need it."

"Thanks." She laughed.

Syrus inclined his head. "You should keep the good luck wishes for your own Keeper buddy. But seriously, my powers don't work like that. They might be my priestesses, but I can't feel where they are, or when they die." "Well that's fucked. I guess we'll have about a thousand containers to search then."

"Don't say that. There's a system to the containers there. Have Blaine see which ones belong to Marrow Industries, Caine is stupid enough to use one."

"I'll call him on the way back. He's probably already thought about it though."

"As well he should. Man isn't stupid. So what's the plan then?"

"Do I look like a guy with a plan?" Dezi rolled his eyes then went back to his food. "Nope, I'm a guy that's been chasing his tail all night looking for fucking Sue Storm."

"Nice analogy. Though Sue Storm isn't my type." he kissed Gwen. "Eat love; you will need your strength."

"Are you queer?" Dezi looked at her. "No offence Gwen."

"None taken, I think." Nervously, she stabbed at the pancakes before picking up a slice.

"Sue Storm was fucking hot." He gestured with the fork full of food. "Any guy would give his left nut to tap that." He waved the food-laden fork again. "Well not me, I wouldn't have to, one look at me and she'd be begging for some action. I'm better than that stretchy dude." He finally stuffed the fork into his mouth.

"I'm not even touching that one. You and your comic book obsessions."

"Eh gotta have something to pass the time when I'm not killing Div or fucking and I don't get a hangover with comics." He tipped his beer back and drained it.

Syrus laughed. "Remind me not to leave my kids with you. Ever."

"What you're having kids now? Fuck Tiamat'll be pissed as hell."

Syrus considered it. "No, but, just for future clarification."

"Ah well by that time I'll be shacked up with my ex hooker current stripper Keeper and her bunny friends." he offered to them. "You prolly wouldn't wanna leave your kids with us."

Syrus looked at him horrified. "Dez, you will not be that lucky. I guess we should get our shit together and head to HQ then? You going home or what?"

"There's nothing for me at home, I'll follow you guys into HQ."

"Pet? You wanna go get dressed? As fetching as you look in that..." "Fetching?" She laughed, shaking her head. "I'll be right back." She stood, kissing him on the cheek then retrieved her bag from the hallway where she'd left it the night before and went off to change.

Chapter Eighteen

Headquarters was quiet as they entered, and Syrus's senses were reeling. They had left the brownstone shortly after breakfast and the sights and sounds of the city were greatly enhanced now that his Godhead was back. Thankfully he had his sunglasses, or his headache would be legendary. It was going to take some getting used to.

Everything was enhanced, his sight, his hearing, sense of smell, things he didn't realize were part of him till he regained them. And his Dark Fire... Oh how he missed it. It cloaked his essence once again, his and Keeper, and bound them tightly. He would have to teach her how to call it, and how to manipulate it to do what she wanted. Those were lessons he looked forward to.

Dezi closed the door to the underground garage. Syrus heard Blaine tapping away on his keyboard. No doubt the other Inferi was hard at work doing what he did best. Syrus turned and grinned at Gwen. "Baby? Since you didn't get to take a shower at the house, you wanna hit it here? I'm going to check in with Blaine," he wrapped his arms around her waist and kissed her, "Then meet you in there? Scrub your back maybe?"

"Mmmmm a very good idea." She leaned into him, kissing him back.

"I thought so. So don't rush out of there..." His smile reached his eyes as he patted her rump. "You know the way."

"Ok but hurry, we need to talk about things... more than we did last night. I feel so different today. Good, but different."

He kissed her shoulder. "You got it."

She walked towards the living quarters and headed down the other way to Blaine's Command center. He knew why she was feeling different, but it wasn't the time to tell her, or his place. Sherri would do it, and in her own good time.

Blaine was sitting, as usual, in front of his digital surveillance equipment, both typing and writing on his ever-present notebook. There were several screens around him all playing different clips of Marrow related information. He looked at Syrus when he walked in and smiled, pushing his wire-rimmed glasses up his nose in a very Blaine like gesture. "So what's good? Dez called you right?"

"Yeah he called ahead from the car, told me to check the containers to see which are Marrow owned." He paused long enough to frown and shake his head. "Something I should have thought of. Anyway, it shouldn't take much longer to get the information."

"I trust you'll do it right." Syrus let out an exasperated sigh.

"You shouldn't." Blaine turned from him typing furiously concentrating on one of the screen pulling things up.

"Maybe, but you always seem to come through. So what got your panties in a bunch?"

"Usual." He told him his voice distant. "I'm weary; I'm just tired of... Ah ha!" he exclaimed as he found what he was looking for. "Here we go, Marrow in blue." He scrolled over a map of the dock containers, highlighting the ones owned by the company. "They own twenty or so, but only three are close enough to our cameras to have showed up." He pointed to the screen. "And they're sitting together."

"Well that helps a bit doesn't it?" he grinned. "So I'm thinking we better saddle up and save my girls, what do you think?"

"Maybe not quite so half cocked." He smirked. "Kaid called and offered to keep Gwen's friend out of the way for the night."

"I'll just bet he did." the shock in his voice was apparent. "Still I'm going to need him I think, Lord knows how much Div are going to be lurking, and since you are going to keep Gwen company..." he cracked his knuckles, "Seeing as you are out of commission anyway. Tell Kaid to leave her at the museum."

"Out of commission?" He quirked an eyebrow.

"When was the last time you went out to kill these fuckers?" "I never did, but you could put it in a nicer way. Like I'm better needed keeping the women folk safe and warm." He shrugged turning to him for the first time taking in his appearance. "Well doesn't godhood suit you, my friend?"

Syrus nodded. "Thank you. You should see Gwen, She is brimming with my dark fire already." Unable to hide the large amount of undisguised pride, he called his powers, letting his hand catch with the darkness that owned him and grinned. The flames had a slight purple color to them, indicating that Gwen was bonded to him, her soul light bleeding through his powers and into the ball of energy occupying the center of his flames. "See? It's strong, Very strong."

"Congratulations. How does it feel to be whole again?"

"Strange as hell to tell the truth. Though it will take some getting used to. Having her lurking in my head is a new feeling that's for damn sure."

"You'll get used to it."Blaine offered and laced his fingers together.

"Yeah I think we will. Speaking of Gwen, I should get back to her." He growled and pushed his mind out to her making her body tingle in her favorite places.

He heard her gasp in his head and grinned to himself. "She's about halfway through her shower."

"Well you guys might have to postpone a little longer. Tiamat wants to talk with you... Sherri's waiting. You should have heard Arlo when he realized he had to sleep alone."

Syrus winced. Arlo sleeping alone meant that Sherri had been in audience with the goddess for some time. It was a double-edged sword though. On the one hand, Tiamat looking to talk to him was good in the way that maybe shit would get cleared up, and on the other, she might be pissed. "Really?"

"Uh huh." he nodded, chewing on him bottom lip. "He threw a fit, the Roman had to set him straight." he said tightly referring to Castor. "You should go. She's been waiting a while."

"Shit. If I'm not back in fifteen, Call the guards." He left Blaine and opened his mind once more to Gwen. *Love, I'm sorry but the shower is going to have to wait. The goddess requests an audience.*

Her sigh came over loud and clear, as did the disappointment in her voice. *I guess I'm just about done in here anyway. Hurry back though; I hope she doesn't plan on stealing you away from me all the time. I might just have to have words with her.*

Good luck with that love, though I think you could give her a run for her money. He sent her a silent caress and walked towards the lone hallway of the soul Keepers domain. Their mind speak had taken him by surprise, but it made sense. He was close to the other Inferi, like brothers, and he spoke with them like that. It stood to reason someone that was the other half of his soul would be able to as well. A partnership. The right way.

Sherri's quarters were a perfect copy of the temple she presided over in the ancient world. Darkened stonewalls, sumptuous pillows and cushions, a large altar where she communed with the goddess. The only modern adornments were the recessed lighting and the large television in her anteroom with her couch and chairs for entertaining. While Arlo spent a good deal of time in the Soul Keepers Inner sanctum, Syrus had only been in the room a handful of times, and usually it was to speak with Tiamat, their goddess in charge.

Sherri was a special human, one that was so devoted to her faith, to a goddess of power, that she enjoyed the perks of her station. Powerful in her own rite, Sherri was their rock, the link to their stunted powers. While Syrus enjoyed rattling her cage, he also knew that she was special, and should be treated as such. She was the heart of the team, and she knew everything the goddess knew, and when she held a divine audience was scary.

Like now. Sherri sat in front of the altar facing him as he approached. Channeling the goddess, she was a sight to behold. Her hair wild around her head, curly and whipping with an invisible wind, and her eyes glowed a bright violet, her pupils lost among the shine.

Tiamat had a flair for the dramatic, but what threw him was watching as Sherri's skin slowly morphed from the creamy mocha it normally was into a steely grey, with scrolls visible over all her exposed skin, which was a lot. When she channeled the goddess, Sherri was sky clad, except for the hammered gold collar she wore, as proof of her loyalty and devotion to her goddess.

Syrus kept his distance, falling to his knees onto a crimson pillow, then placed his hands in his lap.

Normally he would show up for an audience with the goddess in his old ceremonial robes, but they were pressed for time.

He hoped she would overlook his blue leather pants and black fitted shirt, and of course the weapons.

"It is an honor, Goddess, mother of all above and below, to be in your presence this night." He bowed his head and waited for her to speak, steeling himself against the resonation that came when the goddess communicated.

"I'm sure." The goddess drawled sarcastically. "As it always is Osiris."

He nodded. "May I ask why you have chosen tonight to endure physical form?"

"No, you may not, but you're intelligent enough to figure it out for yourself."

"Which is why I said may. What will you have of me Goddess?"

"Tell me of the past few days Osiris." She ordered, moving Sherri's body out of her kneeling position to sit cross-legged in front of him.

"I'm sure you know I found my Keeper, and I suppose I have you to thank, as I did when I was ordered to take Arlo's run. Three of my priestesses have been taken, one, Antonia Ormand, is dead. I'm hopeful for getting the other two back intact, and now that I have my godhead back, I believe it's possible."

"It is, but you must give up your relic to the Div. Things are changing. Now that you have found your Keeper, things must happen quickly. I had hoped for another few centuries. Isis was always an impatient one." she sighed, waving her hand in an odd gesture. "No matter, now is the time that we must be the most vigilant."

Another few centuries? Was she out of her fucking mind? As it was, the guys were all losing hope, Syrus thought it came at the right time. "My relic? Goddess, I rarely protest, but I just found my wife again, and the relic keeps us bound. I won't lose her. Not again. "

"And now this is where I tell you to do as your told and kill our communication," Her eyes burned to a darker violet, "However our bonds are weakening and we cannot afford for you to do something rash. I'll ask you to trust me; this is a sacrifice that you must make. If you do not you will lose everything."

He nodded. "Yes goddess... But I should ask..."

"If you must."

"Should something horrible happen, Please watch over Gwen." he looked right at her. "I couldn't lose the love of my life Goddess, not again. And I won't. I need her. I have done my time."

"You won't lose her, not if you do the right thing. She will be looked after in any event, of that you have my word. Now go and contact the foot soldier, no doubt he's getting impatient."

He nodded and stood. "A blissful night to you dear Goddess. And I will send Arlo in to tend to Sherri."

"See that you do."

He turned and felt the goddess leave the room, as all the air got sucked out of room and then was pushed back in.

Sherri took a gasping breath collapsed forward, her breathing heavy as she coughed.

He left the room quickly, knowing the Soul Keeper wouldn't welcome his help, but would be craving attention from The Etruscan God who normally shared her bed. He made it to Arlo's room and knocked. "Arlo? Sherri needs you." he continued on and heard Arlo's door open seconds later from behind him. Syrus made it back to his own room and walked in, locking the door behind him. The lights were low but he didn't see Gwen. Figuring she was still in the bathroom he walked to it.

Gwen stood in front of the mirror wrapped in a towel studying her reflection.

"See something you like love?"

She met his eyes, "I do now your here. You didn't take very long. I was expecting you gone for hours. I take it you don't travel far to meet the goddess?"

"She communicates through Sherri, it's quite daunting actually. She had something to decree, then she was gone."

"Anything important? We don't have to name our first child after her do we? Somehow Tiamat just doesn't have a childish ring to it. But I could go with Tia... for a girl." She smiled turning to him. "You ok?"

"Kinda. She told me I have to give Caine the relic." he went to her.

"Oh..."

"Yeah." he blew out a breath slowly.

"Well it's not like it was mine to start with and we have to save the girls. Will it undo what we did last night?"

"I don't know, and I'm hoping not. Screw my powers; I don't want to lose you." Syrus pulled her into his arms and kissed the top of her head, breathing in her clean scent. "And I won't. Not now. I still don't even know what the deal is. All I know is we have to get them back."

"We will, I have a lot of faith in you guys. I promise you won't lose me; I'll never leave you. I love you." She kissed him, clinging desperately to him.

The words resonated through him as they sunk home. She loved him. He held her close to him and kissed her harder lifting her up from the floor and turned them, sitting her down on the counter. "I love you too Gwen. You are the Keeper of my soul, my powers and my heart. It was worth the wait for you, love."

She wrapped her arms around him. "Even if you have to give all of it up but me?"

There was no insecurity in her voice telling him she already knew that answer.

"Obviously. Life isn't empty anymore. I would give it all up, my immortality, my powers and my whole world for you. But first I need to save the girls. Caine has to die."

"He does." She pulled the chain over her head her hands trembling. "Maybe once he does we can get it back?" "I'm counting on it. Come on let's get you dressed, cuz I don't think I'll be able to focus with you in that towel any longer. Or out of it." He kissed her sweetly. "We need to reconnoiter with everyone, the sun is going to go down in a few hours, and I want us already in position to save the girls."

"Is Ansley here?" She hopped off the counter.

"No, Blaine is making sure Kaid leaves her at the museum. She can't be here for this, you think she would understand me bringing two possibly naked and beaten women back that I have intimate knowledge of? That woman is fiercely loyal to you. She would probably geld me. And I don't know about you, but I like me completely intact."

She gave him a cheeky grin. "I couldn't agree more."

"I should hope so." he laughed and took her towel from her.

"Gelding you would be such a waste," she winked at him, "Besides then your tongue would be so overworked you'd hardly be able to speak with it." Shaking her head, she walked into his room to dress.

He chuckled. "Such a potty mouth. You do know I'm a God right? I don't get tired, especially not concerning any part of your perfect body, love." He leaned against the doorframe and watched her move around the room, taking in her every curve.

"Brave claim to make Mister God. You know I've got nine years of bad sex to make up for."

"That sounds like a challenge if there ever was one. Believe me I'm sure I can oblige."

"Mmmmm..." Her eyes light up wickedly as she pulled a top over her head forgoing the bra. "But not now."

"No, now is time for planning and rescuing."

"So go plan," She waved him off. "I'll be down soon."

***

Caine stood outside of the container and glowered at the hulking door as if he could see its feminine occupants thought the metal. Fucking bitches. The last thing he wanted to do was pump them for information. Nathan asked too much, he should have given this assignment to that prick Stark especially after his recent cock up. Stark was far too trusting. At least Caine's cock up had been purely on instinct. A Div that trusts and cares is far too weak.

Memory of a goldfish, he'd said, how dare he? It still pissed him off that he'd had to send Brander over to Luther with the blood and organs. Giving up his prizes didn't come easily to him, not when he'd been human and a thief, and certainly not now. It had taken great control to not eat the girls' meat while it had still been warm and brimming with life. Giving it up after all that effort had not came naturally to him.

Caine took a deep breath, reminding himself that Nathan was in charge. Despite his recent questionable choices, his pet human and Stark amongst the few, Nathan was the boss. He was Nebacanezzar chosen and he would lead them. At least he would until the dark gods chose another but Caine was sure that wouldn't happen.

Nathan may not be Div but as the chosen one, he was so much more. He could still flay Caine's own skin from his body and feed him his liver without so much as a thought. His word was law.

Which meant he had to go in there and pump the girls for info just like he'd agreed to. After all, there was no point in standing out here thinking about it especially not now that their so called 'time frame' had been halved. Besides poking fun at the bitches was about the best offer he was likely to get for a while. Killing the other girl had been impulsive, but then what the fuck could Nathan expect from him? For years he's been serving the gods, bringing in new recruits for the cause. Ever since Nathan had converted his human form, everything he'd done had been in the service of the gods. It made him smile to think how often his god's needs and his own coincided.

This time he'd made sure his demon was well fed it would be a waste of time to do this while it rattled around in its cage screaming to be stated. This time it was all him. Grinning, he moved into the locker dismissing the Div on guard. He pulled a recorder from his pocket. Nathan didn't want him to miss anything and this time he wouldn't. He clicked the recorder on moving to the girls and studying them. Both were awake, the little one looked worse for wear. Suspension was doing all sorts of things to her arms. If he'd been a caring man or any sort of man at all he'd have let her down and strung her up a different way. He sincerely doubted that the ligaments in her arms would ever be put right, if she ever lived long enough to work through the therapy.

"That's got to hurt." He said to the other one. Watching her friend die certainly had cowed the mouthy bitch to a point but she still wasn't broken, not by a long shot.

Both he and his demon smiled at the prospect of totally breaking her in this short conversation.

She spit on the ground in front of him. "Please. This is nothing. This is foreplay." She gave him a disgusted look.

"Foreplay." he repeated, amused by her display of defiance. "Now we're talking." He took the lone chair in the room, scraping it over to sit it in front of her. It still had her friends dried blood on it, not that he'd let much escape.

"Cut the shit."

"You have far too much hate in you to be one of the good guys." He kept his tone calm while he sat down. "I don't blame you, mother selling you off as a child into the service of a god. It happened more frequently when I was younger but it still happens."

"So when did you become Freud? I'm not talking to you about this because you can't sway my conviction. I love my life. I serve my god with no doubts so you're wasting your time if you're trying to turn me towards the dark side."

"I'm not swaying, it's not my style. But I would be remiss if I didn't point out that your service to your god soon isn't going to entail very much." he commented off handedly.

"Uh huh... And this is where I ask why right?" he sneered at him. "Lord Osiris will always need me and my sisters."

"For what? Cleaners?" He shook his head sitting back in the chair slouching. "Thing is, he doesn't need you for shit now he has his Keeper." He smiled, letting that food for thought sink in.

Simone laughed after a scant few seconds and shook her head as best she could give her situation. "Yeah, see any other Inferi and I might believe you. My Inferi? Not a shot in hell Div."

"Oh this is going to be fun. Didn't you expect him to break down the door and rescue you as soon as I killed your little friend? Why exactly is it that you think your still alive?"

"Just who do you think you are Dr. Evil? You got the bald thing going and the lazy eye. I'm still alive because you want something from him, I'm not that stupid, and Syrus is a lot of things, but stupid isn't one of them. He never goes anywhere, " She looked down with disgust at Caine's groin and then back to his eyes with a sultry smile, "halfcocked."

"You're still alive because we want his Keeper and his Scarab, and you remain... unrescued, so to speak, because, to him, you're lives aren't worth hers. He's had plenty of time to," He leered, letting his gaze roving over her body. "Fully cock himself. He's had days."

She shook her head again. "And I'm sure you have went above and beyond to hide where we are from him. You talk some talk Caine. Let's say you're right, that after over seven thousand years he found his relic, regardless, he will come for us. We are his. But I don't believe he did find it. Not after all this time."

"Ah denial," A smile curved his lips and he found himself enjoying this far more than he'd expected. "What's that saying about it being a river in Egypt?" Simone scoffed. "Whatever. I'm not stupid Caine."

The falter in her words didn't escape him; neither did the sudden way she held herself, lacking any of her conviction. "Apparently. But you are just human, very human, and in the grand scheme of things very unimportant. I think the term is expendable."

"Looks who is talking." she frowned.

"Yet I can admit it, I'm a little higher up in the food chain than you, precious. My talents are a little more diverse than just fucking the boss.

"Thankfully we have special whores for that particular task, much like you really."

"Name calling is just really pathetic, though I do feel for the poor women you coerced into willingly sleeping with you." Her eyes narrowed. "And the life of a priestess isn't just fucking the boss, we mean much more than that. I have killed oodles of your precious Div. Can your ladies say they do anything buy lie on their backs?"

"You should have asked her before she abducted you, though I'm told she prefers her knees, personally I wouldn't care to know."

"Figures a hot piece of ass like her would be corrupt."

"The boss has his ways. I prefer the old fashioned way of getting my woman. Bitch will do just about anything if she thinks she's getting paid at the end of it. Much like Osiris did with you, I bet you did everything for a crack at immortality with him, for some sense of purpose. Just like your mother would have, and her mother... he has a pretty sweet set up if you look at it objectively."

Simone closed her eyes and took a deep breath. "I love him, always have. Nothing would make me regret my time with him. So can the seeding of doubt. Sy cares for his people, all of us, and you will suffer for what you did to Tony."

He grinned, making sure to show all his teeth. "Bring it on I say." He slipped a phone out of his pocket, her cell. "And on that note, let's see how quick to run to your rescue he is." he held up the phone showing it to her as he stood.

He wasn't going to get any more from the girl. It was clear that she didn't know anything of the Inferi or their doings and if she did it would take a more severe torture than Nathan was willing to allow him.

Maybe after they'd disposed of Osiris he could interrogate her fully but until then, his hands were tied. There was no point in delaying this any further. His demon woke up at the thought and they both were in perfect agreement. Tonight Osiris and his relic would be his.

***

They were running out of time, and everyone was on edge. Castor and Blaine conferred over some video feed. Arlo was getting takeout, and Kaid was on his way in from making sure Ansley was ok at the museum.

"What the hell was Arlo picking up anyway?" Syrus stood when Gwen walked in and went to her, steering her to the couch to sit. He paced.

Castor turned to him. "Osiris that is not helping. You should be more grounded now, hell you have your powers back and a stunning woman of worth. Calm down. The last thing we all need is for you to start throwing off excess power."

Syrus knew he was right, and his agitation wouldn't be helping Gwen out any either. He needed to remain focused. His body sparked and spitted power, and he went up in black flames, with smaller purple orbs rotating around his person. He contained it to himself, but it was still one hell of a show.

"Cas is right," Dezi grinned, throwing himself down on the couch next to Gwen. "You're practically burning up. Cool power by the way."

Syrus grinned. "Yeah I think so, cooler still that Gwen can channel it," he winked at Gwen. "Don't touch her Dez; she's got full control of them."

"Wasn't going to, not that I don't want to," he smiled at Gwen. "But I'm not into cutting someone else's grass."

Syrus stretched. "Just wait till you find your own Keeper Dewi."

"Yeah well you know my thoughts on that. I'm getting a call girl," he licked his lips, "High class with a hot teacher act that'll weaken you at the knees. Blaine's gonna get a nice round soccer mom, with one dying kid which he can save and I bet she cooks all the time. Makes world famous chicken noodle soup." he turned, "Now Cas..."

Castor shot a look at Dezi clearly meant to melt steel. "Watch it devil man... "

"Eh fine," he held his hands up in surrender, "I mean if you don't wanna know about the blonde German chick with the powerful yet surprisingly waxed legs that's your damage. My lips are sealed."

Castor shot him the bird. "Two times devil man. Where the fuck are the other two chuckleheads?" He looked at his watch and frowned.

Syrus wondered the same but said nothing. Suddenly the sound of Syrus's ringing phone was ominous. Everyone in the room stopped moving and looked at the cell phone sitting on the side table. He frowned hard, the ring Simone's. "Who is this?"

Blaine started a tap under Castors watchful eye.

"Did you like my little video Osiris?" Caine's voice sounded particularly smug.

"Someone didn't keep his word. You do realize that you just called open season on all Div right?"

"My word?" Caine laughed, "I kept my word Osiris. I told you that if you killed my minion that I'd kill one of your girls. I didn't mention not killing them if you left him alive. The minions can take care of themselves and if they can't then they're of no use to me. They're plenty easy to replace."

Syrus shook his head. "You're a dead man Caine, you just don't know it yet. What the fuck do you want?"

"I told you, the Keeper and the Scarab."

"You seriously think I'm going to give you my relic and my girlfriend?" he scoffed. Castor and Blaine were whizzing through images on the computer screen. They were getting close...

"For the lives of the girls? I believe you're considering it... but I'll take just the relic. That's all we need. It's a good offer, I'd accept it if I were you, and quickly. Before I have to hang up... and trust me once I do another girl dies."

Syrus growled. "Time and place Caine. Relic is yours, provided that both my girls are not dead, dying or hurt in any debilitating way when we made the drop."

"They'll live, though they'll most likely need help in walking. We'll meet at the docks two lots over from where you nice boys have been running security. Fifteen minutes from now. Any later and I'll start taking limbs from your girls here. Come alone, or bring your Keeper with you if you like. It's about a twenty minute drive from you so you better hurry."

"You drive a hard bargain Caine, considering that's not even enough time to get the Relic and make it to you. Shooting yourself in the foot there buddy."

"You don't have it with you? Surely for spending so long without it you'll have kept it near."

"Much you know about the Inferi Di Div. Once we find it we aren't allowed to keep it. It goes in a vault." He hoped his lie would give them more time to mobilize.

Blaine snapped and pointed to the screen, proving that Caine was lying, that where he said to meet was not anywhere close to anywhere he could hide the girls or bring them with him.

The other screen showed the container the signal came from. If they played it right, they could all get there before the appointed time, and take the girls by force. If not, then they could get there, bluff, and then take the bastard out when help arrived.

Kaid and Arlo both chose that moment to walk in.

Arlo dropped the take out Chinese on the table and went with Kaid over to the sideboard. Syrus thought to them.

Suit up, all of you...

I'm cool. Dezi thought.

Blaine nodded.

Caine growled. "Fine you have half an hour. But I'm warning you I might get bored having to wait so long so you might interrupt me amusing myself," A girls whimper came over the line.

"Caine, I'm warning you, touch one of them and you won't live to scream. Your suffering is already going to be legendary for Tony..."

"That's the thing I like about you Inferi, you're full of such conviction." A loud snap came over the line followed by a blood-curdling scream. "Don't worry it's not life threatening or debilitating. Don't threaten me Osiris, you're not holding any of the cards here, all you have is the Scarab."

"For that Caine, You'll suffer. You need the Scarab, more then you need to torture them. Touch them again, I fucking dare you. See you soon." Syrus hung up and looked at the guys. "Well? What's the plan?"

"Is taunting him wise?" Gwen asked.

"Probably not, but I'm not the kinda guy to just 'yes' him to death either." He looked at her. "Regardless of what we do, you're staying with Blaine." he turned to Castor. "Well?"

Castor nodded. "Agreed. Arlo, Dez, and myself will shadow you. You cool with that?" He asked Kaid "You go with him. I want you close to pull the girls out."

"Like I need to be babysitting more girls? Send the man whore to do it." Kaid growled gesturing to Dezi. "I need some actual action tonight."

Castor shook his head. "Why do you think I'm sending you in? To make sure they get out? Kaid I want no witnesses, your... talents are best suited for that. Bloodthirsty freak." he turned. "All cool? Let's go. I want the element of surprise."

"I'll do what I can from here." Blaine sat back in his chair.

"Mostly I think that's looking after me." Gwen answered dejectedly.

Syrus pulled her up by her hands and kissed her soundly. "I need you here and safe love, so I can do this and get back here to you."

"I know," She blinked, "I'm just worried for you and the girls. Wouldn't it be best to have Blaine there? He is a healer, when if they need help?"

"They will, but it's best to have you here and him as well. Blaine will be able to route any law enforcement away and such..."

"Okay." she kissed him and passed the Scarab over. "I'm just lending you this, I want it back." She kissed him. "And I want you back too."

. "Count on it." *I love you* he thought to her.

I love you too. She sent back hugging him.

"She'll be safe here." Blaine assured him. "Now go suit up you're on a count down."

Chapter Nineteen

The Ignatius dockyard was quiet; and Syrus wished he had Arlo with him. At least he would be able to hide in plain sight, but Kaid was just as good, if not more deadly. He talked to him mind to mind, as not to give away their position.

So you left Ansley?

She's taken care of. Kaid's mental voice came through ice cold and deadly.

I wasn't questioning that. And I'm sorry you got stuck with the chit. Truth was I didn't trust the other guys with her, and Blaine is far too cerebral.

Blaine's a geek, albeit a well-intentioned one. Arlo and Dezi are fuck up's and Castor's the king of delegation. I understand why I got stuck with her.

She hasn't been trouble though right? I mean she hasn't been climbing you like Mt. Fuji has she?

I'm a lot harder to climb than Mt. Fuji.

Syrus laughed internally. *I'll say. Seriously though, was she any trouble?*

Nothing I couldn't handle, though I do plan on billing you for the research material she stole off me.

I'm sure you will be able to get them back. How do you feel about her digging into your past there?

Kaid hesitated before answering his voice sounding unsure. *It kept her busy and she doesn't know it was my past. I can pretend it happened to someone else.*

Syrus highly doubted it. Kaid was celibate for a reason, and that reason was his past. If Ansley dug too deep who knew what would happen. They had made it to the container the cell phone signal originated from and watched from above, with 15 minutes to spare till they were supposed to meet Caine at the other location.

They watched twenty five Div set off in that direction, no doubt supposed to be the first wave, and the one to subdue him and take the Relic. He knew now Caine had no intention of keeping his bargain. Again, he was glad they had compensated and went for the brass ring. He opened a channel to Dezi. *Twenty five Div headed your way guys. No holding back. In ten minutes start fucking killing.*

Will do, Dezi' sounded cheerful. *I've been looking forward to this.*

Once your done get your asses down here. He turned to Kaid, *Keep contact with me through this. The second you get the itch get in there.*

I'll be with you the whole time.

Syrus gave his teammate a pound and walked out of the darkness and rushed the doors, blasting it open with his dark fire.

Caine stood in front of him with an astonished look on his face. The girls were strung up in a corner, and he heard Raine gasp and smiled.

"Ah," Caine smiled recovering quickly. "Very clever."

"You seriously didn't think I was going to fall for your bullshit did you?" He sent a dark fire blast at the Div, which pushed him back against the sidewall.

"You can't blame me for trying." he smirked, eyes focusing on Syrus. "Where's the Scarab?"

"So you think I'm going to hold the bargain when I just saw your little henchmen off to the ambush?" He put himself between Caine and the girls.

"The men I sent will return soon. So for now it's just you and I... and them." Five Div demons walked in behind him, blocking their escape. "So I ask you again, the Scarab? I know you have it on you, I can practically taste it."

Syrus chuckled in his head and sent a thought to Kaid. *5 Div and Caine, you square?* He looked at Caine and cocked his head, then pulled it out of his pocket, dangling it out in front of him.

Game? I'm spoiling for a fight. Good thing to because there's more outside, sixteen maybe more. Kaid growled.

"So much trouble for such a little thing, wouldn't you agree?"

Have at them then brother. I'll stall, the girls are stable though. Syrus looked over at Caine once more. "I didn't come here to shoot the shit Caine, release my girls."

"All in good time, I see the years haven't exactly taught you patience." Caine paced in front of him almost waiting for something.

Something is up Kaid. I'm playing along, tear those fuckers up, but do it quietly. His eyes didn't leave the Div leader as he moved   Syrus kept himself between the girls and the threatcoming from two sides now.

There was a long moment of silence from Kaid but he finally answered. *There's more. A lot more. Syrus I've never seen so many in one place.* Kaid sounded worried. *I can't get in touch with the others. It could just be the distance though.*

Caine snapped his fingers in front of his face as the Div behind him moved closer, flanking him. "I was talking about patience Osiris." He laughed. "And here you are trying mine," he thrust his palm out. "The Scarab."

This wasn't going well. The guys were all screwed. *Kaid, call Blaine if nothing else, have him hide it from Gwen... but this is more than a trap.* He looked at Cain and smirked, tossing the Scarab to him, not feeling anything by way of power now that it wasn't near Gwen.

This is an army; they're looking for all out war. I'll do what I can from here and call Blaine. It's probably not a good time for wistful nostalgia, but back when I had full power I could have taken them all. I killed armies for fun. He gave a wry chuckle. *Who am I kidding, it's still gonna be fun.*

Careful Kaid... If one of us dies... He knew he didn't have to finish the thought. If any of the Inferi Dii fell in battle, and died, the whole thing could be thrown through the gears of time, especially if he didn't find his Keeper and relic. Syrus sent a silent prayer to the goddess, that they would prevail and turned his attention back to Cain. "You got your relic, now release my girls."

"Of course." Caine walked by him to stand between the two girls. "We should have a little fun though, after all this is a nice happy reunion." He ran his hand up Raine's leg, causing her to flinch. The Div flanked him quickly, one distracting him as the other slapped a cuff onto his hand he could feel his powers being blocked. "Yes," Caine smiled, "A very happy one."

Syrus frowned outwardly but chuckled in his head. *The Dornal Shackle? Where the hell did they get their hands on this?* He made a show of wrestling with the cuff. Now that his Godhead was restored, the old magic would slightly dampen his powers, but not enough to be effective. Of course, they didn't know he had them back, and yes, the shackle would neutralize his stunted power. So he would play along, for as long as he had to. He sent a thought to Kaid quickly. *They have the Dornal Shackle, so watch out. Who knows what else they uncovered.* If they had anything similar, and there were objects of power lying around out there, then the Inferi were not going to be the victors in this battle.

"So you're that worried about me that you had to pull this antiquated binding tool out of the closet? Where the hell did you find this piece of shit?"

"You're not the only one putting money into antiquities Osiris. As for being worried about you, I haven't lived this long by being stupid. Now where were we? Ah yes, who should I release first?"

"How about both of them, from their chains, not their lives, and don't you dare touch them. I might be bound here, but I can take your sorry ass in a fight. You touch them and that's exactly what it's coming down to."

"Please, you're as good as human with that thing on." He pulled a wicked looking dagger from behind his back, scraped it along Raines thigh and moving upward. "Now play along."

Syrus growled and watched. "Caine, last chance to quit fucking with them. You got your relic; they are not part of this. Leave them alone."

"You made them a part of this. Choose, or I will."

Syrus wasn't sure what to do. He looked at the girls. "Mone? Raine? You guys ok?"

Raine shivered, her eyes closed tightly, Simone looked at him winking.

Syrus had his answer. Simone would be the best to deal with. She was still strong, and that was their best bet if the asshole tired to fuck with her. "Simone." he narrowed his eyes.

"Ah the perky one, good choice." He moved from Raine turning to Simone. "Such spirit. The fire does add spice to her flavor. Did you know that?" He cut the rope, keeping it in his hand, yanking her arms down.

She screamed in pain through the gag as her arms changed position.

"Oh you're going to pay for that Caine."

"Threats aren't much helping your cause Osiris."

"It's not a threat Div, its fact. I don't threaten."

"Of course, and I should just let her go?"

"Seeing as you probably have some Div milling about outside I'm going to say no. Leave her alone and let her free. Raine too. That was the deal, so do it."

"One or two Div, I admit. So I'll leave her alone then." He cut her hands loose and let his hold on her go.

She dropped to the floor her legs unable to hold her.

Syrus looked at her and then at Raine. "Now Raine."

"But we haven't had our fun with this one yet." He smiled cruelly before dropping the Scarab into her hands. "Here, have a look."

Syrus frowned. "Leave her alone Caine."

"You're not in a position to give orders here; I'm not one of your whores. So hush up before I'm forced to muzzle you, which I'll guarantee you I'll enjoy.".

Syrus smirked and shook his head. "Enjoy this feeling of power Div, it won't last." He looked at Simone fingering the Scarab.

"I'm sure you know all about what that's like." Caine turned to Simone. "You recognize it? It's not yours you know, no matter how much you hoped and prayed it would be... You are not his one. You were just another woman whoring herself for the greater good. Teaching others to do it no doubt."

Simone's body shook as she held the Scarab. "No..." A tear ran down her cheek.

"Oh yes," Caine answered,And now you get to go out and sire a whole new lines of whores to sell to him. Just like your mother gave you away and her mother did the same. You can't help that you were born into madness." He chuckled.

"You know you should come to me, we could do great things together. You won't, mostly due to brainwashing and misplaced loyalty; it's strange when you think of all the pain he's brought to you. At least I'll openly admit that I'm not the nicest guy in the world. I won't dangle a fairy story in front of you promising you something that I'll never deliver."

"I never promised any of my girls anything and they didn't have to come to me, ever. They always had a choice, and they still do." He looked down at Simone, feeling, for the first time, regret. "I'm sorry love..."

"Nothing but words." Caine grinned, stroking over her hair, causing her to flinch. "All this time with humans and he still doesn't truly understand them." He cooed softly for her. "How could any of them refuse when they've been brought up to believe that it's what they want? Hmmm? Not when there's such a pressure from your sisters, your mother, her mother..." He continued to stroke her hair gently. "As for the promises, how could you not share his bed hopping that you were the one? His one. I bet all the girls do, why wouldn't they?"

Syrus looked at Simone and shook his head. "They aren't stupid Caine, none of them... Until that was found none of them had the chance, but they did it out of love, and out of honor and duty, something you know nothing about. My girls are loyal, and beautiful, and that pisses you off doesn't it?"

"He's right though," Simone said quietly, her eyes never leaving the Scarab.

Caine grinned triumphantly. "We all hoped, all of us."

"I know, and I hoped with you love... My trusted my most revered and devastating priestesses..."

"Devastated is a word I would use." Caine grinned. Simone ignored him. "So was it one of us?"

Syrus shook his head. "Not per say...but a lost family." He wouldn't say anymore. Simone's mind might not be broken, but she was close to hysterical. He wasn't sure if she would blurt out that the girl was his lifeline anymore, and that the Scarab held no magic unless it was with the Keeper. If she did it could all turn sour for everyone. Thank the goddess that Gwen was safe and away from this mess.

She nodded as another tear slipped down her cheek, "I'm glad."

Caine snorted, "No she's not, humans say the strangest of things. She's trying to shield you from her distress, silly girl. As if you'd do the same. Loyalty doesn't anger me but it does fascinate me. Experimenting on it is fun...maybe you should have been here when I cut into the other one... what was her name?"

"What did I tell you..? They both come for the Scarab...and you don't touch either of them if you don't wanna die."

"I won't be the one to die, Inferi. I'll hold to our bargain, the girls will go free. We just never set a time limit to when." He laughed. "Just to their condition and most of them will be in working order. Maybe I'll father a few bastards for your line first." He smirked cruelly. "Maybe I already have. Wouldn't that be interesting?"

"It would be a trick of genetics as you bastards are sterile." He opened up his mind to Kaid, to see how he was fairing.

"Maybe that's for the best." Caine grinned.

Kaid's voice came through stressed. *Killing these fucks is harder than I remember. I might have to give over and shift.* He growled.

Syrus sent a silent prayer out for him. If Kaid shifted the world was going to know. *Have you contacted Castor?*

Still no. I talked to Blaine though, he's keeping Gwen safe. If I lose control Sy, you'll have to hunt me down. Not you personally. Dezi will enjoy it. How are you holding up?

Playing the part, but I'm just about done with this bullshit. You just about ready to bring the chaos?

Just about, he heard Kaid chuckle then gasp, *Holy shit, it can't be.*

What? What Kaid! He screamed in his head but something in his being was already telling him the answer.

It's a bunch of Div... They've got Gwen. She doesn't look hurt but fuck she looked scared as hell. There's no sign of Blaine. He said ominously his tone suggesting that he hoped the other Inferi wasn't dead.

Fuck. His plan of busting out of the shackle was moot now, as he would have to play along a little while longer. Gwen was fine, he could feel it, but she was scared as hell. He reached out to her to soothe her, but found a blank void. Her fear had erected walls in her head, and until she got that emotion under control, then he was locked out.

Chapter Twenty

"So..." Gwen said trailing off. Syrus had left her with Blaine.

"So?" His lips curled in a tight smile.

"Nothing," She shook her head. "Sorry it's just awkward being babysat."

"I'm not babysitting; I never go out in the front line anyway."

"No?"

"Nope." He looked back at his computer doing something, most likely playing solitaire.

"Why not?"

"It's just not my thing." He paused to see if she'd accept that as an answer before continuing. "I'm not really swinging in the "dark war god" jungle." He frowned. "I guess that's not really fair to the others, except Kaid. He was king of that jungle." He sighed, reconsidering his words. "What I meant to say is that I'm a healer, not a fighter. I can fight but it's not where my strength lies."

"Oh. But I guess it makes sense for them to have a healer."

"Not really. The guys could heal themselves without me it would just go slower for them. Mostly I get stuck on hangover and come-down duty." He smiled bitterly, then shrugged. "Of course there is the occasional gutting that I get to help out with."

"So how come you're here then? If you're not needed, Tiamat must have had some sort of reason?"

Blaine shook his head raising his eyes skyward. "I doubt I was part of her plan. She demanded warriors of dark origins. I was firmly half and half. My power was rooted in light but it had a dark twist." He sighed.

"My wife had similar powers but she also happened be fucking most of the other dark gods." His voice remained surprisingly bland as if the words held no meaning for him. "She casually suggested at council that we didn't need two healers but, as we were at war with the Romans..." He sighed then chuckled. "My sacrifice was intended as an insult to the Romans."

"I'm sorry." She breathed, horrified at how his pantheon could be so callous. Blaine had never been anything but kind to her. "You don't have to tell me anymore. I know how Sy hates the subject." And if his story was anything like Blaine's he had good reason.

"It's fine," He shook his head again showing no emotion. "I made peace with that demon centuries ago."

"But you were married," He nodded in answer. "And she betrayed you?"

"Marriages were different then. We were paired as we both could heal, her heart was black though, always was. I knew that. She'd always taken sacrifices for her gifts. Mostly she preferred what our people couldn't afford. She was vengeful too. Got her comeuppance though. I have it on good authority that the other gods soon saw her for what she was."

"A skanky ho?"

Blaine laughed loudly, "I wouldn't speak ill of the gods. But yes, skanky ho is an excellent term for her."

Gwen laughed. "Why can't I speak ill of them?"

"Not all of them locked themselves away, but even at that I've heard Castor curse Zeus a few times then regret it, though he'd deny it. They're gone but not forgotten I guess. As long as they're names are still remembered then they still have power over us."

"And you're skanky ho?"

He shook his head still smiling. "I wouldn't worry too much of Bormana. Either way it worked out well for Tiamat. Dezi would have gone insane by now if he'd have to deal with his own hangovers and I do my bit here."

"Like babysitting?"

"Among other things." He flashed a genuine smile. "Aren't you a little curious about your own past? I mean this has got to be all pretty surreal for you, and seeing as you weren't brought up in it, like the rest of his girls." He sighed and ran his hand through his hair. "Don't you want to know why you're here?"

Surreal didn't even begin to describe it. "I know why I'm here. I'm here because I happen to have the Scarab."

"Ah," he gestured with the ballpoint he'd been chewing, "But why did you have it?"

"Why? Honestly, I don't know, maybe one of my ancestors was Indiana Jones with less morals. Because it never ended up in a museum."

"It's possible, but unlikely. You must have it for a reason."

"A reason, right." She shook her head at the doubt in her words.

She could have been any woman at any time. Syrus was amazing and loving, but he could have been just as amazing to any other woman. There was nothing special about her no matter how much she wished it so and she did. Syrus had had a wife before all of this started, his very own bonifide goddess willing to cheat death itself to be with him.

There was no way she could compete with that, no way could she try. She loved him even after knowing him for such a short length of time but, for him, she'd done her part.

He was god now and if he tried to do something godly to find his wife, she couldn't blame him. Well she could, and she would, but a few day old love couldn't compete with age's old one no matter how deeply she felt it. Her eyes started to fill with tears; she looked up to stop them from falling. This was the last thing she needed.

She sighed heavily glancing at Blaine who was pretending to be busy at the computer missing her melancholy. "Excuse me I have to... go for a walk."

"Sure," he said gently. "Try and avoid walking near Kaid's room he tends to lay traps."

Not sure she wanted to get any more into that she started to walk deliberately avoiding where she knew the guys rooms were. In the light of day things just weren't as easy as they had been last night with Syrus. Everything had more complications and implications that she'd ever imagined. His priestesses for one thing, they were lovely and she'd love chatting with them, but could she really accept a whole group of women into her life always looking to her for answers, calling her by Syrus's dead wife's name. Syrus was god with a few millennia's worth of baggage and she just wasn't sure she could cope with that.

It didn't take her long, lost in thought, before she wandered into the heavy smell of incense and the sound on gentle humming. She looked up, seeing Sherri kneeling with her eyes closed.

"Oh I'm sorry, I didn't mean to come this far."

Sherri opened her eyes.

"Nonsense. You're right where you need to be Gwen. Please, come in." She stood and smiled a warm smile at her. "Can I get you a drink? I'm partial to Peach nectar."

"That sounds great, thanks." Something about Sherri put her at ease. That or it was a little more than incense in those burners.

Sherri poured two small glasses and set ice in them, then walked over to Gwen and handed her a glass. "I'm glad we have the chance to talk, without all the testosterone milling about."

"There is a quite a lot of it... and then some to spare."

She shrugged. "Put six men who ruled their pantheons in both darkness and sexuality in one place and its bound to happen."

"Sy said much the same thing. It must get pretty crazy around here," she said absently not needing another reminder of who and what Syrus was. "How do you put up with it?"

"Me? Well... you know the saying Carroll used in Through *The Looking Glass*, 'we are all mad here'?" she drummed her fingers on the side of the cup. "I didn't really have much of a choice. I was favored by the Goddess, and gave up my life in service to her. I deal with everything, but really they are all a bunch of teddy bears. Lonely teddy bears but..."

"Bears none the less," she finished for her. "Including the occasionally grumpy. How was it that you were favored? If you don't mind me asking, Syrus said you were human."

"I don't mind." she offered and took a sip of her drink. "I was Tiamat's main priestess and was one of the only humans present when they imprisoned the Velns. It was a great honor. Soon after we found out I was barren, and rather then lose my line, and me, Tiamat gave me a choice. Serve her warriors and my own prophecy will come to pass."

"Prophecy?" she sipped her drink.

"Umm. Yes, See Tiamat wasn't stupid, she took so much from all of them, and they needed something to look forward to. So she bound each of their powers, and gave them just enough to live, fight and survive. She swore they would each become whole once more when the women destined for them, their soul mates, came in contact with them and their relic. It was enough hope that none of them have gone crazy up until this point. For me, I got my own. My service would gain me my ability to create life when life would once again not be in jeopardy." A sad smile slipped over her face. "I don't know when that will happen. I mean, when is the world not in jeopardy?"

"True, there's always one thing or the next." She felt for Sherri. She was someone Gwen admired, it was obvious she'd been through a lot but she seemed to have come through it well. The fact that she still had hope after it all, Gwen didn't know how she'd have turned out if she'd had to wait as long as Sherri or the guys had with nothing but hope and the word of some goddess. "Soul mates huh?" Gwen felt herself smile. "That doesn't sound so bad."

"It's not, at least it shouldn't be. No one knows how it ends up. If I may say so, Syrus seems to have come out on top."

She struggled to maintain her smile, it wasn't for her to share her doubts, and Syrus didn't deserve that. "Yeah, being first must have its benefits."

"I don't know about that, but I do know he has exactly who he needs to have. We have been waiting for you a long time."

"For a Keeper." She said quietly her hands reaching for the lapis only to remember that it wasn't there. "That's the whole point of the gig, get your godhood back and kick Div ass."

"True, but we have been waiting for *you* a long time." she sighed and took another drink of her nectar. "What were you so deeply thinking of when you wandered in here if you don't mind me asking?"

"I... I guess I don't." She made the decision to share her feelings. "I just don't see how I can be right for him or what he needs... He's never been anything but loving and amazing to me but," she paused trying to put into words how she felt. "He has had this whole other life. He's experienced things that I could only begin to imagine. I'm not refined or sophisticated or even all that worldly. To be honest I couldn't even tell you where Egypt was on a map. I love him, with all my heart, but he deserves someone who could fully appreciate him."

Sherri nodded. "You haven't figured it out yet have you? Tell me Gwen, do you dream?"

Figured out? "Dream? As in goals? Or dream as in I'm naked in front of my high school class dream?"

"As in seeing yourself in another place and time?" she sounded amused.

"Oh..." Her frowned deepened. "Well only once but I'd had a really rough day... really rough."

"None since meeting Syrus?" "Well yes, that was the rough day." And they'd just had the most amazing sex she'd ever had things were bound to have been edgy. "What are you getting at?"

She downed the rest of her juice and went to the side table, then walked back over to her meditation pillow and grabbed a large urn. She started gathering small supplies from around the room. Some incense, some dried sticks, some powder. "What I'm getting at Gwen is that your past is trying to tell you something, the past you shared with Syrus."

"As a priestess?" She wasn't stupid enough to miss Sherri's meaning now but she had to be absolutely sure.

"As his wife."

"Isis?" She paused, blinked a few times. "No I..." She shook her head.

"The one and only." She gave her a big grin and walked over with the urn filled with the supplies she had gathered.

"Are you sure? I mean... wait does he know?"

"He does, to a degree. Parts of you are inherently her. Think about it. Aside from your little buddy Ansley, what woman would be Ok with her lover having a sect of women he isn't sleeping with now that he's found her, but will still interact with? Before Syrus and you came into contact, how did you feel about sharing?"

"I didn't have much of a choice but I hated it." She let out the breath she'd been holding. "I'm not sure how I feel about his priestesses, but I trust him with them... They need him."

"And he needs them. But he needs you more. Isis was ok with the sharing of his body, not his heart. They were gods, they had their intrigues, but they also had each other. Your acceptance of his priestesses comes from her ideals."

"So what else do I get from her?" She bit her bottom lip and fidgeted. On one hand this was the affirmation of everything she'd ever dreamed of but on the other, "I'm not going to turn into her am I? I'll still be me?"

"Turn into her? Gwen, think of yourself *as* her, only better. Think Isis 2.0" She winked. "Let me show you?"

She looked dubiously at her, uncertain if she wanted to see, "Ok."

She nodded and sat on her meditation pillow in the lotus position. "Then come, and sit." Sherri motioned to the cushion on the other side of her.

Gwen sat next to her, curling her legs under her. There was no way she'd be able to make the lotus position.

"Clear your mind Gwen. Let your body relax, and open yourself to all possibilities."

She closed her eyes taking a deep breath and trying to clear her mind as best she could. Shutting her mind off didn't come easy, especially now that she had so much to think about. She slowly counted backwards from twenty-five, breathing in the musky scent of incense. It was as Sherri counted ten that Gwen opened her eyes, relaxation permeating her being. Sherri lifted her hands to the ceiling and closed her eyes. She spoke in words Gwen had never heard. She switched to English soon after and looked toward Gwen. "Great Mother, show us what it is Gwen needs to know. Show us so that she may understand her feelings for your favored Osiris." She lit a match and threw it into the urn, creating a small flash. The flash quickly turned into a curl of white smoke that rose above them, billowing into a misty cloud.

The scene opened up between them in the clouds of vapor coming from the wide urn and Gwen blinked, not sure how she could be seeing something as clear as on a movie screen on billowing white smoke.

The room she spied on was made of sandstone, with torches in sconces, the flames licking lovingly across the walls, darkening them with their luscious soot. A girl raced down the hallway, the front of her shift balled in her hands to help her move without falling. She traversed the hallways of flickering light with purpose, and entered a large receiving room stepping forward quickly to kneel at the feet of a beautiful woman.

She was stunning; her long dark hair in sheets around her slim but curvy frame gave her a more youthful appearance then any of the others in their pantheon. Her eyes were heavily made up in kohl and her lips were fresh, clean of the berried rouge clay many of the others used.

"What will you have of me Great Mother Isis?"

The woman that was Isis smiled indulgently at the woman on the floor. "Rise Amalia, My favored one. I will not have one I consider an equal on her knees."

The girl gave her a confused look but did as her Goddess bade.

Isis inclined her head. "Amalia, I have a task for you. My powers are weak now, and I have one last thing to charge you with before I fade completely."

The girl nodded. "What is your will Great Mother Isis?"

"The Scarab. I do not trust Osiris' priestesses to do what is right to ensure its legacy and my own. When I am gone, part of me will be bound to that Scarab the other, to you. Generations from now in your bloodline, I will resurface, and be born of human flesh, to find Osiris once again. Would you give me this gift?"

Amalia's eyes shone bright with tears. "An honor, Great goddess. To be the vessel of your soul."

Isis smiled. "You have served both my husband and me well, and your progeny shall bear the love we had for each other."

"Thank you great one. What is it I am to do? Dola is the Keeper of the Scarab, and will be entombed with it. Should I beg for a spot in those chosen?"

"No, or my plan will not work. You will steal into the chamber and take the Scarab, and you will leave Egypt, and begin again across the seas, taking and protecting the Scarab relic with you."

"As you wish goddess." She approached the ethereal beauty that was Isis as she was beckoned and lifted her head to her goddess, who bent to her and pressed her lips to hers softly. "I entrust to you the rest of all that I have left, on the hopes that one day I will be back with him."

"An honor..." Amalia said and smiled. "I am ready."

Isis sighed and looked around then, bent once more her lips pressing again Amalia's once more and the air around them pulsed. Isis faded from the room.

Amalia shook herself and looked to the heavens, a tear escaping her eye. She turned and strode towards the grand doorway of the room and the scene dissipated.

Sherri groaned and rolled her shoulders.

"Huh." she said stunned by what she'd just witnessed. "And all this time he thought it was lost."

"Isis was always a sneaky bird when it came to him. I always had my suspicions... Your uber great gran-ma-ma was favored, you should be very proud."

"I guess, I am... and what my Gram said about the Scarab was true. It's weird to think that though, it was passed down for so long. It's a lot to take in though..."

"You said a mouthful. Did this answer your questions Gwen? Ease your troubled mind?"

"Yes," she realized with a smile feeling lighter. "I guess it does, a lot. Thank you." She hugged her tightly.

"Good. I'm glad your mind is at peace then. Now go, sister, and remember. Love him as you would always want him to love you. Unconditionally."

***

Gwen walked into the room, still shell shocked from what she'd just witnessed and looked over at Blaine who was searching through some video when the phone rang.

Blaine kicked the floor wheeling over to answer it in his chair. "Yeah?" There was a pause as he frowned. "Yeah ok, I can try them but there's a good chance they'll be busy." He sent her a suspicious sideways glance before moving away from her for privacy.

Gwen's heart sank, something was wrong. Something had to be wrong. She felt for her bond with Syrus hoping to feel something but he had it tightly locked down. Blaine came back several minutes later, his expression grave.

"What's wrong?"

"Nothing," he shook his head as if trying to clear it. "Everything's going well."

"You're a horrible liar Blaine. Tell me what's wrong," she said more forcefully.

"Things are a little pear shaped but it's nothing to get worried about. Kaid and Sy have lost contact with the others but they're most likely fighting. Kaid's being paranoid."

"Is that something he does often? Gets paranoid?"

"Not under normal circumstances, no. But still the past few days dealing with your friend have been hard on him."

She shook her head. "Ans is hardly taxing. We need to go there!" "There? No way. I'm keeping you as far away from there as possible. No good could come from having you there."

She shook her head knowing in her heart of hearts that it was the right thing to do. "No good can come from keeping their healer from them."

"Their bodies can heal without me."

"Even if it's something really bad? And what about the girls?" His silence was its own answer. "We'll stay far out of the way of any heat. I promise Blaine. Please!" she begged.

He thought it over for several moments before nodding in agreement. "Fine," he ran his hands through his hair. "But you're not leaving the car. Promise me."

"I promise." No way did she plan on running headlong into any situation where she would encounter any Div.

"Even if you see Sy in trouble? You'll only draw attention to yourself and put us all in danger. Get your coat then." He stood.

She followed suit grabbing her coat from the stand. "I promise I'm not about to go running off into a war zone. I'm not stupid enough to think I can take a Div on. I have no desire to be eaten thank you very much."

They marched to the garage.

"Clever as well as stunning, Syrus is a lucky man."

She noted his low whisper and her heart ached just a little for him.

As they entered the garage Blaine walked off to a box, typing in a code and opening it. "Keys," he took a set. "Everyone has their own box. Except me, I don't get out much and when I do I take one of the company cars. That's one of the benefits of being the tech guy though. I know all the codes."

"Ah." She grinned, "Who's is that?"

They walked over to a blacked out hummer. "Kaid's, it's the most armored one we've got." He opened the car doors and got in behind the wheel. "Bulky as all hell though. Good thing we're not going for speed or maneuverability."

She got in beside him as the engine roared to life. "We should hurry though." She felt a sudden sense of urgency.

"I'm with you there." He pulled the car out of the garage.

They drove in silence for several moments as the huge car cut through the sleek night. Gwen let her thoughts wander trying all the while to feel something from Syrus.

Finally, she broke the silence between them. "What do you do?"

"Excuse me?"

"What do you do? The other day you told me that Syrus needed his women to cope with things. That Dezi fucks and drinks, but you never really said what you did." It was something that had been bothering her for a while. He'd told her that he did something far worse. There was something about the way he's said it had struck a chord in her; he'd sounded so lost.

"No I didn't." his grip tightened on the steering wheel his knuckles going white.

"Will you?"

"It's not something I'm comfortable talking about Gwen. I'm not one to air my demons in public. I'll tell you now what I told you then, I'm not hurting anyone but myself."

"Do you actually hurt yourself?"

"No," he shook his head, keeping his eyes firmly on the road. "I don't hurt myself." He stressed the words a little too much for her liking.

She nodded, unwilling to push the matter further. "Ok, but sometimes it's better to talk to someone. If you ever feel like talking I'm here for you. I really don't mean to pry; I was just a little worried."

"For me?"

"Yes," she nodded. "You seem to look out for the others; I just get the feeling that you wouldn't let them look out for you. Maybe bottling things up isn't a good way of dealing after all."

"I don't bottle up Gwen. I wasn't like the others. I don't see myself as better, don't get me wrong, but I wasn't like them. I was an elder god. Well respected by others and loved by my people. I didn't kill anyone or preside over death, I did the opposite, and I saved my people. I reigned throughout all of the highlands and Gaul," he chuckled bitterly. "At least before the Romans started to spread."

"I thought you said that sending you was an insult."

"Tiamat and Castor didn't want healers. Then again maybe I wasn't as well respected as I thought. I certainly share the same fate as the others." He took a deep breath, "I should have seen it coming."

"But you guys are here now. Surely that's better than being dead thousands of years ago. I mean Sy just found me; you have all that to look forward to. A chance for love."

"I guess I just don't have that much faith in love. I'm much like Kaid in that respect. I knew it once and it bit me on the ass. You and Sy are happy, I'm glad for it. But still, I'm too old for fairytales... or soccer moms, round or otherwise."

She was about to argue when he silenced her by pulling over the car. "We're here."

"So soon?" She looked out of the window into the darkness.

It was dark outside. Rain thumped off the window of the car slashing down in rivulets. She thanked god she was staying in the car. *Well this is fun,* she fidgeted with her hands. Blaine ignored her, still looking stiff from their discussion. It was obviously a sore point with him, she shouldn't have pushed it. His face was tight and drawn.

"So now we wait I guess. I don't suppose there's any cards in here?"

He shrugged with one shoulder. "I wouldn't know. Check."

She opened the glove box rooting around coming up empty. "So can you feel them or talk to anyone? I can't   get   Sy."
Blaine had always been easy going. She didn't like this change in him; it was like he was waiting for something wrong to happen.

"No," he shook his head. "I can't talk to them but they're all here. I can feel Dezi and Arlo just over there." He pointed off towards a light. "That was their meeting point so I doubt they'll be too far from there."

"And Syrus?"

He shook his head, his body language easing off a little. "The two of you are linked in ways that I don't think I could comprehend. Close your eyes and look for him. He should be open to you."

She closed her eyes and tried feeling for him, and failed.

"No sorry, I can't feel him."

"Well it'll come to you," he smiled gently. "We've got plenty of time to practice and he might be blocking you. Stands to reason that he'd have a better grasp on it that you would."

"Yeah but I'll get better at it."

Blaine nodded about to say something when he sat up stiffly.

Gwen's heart plummeted. *Was it the boys?* "What's wrong?"

"Nothing." He shook his head to clear it then cried out as if in pain. "Gwen, I'm sorry, do not leave the car." He gasped desperately, before flashing out of the car in a bright light.

What the fuck was that? She shivered. One minute he was there and the next he was gone. She just hoped that wherever he went he was ok because she was going to kill him when he got back, if he got back. She sunk down in her seat feeling horribly exposed for the first time since the Div had attacked her and Ansley nights ago. Gwen panicked seeing movement ahead of her, a group of what looked like boys in the distance. Div. they looked to be scenting in the dark following their cars direction. They were heading right for her.

Don't leave the car, he'd said. Like the car would protect her from the Div. Would the car protect her? She looked around. Staying in the car made her a sitting duck. She didn't think a silly thing like glass and metal could stop the Div from getting to her. Maybe she'd have a better chance of hiding outside. She dug around in the glove box, taking out a knife that she'd seen in there earlier, not that she'd have a clue what do with it in a fight, but it couldn't be that hard. Pointy end in first. She opened the door and slipped reluctantly out of the warmth of the car into the ice-cold rain.

Gwen ran toward the light Blaine had mentioned earlier, keeping to as much of the shelter as she could find and put distance between her and the demons. If she could get to the guys she could hide in relative safety. It'd been a stupid idea coming here.

The cold rain plastered her clothes to her body as she ran. At least the rain would block her scent, or so she remembered seeing once in an old film. Bloodhounds couldn't search you through water, or was it that the scent just pooled everywhere? Either way she wasn't so sure how a Div faired up to your average scent hound.

She ran a while longer and stopped, hidden between two canisters with a view of the light. Her heart pounded in her ears. She peered to her right, her eyes following the sounds of fighting. Castor, Arlo and Dezi were there, surrounded by Div. But instead of looking outnumbered they all looked in their element.

Dezi had transformed, for lack of a better word, his skin a deep red, his hair parting for long curling horns. He fought with ease, using his bare hands with metal claws, ripping into the Div's borrowed flesh. He let the Div in close to him.

Castor and Arlo looked the same, using weapon she'd never seen before. They moved with a fluid grace only a seasoned fighter could achieve. No Div got close to them before they were brutally cut down. She couldn't help but appreciate them as males, even Dezi with his red skin and what appeared to be a tail. They were in danger of being overrun though, more and more Div kept joining the fray.

A small group of them on their way into the battle happened to look up, startling her when they detected her. None of the Inferi Dii noticed as they broke off to run after her. Fearfully, she pushed back out of her shelter and ran stupidly into the first group she'd been running from in the first place.

"Shit!"

One of the Div grabbed her from behind with cold, creepy hands.

She gasped and struggled, throwing her head back. Gwen hit him in the face but he held strong on to her laughing a disgusting, rasping laugh that sent chills up her spine. She pulled the knife out, stabbing blindly.

They quickly disarmed her with a sharp smack to the hand leaving it limp.

This can't be happening, her brain screamed. Visions of Tom's lifeless body came back to her. She retched, her dinner threatening to come back up as tears and rain streaked her face.

"Bitch!" The one in front of her hissed and slapped her so hard her head rocked back with the force.

Gwen staggered, stunned, and two grabbed her securely on each arm. The one who slapped her licked his hand, making a low guttural moan. "Taste better with the fight in them." He grinned, groped her, squeezing her breasts hard enough to make her cry out.

Terrified she struggled harder to no avail.

"Can we have her now then?" One over her shoulder rasped, his mouth full of needle sharp teeth just under her ear.

"No," the one in front of her growled, stopping the other from taking a bite. "She shouldn't be here; we'll take her to the boss first."

She struggled more.

The first Div laughed, pinching her breast painfully. "She'll go quietly or we'll take her right here."

Shedragged to her feet and marched through the containers, her fear spiking with every step closer. It was paralyzing her. The only thing that kept her moving was the Div that held her arms, pushing her forward. After what seemed like hours, they reached a container. The lead Div knocked on the door and pushed it open, and the scene that greeted her stole her breath.

Chapter Twenty-One

The container opened and four Div walked in with Gwen's small form between them.

Syrus turned around and spotted Gwen. She didn't look any worse for wear, but her aura was throwing off hostility of the highest caliber.

He watched Simone look over at Gwen and then back at him, and he saw the pain in her eyes.

Cain chuckled from his stand in front of them all.

Syrus tampered down his powers, and emotions, it wouldn't do to get them all killed from a misstep made out of anger. He kept his mind closed to Gwen, and she looked at him, standing there hiding what he was, and he knew something other than her getting caught was wrong. Where the fuck was Blaine!? The Healer had times when he was incommunicado, and this, of all times was the worst for it.

"Well what have we here? A present?" Caine stepped towards her. "You know how I love them wet, don't you Osiris?"

"Whatever you say Caine... I'm not privy to your preferences, though you seem to be biting off mine."

"Biting?" Caine smirked at him.

"Copying off me? Christ you used to be human Caine." he scoffed. "Shall we get back to it? You going to let Raine down now? This is getting old."

"I suppose I should, She's of no real interest to me now." Without taking his eyes from Gwen, he motioned to one of the Div who moved to Rain and cut her down

Falling hard, she hit her head off the floor, the sound echoing though the container.

Syrus growled. "You're going to pay for that one too... Simone? See to your sister."

Simone pulled herself over to Raine. "She'll live." Caine moved towards a trembling Gwen. "You on the other hand sweetness. You shouldn't be here, lost little lamb that you are."

Gwen swallowed hard trying to back away but two Div stopped her.

"Ah, ah... She's not part of the deal Caine. Lay one finger on her and I'll cut that fucking arm off."

"But you're right; she isn't part of any deal. That makes her mine, you have your priestesses. Take them and leave."

Syrus laughed and shook his head. "No, you got what you wanted for the girls, the Scarab. Ms. Stapleton is not part of this transaction."

"And yet she just managed to wander so helpfully into my arms." He grabbed her spun her around and held her back against him to face Sy. "Ooh she's cold but I'm sure I can manage to warm her up like I did the others." His hands snaked around her waist.

Gwen shook her head tears welling in her eyes. "I'm sorry."

Caine tutted. "Sure you are lover. You know Osiris; she should have been mine anyway. Would have been if I hadn't indulged on that drunkard in the alley... in fact didn't you have some sort of attachment to him love? What was his name love?"

"Tom." Her whole body shook as he sniffed her neck.

"Ah yes... boyfriend wasn't he? Delightful character if you like that sort of thing... you jumped the boat rather quickly onto Osiris here, didn't you?"

Syrus watched her intently, keeping his priestesses in his peripheral vision. He had to play a little longer, till he could be in a position to strike. "Must you be a dick Caine? Ms. Stapleton isn't interested, now or ever. She's mine... Aren't you?"

She nodded and met his eyes. "Always."

"See Caine. Now let her go, or I'll let her take the little switchblade she carries out and cut your dick off." He knew full well she wasn't carrying a blade, but he needed the Div to steer clear of her so he could engage them.

Caine hissed grabbing both her arms and holding them at a distance to him. "Now why would you do that Gwenny?" He twisted her wrist, making her cry out. "Sweet, we were going to have so much fun. I know you wouldn't want to spoil that." Keeping his body behind her, he looked to one on his Div. "Search her, and be thorough about it."

Syrus shrugged off of the two Div behind him and picked at his nail. "Touch her and you're the first to die."

The Div paused then shook his head before moving in front of Gwen, showing his back to Syrus in insult. He brushed his hands over Gwen slowly and deliberately.

She shrank away, making him come forward. Then she stepped towards him, cracking her head forward to butt him between the eyes. She brought her knees into his crotch at the same time, dropping the Div to the floor. Everything was silent for a few seconds then Caine started laughing keeping his grip on her hands.

Syrus grinned. "Well me killing him right now would defeat the purpose of that I think. Still..." he moved in a blur, one second several feet from them, the next he appeared between Caine and Gwen, his Keeper between him and the wall. He grabbed Caine by the throat and launched him across the room, pushing his normal amount of power into his grasp, searing the Div's skin.

Caine crashed to the metal wall.

Syrus was quick about grabbing Gwen and moving them closer to the girls on the floor.

Gwen hugged him quickly, "I was supposed to stay in the car but the Div came and I had to jump out..."

"Save it for later love..." he grinned then looked down to Simone. "Love, you ok? Raine ok?" He kept one eye on Caine, who looked as if he was passed out.

Simone nodded not looking at him, "We'll live. I think I can walk, I'll need help with Raine though."

"I can help." Gwen smiled sheepishly at Simone, moving around to assist her with Raine. "There's more Div outside though."

"We aren't through yet..." he looked at Gwen. "Introductions are in order I'm sure but I don't think this will keep." He looked over at Caine again and saw the head Div stirring. He was ending this now.

Caine shook his head, rising quickly. "Nice trick there." He snarled.

"Yeah, more where that came from."

"Uh huh. Well I can hardly wait. But you have what you came for," He rolled his eyes. "All the girls. Take them while you can."

"No, I think I'll have the Scarab too..." He bent down and picked it up off the floor where it lay since Simone dropped it and spun it around his finger. "There, now that's all done... I think I'll make good on my promises as well..."

Caine laughed, cock as all get out."You plan to kill me?" he shook his head.

"No, I plan to decimate you." He growled and rushed Caine with all his power riding him, and the intensity echoed off the walls. The lesser Div were no match for him using the power of his godhead.

They were flung against the walls, several misting to vapor under the onslaught.

Caine was pushed back by the shockwave, but to his credit stood his ground.

Syrus called his dark fire, cloaked himself in it and stopped a few feet from Caine, ready for full-scale war. His voice was a parody of its normal timbre, resonating with all the powers he finally possessed again. "Get the girls out." he said over his shoulder. "Now where were we?"

Caine smiled slowly his lips peeling back from his teeth. "The Scarab is pointless now; guess I'll just have to take you myself. Don't go too far girls. Once your God here is dead I plan on enjoying you all more than I already have." He backed off slightly assessing Syrus. "I like the fire though, it's a nice touch." He darted to the side, drawing a sword from its scabbard. "Not so well thought out though."

Syrus laughed. "A goddamn sword? When the hell are we? The fucking middle ages?" He launched a swirling mass of smoke and rolling purple lighting at Caine, and caught him on the shoulder.

Caine charged him too fast for eyes to track. He sidestepped Syrus, staying inches away from the flame before slashing the blade up the Gods body. The hilt butting into Syrus' face, knocking him backwards. "You prefer guns?" he growled low from behind him. "Those I have." He pulled out a gun, firing it pointblank into Syrus, making sure to empty the clip into him.

The force dropped Syrus to his knees.

"But they won't take your head." He lifted the sword over Syrus's shoulder the blade going to the throat.

Gwen screamed, running forward and stabbing a blade into Caine's shoulder distracting him. He turned and grabbed her, then threw her across the small room.

She hit the wall hard where she slumped.

Syrus' eyes flashed the fire that made up his soul as he went at Caine full blast. He held nothing back thrusting dark fire at Caine. He concentrated and put all his will into the attack. It bubbled up, wound around him like a living, breathing entity and crashed at the body before him. Syrus felt it slip through the meat of Caine's torso, felt it bleed into his blood stream as he pulled it out.

Caine shook, his eyes going wide. He fell to his knees, taking one gasp for breath, then smiled, raising the hand holding the knife. With one swift movement, he threw the knife at Gwen's stirring form.

Syrus was out of reach but he dove for it, his heart sinking. The knife flew through the air, aiming straight at its target.

Seeing Syrus unable to get to it Simone threw herself in the way, protecting Gwen from the blade as it sank into her gut dropping her instantly.

Syrus screamed and pulled his power out of the Div. He flung him down, putting his foot on Caine's back and leaned into him. "Normally me killing you would mean you went back to the Velns hell realm, but with my power coursing through your veins, you're going to my hell realm, a realm I now have full access to once again. For that last ditch effort, and hurting my priestesses, you're going to be tortured for an eternity. I told you, you would pay greatly for your transgressions. Enjoy the trip." he stabbed Caine between his shoulder blades, the body not misting, but simply dying.

Syrus felt the essence of the Div pass from this realm to his own and smiled. Caine's hell was just beginning.

He turned and went to Simone, cradling her and turned to see Gwen crawling over. "Mone, Wake up... Sweetheart please..."

Gwen joined him followed by a battered Raine.

Simone stirred slowly, opening her eyes meeting his. "A little slow getting to that there Sy," she teased smiling painfully.

"Fucking hell darling... you crazy bitch. Hold on, ok... we are going to get you well..."

She nodded, curling up against him. "Now would be a good time for that healer you guys keep around." she rasped.

I don't know where Blaine is; Gwen's voice came franticly in his head. *I lost him.*

Syrus sighed and shook his head. Fine time for this, but there was nothing he could do. He called out to Kaid as a last ditch effort then looked at Gwen. "It's ok; we are going to get her back to HQ. Why the hell did you do that Mone?" He caressed her face as Gwen held one hand, and Raine had the other.

"You expected me to let her die?" She coughed blood coming out of her mouth. "That's not good." her breath rasped. "You've waited so long to be happy Sy... you deserve it." She took Gwen's hand and placed it in his.

The door opened and Dezi staggered in covered in blood, but he held his human form. He took a second to look over the situation. "Fuck me..." he trailed off when he spotted Gwen. "Where the fuck is Blaine?"

Syrus looked at him and shook his head. If Kaid didn't get there soon with the transport they were going to lose Simone. He held her and looked down into her face. "I didn't mean to hurt you Mone, ever. Please hold on."

"I know," her face contorted painfully.

Kaid's not coming, Arlo's getting the car. Kaid's kind of... well he's gonna be a while. Dezi informed him. "Can I get you anything?"

Syrus nodded knowing what Dezi meant. Kaid had shifted and his bloodlust rode him. He would be getting rid of the last of the Div, but while that was a blessing, anyone seeing Kaid in his altered state would either drive them mad or kill them. That was definitely a bad thing. "We need to get them out of here. And blow this place up. I'm not taking a chance with the body still here." he motioned to Caine's lifeless husk on the far side from them. "Mone, Mone hold on!" He felt her grip slipping. "Baby don't fucking die on me! We need you."

Simone's grip grew weaker. "I'll get Raine, Gwen you ok?" Dezi helped Raine stand.

Gwen nodded silently.

"Mone... Please." he looked down at her and kissed her silently. "Please don't go. We need you. Gwen needs you."

"You'll both do fine without me. Just wish Tony didn't have to go..." A tear slid down her cheek. "Forgive me."

"For what love?" he held her tenderly.

"It's my fault... all this. Please."

"Nothing to forgive Mone... just hang on." He felt tension leave her and watched the light slowly go out of her eyes. He exercised a little power, sending her on her way to his palace in the afterlife, Abydos. It wouldn't be long till he could see her, or take Gwen there, and she wouldn't suffer, wouldn't hurt again and would be waiting for them. He kissed her and said a silent prayer, then looked at Gwen. Tears shone in her eyes.

Gwen cried silently as she hugged him. "She was a brave woman."

Syrus held them both and sighed. Arlo walked in and saw the carnage and his face fell.

Dezi was carrying Raine out gingerly, and Arlo nodded to him.

Syrus got to his knees and then to his feet, cradling Simone's body. "Arlo, clean sweep, no hint, I don't care how many tanks this takes out, but The Velns cannot reacquire Caine's body."

Arlo nodded. "Understood." He threw the keys at Gwen.

She caught them and gave a wan smile.

"Castor is in the front seat of the Hummer, dislocated shoulder and a couple knife wounds. Where the fuck is Blaine?"

"I'm not sure," Gwen shook her head. "He sort of disappeared."

"Fucking figures. Bitch." he muttered under his breath. "Get going, I got my bike here, I'll set the charges, and follow behind." he nodded. "Can you drive that thing, Gwen?" "Sure," She nodded solemnly. "Where's Kaid?"

Dezi came back in having settled Raine in the car, "I'll go after him. I'll get you guys back at the compound."

Syrus watched Gwen and pride swelled in his heart. She was battered, no doubt bruised, but she held her own, and didn't complain. She wasn't jealous that he held Simone, wasn't jealous that he had yet to comfort her. The time would come, but for now, she was more then he or the group had ever expected out of a Keeper. He smiled at her and then looked at Dezi. "Be careful. Come on let's get back to HQ."

Chapter Twenty-Two

The last seven hours had been utter hell. Castor's wounds were mostly superficial, though the dislocated arm was a bit of a problem. It took both Syrus and Arlo to reset it, and even then it was a fight to the finish. Castor was out, passed out soon after the deed was done for a healing rest.

Syrus should be so lucky.

He and Gwen had done the honor of dressing Simone's body together, and Gwen had made the call to Angelica, Simone's mother. Angelica had been distraught, but relieved that her daughter had died in the service of her god and his consort. Syrus had taken the phone from Gwen and told Angelica that Simone was not gone completely, and still in service to them all, and he had felt his old lover and confidante grieve a little less. He knew he would have to take steps to bring Simone back, but it was going to be a while till he could muster the concentration and strength it took to make a soul tangible again. It was doable, well within his scope of powers, and for her sacrifice, he would do it, and give her back a life she deserved, or part of one.

Blaine had shown up after the ritual to inter Simone's body, looking worse than Kaid had at the end of the fight. He tended to Kaid's more grievous wounds, but barely looked at anyone. Syrus waited till after he was done, then cornered Blaine.

"We need to talk."

Blaine nodded gravely his eyes never leaving the floor.

Syrus looked his comrade over and shook his head. "Tomorrow."

Again, Blaine nodded and sighed.

Syrus turned away from him and went to Gwen. She smiled at him.

"You and I both need a rest. Come..."

Syrus nodded to Arlo as they walked through the common areas, and out into the parking garage. With so much death, Gwen needed to see something that would make her happy to be alive.

***

Nathan felt Caine go on to his ethereal rewards with a twinge of regret and a heaping helping of anger. For a man that had spent so much time with him in the organization, working for the cause, to be lost to them all wasn't something he was happy about. The man that was Caine was either being justly rewarded for all the service he had given to their gods, or eternally tortured for disobeying a direct order. Odds are it was the latter.

Losing a lieutenant sucked for the cause, and now he only had Luther and that spineless pissant Stark. He was still trying to figure out why he had brought him into the fold. Didn't matter now, he was going to have to rely on them both... and Caine's protégé, Brander. That one showed a lot of promise. If things worked out, well Stark might meet a sticky end.

He pushed his chair away from his large desk and stood, striding his long legs over to his office bar and grabbed a tumbler. He poured himself a dram from the decanter. The smoky scotch swirled in the glass, his wrist moving ever so slightly to get the effect. He brought it up to his lips and tipped the glass back, downing the swallow in one and then set it down, ready to pour again.

Carina chose that moment to walk in, dressed like a present for him to open. A satin and leather confection covered just her breasts and torso, held on by buckles and straps.

She took one look at the glass and raised a questioning eyebrow, "Bad day?"

"We lost Caine." was all he said and took another swallow.

"Gee that's a loss," she sounded unconvinced. She moved to the bar and poured herself a generous measure before refilling his.

He nodded his thanks and then turned from her, walking towards the windows. "He was a good solider for the cause." He took another smaller sip and then put his arm up on the window, leaning into it. "Is there a reason why your here?"

"Other than to cheer your gloomy mood up? Yes, actually." She smirked, taking a seat swirling the liquid in her glass. "Besides I thought Div didn't really die, don't they just get..." she swirled her hand in the air. "Recycled?"

"Most don't, but someone as powerful as Caine... one that had both helped and hindered our gods; I don't know what they will do to him. Either way, he is lost to us. So what do you have for me, or did you just come in looking for a stiff fucking?"

"Well there is always that," her voice took on a needful throaty tone. "It's been too long. But that can wait; I have the information you wanted."

That got his attention. He pulled away from the window and turned to face her. "Oh? Well give me some good news here."

She smiled happily at him, "The Celt, Dewi, his relic was easy enough to find. Unfortunately he passes it around his women and of those there's far too many. I spoke to one of them, disgruntled stripper, who woulda figured, she's seen it but she isn't the one. I have a list of women, pinning them all down was hard enough this guys had more skirts this month than I've had dicks all year, and that's impressive."

she pulled a piece of paper with names and addresses on it setting it on the table. "There's some he sees regularly and some he just fucks and discards, of those he sees regularly there's five I think may have the Garnet. They don't feel like Keepers though so it's not activated.

"The chalice is being kept in a private collection which I'm narrowing down and the junkie's being kept at their headquarters. Nobody's getting to him any time soon but you know junkies and their habits, won't be long till he steps out of the rabbit hole." she smiled sweetly up at him. "Now tell me I'm a good girl."

Nathan smirked and walked towards her. Yes, there were silver linings to the clouds that rolled in. "You are a very good girl Carina. Such a diligent little bee." He smiled at her. She looked at him with expectancy. *So? Puppy want a treat?* "So what do you think you deserve for your troubles pet?"

"Well it has been so long since I had you... I need," she broke off in a whisper, her eyes locking to him. "Please."

Ah.... He smiled to himself. The woman was in withdrawals. Every time he took her, he bound the darker side of herself to him, making it harder for her to function without him. Soon, she would be completely his, and nothing would change that. He scrutinized her slowly, the little pink tongue that darted out to lick her bottom lip, her heavily made up eyes were at half-mast, the flush to her cheeks. Yes, she was in dire need of him, but he figured he would make her wait a little longer. "Ooh I think we are getting close to you deserving that. Tell me pet, what will you do with the information you have unearthed?"

"I...?" she blinked, realizing she wasn't going to get what she wanted just yet. She sat back on the seat crossing her legs and taking a sip from her glass. To her credit her hands only tremored slightly. "I'm passing it on to you. I've dug up what I can in such a limited time but I'll keep digging... subtlety. I can keep an eye on the Welsh god and see if the garnet passes hands or if it's activated, likewise with the chalice once I locate its final place... unless you want to try and force activation under controlled circumstances? Pay someone to steal it?"

Both were good ideas. "See pet? This is why I pay you the big bucks." he reached out and caressed her cheek. "The chalice, let's see how it works out once you find its location. Paying someone isn't my preferred method but it might be the best way to do it. The garnet, I think flushing out the Keeper might be a good idea. I believe we should start questioning, discreetly, the ones on your list you think are the best candidates. Once we can cross them off the list, take them out. It will bring the Inferi out in the open and maybe his Keeper into his sphere. We will have to take the gamble."

Her eyes fluttered at his touch and she leaned in to it. "We don't actually have to pay them; I'll look into a suitable candidate. I'll take another look at the girls on the list and start crossing them off."

"Good girl. Now stand. You have turned tonight around." He ran his hands down her arms and his fingers traveled to her back. He started unhooking the buckles of her corset. He pulled her closer to him and grinned, letting his power bubble to the surface.

She felt it, and gasped and he smiled. Yes, she was his, and would stay that way. The Inferi's prophecy might have begun, but there wasn't a shot in hell he was letting it completely come to pass. Not when he has so much at stake. "Now... Attend me."

Epilogue

The roof garden was alight with warmth and alive with the sounds of nature as Syrus carried Gwen in from the lower floors. The birds that called the space home greeted the man that fed them and gave them a refuge from the city beyond.

The family of squirrels that had infiltrated the sanctuary a few months before peeked out of the lone copse of birch trees occupying the garden in curiosity. The small waterfall that fell into the pond, the burbling gurgle from the fountains scattered throughout gave a calming effect almost as much as the soft recessed lighting that was peppered through the foliage.

He had always planned it so that when he found his Keeper, she would see it as a Garden of Eden, a perpetually blooming habitat, night and day, all for her. Plants from throughout the ages and world graced this space, Plants rich in exotic scents and colors. He set her down in front of a row of night blooming cactus, their fragrance an intoxicating mix of sweet and spicy. He inhaled and grinned down to her.

"It always reminds me of the scent of the Nile before man destroyed the natural world."

He hit a button on a stand disguised to look like a stump and fan on the ceiling started to move, making the fronds of the palms at the far end of the garden and the lower ferns closer to where they stood sway slightly after only a few moments. Syrus's hands went to her shoulders and rubbed them, the massage slow and deliberate, the action meant to relax her and put her at ease.

The threat to their happiness had passed. They had the Scarab back, and it rested quietly between her breasts, where he knew it would remain the rest of their days. Without her, the relic was only lapis and gold, nothing more than ornate jewelry. Without her, and her essence it wasn't the tie that binded them together for eternity.

No doubt word had already reached the Velns leader through the remaining Div that had limped away during their flight from the container before the explosion. Relics were useless without their Keeper, and that would seriously endanger the women that would fill the positions of the other Inferi Dii, but thankfully, only as long as the Keeper and the Inferi weren't bound, and their godhead released. The guys knew what the deal was now, and would be looking for and protecting their relics and the woman that would set them free.

But none of that really mattered to Syrus. He had his woman and the love of his life in Gwen, and nothing was going to change that, but the victory was bittersweet. Losing Simone was horrible, and he now held Gwen as she shed tears for the woman that didn't ever know her, but gave her life to keep her safe. Simone was loyal to the end, and he would always be grateful for her sacrifice. Without it, Gwen would be lost to him, Isis would be lost to him, and his life would never be whole.

The woman in his arms cried silent tears, and he joined her, the sorrow they both felt almost enough to consume. Syrus knew Simone wouldn't want them to grieve too much, she was full of life and she would have them celebrate their love and finding each other. He was determined to celebrate life with his Keeper, celebrate the second chance his priestess had so generously given them. And show Gwen that Simone was fine in her new incarnation.

"Gwen, love don't cry, she wouldn't have wanted that."

Shaking her head she sighed, "She shouldn't have done that. It wasn't right."

"While I agree with you that she shouldn't have done it, to her it was right. Saving you and I was what she was trained for, to keep us safe, to keep the world safe."

"She was very brave then, I doubt I could have jumped in the way of that thing." She flashed him a wistful smile. "Then again I didn't have to, that bastard had thrown it at me." She cuddled him closer, burying into him.

"Yes. And now he's dead, and can't hurt either of us anymore."

"He's really dead?"

"The human he was is, and his Div soul can't return back to this plane, not while I have hold of him. Normally I couldn't hold a minion of another pantheon in my realm, but The Velns and the Div have been declared rogue, and that helps keep the powerful from returning. We won't be hearing from him again my love."

"Good," she said quietly. "Do you think Raine's going to be ok?"

He nodded. "I do. She's tough, and she will heal. I understand she wishes you to come to the house soon and that Angelica is going to name Raine High Priestess of the cell. They will need to get to know you, and Simone's acceptance of you has gone a long way."

"Sherri mentioned something about Isis. Is that the reason?"

Syrus rubbed her shoulder in a caressing sort of way. "Something like that."

"How the hell is that possible? I mean I know what Sherri told me but..."

Syrus sighed. "Reincarnation isn't just a pleasant thought to comfort those that are alive when losing their loved ones. It's a very real thing. Tiamat said we would get the loves we gave up back, and at least for me that's true, in a sense."

"But I'm not her." She frowned. Being a copy of a woman he loved so long ago wasn't how she liked to think of herself.

"No, you're not her. You're better. You have her soul, but you are still you. She gave you the best parts of her, her powers and her love and acceptance of me to ensure we would be happy and together. Time is cylindrical, and the best parts of her returned to me in a woman I could never share, never harm, never leave. You're it for me Gwen, and the girls know it. They know you will lead them, and love them like I do."

"I'm looking forward to it. I like the girls, I'm sure we'll have some fun together... something I'm sure we all could do with. Did Raine say much about the girl that took them?"

"She didn't know anything that she told me, only that Tony had picked her up at the bar. One minute they were drinking, the next going to a limo, and then everything went black." He sighed. "I believe she did give Arlo a name, though I didn't have time to question him about it."

"Well with any luck the Div ate her."

"I don't think they would. Even the corrupt need women about for their desires."

"Eww," she pulled a face. "Really? Well I don't know what type of woman would do that willingly."

"Ones looking for the bad boy, one who doesn't know any better and is used to being abused, one who is just rotten to the core..."

He ticked off the reasons and then sighed. "We will find her and punish her. I promise you that. Now tell me...How do you like the garden?"

"It's beautiful." She pulled away from him a smile breaking out on her face. "And peaceful. It's just what I needed. What we both did I guess."

"I always hoped my Keeper would like this. It's our little piece of heaven I think. And it comes complete with hidden speakers and a picnic spot." He paused to stare at her beauty. "I'm glad I can finally share it with you." Syrus leaned in and nuzzled her neck.

"Me too. It's wondrous."

He smiled and took her hand, leading her past the cacti and the low-lying ferns further into the foliage. They walked along a small winding path comprised of paving stones, and soon made it to the small pond, and Syrus stopped letting her take in everything. They stood on a small patch of grass, the rocky shore of the pond outlined by a lip of river stones and smooth marble and granite. The lush plant life surrounding them held secrets, and Syrus couldn't wait to show her.

"Check this out." He walked over to a rock and opened it, flipping a switch.

Music filled the air, low, seductive. Syrus grinned and turned to a large bench and then flipped it open, pulling a blanket and a few small throw pillows out. "Music choice ok? You know I never asked you what you like to listen to." He looked at her and smirked. "Please tell me it's not that pop top forty shit, or," he shuddered "Hip hop."

He laid out the blanket and scattered the pillows at the top of the blanket. Her silence made him turn. "Dear goddess, please tell me your not a Cher fan."

"Cher?" she laughed, "Cher's made a lot of good songs in her time. But no, I'm more of a Rod Stewart fan," she giggled.

He looked at her horrified. "Please say it ain't so..."

"Maybe."

Syrus laughed and pulled his shirt over his head and threw it to the side, then fell to his knees on to a pillow. He pulled his sneakers off, then his socks. He turned and cocked his head and thumbed the first fastener of his button fly open.

"Ah..." her gaze wandered over him slowly."Playing dirty are we?" She reached the hem of her top lifting it over her head in one fluid motion. "At least I hope you are."

Syrus growled and smirked. "Just getting comfortable. You didn't tell me about the music you listen to though..." he stretched out and relaxed against the pillows.

"There's not much to tell, if I like it I'll listen to it, besides," she dropped onto her knees beside him, kissing over his hipbone just above his jeans waist. "There's so much more we could be doing than talking about music."

Syrus sucked in a breath and groaned, caressing her shoulder. He added a little bit of dark fire to his touch and watched as it skittered over her skin and down her back, rolling like raindrops. "So it is true what they say then."

"Mmmmm and what's that?" she rolled her eyes up to meet him.

"That people in high stress situations normally become very interested in sex afterwards." he bit his bottom lip and wiggled his eyebrows.

"True that I am highly interested in sex. Though I'm not so sure if that's got more to do with you lying here all sexy than the high stress."

"I'm sure it's a little from both columns." he turned on his side and looked down her body. "You are so beautiful Gwen. Do you regret meeting me?"

"You saved my life," she laughed.

He shrugged. "You saved mine. We are even. But that doesn't mean that you're happy now, with the situation or even with the future."

"I don't think I could ever regret you Sy," Her soft expression turned serious. "I love you."

Once again his heart sang hearing her profess her feelings. She loved him, she said it more than once, and the fates he knew, heard it as well. "I love you too darling." He pulled her up to him and kissed her, and rolled them, pulling her under him, comfortable on the soft earth.

"Mmmmm, you better," smiling at him, she cupped his face in both her hands pulling him down into a long sensuous kiss. "Because I'm not going anywhere."

"Damn right," He murmured and slid his hands down her sides in a sensual caress. He slid his fingers into the lip of her jeans, teasing the hidden skin of her hip.

Her hands reached for his button fly popping the next two and slipping her small hand inside. "And neither are you Mister."

He shivered. "Never. You my love are every illicit dream I have ever had come true. And your touch is sweet torture..."

"Torture eh?" Her fingers swapped around him.

He groaned. "You know it. I get any harder I'm going to turn to stone."

"And we can't have that can we?"

"Well with any other Inferi I would say no, but with me it's physically just not possible. Though those nipples of yours are giving me a run for my money in hardness department. I love how responsive you are to my touch."

"Ummm I bet. You know they'd be more responsive if you touched them," She arched her body up to his.

"I couldn't ever deny you anything, but I'll do one better." He slid down her body a little and wrapped his arms around her torso keeping her arched and nuzzled her left breast, and took her peaked nipple into his mouth, rolling it with his tongue.

She tasted sublime, more so than ever because of the situation. This fantasy, this dream he had mused on for so long, was finally coming true, and he couldn't have picked a better lover to spend eternity with.

Gwen purred under him, wrapped her legs around his hips and pushed his jeans down.

He chuckled into her breast and nipped, drawing a gasp from her with the action. Her legs continued to work the denim down his hips, then thighs, then legs, and in one swift kick of his legs and he was naked. He pulled away from her nipple and then laved the other, never one to not give attention equally, and then looked down into her smiling face.

"How is this fair? I'm here, naked, and you're still in your jeans."

She giggled.

He kissed her soundly, groaning once again at the luscious taste of her. His hands went from around her torso to her jeans and with nary a hairsbreadth between them, he unbuttoned and unzipped them, and slipped then down her legs.

"Now that's a whole hell of a lot better..." he snickered and rolled then so she was on top. "Umm now that's perfect. I like how you tend to always end up on top."

He grinned up at her and licked his lips. "I do love the mark," his thumb caressed the little black flame that mirrored his own. "I think it's much better than a wedding ring." He teased.

"Mmmmm it is... but I still want a ring, if you plan to propose that is."

"Baby I gotta make an honest woman of you..."

"Oh you do?"

Syrus growled and closed his eyes gripping her hips. "But that's for later... the biggest diamond you can comfortably carry on your ring finger... Don't stop moving."

"I'm not moving," she squirmed grinding in to him.

Syrus smirked. "So you aren't." he gripped her hips hard and moved her on him.

"Oh," her body hugged his tightly. "Mmmmm. Moving is much better." She took his hands, bringing them up to her breasts.

They were one, his love on top of him, and her body a sweet caress, undulating in the night. Power grew around them, pulsed as he did inside her. His eyes never left hers, and he smiled up at her. "I love you Gwen." He felt the whisper of power build in her, an echo of his own. He kneaded her breasts, and bucked,.

She sobbed.

"You feel it too don't you?" he grit his teeth.

She nodded opening her eyes looking down at him. "I can."

"Don't deny it... embrace it... "He growled and moved his hands down to her waist again, his thumbs on her dark fire tattoo. "I don't want it to hurt... Please."

"Doesn't hurt." she rode him harder, letting it build within her.

Syrus let his control go, giving himself over to the magic. If she accepted it fully, and him, the process would be complete, she would be his forever, locked as she was now, always beautiful always sexy, Powerful and young. He felt his life force ebbing into the air, the magic that made him a god, made him immortal, being sucked into the aura of his lover, the woman his heart had accepted the second he saw her.

She came suddenly, her body exploding with dark fire. "Syrus!" she cried out with pleasure.

His body arched, the magic finding its way into her soul, and he cried out, feeling his soul become tied to hers. The room went hazy as he lent himself to her, and wavered as he felt some of her come back with his powers. It was less than a second, but her aura now pulsed with a darker light than ever, forever bound to him, forever the woman he was supposed to love.

"Oh wow..." she breathed heavily nuzzling his cheek. "Amazing."

Syrus chuckled. "Well that's one word for it." He wrapped his arms around her as he kissed her shoulder and rolled them over. "Not bad for our first night under the stars eh?"

"Ummm not at all." she kissed him. "The first of many I hope."

"We do have forever now baby..." he grinned and pulled back looking at her dark fire mark. The mark bore a swirl, one that radiated a pale blue color, like Syrus's eyes. He looked down on his own and saw the same markings, and grinned.

"Forever sounds good."

"I should hope so." He grinned. "You feeling better?"

She nodded cuddling to him. "Much... At least better than the girls." she sighed guiltily.

He looked down at her. "Well if you're agreeable to an orgy..." he winked and grinned. "Seriously though, they are always my girls, and they will be ok. Even Simone will be."

She pulled back looking up at him. "How can she be? She's dead... As is Tony..."

Syrus sighed. "Regrettably, I can't help Tony; her soul was gone when we found her. Simone though, I was there as her soul traveled, and I didn't send her to the Darkness. She will now serve in my original temple, where I was and still am a God." He smiled. "And now that we are completely bound, I can take you there." He kissed her sweetly. "I will search for Tony now, but..." he closed his eyes.

"But what? Simone? She's ok?"

"In a matter of speaking yes. Her essence, her soul is. She just doesn't have a physical body. She's like a demi god, without the god part."

"I don't understand." she frowned.

"She's living; she's still Simone," he kissed her. "You wanna see?"

"Oh yes," she nodded.

Syrus grinned and let his newly formed powers surge, enveloping them both in a thick grey hazy mist. He closed his eyes and exhaled, pulling their physical bodies from the plane they existed on, and through the miasma. He held her close, and then pulled away slowly nodded to her. She was clothed in a white shift, attached by a gold Scarab at her shoulder. He looked down to see what he normally wore in his special domain, a pair of black linen pants. "Well what do you think?"

She gasped looking around, "It's beautiful." She touched his chest. "I can feel you, where is this?"

"Of course you can feel me, your part of me." He winked. "This is where I ruled the Egyptian underworld from. This is my original home, Abydos, locked forever in the spaces between the living and the dead. Think of it as our summer house."

"A summer home?" she grinned. "Where are our bodies?"

Syrus grinned and pinched her hard. She yelped. "Right here. Immortality has it perks, and one of them is being able to transcend different planes of existence. This place *is* real love, and we are real here, as real as we are when we are on earth."

"Ow," she rubbed her arm. "Ok so we're really here."

He went to her and kissed the spot he pinched and then nibbled up her shoulder. "So you wanna see Simone?" he nipped her throat.

"Uh huh," she relaxed into him.

He chuckled and guided her through the fire lit sandstone corridors, and entered into a vast receiving room, with large floor to ceiling windows. The night beyond was quiet, and they walked toward the opening and gazed out. Gwen gasped as she looked upon a night-land Egypt, the Nile snaking its way through the plains, the palms swaying softly in the sweet smelling breeze. No moon hung in the sky, though it was awash with pinpoints of light, twinkling like stars. "I fashioned this to always remind me of Earth's beauty." He kissed her shoulder. "We can explore outside the temple another time. Come, Simone is this way."

He led her further into the room, and then through another corridor, and Gwen started to hear music, twentieth century music, coming from beyond.

"I take it the music choice isn't yours?" Gwen grinned up at him her hands wrapping around him.

"It could be. Simone and I have similar tastes in music." They went further into the hall and ended up in a huge room decorated in a more updated style, with a woman sitting on a large pillow in the center of the room in the lotus position. The second they stopped walking she opened her eyes and grinned getting up.

"Syrus! Gwen!" She cried and ran to them hugging them both. "Thank you my lord!" She turned toward Gwen and kissed her fully on the mouth. "And you're ok!" she grinned.

"Thanks to you... You look great."

Simone hugged her again and grinned. "I know right!? I can eat anything I want and not get fat now. Syrus is very generous." She winked at him and then gasped. "Oh! You did it! She's yours now isn't she?"

Syrus nodded and pulled them both close. "She accepted me earlier tonight."

Simone nodded. "And good thing you did!"

"There wasn't much of a choice really."

Simone laughed and then looked at Syrus. "My family?" she looked hopeful.

"Already briefed. You'll be able to see your mother in a few weeks. Once we prepare her and you. It will be a while still till my powers are at their peak for me to give you what you need to survive back on earth but... We can keep you comfortable here till then. Right Gwen?"

Simone looked at Gwen. "And you'll come and hangout with me?"

"Of course," Gwen nodded.

Syrus smiled. "She has the power to come here on her own now." He hugged them both closer and sighed. "Simone will be our eyes and ears in this realm from now on, allowing me to keep firmly planted with you. I have every faith in her."

"Thank you my lord." She sighed and snuggled closer to them both.

"We are going to have to leave though, I'm not up to full strength yet and this took a lot outta me."

"Of course. I understand. Don't be a stranger, ok?" she kissed him on the cheek and then went and kissed Gwen sweetly on the lips.

"We'll see you soon." she squeezed Simone's hand.

Syrus kissed his priestess on the mouth and then took Gwen's hand and brought them back to earth, where less than a second passed between when they left and when they arrived. "See? She's fine..."

"She is," Gwen grinned kissing him. "Do you think you'll be able to bring her back?"

"I do. Soon, but not yet. Being the lord of death has its privileges." He wrapped his arms around her. "Now unless you wanna sleep out here tonight, I think we need a shower and a soft bed."

"I could skip the shower and go straight for the bed." she kissed the tip of his nose. "Unless you want some company."

Syrus grinned at her mischievous smile. "Newsflash Gwen, I will always want company, and now I finally have the woman I want."

About the Author:

Bi-continental, Stella and Audra break all misconceptions about siblings. Writing as a team they have produced well over eighteen novels as well as several novella's and short stories. And nary an argument has come from it.

On their off time from writing, Audra is a makeup artist and Stella is a graphic artist and web designer, as well as the convention director for the Authors After Dark convention. They both love animals and have several including snakes and a peacock.

Audra lives in Scotland with her husband and children, while Stella Lives in South Carolina with her dogs Moo and Poe and her husband.

Other work by Stella and Audra Price/ S.A. Price:

The Eververse series:
Sugar and Sin
Silk and Steel
Frost and Flame
Masquerade
You Burn Me

The Dragon Elementals series:
Fire in His Eyes
Deep Water

The American Satyrs Series:
Of Crimson and Collars
To Collar and Keep

The Knossos West Weresnakes:
Beyond the Vision of Dreams
Surrender in Moonlight
A Gift of Daybreak

Ophidians, Book one:
Entwined by Fate

The Duvall Inc. Series:
The Assassin, The Djinn and the Hundred Year Wish
The Things a Djinn Can Do
A Very Djinn Christmas
London for the Holidays

All available on KINDLE!